The Tracker

Leslie Thompson

Yellow Car Publishing
Cartersville, Ga.

This is a work of fiction. Names, characters, places, and incidents either are the product of the author's imagination or are used fictitiously, and any resemblance to any persons living or dead, business establishments, events, or locals is entirely coincidental.

The Tracker

Copyright: 2007 by Leslie Thompson
Cover design and copyright 2007 by :Nick Cochran

ISBN: 978-0-6151-9586-5

A Yellow Car Publishing book
Editor-in-chief: Susan Cochran
Editor: Laurie Thompson
Cartersville, Ga.

CHAPTER 1

Maddie rubbed her burning eyes and struggled to focus on the paperwork in front of her. The night had grown long and she yearned for the comfort of her beloved family. She glanced at the phone sitting on the corner of her large oak desk and contemplated calling home. She checked her watch and groaned as she realized that it was far too late to call. At this weary hour, Sam and the kids would be sound asleep.

She wrote a few more lines on the page and noticed several stupid mistakes. She tore the paper up in frustration and threw it into the trash, giving the whole thing up as a bad job. She could always write the damn report tomorrow. For now, all she was capable of doing was getting home and snuggling deep under the blankets with her husband.

She gathered her purse and bag and prepared to leave. She'd just returned from a tedious mission spent cataloging the mold that dwelt in the crawl spaces beneath the aboriginal peoples in a very random, very weird rainforest on the eighth world of the second galaxy. She'd spent most of the time dizzy and sick to her stomach from her exposure to the exotic fungi. Not to mention she'd been covered to her knees and elbows in slime and questionable water. She needed a bath.

Because of the mission, she'd been out of town for nearly a week and Sam had needed the car. Keung had arranged for George to pick her up from home and bring her in. So, she needed to find George to take her home. No doubt he'd either be in the cafeteria eating a late supper, or in the gym beating the snot out of some rookie Agent. But Keung could be lurking anywhere, waiting to send her out on a last minute assignment or demand that she stay and finish her report tonight. Which meant that she needed to avoid him like the plague.

She sent out a sliver of her mind, looking for him without letting him know that she was looking. Using mental abilities on others inside the Center was strictly forbidden, due to the friction and occasional infatuations it may inadvertently cause. Keung considered the coercion of coworkers counter-productive and violated their ability to perform their jobs creatively and adequately. But the ban was useless. Everyone had their own abilities and they all guarded against each other's practical jokes, including the Keeper. When she didn't find him, she realized that she should have known it wouldn't work. The man was impossible to track.

Maddie hurried to the elevator and jabbed the call button repeatedly. Behind her, the Control Room maintained its high energetic pace even at this time of night. The room buzzed with whispered voices, the rustle of pant legs moving against each other as they walked and the shuffling of paper work. She kept her head down and refused to make eye contact. If she made eye contact, someone was bound to want to talk to her about something and then she'd be delayed longer.

The elevator finally arrived and took her to the cafeteria with a soft whoosh. Riding it always made Maddie feel a little squeasy because it moved so smoothly and so quickly. She nearly fell on her face when the thing stopped so abruptly. The doors slipped open and revealed the cafeteria. It was lit in friendly golden light; the large eating space was designed to provide the relaxing environment required for efficient digestion. Not that it worked for everyone. Fred and a small group of Agents were sitting in a dark corner and glaring at their food as they brutally stabbed it onto their forks. But then, Agents were a surly and aggressive group of men who thought only of violence and obsessive protection. Of course that was their job, but really, was it necessary for them to remain so morose all the time?

When she didn't see George glaring at his food among his fellows, Maddie turned and walked back towards the elevator. Near the soup bar, Elcia, the librarian waved at her with a nervous grin on her narrow face. Maddie noticed that she was standing a little too close to Mac, the cook, but he seemed pretty happy about it. Maddie waved back and then gave the woman a small thumbs-up the second Mac's attention was away from her. Elcia went back to adoring the bulky man. She batted her large eyes at him and he puffed up and grinned. Maddie smiled to herself and went back to the elevator.

With a whoosh and a sudden stop, she was in the Agent's gym. The place was made for training in the art of defense and attack. Mats were stacked in one corner next to equipment created for the practice of pummeling human beings. Punching bags and bandages used to bind hands and feet were kept in an area all their own. A little space had been cordoned off so that sword training could be taught without an innocent being gouged or impaled. There was space to learn hand to hand combat, a shooting range for target practice, and even a triage area for those inevitable accidents that occurred when large groups of men played with projectiles and sharp pointy objects. Tonight, though, the gym was dark and empty. Normally, the gym always had at least a few occupants. The Agents worked relentlessly to keep their skills and bodies in perfect condition.

Maddie was glad that the gym was empty tonight. The last month had been grueling for the Agents assigned to her use. They'd worked strenuously to keep her butt out of the fire. For the last year, it seemed like every mission was a trial by fire. She had found herself tangled in political intrigue that threatened to leave her rotting in a dungeon. There had been a battle or two when a riot or revolution broke out, and even an assassination attempt made on her. Blood had been spilled, and there had been more than enough lives taken and destroyed. She'd been a little more than freaked out by it, but the Agents constantly assured her that this was the normal pattern of the job.

But she always got the samples she was sent out after. She never failed to squeeze the last bit of information out of a subject, whether they had to be cajoled, threatened or simply asked out right. So what if a couple of Agents were a little maimed at the end of the day? The Quarter got what they wanted so everyone was happy. Maddie's mood plummeted as her guilt rose to an intense tingle in her brain. It wasn't fair that the Agents spent so much of their blood, sweat, and tears for her personal safety. And she never seemed to really know why they did it so willingly.

The Quarter was beginning to feel ruthless and unethical. They didn't seem to care at all for their people, just so long as their goals were achieved. Just what their goals ultimately were was another mystery that no one would or could answer.

Maybe she should drop by the infirmary on her way out and see how the guys were doing. She'd avoided it until now because it was her fault that they were there, and she was fairly certain that they were pissed at her. But in her defense, no one told her that earrings were considered offensive in a bar where everyone had eyebrows bristling with hoops and studs. A patron had insulted her virtue and of course she'd mouthed off. Which then led to the nastiest brawl that she'd ever imagined. She was very nearly been dragged off to be raped when the Agents had finally stepped in. Another brawl broke out, hot and fast, followed by an abrupt and brutal victory for her men. George had dressed her down viciously for the incident and she still felt rotten for it. The right thing to do would be to stop in and check up on everyone, even if they didn't want to look at her. At least none of her people had been killed yet.

She took another elevator ride to the medical floor and had her hand on the door when Keung's voice stopped her.

"I see you're ready to get home," he said casually. Maddie flinched and turned to face him.

Keung's normal expression was either casual or flatly cold. He never showed any reaction or emotion. He was as impassive and unreadable as a granite mountain. Maddie fidgeted with her purse nervously, and looked at everything but the tall man looming over her. Maddie wasn't short; she was five feet six inches tall, a perfectly respectable size for a woman. But Keung stood almost two feet over her, and was too aloof to bend his head to look down at her. His head was held proudly, as if he would break if he bent his neck just a little for her. Instead he looked down his bold nose at her, a small smug smile quirking on his lips. It wasn't much, but on Keung, it was good as a hard laugh.

"I thought I'd go see the casualties before I headed out," she said boldly, trying to ignore his amusement. She could ask him what he thought was so damn funny, but he wouldn't tell her anyway. He remained silent, staring thoughtfully at the door.

"I'm sure they'll appreciate the gesture, all things considering," he said.

"Considering what?" she asked not really wanting the answer but unable to help herself.

"Considering that your foolishness is what put them there. If you had read the file thoroughly like you were supposed to, you would have known that the Alloise consider earrings were obscene, and you would have been spared a battle and a rescue," he replied. Maddie flinched and felt her mouth twist in a wry grimace.

"You could sugar coat it once in awhile," she grumped. Keung didn't respond. He reached into his coat and withdrew a thick envelope from the pocket within.

"Here are the proceeds from the 'artwork' you sent back for personal use," he said. "It appears that you do have an eye for what is fashionable. You've done better for yourself than most Trackers before you."

"Thank you," Maddie said meekly. She snatched the money from Keung, but refused to open it or count the money inside. Instead she tucked the bundle in her purse with a dopey grin. The Quarter didn't pay the Trackers for their services. The post was supposed to be a great honor, to be served happily and without compensation. Maddie had been a lot less than thrilled when she learned that she wasn't going to collect a salary.

Like many of the other Trackers that came before her, she told Keung to kiss her ass and left the Center when she found out that there would be no pay. Later, when she learned the hard way that death was the only means by which she could vacate the position, she'd started a side business collecting the indigenous 'artwork' of the planets she visited and selling them to local galleries and collectors on her own world. Keung handled most of the details. If he kept a cut for himself, Maddie didn't know or care. It seemed to her that if she wasn't getting paid, then it was likely that he wasn't either. And he'd shown some sympathy by helping her make a better living and she appreciated it. If he took a few bucks behind her back, well then, fine. After all, if he'd stuck to the letter of Quarter's law, she'd be homeless by now.

Sam would be pleased to see the cash. He wanted to start renovating the spare bathroom for awhile now, and had begun to become a bit testy on the subject.

"I had the large bills cut down into something more manageable," Keung said.

"Thanks."

"You'll find George down on the Agents floor. I believe he's finishing up the debriefing from the last mission. You should go talk to him now, before he decides to go to bed. The casualties can wait to see you until they're awake," Keung stared at her intently, his vivid green eyes glowing eerily in the fluorescent lights. Maddie shivered and stepped away from the infirmary door.

Her wide eyes never left the Keeper's face. She backed away from the door and all but ran for the elevator. Once she was gone, Keung went into the infirmary, shivering slightly as the cold medicinal air rushed over him. His eyes searched for the Center's doctor, wanting to talk to him about the patients. Andre would no doubt already have a handle on the strange infection affecting some of the men who had returned with the Tracker. There should be a written report ready as well as a verbal presentation prepared. Keung did not look forward to it. The infection was being described as gruesome, and a pair of nurses had been spotted weeping quietly in their rooms. Andre had already assured George that his men would survive, but they would be a long time recovering.

CHAPTER 2

He paced the length of his antechamber, barely noticing the heat that radiated from the massive stone fireplace. Nor did he see the small, frail and ragged creature trembling in the corner. He prowled the room, avoiding sumptuous furnishings and gilded fixtures with blind reflex. He cursed everything around him, even the very air he breathed, and pounded a fist into his palm. The sound of bone meeting flesh made the timid jump in open terror.

It had been a year since the title of Tracker had changed hands, and still he had no more clue of the human's identity than he did that first day. He remembered the exact moment clearly, the Master coming upon him suddenly and cruelly as he descended ruthlessly into His mind. His face was covered over with a tight suffocating presence as the Master settled in, cruelly ensuring that he had His undivided attention. He tried not to struggle, but the way the Master held him ensured a small struggle just to maintain his life.

"The Keeper has found another Tracker," the Master had growled as if it was His fault. He trembled in silence, too afraid to answer the statement. So He waited for his Master to speak again.

"Find it, and kill it. Make sure the job is done right this time. Be sure that all the heirs are put down as well. Clearly, one was missed the last time," The Master spat. He trembled, shaking like the timids he so despised. He was so afraid, so very afraid, and he hated the Master for it.

"Master, I have nothing to start with, no vital knowledge to help me locate the Tracker and its heirs. Please, Master, surely you know something to aid me in my quest." He was begging. He hated to beg. It was a demeaning, weak act. He would not have to do it if *He* were a Master.

"Another lair has spotted Agents in your territory. Watch for them. No doubt they will lead you to the Tracker," the Master replied without bothering to hide his disgust.

"Yes, my Master."

The hold over him began to lift. He could see light, though he couldn't make out colors or details. He still struggled, but not as he had before. Before the Master finally released Him, he was granted the vision of a clock, the hands spinning around its face. The point was clear; he would be given only a certain amount of time to complete his task. If he failed to meet the deadline, his life would come to a messy end.

With that thought, He came to himself and felt the dreaded pressure of the deadline upon him. Soon his time would expire and the Master would be out of patience. With this Master there was no bargaining, no second chances. His command was absolute and final. Failure meant death. Suddenly He ceased in his prowling and noticed the timid cowering in the darkest corner of the room.

The thing was a disgusting, reeking mess. Like all of its kind, it had a fear of water so intense that it never bathed. It smelled of filth and whatever disease was eating at it. It stared at him with wild eyes peeping through gnarled and bony fingers. He smiled at it, making the timid cover its face completely with its hands and whimpering pitifully.

"Remind me, timid." He decided to have a little fun with the detestable creature. "Why is it that we care about the existence of one insignificant human?"

He knew the answer to the question. He wanted to see if the timid knew it. Timids were supposed to be hyper-intelligent, which is why they were tolerated. If it didn't know the answer, perhaps he would kill it.

"Because the Trackers, unlike all other creatures, are capable of many terrible things. They have killed not one Master, but three in their long history," the timid nearly screamed its answer. "Besides which, the Tracker is a crucial member of the Center, which is in direct competition with us. Take away their Tracker and they will crumble. The Tracker title is passed through a bloodline for a reason. There are no other humans who posses the genes that allow them to tolerate the rigors the job inflicts upon them."

He gave it another smile that nearly caused the timid to loose consciousness. It stuffed a boney fist into its mouth and gnawed. Pink blood flowed from around the creature's lips. It didn't notice what it was doing; it was simply too terrified. He wondered if he smiled at it long enough, would it eat its own fist in terror? He chuckled and the timid nearly chewed through its hand.

"Very true," He said at last. "But a Tracker has not crossed our path in nearly a thousand years. Surely it is no longer a viable threat. I doubt very much that the current Tracker is even aware of our existence,"

"But, master, we have been ordered," the timid shrieked.

"Yes, yes," he agreed impatiently. The only thing the timid feared more than the monster in front of it was the Master who controlled Him. It would always speak in favor of what He was ordered and would inform on Him at the first opportunity.

His mind began to plot. There was an advantage for Him in this somewhere. If he just thought through any situation at enough angles, the advantage could always be found. And always he found it. He grinned evilly, pleased with the string of scenarios his brain presented to him.

"Go to the changelings. Tell them they shall be granted a time of play. They shall be allowed to quench their lusts as never before. This way, we shall draw the Tracker to us and it will be ours," he declared. There was more to his plan, of course. So much more. But he would not share it with anyone. It would remain a closely guarded secret, so much the better to get him what he wanted in the end.

He laughed at his own wit, his own genius. It was a terrible and evil sound. It drove the timid, finally, to its feet and it ran shrieking and sobbing from the antechamber.

*   *   *

Sam stirred as Maddie crept into their bedroom and set her bag down inside the walk-in closet. She moved around the room in the dark, growling when she stubbed her toe on the bed and swearing when she banged her hip on the dresser. She made muffled sounds of pain, trying to keep from waking her husband. Sam woke gradually, eventually watching her move through the room with slitted eyes.

He watched as she stripped off her clothing, her shadowy form becoming a nude silhouette against the dim silver light of the full moon. She flung her clothes into a hamper that was near to overflowing with laundry. She turned and took a quick shower in the adjoining bath, muttering under her breath about the funk in the room and making a promise to clean it in the morning.

Somewhere in his sleep-fogged brain, Sam knew he should be pleased that Maddie had finally come home. But all he could do was wonder how long it would be before she was gone again. He was lonely because he spent all of his time with children and rarely got to exchange words with an adult. The children had stopped asking for their mother months ago; instead they went to him with their tears and needs, even when Maddie was at home. The toddler no longer seemed to recognize his mother. He treated her like a stranger and clung to his father for comfort. Maddie took it all in stride even though a sad expression often crossed her face when she interacted with her children.

Months ago, Sam had asked — no, begged — for her to quit her job. He pointed out how the children were disconnecting from her and how badly their marriage was suffering. Maddie had listened silently as he listed his complaints, then quietly refused to do as he asked. She'd pointed out that he was out of work for the moment, so they needed her income to live. And since she was making more money than he could, they also needed her income to finally pull them back from the brink of bankruptcy. Then she refused to discuss it any further; she just listened to him rant with that sad expression on her face until he ran out of steam. He hated that look on her face, and it had become a common expression for her these days.

Maddie slid between the sheets and snuggled close. Sam didn't move; he continued to feign sleep in hopes that she would leave him alone. She whispered his name twice and then lay her head down on his chest. He put an arm around her. After eleven years of marriage it was an automatic response to her movements. Her abdomen was covered with a strange astringent odor that wrinkled his nose. Her skin felt weird where his hand rested on her back. It was too smooth and puffy; as if she'd been badly singed and several layers of skin had been flash fried off her body.

She lay there stiffly for long moments and still he did not move. She finally relaxed and let her body collapse against him. She stretched an arm around him and held him tight. She took deep shuddering breaths and hot tears slipped down her cheeks and onto his chest. He didn't comfort her and he didn't ask what was wrong. She wouldn't tell him what had happened anyway, and he was growing too bitter to care.

CHAPTER 3

It scuttled through the underbrush and frightened the small animals that kept their homes there. It paid no attention to the fleeing birds and rodents. Their useless scurrying held no interest for it. The humans of this time and place had no regard for the movements of the life around them. Instead, they put their faith in the strange devices of their own making that left them fatally vulnerable. Machines did not care if their masters lived or died and had equal disregard for their own functions. They did simply as they were told until they broke. Such machines were easily bypassed and took away that element of unpredictability and left humans open to attack.

It stopped beneath a window and examined the cracks between glass and frame. It smirked, and knew that it had found its entrance into the human lair. It concentrated on its body, thinking about how small and flat it would need to be. The pliant muscle rippled and contorted beneath the loose skin. Its bones grew paper thin, its organs thinner than the width of a hair. In the end, it had to force itself into something much longer than it originally had been but the mass was the same, which was what mattered.

It reared up and pushed itself through the crack and kept pushing until its entire body lay in a folded heap on the plush floor. If any human happened across it in the dark, the fool would think it a discarded blanket and ignore it. But no human came upon it. The house was dark and quiet. It took enough time reforming to its original shape so that it did not become disoriented. Once its vision cleared and it had firmly oriented its center of balance, it peered around the human dwelling. It was much the same as any of the other houses it had ever been inside. It smelled of human and animal musk, of their garbage and their chemicals. It was filled with the cheap possessions that all humans hoarded: couches, chairs, tables, light fixtures, and useless knickknacks littered the human lair like so much trash. The place buzzed with the electricity that powered it, and it shivered from the annoying sensation. The magnetic fields created by electricity being diverted to so many useless and mundane things scrambled the changelings poorly developed wits and made it nauseous and irritable. By the time it found its first victim, it would be in the mood for killing.

When it crept from the window, a large yellow dog padded into the room. The dog stopped the moment it saw it, and stared as if it could not believe its eyes. Its throat rumbled angrily, indicating that the intruder's presence was not welcome. The changeling watched the dog warily, waiting to see what it would do. The animal continued to growl, struggling with its fear for its own well-being, and its instinct to protect its human pack.

The dog's instinct finally overwhelmed its fear and it began to bark in an effort to warn the humans of the deadly threat. An angry voice answered, demanding that the yellow dog shut-up. The source of the voice told the changeling that the humans slept in the rooms just to its right. It lashed out and struck the dog a blow that crushed its skull and sent it flying. The dog fell without a sound, keeping its humans ignorant of their impending doom. It moved in a streak from one room to the next, lashing out and killing the still forms in their beds whenever he encountered them. As the blood splashed and the bodies collapsed delightfully, the changeling felt no real satisfaction in what used to be its favorite sport. In the old days, humans had had fought desperately and skillfully for each breath. They had faced him like fierce warriors, confident that another would conquer should the first fail. They had been brave fools. But now in this modern age, they were just fools. It was disgusting to see how they threw their lives away.

It turned away from the slaughter and called in the grunts for their play. They made a great deal of noise as they clamored and fought over the bodies. The changeling thought about making them be quiet lest they rouse the attention of the neighboring humans. But as soon as the thought came, he cast it aside. It didn't matter if the grunts made too much noise or not. Humans had grown cowardly and no longer involved themselves in each other's lives if they could help it. None of them wanted trouble. The changeling and the grunts it commanded were safe from prying eyes.

It sat and watched as the grunts cavorted in their play. Organs were ripped from corpses and tossed about like toys. They let the blood pool and they splashed about in it, painting pleasing pictures on each other's flesh. Eventually, they feasted on the tender morsels that had once been their toys and lapped greedily at the remaining blood. Sated and weary, the grunts slunk away. The changeling grinned and stepped forward to do the work that hadn't changed in over a millennium. This part was just as satisfying as it had ever been. The goal was to terrify the humans who would stumble upon the corpses later. It cackled happily and set to work.

*　　　　*　　　　*

Maddie lounged on the couch and spooned ice cream into her mouth directly from the quart she cradled in her lap. An all-news-all-the-time channel was on the TV with a ticker running headlines across the bottom of the screen and a pretty newscaster sitting grim-faced and spouting the news as she was told. On-site reporters appeared in little corners of the screen and fed new information to the cameras. Maddie watched avidly, catching up on the events that she missed while she was gone.

This week, a serial killer was terrorizing Atlantic City. The monster spent his time cutting up college girls and strippers, leaving their gooey bodies on display in car dealerships. A Republican Congress had been elected, which meant that the country's democratic president was going to be facing investigations and scandal eventually. Which wasn't surprising, really. Everything in government was about war. If a country wasn't at war with another one, then the country's government was at war with itself. No doubt the Congress would find some illicit dirt on the aristocratic-minded president. It didn't matter that in two years the country would be forever free from the man since he was in his final term of office. The opposing party would see the lying, womanizing, alcoholic but brilliant man absolutely destroyed, or die trying.

A powerful and unseasonable tornado had flattened a small town in Texas, and sent singlewides and rednecks flying. Two people were dead, dozens injured. Of course, the state government would do everything they could to assist the victims just as soon as the Federal government was finished stabbing itself in the back and approved the funding.

An already obscenely wealthy executive was caught embezzling money from his own company, which made no sense to Maddie. Maybe he was doing it to see if he could. It just seemed like such a self-destructive thing to do.

A random gang member shot and killed a young woman in a convenience store robbery. He was pleading not guilty by reason of insanity due to an increase in crack cocaine consumption. Maddie thought that no jury would be stupid enough to acquit the young killer, but she'd been surprised before.

Across the globe, there was violence in the Middle East. Big surprise there. They weren't even using new tactics to make their moldy old political statements. The Muslims simply strapped a bomb on some naïve adolescent and sent him into a strip mall. The mall went up in a ball of flames, killing dozens and maiming hundreds more. The Israelis responded by rounding up anyone who even looked guilty and shot them. Which, since there was inevitably at least one innocent guy in the group, pissed off the Muslims all over again.

Somewhere in Africa, corporations were committing mass murder for the sake of profit while tribal peoples and the impoverished were dying of famine and disease. Across the continent, innocents were dying in the crossfire of small petty wars for control and millions were being infected with or dying of AIDS.

The whole thing felt like an overblown and depressing rerun, so Maddie turned off the TV. Maybe she'd go back to getting her news from Sam. He always weeded out the crap from the real news for her and he was way more entertaining than the people sitting in front of the camera. She put the lid back on the ice cream and wandered into the kitchen.

Sam had his back to her as he did the dishes. She put the ice cream into the freezer and gazed affectionately at him. Sam was a big man, despite being only five feet eleven. He was overweight and, at thirty, had begun to lose his hair. But to Maddie he was still as cute and sexy as the day she first grabbed his butt. Her chest swelled with love and passion as she slid her arms tightly around him. Sam jerked away as if she'd burned him and frowned irritably at her over his shoulder.

"What's wrong?" she asked. Waves of anger and resentment were pouring out of him. She didn't peek into his mind to find the cause of his foul temper. She felt that doing so was unethical at best, mind rape at worst. Either way, she wasn't going to violate his privacy and would only read what was already out there. Sam shook his head and nudged her out of the way. He reached for a dirty pot without speaking.

"Sam, talk to me," she said softly. He sighed heavily and turned to face her. He crossed his soapy arms across his chest and leaned against the counter. His green eyes were cold as they tried to bore a hole into her forehead. He was avoiding her gaze, which meant that he was going to pick a nasty fight. Maddie sighed and shifted her weight uncomfortably from foot to foot.

"You can't be gone for over a week without contact and expect me to be thrilled with you," he said finally. Maddie bit her lip to keep from saying something rude.

This was an old argument. Many missions required her to be gone for long periods of time without contact with her family. It drove her as crazy as it did Sam but there was very little that she could do about it. She had tried to explain her job's policy of secrecy to him as well as the fact that she couldn't always use her phone on the field. But Sam refused to accept it and Maddie wondered how many times they'd have this argument before he finally got the hint that she couldn't talk to him about it in detail.

"I'm sorry. It's my job—," she began, pulling out the same tired excuse she always used.

"Yeah, yeah, it's *always* your job," Sam interrupted angrily. "There's always some dumbass reason why you can't pick up a phone and call me once in awhile."

"No, I couldn't call you," Maddie snapped. "There weren't any phones!"

"You didn't have your cell phone with you?" he asked, confounded.

"Well, if they didn't have regular phones, it does stand to reason that they didn't have cell phones. Which means they didn't have satellites or towers to carry cell phone signals, doesn't it?" Maddie retorted. Sam's big eyes narrowed angrily and his mouth tightened. The truth was that her cell phone would have functioned anywhere. It was a super-powered, high-tech thing that she didn't understand no matter how Bob, the tech manager, explained it to her. But she'd been dealing with a fairly primitive culture and they would have had a conniption fit if they saw a tiny box vibrate or make strange music. After that, everyone would have been dead.

"Where the hell did you go that you couldn't use a phone?" he demanded. Maddie wanted to tell him, she really did, but she couldn't. The Quarter who funded and ruled The Center demanded absolute secrecy. Any time she even *thought* about confessing everything to her husband, she felt a sharp electrical pain down her spine, and she went into convulsions. Which sent Sam into conniption fits of his own.

Sam saw the helpless look on her face and angrily slapped the counter.

"Can't tell me," he hissed. He shook his head in disgust and rolled his eyes. He wouldn't ask her why; he'd learned a long time ago that she couldn't answer that question either. It didn't really matter anyways. What did matter is that she always did what her boss wanted and she kept things from him. The chasm between them was opening wider and he could feel her move further and further away from him. He missed her terribly and he was jealous of every moment she spent away from him.

"Can you at least tell me about the burns and bruises?"

"Bruises? What bruises?" she nearly yelped. Her eyes grew wide with feigned innocence as she pretended to not know what he was talking about. Sam gave her a dirty look.

"Cut the shit, Maddie," he growled. "I'm not blind. I saw the burns and bruises all up and down your left side when you got up this morning."

"It wasn't really a big deal," she said, not really seeing any point in pretending that she didn't know what he was talking about. "I was mistaken for some figure of local myth and they got a little freaked out."

"They were afraid of you, so they beat you up and set you on fire?" Sam asked, trying to clarify the bizarre and vague tale in his mind. "Who are 'they' and what did they mistake you for?"

"Just some primitive mud people," Maddie said lamely. Her spine tingled dangerously. She'd said as much as she was allowed to. Sam looked at her like he didn't believe her. Maddie wasn't sure that she believed it either and she had been there.

She had been collecting mold from the basements of a people whose technological sophistication matched Medieval Europe. They spent a lot of their time in a bog and they were almost always covered in something nasty. They enjoyed piercing their eyebrows but found it obscene to have holes in their ears. They were always plotting against one neighbor or another and had tried to use her and her Agents as pawns in their schemes. There had been a couple of minor conflicts when someone noticed the gold studs she wore in her earlobes. But the community had completely panicked when they saw the Tracker's mark on her finger.

The Tracker's mark was a ring; designed to identify the Tracker to any culture they encountered. It was all graceful curves and whorls, with four white diamonds at compass points of the ring and a fifth blue diamond in the center. Keung had once explained that the symbol signified an ancient Egyptian myth about the Pillars of Creation while the center stone represented the Tracker's home. Maddie hadn't been paying much attention at the time since she had been learning about what she was and she was really pissed off about it.

A few centuries before Maddie's arrival, a very violent, very ill-tempered Tracker had visited the muddy bog people. He had made the mistake of wearing earrings as well and when the locals had tried to correct him, he'd flipped out. He'd killed so many people in such a spectacular manner they'd developed a terrifying myth about the incident. And they had reacted to Maddie's Tracker's mark with extreme prejudice. It had not been a pleasant experience and was one of the reasons why there were Agents in the Center's infirmary.

Sam was stunned and shook his head. He was too baffled to say anything.

"Why in the hell would you be in a place like that?" he asked. "I thought you were supposed to be doing research."

"Sometimes you have to go where the information is," she shrugged lamely.

"You go to the information more often than not," Sam pointed out. His level of agitation was finally beginning to lessen. Maybe because she was finally telling him something. "Seems like pretty dangerous research, too."

Maddie shrugged to cover the sudden spasm in her back.

"I want you to quit. We have more than enough money saved now. I'm sure I can get my old job back. You can stay home and everything can go back to the way it was," Sam said desperately. He nearly cried when that regretful, miserable look settled across her face. She glanced at the floor, unable to look at him anymore.

"You know I would quit if I could," she said, her soft voice thick with tears.

"But you can't." The anger flared back while his voice trembled with restraint.

"No."

"Why not? What is so damn important about this job that you cannot let it go?"

"I can let it go, believe me, I can," Maddie looked at him with eyes shiny with tears. "It's that they cannot let me go."

"Why? What is it that you're doing that no one else can do? What can they possibly do to keep you where you don't want to be kept?" Sam shouted.

"They can get to you and the kids," Maddie replied honestly, not knowing what else to say. Sam's mouth dropped open in shock. Maddie wiped a tear away and offered him a bright smile. The comment was a truth meant to shock the argument into a stand still. It worked. He was so startled that he couldn't think straight.

Maddie wrapped her arms around his middle and squeezed him like an overgrown teddy bear. Touching his body was soothing even if he was mad. He stared down at her with frightened eyes.

"Who are you working for?" he asked. Maddie kept the smile on her face, as if the question didn't matter.

"Let's not fight anymore," she said as cheerfully as she could. "Let's go somewhere and do something. Katie and Chris won't be home for a couple of hours. Let's get Allen and go someplace fun."

She did something she had thought she'd never do. She let out just a little positive thought into Sam's mind, just to push the horror away and to make him just a tad more receptive to the idea of spending some quality time together. His mind seized it and he relented. Finally his face cracked and he gave her a small smile. She began to talk and listed all the things they could do together. She did get the feeling that he was humoring her while still contemplating the nuggets she'd given him. Now he had reason to go behind her back and snoop, looking for a way to get her out of the situation she'd found herself in a year ago. He'd figure out what she was and what she was doing and she wouldn't have to hide anything anymore.

As they began to make their plans, the phone rang. They froze and looked each other in the eye. Both of them knew who was calling and a feeling of dread settled over them. Maddie sighed and pulled away. Sam seized her by the arm and tugged her back.

"Don't answer that," he insisted.

"I'm sorry, Sam." Maddie pulled gently but firmly from his grasp and picked up the phone. Anger boiled back up in him as Maddie's head bowed dejectedly and she rubbed her forehead wearily. She held the phone pressed to her ear for several minutes and then hung up the phone.

"I have to go in to work," she said softly. Sam didn't reply. He gave her a hard look as Maddie silently picked up her keys and purse and left.

CHAPTER 4

Detective Darlene Arnold walked slowly up the gravel driveway that led to the small three-bedroom house embraced by two towering oak trees. As she made her slow way, she was careful to examine every detail of the place. The bushes beneath the windows were wild and unkempt and had begun to show signs of a kudzu infestation. The grass was thin and had dry brown spots. Toys were strewn across the property. Two shiny children's bicycles were propped against the battered family car.

The house was an old one, dating from the 1950s by the looks of it, and by the peculiar layout of the neighborhood. Dirty white paint cracked and peeled from the siding. The decorative shutters were badly tacked up beside the windows and looked undisturbed. A tech dusted the windows looking for prints. The front door remained closed and the dark wood was warped and scarred from long use and weather. There were no signs of forced entry so far.

Arnold moved around the back and took note that the small shrubbery was too thin to conceal a cat, much less a person, and that the windows were old and the frames cracked with rot. She turned to the back of the house with its tiny back yard and the trickle of a creek bordering the property. She stepped up the small cement back porch with its rusting iron rails and pretty wind chimes. The breeze suddenly brushed through the chimes and lent an eerie music to the scene.

The crime scene was being processed as she stepped into the house. Photographers were snapping pictures so fast that the flashes had a strobing effect on her retinas. The forensics crew had people crawling everywhere and they picked up anything that looked remotely like evidence. Arnold moved around them and took care where she stepped and looked at the things the techs were gathering without interfering. No one looked her in the eye. Their complexions were pale and their hands trembled ever so slightly. One or two looked as if they could be physically ill at any moment. Arnold watched them, astounded by their reaction to the crime scene.

Most of the people here were veterans; hell, half the forensic experts here were on loan from Atlanta. Those people were supposed to have seen everything. Or at least that's what Arnold had been led to believe. They were big city cops and were most likely to have seen every cruel thing that humans were capable of. They were jaded, hard and unshakeable. However, tonight they were clearly shaken.

Eventually, she stepped away from what everyone else was doing and faced what she had to. She took one last look around at the shattered home. The tiny kitchen had been destroyed, the cabinets had been shattered like glass and their contents ground to dust. The living room wasn't much better, the couches and end tables had been taken apart and tossed around like tinker toys. Both small rooms had walls with holes punched into the drywall. Insulation, wires, and pipes dangled from the wreckage.

Technicians were poking into the holes, hoping to find any key evidence that might have fallen between the walls.

There was blood everywhere, it streaked the walls as if children had played at finger painting. Grisly chunks of meat clung to the walls and ceiling, and was piled on the floor. Samples were being taken of the material, though no one doubted that the meat came from the victims. Arnold turned away from the destruction and started down the narrow hall where the bodies were.

She passed a small bathroom. That room was untouched, the only room in the house that the killer had overlooked. Or perhaps he had left it alone out of some strange sense of purpose or logic. Arnold stared at it and her profiling training kicked in as she took in the details. She stepped away and decided to make a final analysis of the room's condition once she had all of the facts.

She glanced into each of the two bedrooms that the children had slept in. The walls were in the same state of random destruction as the living room and kitchen. Nothing had escaped intact. Toys were broken and the beds and dressers were upended and splintered. Bloody sheets lay shredded in a heap on the floor. More blood splashed one wall and a small part of the ceiling. The old, cheap carpet was spongy with body fluids. The next bedroom was in exactly the same state. The scatter of toys, furniture, and blood may have been slightly different but the intent had been the same.

She turned away from the rooms when she heard someone call her name. Cooper was walking towards her with his shoulders hunched and his lined face pale and grim. Cooper had received his detective's badge the same year Arnold joined the force, and had been welcoming when she made detective just two years ago. He was a laid-back man, happily married with a mess of kids and dreamt of retiring in ten years on a boathouse. He stared at her with dull eyes and his usually smiling mouth was turned down in a forbidding frown.

"You're late," he said. "What took you?"

"I was in the shower when the call came in," she replied. Odds were Cooper had been at home as well. He was able to arrive on the scene sooner because he was already dressed to leave. He had six kids and he rarely got the chance to even loosen his tie when he got home. The kids mobbed him and demanded his undivided attention until they dropped like rocks into bed.

Neither of them was used to being called to crime scene at a moment's notice. Their small town was growing but they rarely saw the kind of crime that plagued more populated areas. Technically, Arnold and Cooper were homicide detectives, but there was rarely a death in the town that didn't occur through natural causes or traffic accidents.

There were plenty of assaults, though. The local population was poor and tended to drink their blues away. Then they went home and beat each other up. There was plenty of theft, petty vandalism (the water tower constantly displayed the name of some local teen in love) and they had their fair share of car accidents. Once in awhile, a husband grew too violent with his wife, or a battered wife reached the end of her rope, and then someone died. Those cases usually ended with a tearful confession.

Since there was a blessed lack of homicides, Arnold and Cooper often helped out in other departments. Arnold's last bust had been picking up a deadbeat dad who hadn't given her any trouble beyond some sexual harassment.

"Well, you should have gotten here sooner," Cooper grumped. "The call was made by the father's mother. The family was supposed to meet at her place for dinner last night and when they didn't show, she came by to find out why. She found the house a mess and called 911. She didn't actually see the bodies; she had enough sense not to go any further into the house than necessary. A couple of uniforms came in and found the family. We were called from there. The neighbors were questioned, but no one saw or heard anything."

"Where are the officers who found the bodies?"

"Probably still out in their cars puking their guts up. We'll get their statements when they settle down a bit."

Arnold frowned at this but said nothing. It was unprofessional to criticize a fellow officer even if they were overreacting. Everyone on the job had seen a dead body, even if it was mostly dead animals or car accident victims. How bad could the scene actually be?

"You better go have a look and get it over with," Cooper said and stepped aside so she could get by. Arnold sighed and moved towards the bedroom, careful not to step in any blood. The smell of decayed flesh drifted to her nostrils as she got closer to the master bedroom. The stink was thick and it coated her throat. She grimaced and kept walking. The victims had been dead for a day or two by the smell of it.

She did expect to come upon a hideous crime scene. After all, the living room and kitchen had been bloody. She thought she'd see a few bodies, shot or stabbed multiple times, or maybe a murder suicide. What her eyes fell upon was beyond anything experience or training had taught her to expect.

Her mouth dropped open and her eyes widened as she stared in horror at the carnage of the master bedroom. The photographer working the room kept muttering to himself between shots and his hands trembled so that he had to let the camera dangle from the strap around his neck every few shots. Whoever had killed the family had taken sadistic delight in the act. There was almost no precedence to this kind of madness. Sure, there had been plenty of killers who had posed a crime scene, played with their victims or what have you. But this, this went beyond the pale. Arnold couldn't think of a single case she'd read or heard of during or after college that described this kind of depravity. No wonder cops were puking and forensics was badly shaken.

Each of the victims' skulls had been crushed, with deep dents that deformed the tops of their heads. Blood and gray matter clung thickly in their hair. Blood streaked their faces and into their dull listless eyes. An opaque film covered the orbs, a sign that the family had been dead some time. Each body cavity had been evacuated and left the white bone of vertebrae gleaming under the harsh lights. This explained the chunks of meat scattered throughout the house. The skin of their chests had been peeled back and exposed bone and muscle. The scene was gruesome enough but it was the way the killer had played with the bodies that made Arnold's skin crawl.

Once the family was dead and the bodies had been eviscerated, the killer had posed the corpses around the master bedroom in a scene that was as obscene as it was gruesome. On the floor, the father's body had been posed and propped over the daughter's in a mock display of rape. The girl's face was contorted in terror while the father looked as if he slept. On the blood-soaked bed, the mother was propped against the wall with her legs spread open. The face of the eldest son was nestled between her thighs and his corpse was propped up on his arms and knees. Cradled under her arm was the youngest, a toddler boy, who curled against her body. Along the walls, long ropes of intestine were looped around nails and bits of debris to spell a single word over and over: Tracker.

Arnold tore her eyes from the scene in front of her and struggled to swallow the bile in her throat. She took out her notepad and began to write while she struggled not to let her hands tremble too much.

CHAPTER 5

Maddie drove slowly into Atlanta and through the narrow streets towards the Center. She barely saw the elegant office buildings and proud skyscrapers nestled in the autumn foliage of the city in the forest. Instead, her thoughts were concentrated fully on Sam and the cold frustration he felt. She couldn't blame him for feeling frustrated. She'd spent he better part of nine years taking care of home and family while he worked endless hours to get ahead. She had only complained when the loneliness became suffocating or when the kids were driving her to homicide. She'd learned to suck it up and cope, so why couldn't he? Besides, she was doing more than he ever did selling termite treatments to bored housewives. She was exploring the universe, meeting interesting people and finding things that were beneficial to all humanity. Sure, her boss was a bastard about secrecy and obedience, but at least the work was noble.

To be perfectly fair, though, Sam had made it home every night, no matter how late. And he did have the option to quit his job if it ever came between them. He hadn't become some sort of mythical figure complete with unnatural powers funded by a secret society with questionable ethics. He'd never come home covered in someone else's blood or peppered with ugly bruises or stitches. He'd never left the planet and, as far as she knew, he had told her everything.

Suddenly her cell phone rang. Maddie jumped and fumbled for her phone in the passenger seat.

"Hello?" she shouted. She hated driving while she talked on her phone. The sound of the engine made it hard for her to hear anything. It was her sister, and the woman was so busy with her career that she rarely had time to talk. So when she did make an effort to call, Maddie always picked up.

"Don't shout, Madeline. I can hear you," Darlene said.

"I'm sorry," Maddie apologized lamely. "I'm in the car. What's up?"

"I have to cancel dinner tomorrow. I just picked up a nasty case and I want to wrap it up quick," she explained apologetically.

Maddie froze and stopped paying attention the second her sister had said dinner tomorrow. She'd completely forgotten about it and felt like a jerk. So in a panic, she began to babble as cheerfully as she could. Darlene burst out laughing.

"You forgot, didn't you?" she asked.

"I'm sorry. It's just that Sam's mad at me about working too much. It's been on my mind," Maddie said, hoping that Darlene would accept the dumb excuse.

"You do work an awful lot," Darlene chided gently.

"Like you're one to talk. You work all the time," Maddie protested, thinking that her sister was no one to criticize. Darlene was a cop and, ever since her divorce, all she did was work.

"Not half as much as you do," Darlene retorted. "And I never leave town for weeks on end."

Maddie fell petulantly silent. She couldn't argue the point. "My work is important. I'm making a real contribution now," she muttered. Darlene was such a butthead for pointing out the flaws in her work habits.

"Contribution to what?" she demanded. "Nobody knows what you do."

"I'm in research," Maddie protested.

"Yeah, okay," Darlene didn't believe her for a second. "To be honest, I don't think that Sam is half as pissed off about your hours as he is about the fact that you don't tell him anything."

"I know," she growled.

"Look, you've been working there for what, a year now? You should have some vacation time coming. If your boss cares even a little bit, he'll give you the time off. No one can keep up the pace you are and not burn out. He has to know that."

"And if he doesn't care?"

"Then quit."

"You know they won't let me do that," Maddie sighed.

"Then half-ass the job until they fire you. Or go on strike. If that doesn't work, be a total bitch until they give you what you want. If you think the job is getting to be a problem between you and Sam, then stand up to your boss and demand some changes. They can't do this to you. It's not legal."

Maddie bit her tongue to keep from telling her sister that she didn't work for people that she could just take to court. That comment would lead to some awkward and painful questions. Traffic suddenly became thick ahead of her and she had to slam on the brakes and slow down before she hit someone.

"I gotta go. I just hit some traffic and it really sucks," Maddie said, grateful to cut the conversation short.

"Alright. Be safe," Darlene said.

"You, too."

Maddie sat in the traffic and pondered what her sister had said to her. Darlene had made some very good points. She was away from home entirely too much and the job was coming between her and Sam. She loved her husband and didn't want to be without him. She was going to have to mend things with Sam, starting by getting some significant time off from work. She contemplated how she was going to ask for time off. Should she ask as sweetly as she could then throw a fit if he said no? Or should she just come on like a freight train and be a bitch from the get-go? Either way, she couldn't see Keung being nice about the idea no matter what she did.

Failing all that, she could start being "careless" about where she left her work stuff when she took it home. No doubt Sam's curiosity would override his respect for her privacy and he would figure things out for himself. It wasn't like she could come right out and tell him what she'd been doing for the last year even if it was allowed. He'd never believe her and would probably have her committed for having delusions of grandeur. Not that she didn't wonder about her own sanity once in awhile.

She pulled into the Center's parking lot, her soul heavy with dread as she parked and got out of the van. She pushed a button on her keys and her car alarm set with a sharp chirp. A young man sauntered by and noticed her. He stared a minute and began to hurry up to her. Maddie eyed him suspiciously, noticing the bruises coloring his dark skin and the pretty gang colors he wore. She let her mind skim his thoughts, looking for signs that he was on drugs or that he intended violence. Not that it mattered; she was the Tracker, after all. In the last year she had faced men and women far meaner and tougher than this kid looked. She could take him, no problem.

But his mind was clear, which meant that he wasn't high, and his thoughts were colored with concern for her, which meant he didn't mean her any harm. She eyed his baggy clothes hanging over his skinny frame and decided that he wasn't carrying a gun. She gave him an expectant look and wondered what it was that had the young man in such a snit.

"Whatchu doin' girl?" he demanded, coming to a stop several feet away from her. "Dontchu know that place gots some crazy shit goin' on?"

Startled, Maddie turned and looked up at the place. On the outside, the Center looked like a dilapidated tenement on the verge of becoming condemned. The brick façade was crumbling and pock-marked. The fire escapes were rusty and looked loosely bolted to the walls. Even the windows were shabby, the glass cracked and dirty where they weren't completely boarded over. All of it was a stark contrast to the high tech efficiency and cleanliness of the floors within. Maddie scoffed at the young man.

"Hon, you don't know the half of it," she laughed. She began to walk towards the opaque glass doors at the front of the building.

"What's a nice lady like you doin' goin' inna place like that?" he called from where he was standing. He was afraid of the Center and he would go no further, not for her, not for anyone.

"Going to work," Maddie called back over her shoulder. The man was working up to something; his mind was full of curiosity now. He had heard all the urban legends that had grown up around the place and he wanted information that was more real, more reasonable than the things he heard on the streets. Maddie sent out a need to be away from her and, more importantly, away from this place. The young man took a step back but stopped. He fought her gentle influence and kept his gaze locked on the building looming ominously over him.

"Shouldn't you be in school?" she asked, her hand on the door. Time to change the subject and distract him. The young man clicked his tongue and rolled his eyes in disgust.

"Man, school is useless. I ain't learnin' nuthin' there that I can use," he sneered.

"Sure, whatever. Drop out and become another useless statistic. Go deal drugs and live in shitty apartments. Spend your time ducking cops and dodging bullets. Sounds like a *real good* way to go to me," Maddie said sarcastically. The man turned to her angrily. He eyed her clothes and the mini-van behind her.

"Man. You don't know nuthin' about me or my life. You can't go 'round tellin' people what they oughtta do," he yelled defensively.

Maddie shrugged. "Whatever, dude. Have a nice day," she said and went inside. The young man stared after her then finally succumbed to her influence. He turned and ran as fast as he could go.

George was waiting for her by the elevator with an amused look on his face. No doubt he'd listened in on her conversation with the young man. Maddie ignored him as she marched across the lobby. She let her walk show her less-than-pleased mood, her two-inch high-heeled black boots leaving scuff marks on the shabby floor. The lobby, like the exterior of the building, was left shabby lest someone wander in off the street.

The white paint on the walls had long ago turned yellow with age and the once proud decorative pillars were dull where the stone showed from underneath the graffiti. A large receptionist's desk sat, faded and broken, next to the glass doors. The linoleum on the floor was dingy, dirty and badly gouged in places. Litter was scattered around, never to be gathered and disposed of.

Of course, anyone who did come in off the streets and walked a few yards across the lobby would come to the steel double doors that led to the Atrium. The Atrium was a large glass building that housed all the exotic plants and animals brought back from missions for study. As Maddie approached George, a sharp, surprised scream echoed from beyond the doors. George laughed maniacally while Maddie chuckled and shook her head.

The screamer was Harold, the lab assistant. The unfortunate man had the distinction of being considered "most edible" by anything he worked with. Lately, the thing was a very mobile, very ravenous, carnivorous bush. The thing had a rabid taste for Harold and it stalked him relentlessly. So far, Harold had managed to survive all his encounters with only minor scrapes and bruises. Many urban legends about the Center were a result of Harold's loud and terrified shrieking.

"So, how was your time off?" George asked pleasantly as they stepped onto the elevator.

"Brief. Caught up on a little sleep, played a little with the kids, fought with the husband, the usual," Maddie replied as nonchalantly as possible.

"Oh? Are you and Sam having trouble?"

"Sam thinks that the job is getting between us," Maddie said glumly. Sam hadn't come right out and said so, but nearly all their arguments had been about her work. She could take a hint.

"And you don't agree with that opinion?" George asked, as his brows rose towards his hairline.

"Oh, no, I totally agree. I just don't know how to ask Keung for the time off so that I can deal with it."

"Good luck," George snorted. "If I knew how to get anything out of him, I'd have started doing it a long time ago," George replied. Maddie sighed and leaned against the soft padding of the elevator walls.

The elevators were kept beautifully. The call buttons doubled as DNA and print scanners that analyzed the fingers of anyone who touched them. That way, people who weren't part of the Center couldn't accidentally find themselves where they didn't belong. The elevators simply wouldn't work if the wrong people pushed the call buttons. But it wasn't fool proof. Maddie wondered how many people got the bright idea to cut fingers off authorized personnel to gain access to the building. She'd never asked though, she didn't really want to know.

"Has there ever been a Tracker who didn't have marital problems?" Maddie asked. Every Tracker before her had been married, with only one or two exceptions. The Quarter required it, that way they could at least have one offspring who could be guaranteed to be truly descended from the proper blood lines. The very few exceptions to the marriage rule hadn't had any children. Maddie's immediate predecessor had been a bachelor cousin without children.

George pushed a floor button as he thought about it. The elevator dropped, sending Maddie's stomach into her throat. She swallowed and tried to ignore the sensation.

"Sure there has," he said.

"What did they do right?" Maddie asked, hoping for a kernel of wisdom that might just save her ass.

"They married someone who either already hated them or were phenomenally stupid."

"You know, those are marital problem in and of themselves," Maddie sighed.

"True enough. The job doesn't leave a lot of time for the individual doing the work, much less other people. Why do you think I never got married?" George said.

"Cuz you're not allowed to?"

"No, the Quarter *discourages* Agents to get married. It's not the same thing as forbidding us to. What do you think my father did for a living?" George asked.

"I don't know. I thought that the Quarter recruited you guys out of military prisons or bad-ass camps or something."

"Much like your position, Tracker, my title is an inherited one. Everyone here has a long family tradition of service. The previous Tracker was your distant cousin, which is why you didn't have a clue about us when you joined. But you still have blood ties to the Center and the Quarter, just like everyone else," George was lecturing now. Maddie only gave him half her attention. "You should know all this by now."

"Where's the meeting at today?" she asked, changing the subject.

"Keung didn't tell you?"

"Keung doesn't tell me anything he doesn't absolutely have to. I don't think he likes me," Maddie complained.

"Keung doesn't like anyone. The meeting is on sub-basement level two, Agents' headquarters."

The elevator stopped and the door slid open smoothly. The Agents' headquarters housed the training facilities and equipment required by the group of men assigned to protect the Center, Tracker and her heirs. They thought only of the defense of the Center and the well being of the bloodline that spawned the individuals who bore the title and the mark. Many have died proudly in that noble service and it was whispered that many more would die in the service of this Tracker.

George knew that there was some truth to the whispers. Of all the Trackers he had known in his many years of service, only this one remained stubbornly unaware of the dangers she perpetually stepped into. She insisted on playing no roles and she refused to bend knee when the occasion demanded it. The Tracker explained that she was what she was and she wouldn't pretend otherwise. She often said that it was difficult enough just being herself.

George could appreciate the attitude but it wasn't a practical one. He hoped that she learned better before it got her killed.

"There you go, thinking that I'm naïve and foolish again," Maddie said with a false pout. She knew very well what everyone thought of her, she *was* a mind reader after all and no one bothered to shield their thoughts around her. It hurt her feelings sometimes, but she never held anyone's thoughts against them.

"Then stop reading my mind if it offends you so much," he retorted playfully. "Control your gift, Tracker, and you'll never be hurt."

Maddie gave him a wet raspberry and hurried ahead of him. She entered the conference area at the back of the floor. All the other department heads were already gathered. Three had already taken their seats and two were whispering fervently near the ranking Agent's offices.

Elcia, who ran the library and records department, greeted Maddie like an old friend. As the only other woman on staff, Elcia was determined to endear herself to the Tracker out of a strong sense of sorority. Maddie didn't mind. She saw the demure woman as a much-needed ally whenever she needed support against the guys and as a good friend.

Maddie waved politely to Bob, who headed up weapons and technology. While he was unsuccessful at it in the extreme, Bob thought of himself as ladies' man, and took every opportunity to grope any woman who came within his reach. The habit often drove both women into fits and they made a point of never coming within arm's length of the leach. He did tend to stare excessively at them anyway, which continued to drive them both crazy.

George took the chair next to Andre, who was Chief of Medicine. Andre acknowledged him with a nod before letting his tired eyes close. Oscar, a skinny and cantankerous old man, ran Biological research and the associated facilities.   The bird-like geezer was talking to Sherman, Maddie's assistant, and his whispers came hoarse and harsh. He waved his arms furiously and accidentally smacked the younger man in the head when he did so.

Maddie ignored Oscar as a general rule. He disliked her intensely and liked to claim that she was grossly incompetent and shouldn't be allowed near anything requiring electricity. While she did not care for the man's poor attitude, she couldn't quite fault the man's opinion. When she first began her tenure, she'd accidentally crashed the Center's entire network. Not only did the computers lose power but the air conditioning and refrigeration failed as well as the independent air and water filter systems in the Atrium. The locks on cages had disengaged and several dangerous and troublesome animals had gotten free. The ensuing chaos and damage had nearly given the old man a stroke when he saw his research going down the tubes. It had taken a week for the techs to get all the systems functional again. Agents had combed the Center for the lost animals and returned them to their cages. When Maddie had returned from her last mission, she'd given Oscar his hand held monitor in somewhat less than pristine condition. From the harassed look on Sherman's face, it was clear that Oscar was still upset about it.

Keung entered the room as soon as Maddie took her seat. He was a giant of a man, nearly seven feet tall with lean, broad shoulders and long legs. He was dressed immaculately with a finely tailored black suit and green silk tie. Every dark hair was carefully cut and perfectly placed. His green eyes glittered as he scanned the room and his alabaster face showed all the expression of a granite wall. His penetrating gaze took in Oscar mid-rant but otherwise ignored him. Maddie watched his graceful movements thinking, not for the first time, that he looked rather Asian despite his aquiline and Caucasian features.

Keung had a stack of folders in his hands, which he handed out without speaking. Oscar finally ceased his tirade and hurried to take his place next to George. Sherman gave Maddie an exasperated look as he opened his folder and began to read. Maddie felt a little guilty for being the cause of his harassment, but only a little. She was still going to torment Oscar as often as she could.

"There have been some developments on Iza, fourth planet of the third galaxy," Keung began abruptly. The little group settled down and paid attention. "An ambitious young man is attempting to unify the realm known as Rhasta. In this particular case, it means that he is rallying the local population and attempting to bring the local crime lords to justice. Of course, the crime lords are resisting. They don't wish to lose their stranglehold on territory and they don't want to hang.

"We have been asked to assist in the location and capture of the two most elusive crime lords, Ezra Barnum and Iol Cass. The Quarter wants the usual DNA samples from Cass and Barnum plus examples of the recent technology. We have had somewhat limited contact with the Rhasta region, so it is vital that the Tracker makes a full and detailed report," Keung gave Maddie a hard look which said that he didn't like the way she'd been writing her reports lately. Maddie blushed and ducked her head until she banged it on the table.

"Due to the volatile nature of this mission, I will ask for two Agents to volunteer for guard duty for the Tracker," Keung glanced at George who nodded acknowledgement. He'd see to it. "The Tracker needs to be outfitted with mini-cameras and microphones. The Quarter is asking for audio as well as video. And I don't think I have to remind anyone that the Rhasta culture is a male-dominated one, so I expect the Tracker's wardrobe a little more appropriate to the situation. Don't let her go around being mistaken for a whore again, Bob." Bob snorted and slapped the table with unrestrained mirth. Maddie and Elcia gave him dirty looks. Keung ignored them.

"All the bios on Cass and Barnum are in the files along with customs, gender roles and social hierarchy of the region. Elcia, see to it that the Tracker receives updates on the local politics. And Andre, make sure everyone gets their immunizations and first aide kits.

"Be ready to go in two days. It'll be a short trip, so lets not have any mistakes this time."

Taking the last sentence as a dismissal, everyone leaped to their feet and rushed for the elevators. Maddie waited behind, hanging close to the wall and biting her lip.

"What do you want, Tracker?" Keung asked coldly.

"I'm sure you're aware that I'm having some trouble at home," she began hesitantly.

"It's been on your mind lately," he replied, reminding her that he too was telepathic. And that he monitored her very closely. "I suppose you want time off to reconnect with your family."

"That would be nice," Maddie said smiling hopefully. "Of course, I probably wouldn't need any time off if you'd just let me tell Sam—"

"No."

"Why not? He wouldn't tell anyone, and it would make my life a lot easier," she protested.

"No."

Maddie crossed her arms and glared at him. "You know, you can't stop me from spilling my gut to my husband. I mean, what are you going to do, follow me around to make sure I don't tell?"

Keung stepped towards her until she was eye to chest with him. He pulled himself to his full height and glared down his long nose at her. Maddie had to tilt her head all the way back to look at his face. It made her neck hurt.

"Of course I cannot stop you from doing something that you are truly determined to do. But there are consequences to your actions. Need I remind you of the nanite package you carry within your body?" Keung's voice had grown cold and the pitch had deepened until it nearly growled.

Maddie scowled and looked away. The nanites coursing through her body was still a sore topic for her. They had gotten there on her first day when Keung had simply walked up to her and injected them into her neck. The assault had upset her greatly but not as much as the ensuing chaos and illness she suffered afterwards. Her family had been terrified by her ordeal and it had taken months to get Sam to quit treating her like she was dying or going crazy.

The nanites served a purpose as part of what made the Tracker such a formidable figure. They supplied Maddie with everything she needed to know. The microscopic robots were programmed to download information directly into her memory centers whenever she needed it. She now possessed extensive knowledge in geology, chemistry, medicine, biology, botany and the martial arts. She also possessed a great deal of historic memory of each of the worlds and galaxies the Trackers had visited. Unfortunately, most of her historical information came down to her from the memories of other Trackers and whoever had programmed the nanites had not been very discriminate with what they dumped into her head. Sometimes, especially when her mind wandered, she'd suddenly find herself remembering some very personal things that had nothing to do with her. To put it politely, many of the Trackers had been wanton womanizers.

The nanites had served a second purpose to ensure the Tracker's mythic abilities. They worked to repair damaged tissue, whether that meant rapidly repairing injuries or the normal deterioration due to age. Within a couple of months, Maddie had noticed the lines that had appeared with turning thirty were fading away. But to repair biological damage, the nanites took their energy from Maddie herself and increased her metabolic rate. So she was forced to consume more calories in order to survive. The nanites also increased her strength, reflexes, and heightened her other senses.

When the nanites had locked onto her brain cells they had altered her neuro chemistry in order to do as they were programmed, which left her telepathic. Lately though, both Andre and George were heavily hinting that there might be a secondary talent developing in her mind. Maddie tended to just ignore them. She hadn't noticed anything new. She was still learning to deal with the first batch of side effects caused by the nanites.

"Were I you, Tracker, I would be mindful of the fact that the nanites are also used by the Quarter to monitor your actions. You will be most severely punished should you disobey a rule, especially the vow of secrecy."

Maddie gaped at him in open-mouthed disbelief. Keung had just threatened her!

"I believe that we will not be requiring your services for at least three months once this mission is completed. Provided, of course, that there are no gross mistakes that need correcting," Keung turned away from her, seeming to dismiss her. "However, should you be called during that time, you will be expected to respond and do your duty."

And then he left.

CHAPTER 6

Sam stared at the empty bed with his fists clenched at his sides. He was brooding and didn't notice how his fingers dug into the flesh of his palms. His thoughts wandered to the events of just two days before when Maddie had come home from her meeting at work. She had looked haggard and anxious when she had stepped though the front door. She wouldn't meet his gaze and didn't speak unless she had to. It had taken several hours but she had finally told him what was going on. He had exploded when Maddie told him that she was going out of town again after being home for only two days. He threw a fit, yelling at her and throwing his weight around in hopes of shaming her into changing her mind and staying home. Maddie endured it quietly and watched him move from room to room, roughly pushing objects around as he cleaned them, and slamming doors. She wept a little at his frustration, knowing exactly how he felt and feeling guilty for it. But she refused to bow to his wishes. She would not agree to quit her job and she refused to stay home. It didn't help matters when Maddie finally got fed up with his behavior and snapped: "You're acting like a little girl."

Sam gave her a look that should have burned her into a grease spot on the couch. Then he turned and left the house, slamming the door so hard that the windows rattled. He couldn't stand to talk to her right then; he'd take a drive and calm down before he returned. It turned out that it took a long time for him to come home. But when he finally did, he found Maddie still angry. She said nothing when he stepped through the front door. She simply shot him dirty looks and avoided him. She locked herself in her office and only came out to eat and use the restroom. Whenever he walked by the stairs leading into the basement, he thought he could detect the scent of cigarette smoke coming out from between the cracks in the door. He stalked away in anger and disgust, thinking that if the bitch wanted to kill herself by filling her lungs with cancer, it was just fine by him.

After a day of arguing, Maddie finally reappeared and told him that Keung was giving her three months off to spend with her family. The kids had hoorayed and jumped up and down. But the mention of Keung's name set Sam off again and he began to yell. Maddie watched him with her lips pressed tightly together while her left hand played with the ring on her finger. Sam stared at the ring. He hated the thing with all his being. She'd worn it ever since she'd taken the 'research' job and she never took it off. It had become a symbol of Maddie's bondage to Keung and the Center. It was a shackle on her, a constant reminder that Keung was her master and her life was no longer her own. And like all good slaves, her willpower was dribbling out of her until she was just an extension of her master's will. Sam wanted to rip the ring from her finger and throw it down the deepest darkest hole he could find and pile dirt over it.

They eventually fell into an unwieldy silence. They spent the last day before Maddie left going through the motions of happy domestic life and barely speaking to one another. When he woke the next morning, he found the bed empty. She'd left without saying good-bye. He shouldn't have let her leave like that. He should have done something to smooth things over with her. Now she was gone and there was no telling when she'd be back, if she came back at all. Her abrupt absence left an aching hole in his soul that yearned to be filled.

He quickly made the bed and smoothed the wrinkles out of a night spent alone. Maddie had bunked out on the couch. She'd been too put out with him to lie next to him. He went into the kitchen to do the dishes with Allen following him whining and crying. The toddler had picked up on the tension in the house and needed to be comforted and reassured. Sam lifted him onto the counter next to the sink and let him play in the water while he loaded the dishwasher. Once he finished rinsing the dishes and the counter tops were wiped down, Sam took Allen into his bedroom to change his diaper and play until lunchtime. An hour later Allen was full and rubbing his eyes drowsily, Sam put him down and settled in to play video games.

He played the game but his mind kept wandering to the misery of loneliness his life had become. He should have made an effort to make up with Maddie before she left. He should try to be more understanding of how hard she worked to provide for their family. After all, if he had managed their finances better she wouldn't have had to go to work at all. But things had gotten so bad that they had been on the brink of losing the house. They'd been living paycheck to paycheck, and money had been so tight that Maddie had been forced to ask his permission before even buying groceries. But now Maddie brought in an income that not only paid their bills with ease but also left Sam with enough money to spend freely. He really couldn't complain. Then why did he feel so unhappy?

Eventually, he flung the controller down in frustration. Soon after, Katie and Chris got off the bus and the day continued along its usual rhythms. He helped the older two with their homework while Allen vied for his attention. He made dinner, which was inhaled greedily and then the three dashed off for some playtime before it was time for baths and bed.

It had gotten easier over time to get the kids down to sleep. They had stopped asking after their mother after awhile and now Daddy was enough to make them feel safe and secure. It was heartbreaking to see the distance between Maddie and her children developing into an ever-widening chasm. Children needed their mother and it looked like these three would have to learn to do without theirs.

He sat on the couch and bleakly flipped through channels looking for something violent enough to numb the ache in his brain. The phone rang and he pondered whether or not he felt like answering. He answered it but only after being certain that there was nothing on. He paid for two hundred channels and there was nothing on. It figures. He gave the caller a bland greeting.

"Hey, Sam, it's Louise. Is Maddie around?"

"She's out of town," Sam told her as he had told her dozen times over the last year. It had become the generic answer whenever someone called for Maddie these days. Sometimes he forgot himself and told people she was out of town even when she was home. He took it as a sign that she was gone entirely too much. Not that anyone called for Maddie very often anymore. Her family, with the exception of her sister Darlene, called only for important family business. They weren't angry nor was there a lack of interest on their part but because she simply wasn't home to talk to. All of her friends had faded away from neglect months ago, which left only Louise clinging to their long friendship with tooth and nail.

"Again?" Louise snapped. "Does she ever spend time with you guys anymore?"

"When she's home," Sam said in a tone of voice that left no doubt how often that was. Louise only let out a thoughtful "Huh."

"Are you okay with that?" she asked. "I mean, if it was my man, I'd be going crazy if he was gone all the time."

"I do alright," he assured her, not really wanting to talk about it. Louise picked up on his reluctance but couldn't let the subject go.

"You know what you should do, you oughta grab the kids and do something fun," she suggested. "Make a weekend of it. That way you'll get out of the house and take your mind off of things for awhile. You need the break."

Sam promised to think about it then fell into idle chatter. He felt like he was stealing Maddie's friend away from her but then her friendship with her childhood playmate hadn't been the only relationship she was neglecting. He was lonely and he longed for adult conversation. Louise's chatter was a soothing balm to his raw emotions.

She let him go only after reciting Maddie's desperate love for him and making him promise to be patient just a little while longer. He hung up the phone and noticed a note written in Maddie's neat hand sitting on the end table. The message had been blunt and to the point. She would return home as soon as she could and they would talk. There was an apology and a declaration of undying love. To his surprise, there was a phone number where she could be reached at any time. Feeling better, he decided that Louise's advice had been sound. He would take the kids out and have a good time. The time would pass and, before he knew it, Maddie would be home. Then they would have three months to mend things. He could afford to be patient for just a while longer. In the meantime, he would get some of Maddie's hard-earned pay and take the kids to the zoo for the day.

*   *   *

The Agent watched the family wander the zoo from a safe distance. He was always careful that there was a crowd or a piece of scenery to blend into. It was considered something of a faux pas if the Tracker's family spotted an Agent trailing them. There had been awkward and sometimes violent confrontations in the past when a Tracker's spouse thought that she was being stalked. So Sam and his children were happily ignorant of the bland-featured man watching their every move.

He watched as they moved along the cement paths and pointed in glee at the animals on display and stared with pleasure at the exotic foliage. He made notes when Chris tripped and skinned his knee and when Katie ate too much cotton candy and threw up. Allen wandered off while Sam was cleaning up his eldest child. It didn't take long for the attentive father to notice that his youngest had gone missing. It took even less time for him to locate and capture the errant toddler.

The baby had noticed the Agent several times and took to smiling and waving at him. Charmed by the pretty child, the Agent gave him a small smile and a wave. The Tracker's family finally left at sundown, happy and exhausted.

*   *   *

The changeling stared at the crowds of wandering humans that moved through the zoo, its eyes growing dull from boredom. It watched for humans in particular family groups as described by Him. There were several groups that fit the description of two mated adults of opposite gender with three offspring. But none of the groups had the attributes it looked for in its prey. The last humans had been a disappointing kill. There had been no struggle for the last breath, no fight for survival. They had gone to their deaths as meekly as lemmings. It wanted prey that would struggle for every precious second of its terrible end. It wanted to see human teeth, bloody and broken, gritted in the final last grim moments of its pathetic life.

A human male with three small young walked by. The changeling watched them and saw that the family lacked an adult female and promptly disregarded them. Then it saw the Agent lurking near a small herd of humans. The humans varied in ages, from the very old to the very young. Two adult humans, neither old nor young, were haranguing the offspring loudly and angrily. Behind them, the Agent stood against a wall and watched the family intently. It had almost missed it; it was one of the Agent's powers to go unnoticed wherever he went. But the changeling had seen it. It grinned greedily as it watched the Agent regard the family blandly. The family did not notice the man following them around, but then they wouldn't. It was said that the Quarter valued secrecy above all things. It studied the humans, noting that they were an aggressive group, very likely to give it the battle for life it craved.

It followed the family to their vehicle and took to the air as the engine spewed toxic fumes. It followed them home and watched as they went inside their humble home. It fought to suppress its laughter as it plotted its next kill.

CHAPTER 7

Maddie hated traveling in the Threshold. It was a nauseating and painful experience that always left her vomiting and just a little more stupid. She felt anxious and jumpy at the coming trip and not just because of the agonies of the journey. She'd broken another rule by giving Sam her work number and she was still waiting to get caught. The no-call rule had been explained to her on her first mission. As Tracker, she would find herself in extremely volatile situations in which an incoming call could be awkward in the extreme. In those moments, awkwardness could be fatal. But Sam had been so pissed off when she left that she had to throw him a bone. Perhaps if she just made herself more accessible to him he would calm down a bit. She decided that if Sam had been the one with this job, she'd be plenty pissed off too.

She went through the motions of getting ready. She read through the information on cultural customs provided by Elcia. She familiarized herself with the local plant and animal life written up for her by Oscar. She memorized every word, hoping to keep her mind full enough to prevent anyone from finding out what she'd done. That was the problem with working in a place where everyone was a telepath. They knew what you had done the second you thought of it. Which made it difficult to keep from thinking about something. It was like a sore tooth and she just couldn't leave it alone. So her mind was conspicuously blank when Bob walked into her office carrying a box.

He stopped just inside the door and blinked at her. He cocked an eyebrow and tilted his head suspiciously.

"What are you up to?" he asked slyly. His round, fleshy face split in a wide grin. He hoped that she was up to some sort of practical joke that he could be included in. Maniacal antics weren't beyond Maddie's range of activities and hers tended to come off with a great deal of hilarity. Her favorite targets were Oscar and the more cantankerous Agents. Bob had been hankering for an opportunity to take part in one of her plots but she always carefully left him out. He became over-affectionate during group activities and she didn't want her leg humped.

"Nothing," she said quickly. She flinched at the sound of her own voice. It sounded entirely too innocent, even to her. "Gimme my stuff."

Bob came forward and set the box on her desk. He stood there grinning and waited. Maddie just stood there and stared at him like he was a very large bug.

"Come on, Tracker, you're not thinking so hard that I *know* that you're up to something. You're going to get Oscar back, aren't you?"

"What did Oscar do that I have to get him back for?" Maddie asked with alarm. Her hand wandered towards the file on her desk. Had the skinny old fart given her bogus information? Did it matter? She was going to spend most of her time in a city. Typically, cities weren't hot beds of wild life, so what if Oscar had fudged the info? Suddenly Bob's mind was as blank as the expression on his face. Maddie frowned; it was like looking at a freshly painted wall.

"Nothing," Bob squeaked as he began to move slowly towards the door. Maddie gave him the evil eye and tried to get the man to open up and tell her what Oscar had done. It did nothing but encourage the fool to grin harder. Finally, Maddie turned away and let him have his fun. In the end, it didn't matter what Oscar did. The old man was vindictive, true, but his ideas of malicious mischief were pretty harmless. She dug through the box to see that Bob had brought her everything she'd need.

"Where's my weapons and gadgets?" she asked loudly. She expected the man to already be out of the room and on his way back to his labs. The sight of him leaning casually against the doorjamb annoyed her.

"Keung told me to bring them down to the Threshold instead of giving them directly to you," he replied. His dark eyes crawled up and down her body and twinkled lecherously. A very idealized image of her nude body suddenly popped into his head. Maddie snorted rudely and crossed her arms. The ass was hoping she'd forget he was there and undress in front of him!

"Get out," she growled. Bob stared at her with mock innocence.

"Did I say something?" he asked.

"Get out before I slap you silly," Maddie snarled and stomped towards him. Bob grinned and backed away from her. She closed the door in his smug face with a satisfactory slam. She could hear him laughing as she went back towards the box on the desk.

She was almost afraid to look at the clothes that Bob had provided for her. He had a tendency to dress her in the most revealing clothes the mission would let him get away with. She often wore outfits she wouldn't have been caught dead in when she was a teenager and wearing a size two. Those days were long past and she really wasn't shaped for the slut uniforms that Bob forced on her.

She pulled a white shirt from the box, almost expecting it to be nothing but a sheer and thin strip of cloth. Instead it was very modest. It had a plain high collar, long straight and simple sleeves with a long line of tiny pearl buttons running from top to bottom. It was fitted at the waist and had plenty of extra room in the chest, as if Maddie was expected to be very well-endowed. Next out was a long, voluminous, black split-skirt and a pair of matte black knee boots with long white stockings. A simple hat woven from some thick stemmed plant had been dyed black and hung with a white veil. She also found a pair of white lace gloves matching the veil on the hat. At the bottom of the box was a long black coat without buttons or straps to tie it close. Maddie looked the whole thing over, thinking that she was going to look like a very grim beekeeper.

She dressed quickly, her fingers fumbling over the tiny pearl buttons, and stomped her feet in her boots to make the leather conform around her feet. She picked up the hat from her desk and walked out of her office. She made her cautious way through the Control Room, being very careful not to run into anyone or throwing off the rhythm of the place.

The Control Room was the most populated and chaotic place in the Center. From there, everything in the five galaxies was monitored on computers and huge screens by technicians and analysts. The information was sorted, organized, and pored over as the relevance of each event was determined. Two copies were made and one was kept in the Center's library while another was forwarded to the Quarter.

Maddie waved to one or two analysts that she recognized while she waited for the elevator. One saw her waving and stopped to wave back. His act broke the rhythm of the room and a crowd of men went down in an explosion of paper. Maddie stepped onto the elevator giggling at the shouted curses that came from behind her. She pressed a button and the elevator dropped, taking her to the Agent's Headquarters ten floors down.

As part of their duties as the defensive force for the Center and the caretakers of the Tracker and her bloodline, the Agents also stood guard for the Center's most vulnerable point: the Threshold. The Threshold was a mindless thing with just enough consciousness to follow orders and deliver living things and objects from one place to another. Its reach was quite far and it had no difficulties delivering its cargo to any point in the five galaxies. But there were several reports in the library stating that the Threshold could be breached using another of its kind. Since no one knew if there were more or if anyone else had one, the Threshold was held in a steel and titanium reinforced room and was under constant vigilance by six Agents. Should hostile forces cross the Threshold, three Agents would confront the invaders and destroy the Threshold. Meanwhile, the other three Agents would seal off the area, gather reinforcements and make certain key personnel were evacuated from the building.

Maddie nodded at the Agents as she approached them. They stood at attention, three facing the room with the door to their backs, three standing across from them facing the door to the Threshold. They held long exotic guns across their chests and stared sternly ahead of them. The men facing away from the door nodded back at her without looking at her. She slipped between the ranks as one guard shifted his grip on his rifle to open the door for her. Maddie eyed the weapon in his hands, appraising its sleek lines and noting the subtle lights and monitors along the barrel and grip. It was a high tech weapon, clearly too sophisticated to be a native gun of this planet. She wondered briefly where the gun had originated. The Agent saw her appreciative gaze and subtly tilted it so that she could get a better look at it. She made all the appropriate sounds of being impressed and smiled her thanks. The Agent did not respond he simply returned the gun to its proper position in his hands. Maddie stepped through the door to be greeted by the impatient stares of three men. Keung and George stood next to a short bank of computers, while the grim faced Agent she had dubbed Fred stood next to a small steel table across the room.

"You're late," Keung said, gesturing for her to come further into the room.

"Sorry, I had to run Bob off before I could get dressed," Maddie replied and shrugged. Keung had already turned back to the computers and did not respond to her excuse. For several minutes, Maddie was left to stare at her shoes while she waited for something to happen. In his corner, Fred lifted something from the table and approached her with it in his hands.

Maddie looked up in time for Fred to hold the thick belt out to her. It was threaded through several pouches and had several small objects hanging in loops in the belt. She tried to take it from him, but Fred pulled it back with a frown.

"Allow me to place it upon you," his words were polite enough but his tone said that he thought she was too incompetent to do it herself. Maddie scowled at him and thought about saying something insulting. But Fred would most likely make the mission a misery if she went too far. So, for the sake of peace, Maddie lifted her arms and allowed him to wrap it around her waist. It was then that she noticed his clothes.

"What are you wearing?" she squealed, bursting into laughter. Fred scowled and flushed, but didn't answer her. She looked over at George and saw that he was dressed similarly and she completely lost it. She bent over with her guffaws, as Fred grew redder and redder.

As a general rule, Agents were a grim and serious lot and they tended to dress accordingly. The standard uniform was dark and severe and left no room to mistake them for anything other than the dangerous men that they were. But Fred and George had shed their stark clothes and had donned outfits that were decidedly more festive. Fred was wearing a long fitted coat in a brilliant scarlet. The broad collar was embroidered in pastel pinks and blues. Lavender lace frothed at his throat and at his cuffs, covering his black gloved hands. His satin shirt was a deep royal purple with bright pink pearl buttons. He wore skintight indigo pants with gold and yellow curly-cues embroidered along the seams. The pants ended abruptly in thigh-high, glossy black boots with broad four-inch heels. On his head, he wore a wide black hat that sported a broad purple band and a long puffy white feather jutting out of it.

George wore something very much like it but the colors were different. His coat was white and it sported dark blue and orange embroidery along the shoulders and sleeves. His tight pants were pink with green curly-cues and his high boots were a glossy brown. His shirt was forest green with lace in mint green.

"Calm down Tracker," George chided. "It is not that bad."

"I'm sorry," she hooted. "But you guys just look so damn prissy!"

Fred stalked back to his place across the room growling. George tossed something at her without a warning. She caught it with a surprised squeak and looked down to see her cell phone in her hand. The Tracker's Mark was engraved in yellow on the blue plastic casing. She sighed in relief, grateful that, so far, her illegal act hadn't been discovered. As soon as she thought it, she wiped her mind blank. Both Fred and George's head came up and they stared intently at her.

"What?" Maddie asked making her eyes wide and innocent.

"What are you hiding?" George asked while Fred scowled harder. Maddie stepped back and wondered if Fred's face was going to collapse underneath the dark expression.

"Nothing." Her voice sounded squeaky and she flinched.

"Tracker." It was a clear warning.

"What? Do I have to reveal every dirty thought I have about Fred?" Maddie snapped, trying to cover her ass while unable to resist teasing the man. Fred rolled his eyes in disgust while George chuckled at the other man's discomfort.

"I'm sorry, but your butt just looks soo goood in those pants!" she crooned. Inwardly, she sighed in relief that none of them had been paying enough attention to her thoughts.

Keung said nothing about the antics as he stepped to the center of the room.

"It is time," he said softly. Maddie, George and Fred stepped close to him and joined hands. Keung's eyes glazed over as he sank into a deep trance. She caught a whiff of musky cologne. Maddie leaned over to Fred and whispered, "Ooh Fred! You smell so good."

Fred remained stone-faced and refused to look at her. It was just too much fun to tease him. This mission might be a laugh after all. Both men were embarrassed and uncomfortable as hell in their clothes which would definitely make it easier to give them a hard time. Maddie giggled in anticipation of the jokes.

"Quiet, Tracker," Keung's voice was vague and low but she fell silent immediately.

Keung had taken off his jacket and rolled up his shirtsleeves. He placed a big hand on Maddie's shoulder while he made welcoming gestures with the other. At the back end of the room, the smooth black floor rippled as the Threshold responded to Keung's call. It gathered itself into an oblong mass of rippling, sparkling light and began to flow towards the Keeper. He waited patiently as it came to a stop and stretched out a tendril and placed it in the palm of his outstretched hand. Water pooled and then dripped from his hand and landed with wet splats on the floor. Maddie shuddered in anticipation of what was to come next.

A deep buzzing sound erupted from the lumpy watery thing as it prepared to do its job. It pulled slowly away from Keung, leaving a wet trail across his hand. It flowed to the very center of the room where a small point of light glowed in its center. It spun rapidly, the force of its movement made its malleable body grow and shape itself into a cylinder. The white light within it burned brighter and brighter until Maddie ducked her head to protect her retinas while Fred and George shielded their eyes with their free hands. Keung took the opportunity to step away from the three and stand aside to let the Threshold do its work.

Once it reached its full height, it bent gracefully in the middle, exposing its impossibly black mouth as it came ever closer. It paused for just a moment and let Maddie stare fearfully into the void before it lunged and scooped up the woman and two men. She tried to scream but her mouth was filled with the strange nothingness that forced her jaws apart and stifled her cries. She really had to learn to keep her mouth shut.

Keung watched calmly as the Threshold began to collapse upon itself. Its top sank downwards while the bottom lifted from the floor to meet it. It continued in this way until it was only a sliver of brilliant light caught in mid-air at the center of the room. Suddenly the bright light blinked out and it collapsed with a fatigued splash. Keung gathered up his jacket and sent soothing thoughts at it. It responded by sending feelings of contentment for having served its master. He bid it farewell and left so that it might rest for the work ahead.

CHAPTER 8

He sat in his favorite chair sipping bourbon and contemplating the massive tapestry stretched from one end of his private chamber to the other. He remarked to himself that it was incredible how a species as useless and stupid as humans could produce such things as bourbon and tapestries. All His usual interactions with the creatures had led him to believe that they were incapable of anything but eating and breeding. But there it was: the tapestry glowed in the fierce firelight as the bourbon slid down his throat with pleasing bitterness.

He stared at the tightly woven cloth and examined the intricate detail the craftsman had woven into his masterpiece. It depicted a climactic scene from a western European folktale. A medium-sized and wholly unremarkable man held a great and shining sword over his head in a killing stroke. At his feet was the cowering and bleeding image of a Distari grunt. It snarled at the man, baring long fangs and drooling blood. It seemed ready to launch itself at the human while it clutched a screaming human infant to its chest.

It was a portrait of William Demonsbane, the most powerful Tracker the Quarter had ever produced. The artisan who had woven the tapestry had been an eyewitness to the mass murder of every Distari lair for a two-week walk from William's dirty village. William had slaughtered grunts, changelings and timids, but he had also managed to murder three Masters as well. On that day, three of the elite had been promoted to lofty heights with just a few cuts of the sword. When the tapestry had been discovered, the Masters had reproductions made to remind all why they hunted the Tracker. For him, the tapestry represented something else altogether. It reminded him that opportunities did not occur by accident but were made. William had been the catalyst of three elite promotions. No doubt this new Tracker could do the same for Him.

If only he knew where to find the Tracker. But the Quarter was being more protective of this one than any other before it. He thought that very strange. Did it mean that this Tracker was weaker? More vulnerable? Or perhaps he was simply very young and needed more guidance. How old were Trackers when they became Trackers, anyway?

As if reading his mind, which was quite likely, a timid stepped quietly into his chambers and approached him. It made sure to stop its advance well out of his reach, lest He be in a killing mood and strike out blindly. He thought about making it wait there for hours, just to see if it would faint and foul itself in turns. It could be very entertaining. But the stink would get irritating.

"What do you want?" he asked harshly, just to watch the timid squirm. The timid jumped because it hadn't expected to be recognized so quickly. It bit its lip until it bled and struggled not to pee on the floor. Fouling His rooms meant a swift and messy death.

"One of the changelings has discovered an Agent trailing a family. He believes that the humans in question may be the Tracker and his heirs. He has sent directions to their location," the timid shrieked. He considered the information and wondered if it could be true. Had some happy chance simply dropped the Tracker into his lap? Stranger things had happened but it seemed too good to be true. Still, it was too good an opportunity to pass up. He began to plot, formulating the plans that would draw his Master and the Tracker on a collision course. It would end in a battle, of that there was no doubt. The Master and the Tracker were simply what they were and they would never be anything else. There would be an ultimate battle, and if the Tracker were triumphant, then it would be a simple thing to slip a dagger between his ribs and claim vengeance. Should the Tracker fall, well, even Masters die of their injuries. It would be easy to make sure that he did so. Who could doubt his claim that the Tracker had struck the fatal blow?

The timid's whimpers broke through the reverie He had sunk into. Its pathetic cries were punctuated with squealing shrieks that set his teeth on edge and frayed his nerves. He turned in his chair and leveled the thing with fire in his twisted eyes.

"Get out," he snarled. The timid turned and ran for the door as fast as its half-crippled legs would carry it. He settled back into his chair and drank his bourbon until he no longer felt like killing anything. Then he carefully thought about his next move. He recalled the weeping timid and ordered it to bring a changeling to him.

CHAPTER 9

Arnold sat at her desk and stared at the medical and laboratory reports in her hands. Scattered across the scarred and stained desktop were other reports analyzing the evidence of the Anderson crime scene. Her day had been spent chasing paperwork and useless leads. The Andersons had been the most ordinary and boring people possible. They had been poor and living from paycheck to paycheck. They hadn't had any real assets; the only thing that they owned had been their very old and battered car. Their home had been rented and the furnishings had been aging hand-me-downs. Their bank account had been empty and the bank statements had accounted for every penny. They had no savings. They hadn't had money to pay for life insurance. By all accounts, their marriage had been a good one and they were well-liked by everyone who knew them. The children had been average students, the mother had been a loving housewife and the father a good mechanic.

The house itself had been examined for any clues to the killer. The officer who'd been first on the scene stated that he had to break down the back door to get into the house. Technicians had checked to see if any of the windows or the front door had been compromised but they were all locked securely. Two house keys had been found on key chains owned by Mr. and Mrs. Anderson and their spares were with the Anderson's parents. After learning that both of the grandparents had been out shopping and were vouched for by a cashier, Arnold had lost her only suspects.

Arnold set the reports aside and rubbed her burning eyes. The reports had been as vague and useless as all the other information. The autopsy said that the victims' heads had suffered blunt-force trauma, which was just a clean way of saying that they'd had their heads bashed in so hard that their brains had liquefied. And after a thorough examination, no one could say what had been used to strike the victims. Their bodies had been savaged, their throats ripped from the bone and their abdominal cavities emptied as if the organs had been chewed out. The medical examiner thought that an animal had gotten to the bodies but couldn't say what kind.

The laboratory analysis had been less helpful. All the samples brought out of the house had been combed through and sent through a battery of tests and put under the microscope. They found almost nothing. There had been foreign DNA on the scene but it had been so badly contaminated that no one could say what animal it came from, much less who it belonged to. There were no fingerprints, no organic fibers and no synthetic fibers. They had been unable to find any metallic or chemical residue. It was as if the entire family had been slaughtered by a bald, naked psychopathic neat-freak.

Frustrated and fatigued by the long day, she put the reports in the file with the crime scene notes and put it away. It felt wrong to set the file aside for the night. The job wasn't done yet but still she was going home. Her mind was overworked and she couldn't think straight. She decided that she could go back to the scene in the morning. The bright light of day would chase some of the terror away and keep her from adding to her nightmares.

She went about her usual routine of cleaning up before she left her desk for the night. Unfinished paperwork was carefully stacked and put into the tray at the side of her desk. Pens and pencils were put in their caddy and her computer was turned off. She picked up her mail and began to sort through it.

It had long been her habit to pick up her mail on her way to work and sort through it on her lunch break. Today she had not taken the break and the mail was left until now. She tossed out the usual advertisements and junk. She tucked her two bills into her purse. As the last ad passed through her fingers, she saw the decorative envelope and froze. Delicate handwriting covered the snow-white envelope trimmed in pink and bordered with little silhouettes of fat angels. A stamp depicting angels and the word love written at the bottom was glued to the upper left corner. The whole thing was so precious and tacky that it made her ill. She glanced at the return address and saw her ex-husband's name there.

She let out an angry breath. She wondered what the bastard was up to now. He had recently exhausted all avenues to harass her through the legal system and had backed off. The last few weeks had been blissful without having to wonder what Jacob Arnold was going to try to do to her next.

She tore open the envelope and pulled out a pretty pink and white card. It was embossed in gold and trimmed in lace with a pretty bible scripture written across the front. Arnold opened it and glanced inside. She growled low in her throat and tossed the wedding invitation away.

She wanted to say that it didn't matter to her that her ex was remarrying only six months after the divorce. That she couldn't give a crap about anything that the man did. But it did hurt, not because he was getting married but that he was getting remarried before she was and rubbing her nose in it. There was no other reason for the invitation. They hadn't parted on good enough terms to discuss the color of the sky without fighting let alone to justify his inviting her to his wedding. It was designed to make her feel inadequate and angry. She knew it but it didn't make her feel any better. She just wanted to call someone about it and cry.

She walked out of the police station and pulled out her phone. She dialed Maddie's number and pressed the phone to her ear. She kept her head down and avoided eye contact with other cops. She had tears in her eyes and didn't want them to see her cry. The phone rang a few times before Sam picked it up.

"Hey, Sam, is Maddie around?" she asked, struggling to keep the tears out of her voice. She got to her car and unlocked the door.

"No, she had to go out of town on some last minute business," Sam replied. "Are you okay?"

Arnold fell quiet, wondering if she dared to dump on her sister's husband about this. No, this was an issue designed for bitching by women only. Sam would only try to be logical and give Jacob the benefit of the doubt. Jake and Sam had been buddies once, though Maddie swore that they didn't talk anymore. Still, Arnold didn't want to hear half-assed man-excuses right now.

"Any idea when she'll be home?" she asked without answering the question.

"No. Do you want me to call her and have her call you back?" Sam didn't pursue the issue. He was always a good man. She wondered how Maddie could stand to be away from him as much as she was.

"Could you? I really need to talk to her."

"I can call her. But she might not call you back right away."

"That's fine, I don't think I'll sleep much anyway," she said wearily. God, she hated Maddie's job.

"New case got you down?" Sam was making small talk, inviting her to engage in a deeper conversation. She thought it was weird and a little sad. She and Sam had never really been close. He was a nice guy, and she liked him because he treated her sister like a queen but she could never really relate to him. The fact that he was trying so hard to keep her on the phone showed how lonely he was getting.

"It's been rough. I'm not really allowed to talk about it," she said. She was getting a hold of herself now. She got into the car and jammed the key into the ignition.

"Oh, okay. Well, I'll have Maddie call as soon as she can," Sam said. They said their good-byes and hung up. She hoped that Maddie would call soon.

CHAPTER 10

A sharp yelp and the painful thud of a body hitting the ground broke the quiet afternoon. Seconds later, two more thuds struck the ground and everything fell silent. For a long moment, only the musty breeze rippled through the high dry grass and graced the air with a soothing rush. A low animal noise rose curiously. Something had happened, something strange and new and none of the herd could imagine what it was. They sniffed and lowed, trying to detect whether the newness was a predator or if it was simply more antics of their caretaker. When nothing happened, they bent their heads back to their grazing. If it had been a predator, it would have eaten one of them by now. Surely, whatever had joined them in their pasture was harmless.

Maddie lay where she landed as she struggled for air that had been driven from her lungs when she'd hit the ground with bone-jarring force. It seemed to take a long time for her breath to grow even but when it did she sucked in the oxygen with deep hungry gulps. She groaned and rolled over onto her hands and knees. She had grit in her mouth that was caked between her teeth and coated her tongue. She spat it out, not caring if she got it on her blouse or if anyone might be watching.

She felt horrible. Her head was spinning and her stomach had decided to declare war. She was fairly certain that it was going to open fire on her at any moment. Maddie closed her eyes in an attempt to ignore the way the world was spinning around her but it only made it worse. Her belly erupted in time for her to loose her balance and fall over onto her side.

George and Fred appeared over the grass with their faces twisted into grimaces as they stretched to work the kinks out of their backs and joints. Pops and cracks rippled the air as they limbered up. The vomiting noises continued as they brushed the dirt from their clothes and searched around for their hats. They were checking the contents of their bags when Maddie finally appeared above the tall golden grass and gasped. She scowled down at her clothes, disgusted with herself and with the mess. She wiped gunk from her cheek and neck and flung it aside.

"Oh, god, I vomited in my hair!" she groaned. George snorted with laughter while Fred regarded her scornfully. She shot them both with a dirty look and took an impotent swipe at her face. The slime streaked across her cheek and made her dark hair hang in wet clumps on one side of her head.

"It's not funny, George," she snarled. Then her eyes widened in surprise and she disappeared in the grass and made more retching noises. Somehow, she lost her balance again and she fell with a gagging cry. George laughed out loud.

"Why does she call you George?" Fred asked, completely disregarding the agonized sounds coming from Maddie. "It's not your name."

"She calls me that because I won't tell her my name," he replied. "She seemed to think that she needed to call me something."

"Why didn't you just tell her your name?" Fred asked.

"For the same reason why you didn't tell her when she asked you," he replied. "Because we are not individuals but a whole entity; homogenized and equal unto one another. If the Tracker chooses to name us to make it easier on her, that's her prerogative."

"Couldn't she come up with something better than George?"

"Wait until you hear what she's named you."

"What's that?"

"Fred," George waited for the other man's indignant reaction. He didn't have to wait long. Fred began a long and furious tirade. He bitched enthusiastically about the indignity of such a moniker when he had such a grand one given to him by his mother upon his birth. If he couldn't be addressed by his true name, then he preferred 'Agent.' Maddie, however, had felt differently. She'd found the Agents too intimidating and needed to humanize them more for her own comfort. So she'd taken to calling any Agents with easy demeanors 'George,' and any who were grim or surly, 'Fred.' All of the Agents responded to either name although there were more than a few who griped that the names were undignified. Personally, George felt that his men could do with a little less dignity. It was making them stiff and reckless.

"This is why women shouldn't be Trackers," Fred finished his tirade with a growl. George turned on him and prepared to give the man a reprimand for the disrespectful remark. Fred could think what he wanted, but his job was to shut up and do as he was told regardless of the gender of the Tracker.

"I heard that!" Maddie snapped before George could get a word out. She was pale and covered in a cold sweat and the slime that had once been the contents of her stomach. She held her travel bag in one hand and a towel in another. And she looked pissed. George closed his mouth with a snap and took a large step away from Fred. Unlike most Agents, he had seen the Tracker in a temper. It wasn't frightening in the least but it could be humiliating if she was angry enough.

Maddie stormed up to Fred, her eyes full of self-righteous fury and ready for a fight. Fred frowned slightly at her and sneered. It was just so difficult to take a woman seriously when she was covered in her own barf. She seemed to have forgotten about it as she violated all of Fred's personal space in an attempt to appear threatening. His nose wrinkled when the smell hit his nostrils, but he stood his ground. He glared disdainfully down at her and crossed his arms over his chest. She didn't say anything; she just fumed at him, her breath hissing loudly in and out of her gooey nose. Both men waited to see what she would do next.

She moved so fast and did something so unexpected that Fred didn't have time to react. Her slimy hand had shot out and wiped across the entire length of Fred's face. Then she danced back, laughing. Fred's mouth opened in disgust as he scrubbed at his cheek and yelled outrage. George burst into a fit of laughter. He had expected almost anything from the

Tracker, from a shrieking hissy fit to outright blows. He hadn't expected her to do something so hilariously gross. She stood back from Fred and looked smug. Meanwhile, Fred was having a hissy of his own, scrubbing fiercely at his cheek with a lacey handkerchief (provided by Bob) and making gagging noises of his own.

"Who's the big girl now?" she said hotly. "Bitch."

It took time for Maddie to clean up and the Agents were forced to wait with their backs turned while she did it. She'd done her best at cleaning up; her face and hands came clean with a towel and a little water from the canteen. But her hair was foul with gunk and refused to come completely clean no matter how she rubbed at it. Finally, she decided just to shampoo it the first chance she got and she tied it back and slapped her hat on top of it. The veil obscured her vision so she tossed it over the top of the hat and out of the way.

"You're going to have to put that over your face as when we reach the city," George said. Behind her Fred growled something inaudible and most likely insulting. Maddie chose to ignore it since he wasn't talking to her anymore, which suited her fine since she didn't really want to hear anything he had to say anyway.

"I know," she grumped. "But it blocks my vision and I need to see so I don't fall over. I get the feeling that Chuckles back there wouldn't catch me if I did. I'll just keep it out of my face until we get there."

"As you wish," George smiled and shrugged. Maddie thought he might have winked at her but wasn't entirely sure. So she ignored it. They shouldered their packs and began to march across the field towards the low rocky wall along its borders. Maddie walked just a couple of steps behind George while Fred pouted several feet behind her. She kept her head down, and watched every step. She still felt sick and disoriented. She had enough experience riding the Threshold to know by now that the dizziness wasn't from the traveling. It was the experience of traversing an alien planet that she found so disorienting. The pull of gravity was only slightly more powerful than her native planet but it still made her limbs feel heavy and her steps clumsy. She slowly lifted her head. Moving too fast would make her stomach angry and she didn't want to foul herself again. Slowly, she tilted her head all the way back until her eyes looked upon the sky.

The sky was a pure, unbroken sooty haze that obscured the glow of a pair of blood red suns. The light made everything look weirdly pink and made her eyeballs ache. The nanites that swam through her brain told her that there were four moons, each with an orbit that brought it perilously close to the other satellites. It was believed that two or more of the moons would eventually collide and send the population into the chaos of mass extinction. It was the unfamiliar pull of the astrological bodies that had Maddie all out of sorts. If she could spend years on the planet, she would eventually adjust to the weird environment. But she would only be spending a day or two and they would be a misery of nausea and fatigue.

She lowered her head as slowly as she had raised it and felt the dull pounding of a migraine.

"Great, just great," she thought angrily. It was going to be hard enough chasing down wanted criminals. A blinding migraine would make it nearly impossible.

She squinted in the strange light and really looked at the world around her for the first time. She stood in a field of high yellow grass that rose to her waist. It was dense and hid the various holes, rocks, and large piles of what looked like cow poop in its depths. All around her stood a herd of dark humped beasts. They were a brown so dark it was almost black. They had thick pebbled and wrinkled hides like elephants. Their small heads were bent to the grass as their long nimble lips foraged for the morsels that sustained them.

Far beyond the rock wall surrounding the pasture was a city jutting sharply from the earth and clawing at the dismal sky. Thick black clouds hung at the city's knees and made it look seedy. Maddie shuddered. She didn't like the look of the place and wondered what kind of people could live there. The air stank of burning material and strange toxic chemicals that were carried on the wind. Maddie pondered the stink and what it meant. It wasn't a healthy smell and she wondered what side effects she would suffer from breathing it.

Suddenly the air trembled and Maddie tasted the sharp metallic tang of electricity in the air. The hair on the back of her arms stood up from her tingling skin. George and Fred stopped in their tracks and stood eerily stiff and still. Their mouths were partly open as if they were trying to taste the wind.

"We have a problem," Fred said in a voice so soft that he wouldn't have been heard if the breeze hadn't carried his words to them. Maddie looked where the men were looking. Her heart pounded in her chest and her ears tried to hear every nuance of sound around her. But the land was deadly silent so that the only thing she could hear was the sounds of her own heartbeat.

A string of bright flashes appeared in the dense yellow grass along the horizon. The herd flinched and bellowed in fear. The Agents jerked as if they'd been slapped. Maddie stared wide-eyed at the rumbling beasts and wondered what they were going to do next.

"How many flashes did you see?" George asked with his voice low. Maddie pulled her eyes from the herd and stared at the strip of land the men were intent on. Their thoughts pulled at her, feeling tense and chaotic, but telling her nothing of what was happening.

"I counted seven, sir," Fred replied.

"That's a lot."

"Yes, sir."

The Agents became tense as they continued to watch the horizon. Maddie felt it like a shiver along her arms. She had grown as still as the men and the effort of that stillness began to make her tremble. Something was wrong. Something terrible was near. Something deadly, something that wanted to eat her. She fought with her panic and choked with the need to fight or run. The men were no better. Every muscle bulged under their prissy coats. Their faces grew hard and their fingers caressed the guns hidden discretely at their hips.

Suddenly, unable to remain still in the face of the unknown danger, the herd turned and ran. On one side they ran away from the three in their midst; to the other, they ran towards them. Maddie stared at the oncoming rush of massive bodies with wide terrified eyes and her limbs locked dumbly in place. The beasts rushed past them, their hooves pounded the earth and made it shake. Pale dust rose up and blanketed the land.

Dark shapes had appeared in the grass where the flashes had been. There was a horde of them, writhing and jumping in the tall grass. The wind changed direction and brought with it the reek of filth and death. The herd smelled it too and it fueled their terror. The terror brought them to a stampede and they moved blindly. Fred jumped back and avoided a hulking beast twice his height as it stumbled and fell where he had been standing. The beasts screamed a piercing bleating cry. Maddie spun in place as she struggled to look everywhere at once.

The horde began to separate itself out. Individuals appeared dark and twisted within the thick yellow grass. Large eyes shone as they looked around at all the frantic movement. Gleeful bloodlust filled the air like a terrible keen. Maddie clapped her hands over her ears and shut her eyes tight. Her breath rasped hard in her ears as she panted in her fear. The horde regrouped and moved as one living entity upon the herd and attacked. They dragged down an animal with tooth and claw and fed on its terror as well as its blood. They did not stop to fully consume the thing they had killed. They had killed it to see the blood flow, to watch something die. The tall grass was stained with the beast's dark blood. The monsters watched it twitch and bleed for just a moment before moving to the next victim. The animals screamed when another of them fell and its piteous cries were followed by the sounds of joyful bloodlust.

"Run!" George hissed. Maddie stared stupidly at him. She couldn't move, couldn't register the words he'd spoken in her mind. She was shutting down, unable to grasp the horror she was witnessing. He grabbed her roughly by the arm; the pain of his blunt fingers brought her back to her senses and made her gasp. "Run!"

His yell finally jolted her into motion and panic burned through her veins. It powered her dull and heavy limbs and she ran as fast as the wind. Fred stayed behind her, his breath rasped hotly on the back of her neck. George kept a hard grip on her wrist as he pulled her behind him towards the rock wall. They dodged and wove their way through the moving mass of animal flesh, as desperate to avoid being trampled as they were to avoid being seen by the ugly creatures behind them.

Maddie dared a glance behind her and immediately wished she hadn't. The horde was still cavorting among the grass, slaying animals with great splashes of blood. The red stains were garish and ugly among the high gold stalks. Seven sets of large gleaming eyes lifted from their play. And the eyes tracked the movement of the three people running away from them.

They grinned and exposed impossibly long teeth that drooled blood from blackened gums. They hunched their deformed backs in a grotesque arch as they rose up on the tips of their knuckles and toes. The monsters sprang forward in a loping, ground-eating gait. Maddie choked on a scream that she was too breathless to release. She returned her eyes forward and put on another ragged burst of speed. The rock wall was hopelessly beyond their reach. They would never reach it in time. And if they did reach the wall alive, what then? They couldn't possibly outrun the monsters forever. The thunder of the fleeing herd pounded in her ears and echoed in the frantic pounding of her heart.

Suddenly, Fred stopped dead in his tracks and a pair of pistols appeared in his hands. He spun, took quick aim and fired two shots. Two monsters shuddered mid-stride and dropped to the ground. The crack of the guns frightened the nearest animals and they swerved in their flight and changed the direction of the herd. The animals spread out in a wide arch away from them and left the exposed and vulnerable animals to the insidious monsters.

Fred turned and ran. He took hold of Maddie with a suddenly empty hand and pulled her ahead of George. George pulled his guns and fired, dropping two more of the monsters before turning back on his heels and running for it. The creatures screamed in rage. Maddie felt their rage and hate coat her skin like thick oil. The creatures moved faster, the distorted muscles beneath their skin writhing along their humped backs.

The three hit the wall and vaulted it, almost without breaking their stride. Maddie would have kept running but Fred pulled on her wrists and threw her back against the barrier. She hit the stones hard, driving the breath from her lungs and bruising her face and side. She dropped into a crouch next to Fred and dug frantically into the opening in her pocket and grasped the long rod strapped to her leg. Both of Fred's guns were up as George jumped over the wall and crouched behind it. Maddie ripped the weapon from her leg and held it out at her side. She flicked a small black button set in the center of the metal shaft with her thumb. The rod extended at both ends until it reached three feet in length. The bottom remained a smooth blunt shaft while the business end of the weapon became pointed with four sharp edges. She crouched low and settled the blade properly in her hand as she waited to be attacked.

The remaining three monsters jumped the wall and sailed over their heads and landed several feet in front of them. They had suddenly lost their prey and it confused them. They wandered in small circles and grunted, dumbfounded. Fred and George aimed their guns and their faces grew blank and cold. Maddie cringed a little at those expressions. It wasn't that she had ever seen the men kill before but she'd never seen them do it with such brutal purpose. They fired on the beasts, cutting them to ribbons and dropping them limply to the ground.

The land had grown quiet and the air was still. Maddie panted heavily, her system still overloaded with adrenaline and fear. Her limbs trembled from the hard run on a world that had greater gravity. She felt loose and liquid and ready to drop. Fred and George hadn't lowered their guns. They kept careful aim on the new corpses as if they expected them to leap to their feet and attack them. Finally, the guns disappeared from their hands. The men stood and exchanged grim looks as they began to brush wrinkles and dirt from their coats.

Maddie rose on shaking legs. She watched the men swiping at their clothes and exchanging hard looks and shook her head. They appeared to have been trying to stare each other down but she knew better. They were speaking mind to mind about a subject that they didn't want her to know. It happened a great deal more than she liked. She felt inadequate and stupid every time they did it. It wouldn't do her any good to try and eavesdrop. Their shields were solid enough to keep her out of their conversation. If she asked them what they were talking about, they would simply ignore her until she quit pestering them. She had once asked George why the Agents felt a need to keep secrets from her. She'd been irritated by the men's habit of leaving her out and her tone of voice had been ugly. George had simply given her a cold look and said, "There are something's that are better left unknown."

The men finished their conversation and began to settle their packs more comfortably around their bodies.

"Come Tracker. Its time to get to the city before uglier things come out to play," George said grimly.

CHAPTER 11

George and Fred pulled their hats down on their heads and waited for Maddie to replace her weapon in her leg holster. It was difficult because she couldn't see what she was doing and the skirt's material kept getting in the way. She finally gave up and jammed the thing in her belt. She turned to the Agents and leveled them with a look.

"What the hell were those?" she demanded pointing at the stinking corpses. "And what the hell were they doing chasing us?"

The men exchanged looks and then looked down at the ground. She shuddered and stepped nervously away from the wall. The sounds of the panicked herd were growing fainter as they continued to flee further away. Neither Fred nor George would meet her gaze. Maddie scowled and stamped her foot in frustration.

"Tell me what you know now," she snarled. Fred simply turned and walked away, while George lifted his eyes to hers. His face was pale and grim making and it made the faint lines of his face deeper and added years to his appearance.

"Look within for your answers," he said before he turned and followed Fred. Maddie stared after them, anger rising high in her chest. She had enough of the cryptic bullshit. She knew that they were holding out on her. There was something dark and dangerous that she needed to know, and the men weren't going to tell her. She stared down at the monsters lying in the tall grass. Their horrible mouths gaped in death and their twisted limbs contorted with their final agony. They were disgusting filthy things and it seemed good that there were a few less of them in the world.

Her brain teased her and gave her fleeting images of other men's dark and bloody encounters with the monsters. She got images of dead children and the ravaged corpses of women. Her stomach lurched again and she shook the memories of the other Trackers away. She swallowed bile that had suddenly rose in her throat and shivered from the horror of the visions. She wiped the cold sweat from her forehead and hurried to follow the Agents before they left her behind

She stared at their backs as they walked. The men kept their eyes locked on their destination as they walked, as if they it would be lost if they took their eyes away. Soon Maddie had to jog to keep up. She was panting from exertion and was forced to keep her eyes on the road to avoid tripping.

"Slow down," she panted after a few minutes. "What's the rush?"

"We must reach the city before nightfall," George replied with his eyes forward. "When the suns set, native beasts come out of their dens to feed. And there are tales of a strange toxic spore that fills the air every night. We must be within the confines of the city before that happens."

"Beasts like what chased us in the field?" she was fishing for details, anything that would tell her what those monsters were and how they were connected to her. The thought startled her so much that she nearly stopped moving. Before, it hadn't occurred to her that their encounters with the monsters were anything but chance. Now she was certain that those things had had something directly to do with her, but the how still eluded her. Her inherited memories filled her sight again. Dead children and corpses of women danced merrily in front of her. Her stomach lurched in protest of the horrible visions and she shook them away.

She saw that she had fallen behind and she hurried to catch up with George. She waited for him to answer her question. He simply kept his eyes ahead and kept walking. He ignored her hints and outright questions on the subject. Eventually she gave up and just concentrated on keeping up.

The dirt road became a badly cobblestoned street with deep ruts carved into the center of the road. It was poorly kept and muddy water gathered where stones had been lost and weeds grew between the cracks in the stone. The road began to tilt in a slight incline so that Maddie slipped and fell several times and George had to stop to help her up. The gravity of this place was getting to her. The migraine and dizziness were intensifying now that the pain killing effects of the adrenaline had finally left her system.

They came to a stop at the crest of a hill and looked down at the city. It had been Maddie's experience that cities often seemed closer than they actually were in dry arid environments. But perhaps because of the strange light from the red suns or because of the pollutants filling the air, the city seemed very far away despite the details she saw clearly.

They stood on the crest and stared down at the metropolis at their feet. Tall, narrow buildings with sharply pointed roofs bristled from the heavy smog and thrust like daggers at the hazy sky. Smoke boiled out of narrow stacks and chimneys and fell like slow liquid to the earth. Dim flickering lights peppered the darkness at the city's knees and added some small visibility to the pallor of the polluted land.

There were several other roads much like the one the Tracker and the Agents stood on. All of them wound around the curves of the land and led directly into the city. Maddie could see the people like dirty ants moving in a curving line. The travelers stopped and gathered in huge crowds outside the city gates where tired and frustrated guards and city officials tried to sort them out. Lizard creatures that were the size of horses and carried packs and people upon their backs moved as a caravan through the crowds and towards the gates. The crowd was unhappy with the caravan's preferential treatment and began to mutter angrily. The guards shouted for the people to pipe down and issued cruel threats to those who did not become silent fast enough. The lizards chirped happily and added their musical call to the human din.

Without a word, the men started down the hill. Maddie sighed wearily and followed. Several times she nearly tripped and fell on the ragged street in her effort to keep up.

They were at the city gates well before sunsdown and had to endure the screams of an ugly, squat little man in clear need of a bath and a dentist. Maddie frowned at the guard through her thick veil in confusion and wondered what she had said this time. She'd only told the man what she'd been ordered to say in exactly the way she'd been instructed. Yet the guard was completely pissed off. She took a deep calming breath and tried to remember that she was a woman in a patriarchal society. It was going to suck to be a girl.

The culture of Rhasta was so rigidly male-oriented that the way they restricted their women made the Afghani attitudes regarding females seems absolutely liberated. Just speaking to the man, no matter how politely, was a violation of several gender laws and could get her stoned to death. Maddie had no idea why *she* was the one who had to talk to the ass-face and devoutly wished she could stop.

She forced a pleasant smile on her face and broke a few more laws. She figured, what the hell, if she was going to go around breaking the law, she might as well as break it spectacularly. She stared the enraged guard straight in the eye and tried to remember to breathe through her mouth. Why did he have to stand so closely? The little dude stank!

"I said, I'm the Tracker and I've come in response to a request for assistance from your local law enforcement," she said as cheerfully and pleasantly as she could.

"I heard what you said, I just can't believe *you* said it," the guard snarled. Maddie sighed and thought that the little turd was overreacting. Behind her, a wave of amusement came from Fred and George as they quietly snickered at her predicament. She almost turned around and told them to help out or shut up. But that would be counterproductive to what she was doing, which was to get them into the city, not to get them arrested and thrown in a dungeon.

She watched the guard's face turn from bright red to deep purple. Alarmed by his color, Maddie wondered if the man would drop dead from a stroke. She waited for the Agents to come to her rescue but their chuckles let her know that she was on her own. She silently sent hateful thoughts their way as she boldly faced the guard. Their quiet chuckles grew merrier.

"Forgive me if I have offended you, sir," Maddie said dryly. The narrow-minded jackass was thinking very hard about a woman's place and none of them were very nice. But she continued on as if reading his mind hadn't been so ridiculously easy. "But I'm afraid that the gentlemen behind me have grown quite mute and I'm the only one left to speak for us."

"Silence woman!" the guard bellowed. All around them, people stopped and stared at the scene he was causing. The angry guard stepped forward and tried to put his face into hers. It was difficult for him since Maddie was a good four inches taller than he. He began to scream obscenities as he trembled with rage. Maddie fought the urge to grimace and cringe from the verbal assault. The man didn't smell any better up close and personal, and he spit like a rain cloud when he yelled.

After being insulted for the third time in a single breath, Maddie lifted her veil and glared viciously at the guard. The man stopped his tirade mid-sentence and stared with eyes wide with shock.

"You listen to me, you filthy little turd," she snarled. Her temper was finally getting the better of her and she decided that she didn't care. "You had better step off and watch your mouth before I try to see if I can fit my foot in it!"

George and Fred had grown quiet when the guard had gotten into Maddie's face. Now, as the man sputtered in an incoherent rage, they became as tense and coiled as a tightly wound spring. She could feel the potential violence pour out of the Agents like sweat from their pores.

The guard finally got himself together. He took a step back to give himself room to maneuver, but he was underestimating his opponent and didn't give himself enough space. Maddie, however, had all the space she needed. She wasn't counting on Fred and George to help her. Hell, they'd been damn near useless the second they had crossed the city boundaries. Her hand went to the weapon at her belt. The little man saw her move but disregarded it. She was a woman and therefore weak, stupid and unskilled.

He raised a leather-clad fist to strike her. She let her feet part just a little in a subtle defensive stance. Maddie watched his fist carefully and prepared to sidestep the blow at the last second. The man's lip curled in an evil grin at the thought of her cowering at his feet, her mouth bloody and her face swollen and bruised. The mental image aroused him and he contemplated rape as he swung his hammy fist at her face.

Maddie felt Fred move behind her. She leaned ever so slightly to the side and gave him the room he needed to step around her to intercept the guard. He caught the guard's fist easily in his own palm just as it came close to her face. He had come within a breath of striking her but she hadn't flinched. Her eyes hardened and she smirked haughtily. She pulled the rod from her belt in an easy motion and hefted it in her hand.

Now that a man had intervened in the confrontation the guard finally saw Maddie as a potential threat. It gripped her ass that she needed a man in order to be a threat so she flourished the rod and threatened the idiot. He watched her handle it expertly and swallowed so hard that she could hear it. Fred stuck his face into the guard's and snarled ferociously.

"It is death for a woman to strike a man," the guard croaked in fear.

"Then I'm sure you'll give the Tracker every reason not to strike you," Fred growled. The little man cringed and whimpered.

At that point, the local law enforcement arrived. They took in the scene before them and all broke into grins while two of them snickered behind their hands. They had plenty of experience with this particular guardsman. They were often called to scenes where the man had started fights with other men or when he'd been to rough with a woman and her pimp wanted someone to clean up the mess. Finally, here was someone that the bastard couldn't bully and he was finally getting what was coming to him. They measured the man that held the guard in his grasp. He seemed ordinary enough but his body was long and strong and it bent like that of a hardened warrior. The woman standing next to him was clearly not one of the native ladies although she was dressed in local costume. She stood tall and proud, her face naked without its veil and her strange light eyes glared angrily at the man cowering in front of her. She held a weapon but didn't look as if she meant to use it. There were many laws that the woman was in the process of breaking but the sergeant of this little group thought that they could probably overlook them. More often than not, women were forced to ignore the gender laws in the interest of self-preservation. If this woman had been dealing with the guardsman at all then she had probably had to act to defend her husband's honor.

Maddie turned to the police officers staring in amusement and hid a smile of her own as their thoughts crept into her head. The men were dressed in identical uniforms with padded dark blue tunics and skintight red pants. The tunics were decorated with golden braids and fringe at the shoulders and the red pants were embroidered with silver crescent moons. On their feet they wore glossy black boots that ended at mid-calf and lacked the high broad heel favored by the men of the region. They had gold-tooled swords in thin scabbards on their hips and single shot pistols tucked in their belts. Their heads were bare of both hair and hats. Instead, they had sharp geometric tattoos covering their scalps. Their grinning mouths exposed very white teeth that had been filed into fine points. Maddie held on to her neutral expression even as her guts reacted to the savage appearance of the policemen. They saw her looking at them and they cast their eyes down in embarrassment.

"Please tell me one of you has enough brains to talk to a woman without getting distracted by a pair of boobs," she said to the approaching group.

"It is not the 'boobs' that are so distracting, but that your face is naked for all to see," a short, middle-aged man replied. He was slightly taller than the rest and had fine lines framing his dark brown eyes. Maddie sighed impatiently and lowered the veil on her hat with her free hand.

"You can look now," she said dryly. The men lifted their gaze and let out a breath of relief. They were much more comfortable now that the woman was decently covered. Maddie had to throttle her anger and stuff it down until it simmered painfully in her belly. She had to remember that different cultures had different ideas about modesty and nudity. None of them were necessarily wrong; some were just a bit extreme.

"What has happened here?" the sergeant asked looking around with cold eyes. He had a pretty good idea what had happened, he just needed to make it official.

"Is there a ranking officer I might speak to?" Maddie asked, looking from one man to the next. She didn't want to get into a confrontation with the police. She just wanted to get on with her work so that she could go home.

"Oh? Do you wish to press charges?" the sergeant's voice sounded hopeful. He glanced at the guardsman still held in Fred's grip. The dirty guard was giving the sergeant hostile looks. No doubt he had expected the police to side with him since he had been fighting with a woman and a woman was always at fault. But the woman hadn't struck him and, so far, all she was guilty of was public indecency. No doubt because she didn't know any better. But this little fool would not be escaping a night in jail this time, not if he had anything to say about it. He was tired of speaking with bloody barmaids and half-dead whores.

"Does he need it?" Maddie asked. "I mean, we did embarrass the hell out of him. That might be enough."

"If you do not press charges then he will be free to take his embarrassment out on some poor woman later on," he replied.

"Oh, by all means then, let him cool his heels in jail."

"Very well, then. I shall take you to our headquarters so that you may make your complaint," the sergeant sounded very pleased with the idea. He made a gesture and two of his men stepped forward to take the guard from Fred. Fred let him go and took a step back to stand next to George. The policemen gave them startled looks but didn't say anything.

The sergeant led them away and another, cleaner guard appeared from behind the gate. He assumed the position so recently vacated by his comrade and continued with business as if nothing had happened. He didn't even spare a glance for the departing group.

Maddie was careful to make sure she switched to English before she spoke to Fred and George. Sometimes, Maddie forgot what language she was using because the nanites located in her brain made translating so easy. She rarely had to change her thought process when she spoke to alien peoples. But the ease in translation did mean that she had to make a conscious effort to remember what language she needed whenever she had to switch back and forth.

"You could have helped out back there," Maddie growled. Two of the policemen glanced back at her over their shoulders. She smiled at them before she remembered that they couldn't see her face through the veil. She cursed the thing; it made it very difficult to see anything. If she didn't want to bump into stuff she had to look through the opening at the bottom.

"You had enough help," George replied coolly.

"Oh, really? Because I thought it could have gone a lot better with that guard back there," Maddie said.

"You are the Tracker," George said impatiently. "It is your place to deal with the local population. We are your assistants and bodyguard. We come to your aid only when we must. If you have trouble with the local people, it is up to you to solve it."

Maddie fell to growling and muttering under her breath for the rest of the walk. The policemen kept giving her looks over their shoulders. They were uncomfortable with a woman who did not make herself meek in the presence of men. Maddie spoke with men as if she were their equal. She spoke plainly and without deference, allowing her displeasure to show even when she spoke the strange language. Their discomfort grew to irritation which grew into anger as she bitched more and more. Maddie ignored them; she was in no mood now to deal with their preconceived notions of a woman's proper behavior.

They arrived at a squat stone building constructed from long flat stones held together by a thin but strong mortar. The little round windows and main door held thick glass in carved stone frames. More of the strange lizards loitered around the front of the building. They were as tall as large horses and as broad as bulls. They wore leather saddles and harnesses for riding. They appeared docile enough despite the vibrant red and black stripes and long predatory teeth that often meant carnivore back on Earth. They were tied by their reigns to a hitching post with a long, deep trough filled with a red chunky substance.

Maddie shuddered as one of the lizards delicately dipped its pointed snout into the trough and brought up something limp and meaty. It tossed the morsel in the air and caught it in its mouth. It made a musical purring sound as it chewed and blinked its blood red eyes contentedly. Maddie fought the urge to upchuck and hurried after the policemen.

The door led to a small reception area where men with thick, spiky hairdos complained loudly to a bald man wearing a police uniform. The policeman took it all in stride, nodding his head as he scribbled furiously on a wax pad. There were only three women among the crowd of angry men. They stood quietly in corners, their heads bent down and their delicate hands clasped in front of them. They did not speak and if they moved, it was only to get out of the way of a man that might bump into them.

Behind the reception area was the general workspace for the police force. It was small, insinuating that there weren't many men policing the city. Men hurried through neat rows of stone desks and metal and leather chairs. They exchanged information and evidence before moving on to another destination. To the right, a young man sat at what would have been an old-fashioned switchboard back on Earth. He had little receivers jammed into his big ears with copper wires leading from them into the board. He spoke into a round handheld transmitter as he jammed pegs in and out of the switchboard in front of him.

The sergeant led them to the only enclosed room on that floor of the building. It was made of dull gray stone and had an opaque glass door to obscure their view of the occupant. The two men guarding the prisoner suddenly broke off from the group and headed for a flight of stairs leading into the floor. The dirty guardsman dug his heels in and cried when he saw where he was being taken. The police officers simply gripped him tightly by the arms and dragged him away. He blubbered as he went, promising to behave himself if only they did not put him in the hole.

Maddie turned a blind eye to the man's terror. He had wanted to beat and rape her; he had even thrilled at the prospect of it. Surely he had already done something to deserve being put in that place he so feared. The police had certainly been happy enough to take him. They hadn't even asked what the man had done. They'd simply taken him away on her say so. She suddenly saw images of brutalized women in the policemen's heads as well as other bloodier confrontations with off-duty officers. They hadn't been able to jail the guardsman before simply because everyone had been too frightened to press charges.

The sergeant and his men stopped at the opaque glass door. They waited while the sergeant knocked on the door and was answered by a gruff, "Come in." The sergeants pushed the door open and ushered Maddie and the Agents inside. Maddie turned to thank one of the remaining police officers, but his thoughts were so alarmed at the prospect of being spoken to by a woman that Maddie remained silent.

The occupant of the stone office was a large, middle-aged man who glared at the group with small, tilted black eyes. He was as bald as the rest with a more elaborate tattoo on his head. He sat back in his chair and laced his fingers over his flat belly as he took in the merits of his visitors. The sergeant addressed the man as Captain and launched into the story of how they had finally captured the guardsman. The Captain's expression didn't change as he listened to the report. He stared hard at Maddie and waited for her to become unnerved by his gaze. But she refused to be intimidated by the man. She nearly pushed her veil over her head and gave the man a look of her own. But doing so was the local equivalent of flashing the guy and now that she knew better, she wasn't going to do that.

"The man assaulted you?" the Captain's voice sounded like gravel. He directed his question at Fred and George as if Maddie was too simple minded to answer for herself.

"*Answer the man,*" George's faint mental voice said in her head. Maddie sighed heavily, knowing that the Captain was not going to be happy being addressed by a woman.

"He did attempt to attack me, sir," Maddie said politely. "But my men stopped him before anyone was injured."

The Captain's expression darkened with rage.

"What did you just say?" he hissed with intense outrage.

Maddie groaned inwardly. She could hear George chuckling in her head. She reached under her veil and rubbed her aching forehead while the Captain ranted in a fury. This was getting old fast and she needed to put an end to it before it got completely out of hand.

The big man's gravelly voice faded into so much white noise while she consulted with George and Fred.

"*How far out of line would I be if I just jacked this guy's brain?*"

"*That's a pretty extreme solution, Tracker. You'll make more enemies than friends. Not to mention that you run the risk of killing the man if you try it. I suggest that you try something more subtle,*" George suggested calmly.

Fred just sent her an image of the Captain weeping at her feet with a bleeding mouth. He was getting tired of the hold up as well and Fred was not a subtle kind of guy. She decided on a compromise between the two.

"*Silence!*" Maddie snarled the word both verbally and psychically so that it echoed in everyone's mind eerily. The Captain and the sergeant jumped and gaped stupidly at her. She had just a few seconds before the two became really pissed off and she found herself spending time with the dirty guard in the hole. Fred and George were already plotting her jailbreak.

"I am the Tracker and I have come in response to your request for assistance," she yelled, putting her fists on her hips and leaning toward the Captain aggressively. A sensible voice in the back of her head whispered that this tactic might not have been the best idea she'd ever had. She ignored it. "I have not come all this way to be insulted and railed at because you two jackasses have gender issues! Now either let me do your job catching the criminals that you have been too much of a pussy to get, or do it your damn selves!"

Both Fred and George groaned.

"Don't you ever listen?" George complained. Maddie ignored him and leveled the Captain with a nasty glare that he couldn't see.

"The title of Tracker is quite a claim, especially for a woman," the Captain said quietly.

"Not if it's true," Maddie replied coldly.

"Then you have the Mark?" he was challenging her, thinking that the uppity bitch was a liar. He believed Maddie was a disease that needed to be cut out before she spread to the minds of the other, more impressionable women. Maddie pulled the white glove off her right hand and waggled her fingers under the arrogant man's nose. His skin drained of color as he stared in horror at the ring on her finger. He knew the significance of the golden knot and the white and blue diamonds. He also knew the power that was associated with the bearer of the Mark.

"Forgive me, madam Tracker, I had no idea that a woman was capable of holding the title," he said breathlessly and irked to no end that he had to apologize to a girl, no matter who she was.

"Not all ways are your ways," Maddie scolded. "I suggest that you remember that next time and save yourself from further embarrassment."

The Captain nodded with all the humility he could muster for a woman, which really wasn't that much. He stared at her feet with all the rage and hatred in his soul. He clenched his teeth and said the words he never thought he'd speak to anyone but a man of higher rank than himself: "How may I be of service to you?" He nearly choked to death on the words.

CHAPTER 12

Arnold knelt down, not because she needed a closer look at what she was staring at, but because if she didn't get lower she was afraid she'd fall into her crime scene. She closed her eyes against the sight of so much blood and body parts and silently repeated the mantra, "I will not pass out, I will not pass out." She pressed the back of her gloved hand to her forehead in an effort to squash the growing headache away. She opened her bleary eyes and just managed not to breathe too deeply. The presence of so much blood and gore made the room rank with the fetid odor of death. It was oppressive and it weighed on her shoulders like a dead weight.

She saw the victims strewn around the large bathroom, with their limbs ripped from their bodies and piled into the bathtub. They had been tortured and strips of flesh was peeled from their bodies and tacked to the walls with blood streaming from the torn stubs. The mother had her eyes gouged out and one of the children was missing her lower jaw. The mother still had most of one of her daughters clutched in her remaining arm. An infant, no older than six months, had been torn in half and her internal organs were missing. The father was hung by his entrails from the door with a blood-spattered shotgun beneath his feet.

The scene was as fresh as a murder scene could be without a cop actually walking in on the murderer in the middle of the act. A neighbor had called 911 when he heard screams and a gun being fired. A unit had responded within minutes and had arrived at the Escobar home while the family was still screaming. The front and back doors had been locked and Officers Martin and Jerome had been forced to kick the back door down. They had entered the home with their guns drawn and rushed toward the sounds of the terrible shrieks while electric sparks from exposed live wires rained down on them. They stumbled more than once since the floor was covered in water and broken bits of the home. By the time they'd reached the master bedroom, the screaming had stopped and was replaced by the animal sounds of grunting and eating. Someone laughed, and the two men burst through the door, prepared to have the killer in their sights.

Instead the bedroom was empty. There were signs of a struggle, the bed had been overturned and there were bullet holes in the walls. Blood stained the carpet red in large, hideous spots. It was suddenly quiet; the silence was so profound that it nearly hurt their ears. Their breathing came harsh and dry in their throats as they took a precious second to gather their nerve. Then they burst through the door leading to the Master bath with a slam, their guns held forward in two-handed grips. They used the doorjambs as cover as they scanned the room in search of the killer.

But there was nothing they had learned or experienced in their lives that could prepare them for what they saw when they stepped into that bathroom. The sight sent Martin to vomiting on the floor behind him while Jerome went immediately into a hysterical panic. It took several minutes for Martin to pull himself together enough to drag his horrified and screaming partner from the scene. From his car, he called for the homicide detectives and waited for help to arrive.

Arnold took some last minute notes. She kept her personal observations in a separate notebook so that she could compare them to later revelations when she reviewed the case over and over. Her most prominent thought had been that this family had fought valiantly for every remaining second of their lives. She heard footsteps pull away from the silent crowd behind her. He came toward her, the rubber soles of his cheap shoes scraping the thick synthetic fibers of the carpet.

"We found the missing organs," Cooper said softly as if it was painful to speak. She turned and saw that his face was drawn and ashen. His eyes had gone flat, a pair of tiny mirrors that only reflected the outside world and never revealed the things inside his mind. She opened her mouth to speak but he turned away and began to slowly walk off. She tucked her notebook back into her coat and followed him. He led her out of the master bedroom and down the hall.

The carpets still felt heavy and spongy from the flooding caused by destroyed plumbing. The city had been out over an hour ago and they had turned the water and electricity off to the house so that the police could go in and investigate without risk of electrocution from the shredded wires sticking out of the broken walls.

Cooper stopped in front of a narrow doorway and stepped aside so that Arnold could see inside the shattered room. She looked past the open door but did not go in. She just stood there and stared and waited for the things in front of her to start making sense. After a time, she realized that none of it would ever come near the realms of logic and when she finally spoke, she only talked about the facts as she could grasp them.

"There had to be more than one, maybe more than two," she said softly. Her eyes had grown as flat and vacant as Cooper's. Her voice was soft and even, without inflection or emotion. "It happened so fast. There was what, five, six minutes from the time the neighbor called 911 to the time Martin and Jerome arrived. Then it took them maybe two minutes to clear the house and find the victims already dead and no signs of the perps."

She shook her head, completely confounded.

"I mean, how long does it take to dismember a human body, much less five of them? And then to take the internal organs and do this," she gestured inside the room and to the gruesome message spelled out on the walls: *Tracker.*

"I don't know," Cooper replied. "You're the one with the fancy degrees."

They got out of the way so that the reluctant photographer could get in the room to do his job when Officer Jerome approached them. He was still pale and shaken, his glassy brown eyes avoiding the room. He kept his head down and his impressive shoulders hunched like a dog that had been beaten too much.

"The press just arrived," he said softly.

"Shit," Arnold groaned. Cooper began to fiddle with his tie. It was a nervous habit, one he rarely indulged in, which showed how troubled he was.

"Have some uniforms cordon off the area and keep them at a very safe distance," he said into the tie.

"Already did, sir," Jerome replied. "But they're demanding a statement from you."

It was Cooper's turn to swear. He was the lead detective on the case and therefore had to face the press as the on scene representative.

"No one talks to the press," he said. "Things are bad enough without starting a panic."

Both Arnold and Jerome nodded agreement. Jerome hurried away to spread the order before someone talked. Arnold silently went back into the master bedroom to see if the CSI team had come up with anything yet.

They did manage to get through the rest of the night without anything else leaking to the press. Maybe everyone there was too stricken to talk or maybe no one wanted to admit that they didn't know very much. The press did manage to get footage of Cooper and Arnold working the scene and then took pictures of the victims as they were brought out in body bags.

Arnold was driving home when her cell phone rang. She picked it up immediately and checked the caller ID as she did. Her sister's number came up and she wondered if Maddie was finally calling back. It was strange that Maddie would call at nearly five in the morning but not unheard of. She flipped the phone open and answered the call.

"Darlene? Are you still working?" Sam asked anxiously. Arnold frowned in confusion.

"What's wrong?" she asked immediately. Sam had a problem and it could take him a long time to feel her out to see if he could even ask for her help. Half the time he only made small talk and never asked for the help he wanted. She was too tired to beat around the bush with him.

"I think someone tried to get into Katie's room tonight," he said hesitantly. Arnold's heart lurched. Her first thought had been the murder scene that she'd just left. It had the feel of having been interrupted and the killer might be on the prowl for a better fix.

"Did you call the police?" she asked.

"No," he was holding back. He wanted her help but didn't want to say why.

"Why not?" she was irritated and sounded it. He hesitated for a second. She could hear him breathing as he thought about it. Katie was crying in the background and the boys were chattering in a whining monotone. Something had certainly happened.

"What is going on, Sam?"

"I don't really know. Just come over and see for yourself," he replied quietly. He sounded afraid.

"Alright, I'll be there as soon as I can," she said. She turned the car around and headed back the way she came. Sam and Maddie lived just a few minutes down the road. She could get there, look at whatever he wanted her to see and talk him down. It was strange, though, since she never thought of Sam as the type of person who needed to be talked down.

She got to the house just a few minutes later. Every light in every room of the house was lit until the windows were bright with lights. Even the front porch was well-lit. She could see Sam cuddling with the kids on the couch through the living room window. She approached the house, part of her eager to get this done and on her way home, the other part of her felt the hard press of the dark night on the outskirts of town.

Maddie and Sam had chosen to live in what they affectionately called po-dunk. It was a residential area just beyond the town's official limits but was included in most of the benefits. It was thirty minutes from anywhere but the neighborhood was filled with old oak trees and thick with kudzu. It had its charm in the daylight but when the sun set, the night blanketed the land with thick, unwieldy darkness. It didn't usually bother her but tonight it felt as if eyes were boring into the back of her head. She examined the dark, making her eyes wide to absorb as much of the light as possible. When she didn't see anything, she shook herself and said that it was simply the lingering horror of the murder scene that bothered her.

Sam had the door open before she finished climbing the steps to the front door. He held Allen in his arms while Katie and Chris clung fearfully to his legs. Both the older children's faces were swollen from crying. Sam stepped aside to let Arnold pass before quickly closing the door behind her.

"What's going on?" Arnold said, still haunted by the feeling of eyes on her. It made her edgy and eager to get away from the place.

"Katie saw it first from her bedroom window," Sam began slowly, as if he didn't quite know which words to use. He watched her face intently as if he were afraid that she wouldn't believe him.

"It?" she prompted, hoping that he'd hurry up with the story. He ignored her and moved across the house to the sliding glass doors leading out to the back deck from the kitchen and breakfast nook. He looked outside, but didn't open the doors. The children had let go of his legs but they hung on him like ghosts. Their large blue eyes were haunted.

"She freaked out and woke everyone up, screaming that there was a monster trying to get into her window. When I went to her room, I didn't see anything. Then Chris began to scream here in the kitchen. When I came out, he was pointing out the window.

"I thought at first that some animal had come up to the porch and had just startled him. But it wasn't like any animal I ever saw, and it smiled at us," Sam shuddered and stared out the glass door.

"An animal smiled at you?" Arnold said skeptically. He had called her here for that? She almost walked out in disgust. Sam looked slightly embarrassed but held his ground.

"It wasn't just an animal," he said softly. "Go outside and look."

Arnold sighed, just to let him know how put out she was, and put her hand on the door handle. Katie squealed a sound like a small scream held forcibly behind her teeth and lips. Sam put out his arm and swept the girl around the shoulders and held her tightly against his hip. Katie's arms went up around his waist and she trembled.

Arnold turned away and shook her head as she pulled the door open. It made a light scraping noise as it rolled across the tracks. She stepped out onto the deck but couldn't see anything. Again she had that sensation of being watched. The wind shifted and stirred her hair and brought the thick smell of sick and decay with it. The scent was so out of place in the dark and cozy neighborhood that she inhaled in astonishment. It thickly coated her sinuses and throat. She coughed and gagged as tears poured down her cheeks. Arnold looked over her shoulder and saw Sam and the kids staring at her from the other side of the glass door. Sam had quietly closed the door behind her.

Sudden panic filled her chest and gripped her heart, and she spun and grabbed at the door handle. In her desperation to get away from the wretched stench, her fingers fumbled uselessly, unable to get her hand around the slender piece of wood. She was panting when she finally managed to grasp the door and yanked on it with fingers going numb. She coughed painfully and she was blinded by her own stinging tears. The wind gusted again, lifting her thick blond hair off her neck and pushing it against the sides of her face.

A low, ugly growl drifted up from the darkness behind her. Her spine stiffened in a terrified spasm as her blood froze in her veins. She found herself staring into Sam's wide green eyes. Allen clung to his neck and trembled while Katie and Chris huddled against his legs and wept. They saw what was behind her and it made them terribly afraid.

She fought the urge to look over her shoulder and see what they saw, see what was so terrifying. She knew if she looked her pounding heart would burst from the hideous sight of the evil thing. She squeezed her eyes shut to keep from looking and she yanked on the door handle. The door remained tightly closed and she fought the panicked sob that rose in her throat. The low growl erupted again and it vibrated in her chest, filling her with the terrible bitterness of bile. She pulled again, her heart beginning to flutter like a weak and caged thing, frightened, so frightened, and so desperate to get away. But the door would not open, damn it, why won't it open?

She looked at Sam, imploring him to help her, to please open the door and let her back inside. His face was confused, as if he didn't know who she was or what she was trying to do. She heard the growling again. It was like laughter, hideous hungry laughter. She could feel the heat of its rank breath on her neck and still she didn't dare to turn around and look.

Something hit the glass in front of her face. She jumped and screamed and let go of her precarious hold on the handle. She had to fumble for it again. The growling was upon her now, in her mind's eye she could see the thing's gaping jaws, posed over her head. She looked through the thick glass and saw Sam's pale face. His brow was furrowed and his teeth were bared.

"Stop pulling on the door!" he shouted through the glass. Arnold nodded and forced her arm to relax though she couldn't bring herself to let the handle go. Sam yanked the door open, nearly pulling her off her feet. He reached through the opening and grasped her roughly by the arm and pulled her back into the house. Her knees gave way and she collapsed onto the floor. He slammed the door closed and locked it.

She panted where she crouched. The air of the house was cleaner and it purified her lungs of the stench. Sam moved above her. He dropped a length of wood into the door's tracks, keeping anyone from opening the door enough to enter. She knew that such precautions were futile. Whatever had been outside would have no problems breaking through the heavy glass anytime it pleased. But Sam was doing everything that he could to make his home secure. The act of doing something, anything, to protect himself and his family made the place seem safer than it really was. And emotionally speaking, it was enough.

"Do you believe me now?" he asked, bending over her.

"What was that?" she gasped.

Sam shook his head, not knowing what to say even if he knew how to say it. He went to his frightened children and gathered them gently to him. They burrowed deep into the comfort of his arms and clung tightly to him.

Arnold got shakily to her feet and supported herself against the dining room table. She thought briefly about calling dispatch and having a car sent out to watch the house. But she couldn't explain the need for it, at least not in a way that anyone would believe. How could she explain to the lieutenant that something she hadn't seen and had no evidence of had threatened her brother-in-law and his children? But she didn't feel right leaving them alone, either, no matter how much she wanted to get into her car and get the hell out of here. She swallowed past the lump in her throat and decided that she could spend the night on the couch.

CHAPTER 13

The Agent stood in the shelter of the deep shadows of the tiny stand of pine on the Tracker's property. He watched the changeling as it crouched in the pear tree just in front of the living room window. It sat in a tense crouch, its gangly limbs trembling eagerly as it watched the family moving just beyond its reach. The Agent studied it, trying to decide what the thing was doing there. It was slavering greedily and licked its oversized jaws whenever the long strings of saliva grew too long.

It had been a very long time since a Distari had gotten this close to the Tracker's heirs and even longer since an Agent had to even contemplate the possibility of doing battle with the beasts. He wondered what had brought this one so close to his charges and what exactly it was planning to do.

There had been several murders in the area that could be easily attributed to the bloody monsters. They had gone overtly active for the first time since the Spanish Inquisition, when so many of them had been hunted and killed. They were killing for sport again and it was only a matter of time before the Quarter got to the report about it and finally ordered a new war against them. The Agent shuddered at the thought. There were still stories being told of the last war, when the Center was under constant threat and so many Agents and civilians were slaughtered.

There were rumors amongst the police that tonight's murders had been interrupted. Though the victims had been slaughtered and feasted upon, the Distari hadn't been allowed their play. Without the crucial entertainment, they would be quick to scout new prey in an effort to slake their thirst. Perhaps that was all they were doing at the Tracker's home. It was very likely that they had no idea of the Tracker's identity and where her heirs could be found. If the Distari was scouting the family with the intent of feasting, he still couldn't allow it to attack. It must be persuaded to look elsewhere for its play.

But the Distari elite kept their pets on short leashes and always knew where they were. If one were eliminated, it would not go unnoticed. Surely, the elite would realize where its changeling was and use it to locate the Tracker's heirs. He hesitated, wondering what the right decision would be and wishing that he could call in and ask for orders. He couldn't call in; if he tried, the changeling would certainly hear him and attack, which would mean that the Distari would learn of Agents' presence in the area.

It was when the changeling began to inch along the thin, flexible branches that the Agent finally made up his mind. He moved fast, so fast that the monster didn't see what hit it. It was painfully easy. The genetic manipulation that his ancestors had endured held true in him even now. Muscles worked, ligaments stretched and the changeling was in his grasp. It struggled briefly, sending a shower of golden autumn leaves to the ground. It was simple enough to wring the thing's neck with it caught as unawares as it was. He dragged the heavy, limp and stinking carcass back to the shadows and let it slump awkwardly to the ground. He looked back at the window in time to see the man and woman appear there and look out.

He recognized the pair. The man was the Tracker's husband and the woman was her younger sister. The Agent frowned, wondering what the woman was doing at the house at so late an hour of the night. He shook his head and decided that it was none of his business. If the Tracker's husband was having an affair with her sister, it was not for him to interfere. Such a thing brought no mortal danger to the heirs. Besides, he would not be the one to tell the Tracker that her beloved spouse as unfaithful to her. He lifted the body and began to drag it away. He would leave it someplace where its masters may assume that it met with an accidental death far from here.

*   *   *

"Where is it?" He demanded of the weeping and hysterical timid. The creature tore at its rags, unable to contain itself.

"The changeling is not in the lair! Perhaps it was caught in the daylight and it was forced to hide!" The timid cried. It trembled and cowered as it waited for the killing blow to fall.

The changeling had blinked out of His awareness so abruptly that it was likely that the thing was dead. He had recognized what it meant immediately and flew into a rage. He hated it when one of his beasts disappeared like that. It made him look weak and threatened his standing among the other elites. The event could uncover his secret. Unlike most of his particular status, He couldn't know where the changeling had been or what had been done to it or what it had done before it died. For all he knew, some religious zealot had gotten a hold of it and listened as it babbled all its secrets to it. That would be a disaster. No doubt the human would use the information to hunt down every lair in its crusade to erase what it thought was demons from the face of the planet.

"Stupid!" He snarled. "It is a changeling! It does not hide at daylight! It does not need to! It would merely change its form and return! Where is it?"

"It must be dead, then!" the timid wailed, certain that it was about to die a horrible death. He already knew that the changeling was dead. The question was where and how. A thought suddenly occurred to Him and he grew calm.

"And how do you suppose that happened?" He asked smoothly. He grinned and revealed long white teeth. He continued to speak, answering his own question. "Changelings do not become ill and because of their malleable constitutions, they do not injure easily. They can heal themselves with a thought. Tell me, what can attack a changeling so quickly that it cannot heal itself and so quietly that I don't hear of it?"

"An Agent! Or the Tracker!" the timid screamed. He grinned wider, exposing even more teeth. The timid swooned.

"Find the changeling and scour the area around it. The Tracker will be close. I want him found!" He ordered, dismissing the timid with a wave of his hand. The timid ran screaming to do as it was bid.

CHAPTER 14

The first thing the Agents insisted upon doing once the Rhasta police force let them go was to stop at a local inn and speak to one of their contacts. Maddie didn't argue with them. Even on worlds where the Tracker was relatively unknown, there was a network of carefully maintained spies and informants. These people didn't just provide up-to-date intelligence that Maddie needed in order to easily a complete a mission. They also made sure that she had shelter, food and enough money to get by while she was in town. Most of them were nice enough, even if they were a little on the criminal side of things. But over the last year, too many of these contacts had looked down their noses at her in disbelief. Most of them thought she was a joke at first and almost all of them were certain that she would be killed in some ugly and embarrassing manner before she completed her fifth year. Since she was becoming familiar with the local attitudes about a woman in the role of the Tracker, she was not looking forward to meeting this contact. She wondered if she would be allowed to smack the guy if he pissed her off.

She walked between Fred and George and let the sounds of their boots stomping on the pavement guide her along. With the veil pulled fully across her face she was effectively blind. She could see vague shadows of the people and buildings around her. She just couldn't see the details at all and the thick folds of the vaguely sheer fabric also distorted the sounds and smells around her. She felt crippled by the damn thing and all she wanted to do was rip it off and throw it away.

"Be at peace, Tracker," George said softly, reading her mind. "Please, do not remove your veil. It will attract much unwanted attention and require another visit to the police station and I do not think you will enjoy it quite as much as you did before."

Maddie growled furiously under breath and concentrated on keeping her hands away from her face. It seemed an eternity of stumbling and ricocheting between the two men before they finally reached the inn. Fred held the thin stone door open while George led her over the worn and cracked threshold. He took her by her elbow and gently guided her through a maze of pink marble tables and chairs. She tried to move gracefully but she banged her hip painfully on a table she never saw and stubbed her toe on a chair. She nearly strangled on the violent cursing she struggled to repress as George steadied her on her feet. He chuckled and shoved her into a chair where she swore under her breath and rubbed her foot.

"She's a charmer," a sultry feminine voice drawled. "Who have you brought me now?"

Maddie sighed irritably as George introduced her to the unseen woman as the Tracker. The woman exclaimed in surprise while Maddie gave her a weak wave in no specific direction. The woman chuckled wryly.

"You can remove the veil, milady," the woman said. "You are in the women's section of the inn and it is quite acceptable to go bare-faced here."

Maddie gratefully yanked the entire hat from her head and threw it down on the sleek marble tabletop. She rubbed her face and neck, closing her eyes and sighing with relief. After a few seconds she opened her eyes and looked around. She was in a small cubicle made from thin, white marble walls and delicately carved to look like intricate lace. Beyond the latticework of the stone, Maddie could see dark figures passing the walls and moving about somewhere in the room beyond her own. A dim orange light lit the cubicle from an oversized light bulb hanging from the stark and low ceiling.

"I always itch when I wear the veil too long," the woman said sympathetically, watching Maddie scratch at her face. The woman smiled down at her, her large almond-shaped brown eyes twinkled merrily. Maddie smiled back at her, relieved to finally be dealing with a woman and not another pig-headed, narrow-minded man.

"I am Abiah and it is very pleasing to meet you. I am very sorry for the loss of the master Tracker, your father."

"He was my cousin, actually," Maddie replied nonchalantly. Abiah was a pretty woman about Maddie's own age, with broad hips, lovely porcelain skin and very black hair tied severely into intricate braids at the back of her head. Abiah cocked her head curiously when Maddie answered her so frankly. She opened her mouth to say something but Maddie beat her to it.

"How did you know that the last Tracker was dead?"

Abiah had a sweet musical laugh that rang of sex. Fred suddenly sat straighter in his chair and the surly expression relaxed from his face. Even George gave the woman his rapt attention as her delicate long fingered hand flew to her pretty mouth in mirth. Maddie looked at the Agents and felt suddenly like the frumpy housewife she really was.

"My family has been in the service of the Tracker for generations. We have learned that when another replaces one Tracker, it means that he has died. This is the first time any of us has served a lady Tracker. I must say, it will be very…interesting," she replied cheerfully.

"Well, it's nice to finally talk to someone who doesn't assume that I'm stupid just because I'm a girl," Maddie said smiling. Abiah grinned in a knowing manner that said plainly between women: Men are stupid. Maddie suppressed a wicked grin and noticed that Abiah's two front teeth had been filed into long points. Maddie thought it was a shame, it ruined a little of the woman's delicate beauty.

"So what can I do for you?" she asked, not to Maddie but to Fred and George. Maddie rolled her eyes and decided that some habits were just too difficult to break. She put her chin in her hand and waited for things to just take care of themselves. George knew what he was about and so he didn't need her to get things done. She wondered absently what she was doing here, anyway. It wasn't like she could do anything on her own if she had to.

"Just the usual," George said, putting his arms on the table and leaning on them. He smiled smoothly at Abiah, showing a lot of white, even teeth. "A decent room, some dinner, and information."

"Oh, is that all?" Abiah said wryly. "Do you want gossip or something more tangible?"

"Just what you have on Lords Barnum and Cass," he said, reaching out and taking her small hand in his. He let his thumb rub lightly along her knuckles. His eyes sparkled with lust and good humor. Abiah giggled and blushed but didn't pull away. Maddie watched with eyes gleaming and her mouth open in an astonished smile.

"I'll see what I can do," Abiah said in a breathy voice and she opened the door behind her. She gave the men one more flirtatious glance over her shoulder and glided out the door.

"Laying it on a bit thick, aren't you?" Maddie said grinning like a fiend. She'd never seen this side of George before. She could see that he was a man and assumed that he had all the usual needs and urges as all men did. But he always seemed a disciplined celibate, as if sex and women seemed to distract from his job or too far beneath him. Seeing him actually flirting with a woman was shocking and it amused the hell out of Maddie. George gave her a flat unreadable look.

"I'm sure I don't know what you mean," he said dully. Fred was conspicuously silent, his face carefully neutral. Oh, yeah, he'd seen it, too.

"Oh, please, you couldn't be anymore into that woman if you climbed up her butt," Maddie laughed. George maintained his level stare.

"Perhaps, but she liked it," he retorted. "Jealous?" Maddie laughed until she cried and her sides hurt.

Abiah brought them a light meal of gritty flat bread and a stringy vegetable that looked like celery but tasted like a nasty mutant hybrid of bananas and squash. The food stuck to her teeth in a gooey mass and the wine she drank to wash it away tasted medicinal and was as gritty as the bread. She sat back in her chair with her meal half-eaten and thinking that her teeth were going to hurt for a week.

Afterwards, Abiah appeared and led Maddie to a simple stone enclosure. It had copper pipes sticking out of the walls and little glass knobs beneath that. The walls were lined with stone benches and two brass stands held long metal rods with felt tied to the end of them. A large, square grate in the middle of floor served as drainage.

Abiah explained that this was the women's washroom and that Maddie could cleanse herself here with out reprisals. Maddie thought that last comment was rather odd and would have asked what she meant by that but she turned and found herself alone in the room. Maddie shrugged and decided that it was just a weird cultural thing and didn't want to worry about it.

She stripped down and set her clothes neatly on a bench near the door. She figured out that the pipes worked by pulling up on the glass knobs. Fragrant steam blasted out of the pipe and startled her so badly that she slipped and fell on her butt. She expected the steam to be scalding, or freezing cold. But it was a comfortable temperature and rather pleasant to stand in. The steam condensed quickly on her skin and ran in oily streams to the floor. Maddie used the felt on rods to wash the filth from her body. She used her fingers to rub the dried vomit from her hair and it flowed across the floor and down the drain.

Felt towels had been left discreetly inside the door. Maddie dried the strange water from her body and reveled in the thick softness of the brown material. She left it draped on the bench to dry as she dressed. She felt a great deal better for finally getting clean and smelling like a person again instead of a hospital toilet.

Abiah was waiting for her as she emerged from the washroom. The woman beamed and bared her bizarre dental work. Maddie smiled back and fought to keep from staring rudely at the other woman's mouth.

"Your men await you in your rooms. Come, I will take you to them and you can take your rest," Abiah walked brusquely down the hall without looking back. She moved like a woman used to having people following her around and expected them to have the sense to stay close or get lost. Maddie took the opportunity to examine the building without the encumbrance of her stupid veil.

Like everything else in Rhasta, the inn was built almost exclusively in stone. Each large block was dressed and smoothed evenly and locked into one another almost seamlessly with iron struts and pins instead of mortar. The roof lifted into sharp peaks that were supported by ribbed arches and long ivory beams. Maddie contemplated the ivory pieces and wondered what kind of animal could have donated the impressive materials.

The interior hallway was made from smaller-cut bricks and held together by even layers of white mortar. Stone doors punctuated the walls and were framed by graceful archways. Copper wires lined the floors and ceiling and fed into small holes that led to individual rooms and into the ornate sconces next to each door. Large light bulbs were screwed into the sconces and shone a strange orange light through the corridor. The floor was a seamless and gleaming green stone over which a bright yellow and green runner ran down the length of it.

Abiah stopped at a door near the end of the hall and lifted the latch with just a gentle press of her delicate hand. The door was perfectly smoothed and polished, and had a series of lines across the top denoting the room's number. Beneath the latch, a heavily ornate brass lock was set into the door. Abiah held out an equally ornate key as she pushed the door open enough for Maddie to pass through. Maddie accepted the key and politely thanked Abiah.

George and Fred were examining a map spread across a white marble table. They had removed their absurd hats and coats and left them draped across the backs of leather chairs. They leaned on the table in their lacy shirtsleeves and looked more uncomfortable than they had before. Maddie approached them with a grin and a bad joke about their masculinity on her lips. George lifted a leather-wrapped packet from the table and held it out to her without looking up. Maddie took it, her curiosity overwhelming her need to tease the Agents. The leather had been oiled until it was waterproofed and was bound together by a piece of rawhide.

"Looks like we have our work cut out for us," George growled. Maddie opened the packet and revealed a thick roll of skins bound by more rawhide sewn through the top of the pages. The skins had been bleached almost white and worked until they were soft and smooth. Neat feminine writing covered the skins front and back in thick black ink. Her brain tingled as her nano pack automatically translated what was looking at.

It was a report outlining the possible locations, businesses, activities and gossip about Barnum and Cass. Abiah had described in minute detail what she knew of Barnum and Cass personally, their known habits, their personalities and exactly what territories they claimed or fought over. They were both involved in extortion, prostitution, gambling, drug dealing, smuggling of every kind and murder. The two got into each other's way frequently and with bloody consequences. They terrorized the city they fought to control, leaving battered hookers, burnt businesses and homes and piles of dead in their wake. None of the citizenry wanted them around but none of them were either willing or able to do anything about it.

Now the balance of power was shifting, not only in this particular city, but also across the entire continent of Rhasta. What was before a series of corrupt city-states governed by "mob bosses" and warlords was now being consolidated into a single entity by a young self-proclaimed king and savior named Kadar.

Of course, Kadar wasn't carrying out his quest of unification through peaceful diplomacy. He was rampaging through the barren landscape, making bloody conquests and looting the local populations into submission. He did have one discerning tendency that made him stand out from other conquering tyrants. He tortured, hung and displayed the crime lords he found in his newly conquered territories. Because of that tendency, many crime-riddled territories had simply opened their gates to Kadar's advancing army, showered him with tribute and handed over their undesirables. In return, Kadar committed no violence upon those populations and allowed them to continue with business as usual as long as they followed the new laws he set down for them.

By all accounts, Kadar never overlooked a single criminal and, once captured, none ever escaped custody. Their bodies lined busy roadways and served as gruesome reminders of what happened to those who broke the new laws. Maddie shook her head in wonder, thinking that it was a miracle that no one had managed to assassinate the young king yet. But it proved George's statement all the more accurate. They did have their work cut out for them. Kadar was now marching in the direction of this city with his army in tow. Abiah reported that his spies were already combing the streets for Barnum and Cass and three had already been found mutilated and dead, left to hang on the walls of public buildings.

In response, Kadar had found one of the Center's many contacts and requested the Tracker's assistance. Not because he was afraid of the crime lords' considerable power in the region but because his army had been on the move for three years and were growing anxious to return to their homes and their families. He needed to cut his war short for the time being and if he could visibly display an allegiance with a figure as powerful as the Tracker, then it would strengthen his hold on his power and allow him to gather a far stronger army when he returned to his conquests.

Maddie set down the information packet and rubbed her eyes.

"We're being used, you know that don't you?" she said.

"Nothing new, Tracker," George replied. "Just follow orders and try not to think too hard about it. Tell me what you think about the info."

"Well, it looks as if Barnum and Cass have been enough of a problem for a long enough time that the Quarter has decided that they'll take any excuse to get rid of them. Kadar made it public that he got my help because my allegiance will help legitimize his kingship and make him more powerful. On a more personal note, my assisting Kadar will piss off Cass and Barnum enough that they may become a threat to my life and well-being. So I really don't have a problem with the politics of the situation since it benefits us, anyway. Except, I don't like Kadar going around and telling everyone I'm taking orders from him."

"I don't like it when the local kings think they can command a Tracker, either. It makes us look like mercenaries but this is the mission and we follow orders whether we like it or not," George said. "There's another report here that says both Barnum and Cass already know that we're here and have put a rather sizeable bounty on your head. We're going to have to move fast and take these two out before someone starts taking pot shots at you."

"Peachy," Maddie growled. "Let's do it so I can go home."

CHAPTER 15

Arnold hadn't slept well that night. Sam had given her pillows and extra blankets and tried to make her as comfortable as possible. But it was useless. She lay on the couch and strained to hear any sounds that might mean that whatever had been outside had somehow made its way into the house. Her hand kept wandering to her gun, tucked carefully away beneath her pillow with the safety on. She jumped whenever the house creaked or when the wind whistled through the chimney. When she did sleep, it was in fits and she had terrible nightmares. She saw a monster standing over the mangled corpses of her brother-in-law and his children. It lifted its head and grinned at her, exposing long teeth dripping with their blood. She'd start awake and stare in terror at the deep shadows. Eventually, she turned the TV on though its harsh glow did little to ease her nerves.

She rose with the sun beginning to peek over the horizon. Pale yellow light graced the dark corners of the living room and chased away the terror of the lingering night. She pulled her gun from under the pillow and tucked it back into the belt holster and put it on. The house was silent; there were no sounds that indicated that the family would awaken any time soon. So she crossed the living room and went into the kitchen to the sliding glass door.

She pushed down the lock and moved the bit of wood before she opened the door and waited. There were no rank smells of death and decay and the only sounds were the chirps of birds and rustling of small mammals in the bushes. She took a deep breath and stepped out of the house and onto the back porch. The wood was richly varnished and clean, showing no signs of anything that might have caused the fear she'd experienced the night before. The wind lifted and brought with it the clean country smells of small town life and the crisp coolness of autumn.

She went down the steps of the deck and into the yard. She began a circuit of the house, looking for evidence of the threatening presence she felt the night before. But the grounds and foliage surrounding the house were undisturbed. There wasn't even a sign of the animal life that frequently wandered across the property during the night hours. She finished her circuit and stepped back up the porch.

She didn't know whether she should be relieved that she hadn't found anything or not. On the one hand, evidence of nothing meant that there had been no real threat to anyone in the house. But the sensations of terror had been so intense that she was convinced that something had been there. Arnold wondered if she were losing her mind.

The sun had fully cleared the horizon and it spread its warm light through the trees. Arnold watched small animals and birds move around the yard and wondered if the whole thing hadn't been in her mind after all. She was stressed out and the gruesome murders of two families were enough to give anyone nightmares. It was silly, really; she couldn't believe that she'd let a few strange smells and the dark spook her so badly.

Feeling somewhat better, she went into the house and found Sam pouring cereal into three bowls. The children were sitting on the couch all huddled together and looking tired and afraid. Sam didn't look any better. He was haggard and had dark shadows underneath his bloodshot eyes. He hadn't shaved yet and the auburn stubble on his chin emphasized the gray pallor of his skin. He smiled at her weakly as he set the box aside.

"Find anything?" he asked. Arnold shook her head. Sam sighed and rubbed his face with his hands.

"I don't understand," he finally said. "There was something out there. We saw it, we smelled it. You smelled it and you heard it."

"I don't really think there was anything out there," she began softly. "I think both of us have been dealing with an awful lot lately. You're stressed because Maddie's been out of town all the time and I'm stressed because I have a nasty murder case that's not going well. Combine those with a smelly animal passing too close to the house and things are bound to get blown out of proportion."

Sam looked at her in disbelief.

"I guess..." his voice trailed off reluctantly. His mind was too tired to think for itself. He was ready to latch onto anything that Darlene handed to him to explain what he saw last night so long as it was rational. And her explanation was certainly more rational than what his nightmares tried to tell him. He didn't believe in demons and monsters. He believed in real things with real solutions to irrational fears.

Arnold stared at him with big imploring eyes, as if begging him to accept her explanation. He smiled weakly and nodded his head agreeably.

"Of course, you're right," he said. Arnold sagged with relief and felt tension that she didn't know she had draining from her body.

Things returned to normal after that. Sam called the kids to breakfast while Arnold ducked into the spare bathroom for a shower. She wound up borrowing some clothes from Maddie after she decided that it would be a bad idea to show up for work wearing the same outfit she'd worn the day before. She could imagine the relentless teasing she would receive at the hands of her fellow cops. Cops were pretty much the same in small towns as they were in big cities. They were overworked, stressed out and tended to latch on to anything that brought relief to the monotonous stress of their lives. If she arrived to work looking as if she'd taken a man to her bed, they would never let up. And denying it would only encourage the behavior. Best to just borrow the clothes and avoid any incidents altogether.

She kissed her niece and nephews goodbye and encouraged Sam to relax and get some sleep. Sam promised to take her advice as he escorted her to the door. She said goodbye again and told him to call her if he saw or remembered anything, just in case. Sam looked worried but promised to call if he needed anything.

Arnold was making her way towards the downtown area and the police station when her cell phone rang.

"This is Arnold," she said automatically.

"We have a witness," Cooper's voice said excitedly. "A Dr. Shorn called just a few minutes ago claiming to have seen the persons responsible for the Anderson murders. He lives across the street from the murder scene. I think you ought to be there when I question him and see if you pick up on the stuff I might miss."

"What did he say?" Arnold asked excitedly. Her heart began to pound in anticipation. This could be the break in the case they were waiting for. She hadn't realized how hopeless she had felt about the case until she began to believe that they might be able to solve the case after all. Then she remembered the morning news she had watched as she had gotten dressed. Details about her case had broken on the a.m. news and, no doubt, the nuts would be coming out of the woodwork now. It was very possible that this Dr. Shorn could be one of them. The doctor was not listed among the witnesses the police talked to when they canvassed the neighborhood during the initial investigation.

"He didn't say much. Just that he saw some people going in and coming out and he had times that corroborated with the coroner's estimate of time of death." Cooper said. Arnold tried to sound optimistic as Cooper gave her Dr. Shorn's address. He told her to hurry up and then the connection was lost.

Dr. Shorn lived in a small house that dated back to the 1940s. It would have been a charming little place with its towering oaks dripping with moss and the flowering bushes and trees bordering the property with the neighbors. But the house was in desperate need of maintenance and repairs so that it looked bleak and run down. The paint was faded and peeling from the exterior walls and the shutters had long since fallen off. The tall, weedy grass hid trash and the roof was sagging and missing shingles.

Cooper was waiting for her when she arrived and got out of his car as she parked on the other side of him in the driveway. He looked the same as he always did, his cheap suit was neat and pressed and the colorful tie featuring cartoon characters had baby barf on it. His brown hair was neatly cut and combed in the same manner in which he'd always kept it since he was twelve years old.

He smiled at her as she got out of her car and went towards him.

"Are you ready to solve this case?" he asked, ever the optimist.

"Sure. Let's go see what Dr. Shorn has to say," she replied. She wasn't quite the optimist that he was, but then, who was she to ruin the moment for him?

They made their way up the cracked and buckling walk leading to a rotting and peeling wooden front porch. Many of the posts supporting the railing were broken and missing and some of the boards creaked and cracked when they stepped on them. Arnold widened her eyes in alarm and both detectives paid close attention to where they placed their feet.

Cooper knocked firmly on the warped wooden door. It was immediately flung open by a tall, gangly old man with white hair that stuck up in clumps. He wore small round spectacles that sat on a big bulbous nose. He was dressed in a ragged flannel shirt and t-shirt over faded blue jeans and worn slippers. Dr. Short squinted at them with small, watery brown eyes.

"Are you the detectives?" he asked in a loud nasal voice. Arnold put on her best friendly neighborhood authority face and Cooper smiled and showed too many teeth.

"I'm Detective Jeff Cooper and this is my partner, Detective Darlene Arnold. We understand that you have some information regarding the murders of the Anderson family?" He made it a question so that he wouldn't be the pushy, obnoxious cop when he wanted to be the friendly, understanding, and polite detective. Shorn glanced over their heads at the Anderson home across the street. He nodded anxiously and stepped back while opening the door wider to let them in.

They stepped into a dark room as equally unkempt and broken as the outside. The carpets were threadbare and stained and the furniture that littered the living room was frayed and half-broken. Dirty blinds covered the windows and blocked the room from the sun. Tall piles of papers and books covered the warped coffee table and were stacked on either side of the couch. Dusty and faded framed photos hung on walls covered with faded and peeling wallpaper.

Shorn muttered apologies as he scooped up an armload of papers and books, and relocated it to the already overburdened end tables. Cooper and Arnold sat in the spaces he cleared for them while Shorn remained on his feet and fidgeted. He didn't seem to know what to do with the detectives now that he had them at his house.

"So what can you tell us about what you saw?" Cooper said still smiling too broadly. Shorn looked at him like he was a particularly exotic-looking bug and blinked rapidly.

"I already told the other officer dates and times and he must have told you or otherwise you wouldn't be here," Shorn said impatiently. He began to pace the short length of the room and rubbed his large forehead.

"Why don't you just tell me what you saw?" Cooper said gently.

"I saw *them*," Shorn said with a tremor. "I saw one slip through one of the front windows. Then the dog barked and then it stopped. I saw blood splash on one of the bedroom windows and then it let the others in and then they played. I could hear howling and laughing. I watched as they licked the blood off the windows."

The man dropped to a chair without noticing the pile of the papers or the books that he crumpled. His already pale complexion had turned gray and his hands trembled violently. He stared bleakly at the carpet between his feet. He swallowed rapidly as if fighting the urge to vomit.

They waited for him to gather his wits enough to continue speaking.

"I'll bet you're wondering why I didn't call the police when I saw that poor family being murdered," Shorn's voice cracked as he struggled for control. "But if you had seen the things I saw, you would be afraid, too. I don't mean the kind of afraid that happens when you know you're about to get into a bad car accident. This is afraid so bad that your limbs are paralyzed and you cannot control your own functions. You can't move you can't breathe, and you can't hear, see or even think. These things do that. They rob you of everything that makes you human and leave you with a dry shell of yourself."

Arnold and Cooper stared silently at the man, somewhat stunned by his statement. It was clear that the man had seen something but whether or not it was tangible or imaginary had yet to be determined. Shorn had lowered his face to his hands and was weeping bitterly. Arnold and Cooper exchanged glances, their eyes asking the other what they thought they should do. Finally, Arnold cleared her throat.

"Can you describe the individuals you saw?" she asked gently.

Shorn looked up with tears streaking down his sagging cheeks. He looked at them with mournful, uncomprehending eyes. She was about to ask him again when he sprang to his feet.

"I have pictures," he murmured. He rushed off to the back of the house. Cooper and Arnold waited and listened to him mutter and the sounds of rummaging coming from the back of the house. Shorn returned a few minutes later carrying a battered shoebox in his big hands.

He pulled the top off and revealed that the box was filled with snapshot pictures. He sat down with it in his lap and began to dig through its contents.

"I took maybe half of these pictures," he said.

He lifted two pictures from the box and held them out to the detectives. Arnold accepted the pictures and stared at what she saw. Shorn had returned to rummaging through his box and he kept talking.

"This isn't the first I've seen them," Shorn said. "The first time was about twenty years ago. I was at Red Top Mountain, not to far from here, actually, and I was taking photographs of some of the wildlife there to show for a lecture I was doing on mammalian biology. I saw some movement in the foliage and I managed to snap a couple of photos of it before it attacked me. I must have been screaming pretty loudly because a man came and ran the thing off and called an ambulance for me.

"But when I got out of the hospital, I went through the photos I took that day and saw the monster that had attacked me. I've been chasing them ever since. I've taken pictures whenever I see them and I've talked with people who have seen them too." Shorn's voice trailed off.

Arnold barely heard the man speak. She was staring at the pictures he had handed her. The first photo was of the Anderson house. It was nighttime and the house was shrouded in shadows. The streetlight in Shorn's front yard was lit and it spilled a dark yellow pool across the Anderson's yard. Everything was as it was when Arnold first arrived. Toys were scattered across the yard and the bicycle was leaning against the old car. But there was a strange figure crouched below one of the windows. It looked like a man, but the way he held himself indicated that he was badly deformed in some way. His arms were too long and he didn't look as if he was wearing any clothes. He had one long hand resting on the window beside him as he looked away from the house. His large eyes caught the streetlight strangely and they seemed to glow. The strange light warped the features of the twisted face.

The next picture was taken in the daylight. It featured another twisted and deformed man, only this time he was close enough to touch. He was rushing the camera, his long twisted arms reaching out with big hands tipped with curved black claws. The face snarled out from between the arms, exposing long yellow teeth protruding from an impossibly yawning mouth. His eyes were too big for its head, and one was much higher than the other was. His hairless skin was covered in filth and was sick with boils and sores.

Arnold tore her eyes from the picture and turned to Cooper. He was flipping through more photographs and scowling. Shorn clutched his shoebox to his chest and watched the detectives with round anxious eyes.

"What is all this?" Cooper asked, angrily throwing the pictures down on the coffee table. Shorn flinched and seemed to fold into himself.

"It took me years of study to learn what they were and what they did," Shorn said. "And when I heard of a family in Germany who had been murdered, I went to go look into it myself. As it would happen, the father had managed to survive the attack. His name was Jacob Fleicher. He was a high school history teacher with a wife and four sons. They were slaughtered in front of him. He spoke to me of how the monsters bragged about how easy humans were to kill and how they'd do the same to one they called the Tracker. They told him that they were dying so that they could draw the Tracker from his hiding place and kill him. I have assumed that that is what they're doing now."

"Who?" Arnold got the feeling that her only purpose for being here was to motivate some strange plot. It was an annoying sensation. Shorn's eyes took on a haunted look.

"They are the Distari," he whispered.

After that, Cooper became fed up and took over the conversation and kept rigid control of it. He managed to get Shorn to tell him which window the perps had used to enter the home and which window had had the blood licked off. He had Shorn repeat his statement regarding the Anderson murder and made sure of the sequence and time of events. He stood to go and thanked Dr. Shorn through clenched teeth. Shorn escorted them to the door and promised to call if he remembered anything else despite the fact that they hadn't asked.

"That guy is nuts," Cooper growled as they made their careful way down the walk.

"Maybe, but I think he definitely saw what happened to the Andersons," Arnold replied studying the picture of the house that Shorn had let them keep.

"If he did, he's too crazy to be a reliable witness or to make a positive identification. I'll have a crime scene unit come out and take a look at the windows. Call Interpol and go look into the Fleicher case. See if there's anything to it," Cooper said. He pulled his car door open and leaned against it.

"I'll be in touch," Arnold replied, getting into her own car.

CHAPTER 16

Sam sat on the deck set against the back of the house. He tried to relax in a chair with his feet propped up on the table in front of him. Behind him, the house was dark and quiet. The kids were tucked safely in his bed, finally asleep by the light of the television sitting on the dresser. After the events of last night, the children had clung to him and were afraid to sleep.

The moon was full, casting silvery light through the neighborhood and deepening the shadows that eluded the lunar light. A large, fluffy cat stalked invisible prey through the grass. A cold breeze blew in; bringing with it the full promise of winter and making him shiver. He didn't move from his spot despite the goosebumps pebbling his skin. He was just as frightened as the children and he was just as reluctant to sleep.

Besides, he was too angry to do much more than just sit there and stare at the nighttime sky. It had been three days since Maddie left and she still hadn't called home. He knew that he could have called her; she had left him a phone number so that he could do so. But he wanted to see if she would call him first. He wanted to see if she ever thought of him while she was at work and doing other things.

A wretched thought popped into his head, one that he had been trying not to think for some months now. Maddie traveled so much and she never told him where she was going or how long that she'd be gone. When she returned, she had odd marks on her body and she didn't touch him very much anymore. She let him spend money to his heart's content but she was critical of his housekeeping skills and the way he handled the children. He felt like a fool for not thinking of it before. His wife was having an affair while he stayed at home with their children and wallowed in his painful loneliness.

Another gust of wind brought a smell that drove the rage from his mind and made the hair on the back of his neck stand up. The smell was faint but grew stronger as the wind continued to blow. It was the smell of death and decay that was held in the otherwise clear night and it felt horribly familiar. His heart pounded in his chest and his breath rasped painfully in his throat. His instincts screamed at him to go into his house gather up his children and hide. But his brain burned with a sudden intensity. He had an unknown enemy that was stalking him, violating *his* property and threatening *his* children. He was outraged and all he wanted to do was find the source of that pain and destroy it. He would not run and hide like a frightened child. It was bad enough that he was a cuckold, he would not be a coward as well.

He stood up and slowly examined every shadow for the source of that terrifying smell. He tried to swallow in a mouth gone suddenly dry. His palms sweated and his body trembled, but not from the chill. Still, he didn't move; he had to see what it was. He would not run, *he would not.* The smell grew stronger and stronger until his stomach churned from the bile of it and he was choking.

A creature separated itself from the shadows in the neighbor's yard and moved towards the chain link fence dividing the properties. His eyes were pulled to it, and he watched as it approached the fence with long liquid movements unlike anything he'd ever seen before. It moved all wrong, as if its joints were hinged in the wrong direction and attached in all the wrong places. Large eyes, luminous and hungry, scanned the land around it.

Sam blinked and it was suddenly on the other side of the fence and in his yard. It kept itself hunched in a tight ball, disguising its true size and shape. Then it moved, lifting its body from its tight crouch and stretching to its full immense height. Sam stood frozen as the predatory smell intensified and robbed him of all sense and instinct. It lifted its hideous face and sniffed the wind. Those terrible glowing eyes turned towards him and seemed to see him clearly despite the darkness. It smiled at him, exposing long, blunt teeth.

Its eyes met his and tried to hold him in its cold stare. Sam shook his head violently, tearing his gaze from the monster's and staggering several steps backwards until his shoulders touched the door behind him. He squeezed his eyes shut to keep from having to see those terrible eyes. It had looked humanoid but its upper parts were too long to be human and the lower bits were too short. It was built for shear brute power and it showed even in the thin, ropy muscles of its stooped back that were as twisted as the limbs it held together.

Sam's hand fumbled for the handle as the monster began to move slowly towards him. It growled, filling his ears with the same sounds that filled his dreams. It haunted him, tormented him and *it was coming toward him!* He had to move. He had to grab his children and run. There was no way he could fight this thing and survive. It would tear him apart and then do the same thing to his children. Terrified screams came from his bedroom and penetrated the shell of terror that engulfed him and shattered it.

Sam spun and flung open the door and ran inside the house. He hit the bedroom door with all of his impressive weight and broke the knob and doorframe. The children screamed in terror from the corner furthest from the window. The boys clung tightly to their sister while she wept and put her arms around them. Blood-red eyes and long teeth glimmered against the window. Its growl filled the room and rattled the glass. His heart stopped in his chest as he reached for his children and hauled them to their feet. Black claws touched the glass and were dragged across it with a shriek.

Suddenly it was gone. Without warning or sound, it disappeared. One second it was snarling at them through the window and the next it was gone. They fled anyway. Sam led his children to the front door. His hand grasped the knob and then he stopped. So far, those monsters could not or would not come into the house. But they were still out there in the darkness, waiting for them.

"Daddy? What's wrong?" Katie asked fearfully. "What are we going to do?"

"I don't know." His voice came out a raspy whisper. His hand tightened around hers and he let go of the knob and stepped away from the door. Where could they go? What would they do?

The phone rang. The sound was shrill and harsh. The father and children jumped and stared at the source of the sound. The phone rang again from where it lay carelessly on the couch. It was quiet outside. There were no monsters pressing against the windows or pounding on the doors. Where had they gone? The phone rang again and this time Sam moved. The children moved with him, their breath coming in hiccups as he scooped the phone up and answered it.

"Sam? It's me. How is everything going?" Maddie's voice sounded cheerful. He held the phone pressed to his ear and listened to her voice and trembled. It was so familiar, so normal in the terrible distortion of the moment. She did think of him while she worked, just not as often as he liked. He glanced out the windows and saw that the night had returned to peace and normalcy.

"What's wrong? Are you still mad at me?" her voice was anxious.

He licked his lips with a dry tongue. He collapsed onto the couch and the children gathered around him and snuggled close. In a trembling voice, he told her everything that had just happened.

CHAPTER 17

Maddie listened with shock and dismay as Sam described the events of his last forty-eight hours. To her, she'd left her family just that morning, but three days had passed at home and Sam wanted her back. She promised him that she would hurry and that she would figure out what to do about what was happening to him. In the meantime, she advised him to get a gun and keep it with him at all times. His breath caught at that last part but he didn't argue. She made him promise to call everyday and tell her how everyone was doing. They exchanged endearments and Maddie hung up the phone. It was time to ask George some hard questions.

The Agents were back in their flamboyant hats and coats, waiting for her when she emerged from the bedroom suite. They were grim-faced and dangerous looking despite their garishly colored clothing and the frivolity of the feathers and lace. Their guns bulged slightly under their arms and their decorative swords glittered at their hips.

"It is time to go," George said.

"In a minute. I have something I want to discuss with you," Maddie said, folding her arms beneath her breasts as she squared her shoulders. "I just got off the phone with my husband. The things he told me curdled my blood. I have to say that if I hadn't seen those things in the field this morning, I wouldn't have believed him."

"Your husband saw those particular beasts?" Fred asked incredulously.

"He said they attacked the house," Maddie replied coldly.

Both men jerked as if they'd been slapped. Maddie looked from one to the other and leveled them with the same stare she gave her children when she knew they were lying to her. Her lips were pressed firmly together as she narrowed her eyes at them.

"Is he certain of this?" George asked softly.

"He's scared shitless, George," Maddie snapped. "He thinks he's going crazy and that the children are going with him. I had to talk him out of having himself committed, then I had to fast talk to keep him from calling our pastor."

George and Fred exchanged a look. Fred shrugged and turned away.

"Your family is being carefully guarded against your enemies, Tracker. No harm will come to them," George said.

"Yeah, that's what you guys have been telling me since I started doing this crap. Trouble is, they are coming to harm and I don't know what to tell them."

"There are Agents guarding your home and family at all times," he replied.

"Fine. Why don't you start telling them to do their jobs," she snarled. She was angry, not just because her family was being threatened but also because they refused to tell her anything.

"They are doing their jobs, Tracker. Your family still lives," he snapped back.

Maddie ground her teeth in frustration. "Those things were at my house! What are they doing at *my house?* If the Agents were doing their jobs, then my family wouldn't even be seeing them!"

George didn't say anything to that. There were no words to say. Maddie had scored a point against him and he couldn't defend it.

"Of course, *madam Tracker*," he hissed in a mockery of subordination. Fred had turned back around and was glaring at Maddie now. She ignored him and kept her anger focused on George.

"They have always stalked the Trackers. And Agents have always fought against them. We are practiced in battle against them. We will not allow them to harm you or your heirs," he said finally.

"Who are they?" She nearly screamed the question, she was so frustrated.

George was silent a moment, thinking about whether or not to finally answer her. She should know the answer to that already. The memories she inherited from her predecessors should have already explained everything she needed to know. But somehow she had avoided that terrible information and she remained dangerously ignorant. Finally, he spoke.

"They are the Distari."

A barrage of information battered Maddie's brain, flooding her consciousness with gruesome and terrifying images and sending her reeling. She staggered and would have fallen if George hadn't steadied her with a hand.

"My god, what am I going to do? How can my family survive that? I've got to go home!" she gasped, staring up at George with tears shimmering in her eyes.

"You will do as all the others before you have done. You will do your job and trust the Agents to do theirs," George said gently. "We have never lost a family and we never will."

"But you've lost Trackers," she whispered fearfully. Her mind was still feeding her hideous scenes of bloody death and mutilation.

"Trackers tend to be a bit more reckless than their heirs. Many of those we lost had gone to confront the Distari on their own. Like your most recent predecessor."

"So I guess I shouldn't try to go after them by myself," Maddie sniffed. Her brain still reeled with the bloody death of Gustav Haughmein. He had gone after the Distari, not from any sense of revenge or noble desire to rid the world of evil, but because he was dying of cancer and hadn't wanted to suffer any longer. She swallowed bile as she recalled the feeling of being torn limb from limb and let George gather her against his chest and hug her. His heart beat rapidly against her cheek and he smelled of musky cologne.

"No, Tracker. Don't go after them yourself. Should a lair need exterminating, Keung will send Agents to do the job,"

"Call Keung, tell him that there's a lair that needs exterminating," Maddie said coldly. She pulled away from the hug and went in search of a handkerchief.

"Indeed."

It took Maddie only a moment to gather herself and make sure she had everything she needed to do her job tucked carefully on her person. She was frantic about her family but at least she could concentrate on the matters at hand. After all, she was on an alien planet and couldn't do anything for her husband and children until she got home. And she had learned from bitter experience that she wouldn't get home until the mission was completed. The best she could manage was to do the job she was ordered to do as fast as she could and get back to them. In the meantime, George promised to notify Keung of the situation at Maddie's house and make sure that the problem with the Distari was solved.

"Let's get this over with," she growled, finding her work more distasteful than ever. She jammed things into the thick belt around her waist. The men didn't argue with her. They watched in silence as she fixed the cumbersome hat to her head and followed her out the door.

Abiah was waiting for them at the bottom of the women's stairs. The woman grinned at them and held out her slender arms in greeting.

"Are you going out this evening?" she asked pleasantly.

"We have some business in the city," Maddie replied crisply, not wanting to be delayed any longer. She felt the woman's curiosity vibrating from her mind. "I would appreciate it greatly if you would have our rooms prepared for sleep and have a hot meal waiting upon our return."

Abiah bowed her head, bending her long neck gracefully. Maddie saw that she had changed her clothes to something more revealing than what she had worn earlier. She was wearing a blouse that scooped at the neck and revealed a plump wealth of cleavage. Long earrings dangled from her lobes and glittered in the weak electric light. Abiah glanced lustily at George who was suddenly pretending not to see the beautiful woman.

"As you wish, milady," she murmured prettily.

Maddie nodded and moved past the woman with George and Fred trailing behind her. Abiah stopped the three with a polite clearing of her throat.

"I know that a woman Tracker has never graced our establishment and therefore it makes sense to me that you do not know all of our ways," Abiah began loftily. Maddie sighed at the woman, indicating that she wanted her to get on with it. Abiah took the hint and started speaking faster.

"During the day, a woman must veil herself modestly so that the lecherous eyes of men may not touch the divine grace of her face. But at night the shadows shroud her beauty so she may remove the veil that guards her virtue. The night is the woman's true time, where she might face the world with all due honesty and breath freely of the healthful fumes of the night air."

Maddie frowned, wondering what the woman was babbling about. She had quickly understood that Abiah was telling her that she could take off the veil at night but she couldn't quite grasp the reason why. But she was being delayed, so she didn't bother asking what would clearly be stupid questions of the woman. Instead she pulled her hat and veil from her head and held it out.

"Would you please return my hat and veil to my room for me please?" she asked as politely as she could manage through clenched teeth.

Abiah took the hat graciously with a bow. She murmured that she would personally see to it that the hat was properly returned to the Tracker's room in all due haste. But Maddie hadn't waited long enough to hear the woman out; Abiah was just too long-winded. Abiah quickly found herself talking to Maddie's back as she left the inn.

The city was alive in a way it hadn't been while the suns were still up. Now, the moons hung full and pregnant in the sky, the lingering haze diminishing their eerie light. Gas streetlights were lit and the exposed flames danced in the open air. Periodically, a gust of wind swept a flame from its perch on the end of a pole and sent it into the passing crowd. Whenever a person let out a yelp of fear and pain, a man bearing a tank on his back appeared from the shadows of the alleyways and extinguished the enflamed victim with thin mud squirted from a patched hose. Money would then change hands and the two parties went their separate ways. In one case that Maddie saw, a young man refused to make payment when he was extinguished and the tank man badly beat him. Two of Tank Man's comrades appeared and hauled the young woman who had accompanied the young man off to the darkness of an alley. Their brutal minds were full of the thoughts of glee. If the young man would not pay for the service, then his lady friend would pay with whatever could be found underneath her skirts.

People caroused in the streets, men propositioned the whores who had suddenly appeared on street corners and engaged in fistfights in front of the pubs. Men stood in front of buildings, crying out to the multitudes of entertainment and services his particular establishment engaged in while telling elaborate tales of the events that took place within its walls. People stood in groups in front of the various gambling halls, brothels, inns and pubs and laughed as they listened to the eager barkers. They heard the entertaining harangues and paid the criers for his tale whenever they disappeared into the smoky dens of happy sin.

Others simply passed through the entertainment center of the city and took their money to the marketplace that ringed it. The marketplace was segregated according to social class and wealth, the better establishments and vendors separated from the rest with decorative bushes and fences. The places frequented by the poorer citizens of the city were left to their own devices, most of which meant that the establishments fell into seediness and disrepair. Booths and stands competed for space with the more permanent and established business while people, mostly women, examined the vegetables and wares they displayed. Food and drink stands dotted the market as well as wandering vendors carrying their goods and hawking their services.

From the market district was the residential district of the city. Like all cities, the neighborhoods were divided according to wealth and social standing. The privileged enjoyed large houses with carefully manicured and sprawling estates. Their streets were clean and well-maintained. The people who wandered the immaculate sidewalks were prim in their finely cut clothing and pristine grooming. They smiled genteelly at each other and nodded their heads and exchanged polite words.

On the opposite side of the city were the slums. It was made up of randomly-placed and haphazardly-constructed shacks and tenements that always seemed on the verge of collapse. Their clothes were the tattered cast-offs salvaged from the garbage heaps of the rich and middle-class. They looked sickly and beaten, as if they had known from the cradle that they would never escape the crushing poverty that bound them to their misery. They did not speak except to fight and they rarely made eye contact, as if doing so would provoke the fury of their financially-oppressed brethren. The children played in empty lots strewn with trash and the streets were cracked and rutted from neglect.

The middle-class made up the largest economic population in the metropolis. Their homes acted as the buffer between the rich and the poor. They kept their doors locked at night and they spoke softly and carefully whenever they met someone on the street. Their homes were modest and they did their best to keep their neighborhood neat and clean. It was difficult since they were forced to deal with the spill-off from the impoverished and the refuse from the rich.

It was at the boundary between the slums and the middle-class that Maddie found herself swaying on a street corner. The sidewalk beneath her feet was littered with trash and wasted whores, the defeated poor and the frustrated ne'er-do-wells. The men who walked past her found ways to jostle and bump her so that they could briefly lay their hands on the more sensitive parts of her anatomy. She didn't notice. She was too busy discovering what Abiah had meant by fumes.

About twenty minutes before, the fourth moon cleared the northwestern horizon and began its climb towards its zenith. With the small orb's appearance a sweet smell had lifted and Maddie turned her face into the breeze and breathed deeply of the intoxicating smell. She couldn't have stopped had she wanted to. It was just too delicious. She looked at the two men accompanying her to see if they had noticed the smell too. They looked completely oblivious to the air. Fred saw her gaping stupidly at him and gave her a dirty look.

Maddie shook her head to clear it and nearly fell over. It made her laugh as if she was having the time of her life. The wind gusted and she took a deep breath and let it out in a satisfied sigh. God, it smelled so good. As a matter of fact, she felt pretty damn good, too. She opened her eyes and barked out a laugh. Both men were staring at her now, with concern crinkling their faces.

"I'm okay," she chirped. She realized that her balance had gotten horribly skewed. Maybe it was because the ground insisted on moving up and down beneath her feet. She blinked at Fred and George and wondered how they kept their balance so well with the sidewalks wobbling so much. She supposed that it was because they were Agents. Couldn't be an Agent if they couldn't stay on their feet. She giggled at the sudden image in her head of squads of Agents suddenly staggering on their feet and falling over in big piles.

The men exchanged looks and George stuck his face into Maddie's and stared intently into her eyes. She grinned and wondered if he was about to kiss her. What should she do if he did that? Kiss him back? Punch him in the face?

"Are you high?" he demanded.

Maddie laughed at the absurdity of the question.

"Of course not!" she exclaimed. "I'm a good girl! Good girls don't get high!"

Fred let out a rude snort and rolled his eyes in disbelief. Maddie stuck her tongue out at him and blew a raspberry. George smiled broadly at her but his eyes remained cold and intense. Maddie stared back in confusion and thought that his face suddenly looked strange. How can someone smile with his mouth but not with his eyes?

He put his arm around her shoulders and steadied her against the side of his body. She caught the smell of his cologne again and fought the urge to wrap her arms around him and bury her face into his neck. That sort of thing would be terribly inappropriate. She was a married woman! Married women did not bury their faces into the necks of men who were not their husbands. At least, not if they expected to stay married. Still, it felt good to have George's strong arm around her so she didn't move away.

"Let's get her inside," he said, nodding to Fred to lead the way.

Without comment, Fred stepped off the curb and walked confidently down the street. George's arm tightened around her as they walked and tugged on her whenever it looked as if she might fall. She began to hear voices, thousands of them and they battered loudly away at her. She tried to stop and listen, to try to figure out where they were coming from. George pulled her forward and kept her moving in the direction he wanted her to go. How could she hear so many at once? Then she noticed that she could hear those closest to her more clearly. That made sense since those speaking next to her ears were louder than those further away were.

A man walking by in the opposite direction pondered his reasons for going home and facing a nagging wife and screaming children. His face was troubled and he stared at the ground as he walked. A smiling woman made jealous comments to Maddie and plotted ways she could separate her from the man with his arm around her. A bland-faced man loitered in a doorway while making obscene comments at her. He hoped that she would allow him to watch her have sex with George. She gave the pervert a hard and nasty look and felt George's arm drop from her shoulders to settle protectively at her waist. Had he heard the man too? She came to a third man who thought she was too mannish for his tastes and a scowling whore thought she might be willing to give Fred a freebie as he passed her by. Fred didn't seem to have heard her.

Maddie realized then that she had lost control of her telepathy and the voices that thundered in her ears were actually in her head. Frightened, she wrapped her arms around George and buried her face into his chest. He thrilled with such pleasure that she gaped up at him in astonishment. He looked blandly down at her and wondered if he could get away with pressing his lips to hers. She was *hallucinating* thoughts now. It was too much. She shook her head and buried her face into his coat and let the manly smell of his cologne soothe her. George held her and let her cling to him like a frightened child.

Soon she began to feel like herself again and she pulled out of George's arm. He let her go reluctantly, watching carefully to see if she could continue on her own. She walked between the men, Fred in front and George behind her. Her head cleared and the voices stopped yammering at her. She followed Fred steadily and without stumbling. A sense of relief filled her as the wind blew through the streets and kicked up the dirt and dust. She smelled the delicious scent again and she felt even better. Soon she was skipping happily and beaming at the strangers who cast indulgent looks her way.

"Okay, step into the next alley," George called to Fred over Maddie's shoulder.

Without question Fred took an immediate right turn and ducked into a dark alley with the other two on his heels. Once deep into the shadows and away from the noise of the streets, Fred stopped and turned. Maddie was hearing voices again. They were standing next to an illegal brothel that catered to a rather more…aggressive crowd. She cocked her head and listened to men and women make unscrupulous demands upon one another. Maddie blushed and giggled at the things she heard.

George cupped her face in his hands and stared at her. Then he kissed her. Maddie's brain stopped. It just stopped from the astonishment it felt at what was happening. The idea of George actually putting his mouth anywhere near hers had never occurred to her and it blew her away. Suddenly there were no voices, no giddiness. Just the sensation of his lips against hers in a chaste kiss. No tongue and his mouth held tightly closed. She stood frozen and breathed the strong smell of his cologne on his face and neck. Fred cleared his throat.

"You could have done that at the inn," he said dryly.

Maddie stiffened when he spoke, her mind suddenly snapping back into focus. She shoved George away and scowled at him.

"What the hell?" she snarled, wiping furiously at her mouth.

"She's getting intoxicated by the air," George said to Fred, ignoring Maddie's indignation.

"How?" he scoffed in disbelief.

George sniffed and looked around, trying to find the source of the intoxicant. He bent at the waist and dug through something against the building next to them. He came up with a handful of dirt and sniffed at it. He held it under Maddie's nose. She sniffed and immediately felt very happy. George threw the dirt down and wiped his hands on his pants.

"Fungus," he said to Fred. "It blooms at full night and releases spores. The spores have an intoxicating effect."

"Then why are we unaffected?" Fred demanded. "And the local population doesn't seem bothered by it at all."

"You used the lotion Bob gave us?" he asked. "You did as you were told and rubbed it all over your body and in your hair?"

"Of course."

"The lotion prevents our skin from absorbing the spores, and the perfume kills it as we breathe it in. I can only assume that the locals have developed an immunity to it," George explained. Fred sighed in disgust.

"It'll be a real pain in the ass if we have to drag a drunken Tracker everywhere we go," he growled. George shrugged.

"Did you bring along any of your lotion?"

"No. It's in my bag at the inn. I didn't think the stuff did anything useful."

Maddie had lost interest in the conversation. She was too busy listening to people make love and giggling.

CHAPTER 18

The Control Room was a swarm of activity. The personnel, who spent most of their waking hours within its confines, hurried through the narrow walkways carrying information destined to be scrupulously organized and filed away for future use. Analysts sat at computers and picked through the constant stream of information, sorting out the things that needed to be brought to the Keeper's attention immediately and putting away the things that could be casually looked over later.

The giant monitors mounted high on the walls at the front of the room displayed either written data or showed the video feed that transmitted the newest life-altering events of another world. Periodically, a few people would halt in their rushing and watch the drama unfolding on the monitor before them. Then, they would remember themselves with a shake, cast a guilty look at Keung and scurry back to their work.

Keung stood at the center of it all, his big hands clasped behind his back and his large green eyes locked on the screen in front of him. His face was unreadable and his posture was stiff and prim. None who looked upon him could tell that the man had not rested in over two days.

He barely saw the tragedy taking place at that moment on another far off world. In the back of his head, a small voice told him that he should be planning another mission for the Tracker. The planet needed intervention before one culture completely destroyed another. They needed help with dealing with this new crisis and they needed someone to see to it that the threat was eliminated. But his thoughts kept wandering to more personal problems closer to home.

There was Distari activity uncomfortably close to the neighborhood where the Tracker kept her home. Reports from Agents and informants stated that there had already been murders of ten people and the beasts had left taunts to the Tracker written in the victims' entrails. To make matters worse, the Tracker's sister was closely involved in the case and Keung feared that it was only a matter of time before she put the many pieces together and realized who her sister was and what she was doing. It would be a catastrophe if an officer of the law learned of the existence of the Tracker and the Center.

In the beginning, when Keung was searching for a new Tracker to replace Gustav Haughmein, Darlene Arnold had been at the top of short list prospective candidates. She was intelligent, creative, resourceful and flexible. She and Madeline had been the closest genetic relatives to the man since he had refused to have children. Darlene had already known much about self-defense and firearms from her training on the police force and she took orders well. But a DNA test had shown her to be infertile and she carried a gene for schizophrenia that might be triggered if she was exposed to severe trauma or the wrong toxic gas. And so, the title had passed to her sister who already had children of her own and showed no genetic tendencies for mental illness.

Sherman approached him quietly and did not speak until he was ready to acknowledge him. Keung turned his eyes from the screen in front of him and calmly regarded the skinny youth. Sherman licked his lips nervously and fidgeted.

"You're needed in your office," he said quietly. "The Quarter wishes to speak with you as soon as possible."

Keung moved from his perch in the center of the Control Room and hurried towards the glass double doors that separated the offices from the noise of the Control Room. Personnel jumped out of his way as he got close to them, sending paper and disk flying in their panic. Keung was capable of bowling people over without noticing that he had done it.

He stepped into his office and closed the door behind him. Sherman had stopped just beyond the glass doors. The young man didn't want to be involved with anything directly involved with the Quarter. Admittedly, the figures were startling and most of the lower personnel went out of their way to avoid them. Sherman would wait patiently for his orders as he always did. Meanwhile, he would most likely catch up on some of the Tracker's paperwork.

The dark figure in the middle of Keung's office seemed to turn towards him as he entered. Or maybe he turned away. Members of the Quarter are an eccentric lot and they tended to go to extremes to keep their identities and appearance a secret. They were always shrouded in darkness no matter how bright the light in the space they occupied. No feature was ever discernable, not even the color of their shoes. They kept their voices, physical and mental, low and sexless. Keung never knew which individual he was dealing with at any given time. They were all the same height, weight and build. Only his father's insistence that there as more than one of them kept him from believing that the Quarter was but one individual.

They rarely left whatever place it was that they made their home. They communicated with Keung mostly through telepathy and only spoke with their voices when they had to. They were unfailingly polite, slow to anger and they treated the people who served them with great dignity and respect. Many meetings were called to ask after the welfare of the occupants of the Center and to inquire if there were anything that might make their lives and work more bearable.

Despite the secrecy and their taste for extreme isolation, Keung was certain of their benevolence. They always made it clear that their only goal was the peace and prosperity of the humans spread across the five galaxies. All of the Tracker's missions over the centuries were centered on that one goal. They studied the DNA and the evolving technologies of the cultures to help gauge the progress of the people's development and their general health. Many times, a Tracker had introduced a new technology or medical advancement to achieve the Quarter's goal.

The Trackers had done heroic things in the name of the Quarter. They had stopped wars, riots, brought murderers and rapists to justice and rescued entire populations from natural disasters. But almost as often, the

Trackers found themselves completing far more distasteful tasks. Many a man and woman had returned to the Center nearly broken because they were successful in an assassination attempt or because thousands were about to die from a war they had started. One Tracker went mad after releasing a gruesome disease on an unsuspecting population. In such times, Keung reminded himself that it was all for the best of the humans involved and then force it from his mind.

"We have been monitoring the events occurring in the vicinity near the Tracker's heirs. We have some concerns regarding the movements of the Distari in that area," the figure said in a soothing tone.

Keung took a deep breath before he spoke. He knew that the Quarter used other means to monitor the planet that the Tracker called home. Due to the Trackers' personal attachments to their homes, they weren't allowed to influence the events of their native world. They could not take a government office nor could they serve as members of law enforcement. They were instructed to appear as bland and ordinary as the population in which they lived.

Keung did not know who it was or in what capacity that the Watcher served. He suspected that it was an individual much like the Tracker but it was only an assumption. He had never seen a sign that the Quarter kept a retainer for the purpose of guiding the Earth. Whoever it was wasn't as capable as the Tracker. Matters on Earth were a mess. If the Tracker were unleashed here, certainly things would settle into a more peaceful rhythm.

"It is my belief that the Distari are killing in order to draw the Tracker to them," Keung replied. "Two families of five have been killed so far."

"Are the police involved yet?"

"Of course. The law enforcement agencies of this time are more efficient than they have been in the past. Unfortunately, the Tracker's sister is involved with the investigation."

"Watch the sister closely. It would be inconvenient if she discovered what her sister was doing. She could be a formidable enemy if she sees us as a threat to her family. Is there anything else?"

"Agents have reported Distari trespassing on the Tracker's property. They have been forced to kill two of them. The Agents also believe that the spouse and the sister have both seen the beasts. I have ordered an increase in the guard on the Tracker's family."

"It would do no harm if the husband had reason to become more protective of the Tracker's heirs. But again, watch the sister closely. She may not speak of the events for fear of her reputation, but it may cause her to become more driven to learn the truth."

"Yes, sir."

"As for the Distari, send a complement of Agents to locate and destroy the lair. Once they have been exterminated, the murders will be forgotten and the sister will have no reason to become further involved."

"Very well."

"Is there anything else?"

"The Master Agent has reported that the Tracker was attacked by Distari shortly after arriving on the planet Iza. He does not believe that they were there for any other reason but the hunt. However, they were forced to kill six of them in her defense."

"Then it is likely that the Tracker has begun to remember what the Distari are. We had hoped that she would come to those memories later rather than sooner. This Tracker is still too inexperienced and volatile to be exposed to the monsters. Keep a tight leash on her, Keeper. She is not ready for a confrontation with them, not yet."

"Of course."

"And Keeper? We have also noticed some changes in the Tracker's biology. We believe that she might experience a new gift soon. Keep her under constant medical monitoring."

"It will be done."

The figure fell silent then. Keung could feel the eyes he couldn't see boring into his skull. He knew he was being judged but couldn't understand why. He had served loyally for three generations and had never had a moment of serious misjudgment.

"Is there something wrong?" he asked finally. The figure shook his head, no. He began to slowly fade until he disappeared completely.

Keung collapsed into the chair behind his desk, finally feeling the fatigue of the last few days. He took a moment to rest and catch his second wind before standing up and returning to work.

CHAPTER 19

Katie had always thought of herself as a happy girl. She never felt bad about herself or her family. She had a Momma and Daddy who loved her and told her so all the time. Even though she only wanted sisters, she had two little brothers, but they were pests only some of the time. She did good at school, learning was easy even if it was boring. She had lots of friends, but she had yet to choose her best friend. It was just too hard to decide from all the boys and girls she played with which one was her favorite.

But lately, things had become very hard and worrisome. It was getting too hard to sleep alone in her room even with the night light on. She would lie in bed and worry that the monster would get into her house. Or that it might get into Chris or Allen's rooms. She worried that Daddy might have to fight the monsters and she was pretty certain that Daddy would lose and the monsters would kill him. She worried about who would take care of her and her brothers if Daddy died. Momma worked all the time now, so she couldn't be around to do it. All the worries would build up until she was hysterical and crying hard. Finally, Daddy would put her to bed in his room and let her fall asleep with his television on. But as soon as she was settled in, her brothers would come into the room and they would bed down in there, too.

Katie moved slowly, her body feeling heavy and tired as she got ready for school. She'd had another night of bad dreams and she hadn't slept very much. She kept waking up so very afraid and she would have to snuggle up with her nearest brother and try to calm down. She kept looking for the monsters at the window and listening for them at the doors even though they hadn't seen them in a couple of nights. Katie wished that Aunt Darlene would come sleep at their house again. She was a police officer, so she had a gun. If anyone could keep them safe, it would be Aunt Darlene.

She ate her breakfast, her eyes drooping with fatigue as she shoveled cereal and milk into her mouth. Daddy wandered into the kitchen with Chris walking behind him and sternly admonished her to hurry up. Katie silently quickened her pace and finished her breakfast. She put her bowl in the sink and hurried to get her coat and backpack. Minutes later, she found herself standing at the end of the driveway and holding Chris's hand. Daddy sat on the porch and watched them wait for the bus. He sat with his back against the glass door so that Allen, with his hands and face pressed against the glass, couldn't get out. Allen was rubbing the front of his face along the door smearing slobber and baby goo all over it. Katie giggled at him and waved. Daddy, thinking that she was waving at him, smiled and waved back.

The bus arrived shortly after that, its brakes squeaking as it came to a stop in front of the house. Katie rushed across the street and dragged Chris along behind her. She left her little brother in his seat behind the driver and she went to go sit down several rows back. Once the bus was moving, she finally began to relax. There had never been any monsters anywhere near the bus or the school. Those places had become safe since she never had to worry about bad things while she was there. She began to drift off to sleep with her head resting against the window next to her. The bus stopped, let on some more kid, and it was on its way again.

She heard sniffing and crying coming from the girl who was suddenly sitting next to her. She opened one eye to see Allison crying and wiping her nose on her sleeves. Katie though about ignoring her and going back to sleep. She was very tired. Besides, she didn't know Allison very well and the few times she had talked to her, Allison had called her names. Eventually, Katie decided that she had to know what made Allison cry.

"Why are you crying?" her voice sounded very irritated even to her. She decided that it didn't matter in the end. Allison had called her names and so Katie didn't have to be all that nice to the other girl. Allison looked at her with puffy red eyes.

"Somebody killed my dog," she cried. She wiped at her nose with her sleeve and smeared snot on her cheek. Katie wrinkled her nose and fought the urge to say, "eeww." Instead she tried to cover her disgust by pretending to care about Allison's dead dog.

"What do you mean?" she asked. Allison wasn't looking at her anymore. She just stared at her hands in her lap.

"I mean, somebody killed my dog! They cut him up and left his bits all over the yard!" Allison made little hiccupping noises when she talked.

Katie stared in shock at Allison. She couldn't believe her ears. Sure, Allison was a brat but she could have a very nice dog. Why would someone do that to a helpless dog?

"Do you know who did it?" Katie asked.

All Allison could do was shake her head.

"My Mom said that it is the sort of thing that the mean old redneck across the street would do. But I know he would never kill my dog. He loves dogs. He has four of them at his house."

Katie was temporarily distracted by the idea of owning four dogs. A boy sitting behind them, Dylan chimed in then and got Katie's attention.

"His dogs were killed, too," he said. "My cousin lives behind him and he says that the dogs made an awful racket last night. Then that man started yellin' somethin' fierce. I heard that there was blood and guts everywhere."

Katie stared at Dylan in horror.

"You're kidding!" she gasped as Allison began to cry harder.

The talk quickly changed to stories about old pets and the pets of friends and family. Allison eventually stopped wailing and fell to silent crying. Katie didn't know what to do to comfort the other girl, so she ignored her. She knew that all the kids who rode on her bus lived either in her neighborhood or in one of the neighborhoods next to hers. She wondered if the monsters she'd seen at her house could have killed the dogs. She was pretty sure that they could have. Suddenly, she was very glad that Momma and Daddy hadn't let her have a dog yet.

Allison stopped crying by the time the bus got to the school. All the kids filed out of the bus and walked towards their class. Katie made sure that Chris was in line with his teacher before she left him and then she wandered to her classroom.

She managed to get to her desk without incident and put her head down on the desk. She was almost asleep when the bell rang and the teacher began to take attendance.

Katie liked Ms. Tyson. She was pretty, she never got mad and she touched Katie like her mother used to. Ms. Tyson gave her a concerned look when she called her name but didn't say anything. The day went along as usual.

During recess, Katie sat against the building and watched as the other kids played on the playground. She'd refused offers to join in the fun. She just felt too tired to be running around and screaming. So she sat in the shade of the school and just watched. She thought about telling her teacher that she was sick so that she could go sleep in the nurse's office.

Her eyes followed her friend Courtney as she ran screaming from Austin. They were laughing as they dodged through the playground and the other kids. Behind the fence near them, she saw a man standing on the other side of the chain link fence. He was dressed in dark blue and he had on black shoes. He had brown hair and his brown eyes looked mean and angry. His arms were held tight against his sides and his hands were clenched into fists. He scanned the playground without moving his head or body to see. Then he looked straight at Katie. He looked into her eyes and just stared. Katie felt afraid as the man stared at her and didn't take his eyes off of her. He didn't blink! He just stared at her for what seemed like forever and he didn't even blink once!

Katie got to her feet and never took her eyes off the man as he watched her. He made her afraid. Not as afraid as the monsters at her house, but definitely nervous. She remembered what Momma and Daddy had told her about strangers and the things that they liked to do to little girls. She shuddered at the thought of what her parents had told her. She was truly afraid as she hurried to the nearest teacher. The teacher wasn't one that she knew very well, but she'd seen her around the playground lots of times, so that meant she was okay to talk to. Katie ignored several commands to go and play as she tugged on the teacher's shirt to get her attention. The man was still watching her closely.

"What do you need?" the teacher demanded, finally looking down at Katie.

"That man is staring at me," Katie whispered anxiously. The teacher frowned and stared in the direction that Katie pointed. The man stared boldly back, completely unafraid of the teacher and her fierce look. The woman squared her narrow shoulders and began to walk towards the man where he stood at the fence. As she walked, she made a subtle signal to another teacher, who pulled a walkie-talkie from her belt.

Katie watched wide-eyed as the first teacher spoke with the man. He looked at her with cold, flat eyes whenever he talked back to her and he looked over her shoulder at Katie. Suddenly, the teacher shouted something angrily and jabbed her finger away from the playground. The man shot Katie a dirty look before he turned and stalked off. The teacher with the walkie-talkie began to speak into the machine, turning her back to Katie as she did so.

The first teacher appeared in front of Katie and knelt down to look in her face. The woman was afraid although she was trying hard to hide it. She talked in that too sweet, high-pitched voice that grown ups used whenever they knew something was badly wrong and they needed a kid to tell them what it was.

"Do you know who that man was?"

"No," Katie shook her head. What had the man said? Had he been trying to talk the teacher into letting him have her? The teacher smiled at her and put her hand gently on Katie's shoulder.

"Come on, sweetheart. Let's get you inside," the teacher said calmly, though Katie could tell that something really bothered her.

The teacher with the walkie-talkie was busy getting all the other kids lined up to go inside. The kids all protested loudly. Recess wasn't supposed to be over yet and none of them wanted to stop playing. What had the man said?

Katie was marched into the school before the other kids were even finished lining up. The teacher kept her hand protectively around her shoulders as she guided her to the office. She saw security guards rushing toward the playground, all of them with serious looks on their faces. Katie began to feel calmer. All of the security guards looked big and strong. Surely the man would be beaten with so many strong men going after him.

The principal was a nice lady, older than Momma was but not as old as Katie's Nana. She smiled reassuringly at the little girl and offered her some candy. Katie took it to be polite but could only hold it in her hand. She was too nervous to eat. Her tummy rolled and she thought she might throw up. The other office ladies began to wander in and out of the principal's office, saying nice things to Katie and talking over her head as if she wasn't there. Which meant that the things they were saying to each other was none of her business. Katie stopped paying attention and stared at her dirty sneakers.

Someone put a cup of juice in her hand so she drank that while she waited for someone to tell her what she was going to do. A little while later, she saw that the candy she had held in her hand had disappeared and the juice in her cup was gone. She felt a tingling pressure between her legs and knew that it wasn't long before she was going to have to pee. First she tried to get someone's, anyone's attention by making eye contact. When that failed, she began to squirm in her chair and whine.

"I gotta go to the bathroom," she cried plaintively. Every head in the room swiveled in her direction when she spoke.

The lady who usually sat behind the big desk in front of the doors smiled sweetly at her.

"I'll take you to the bathroom sweetheart," she said, offering her hand.

Katie thought about telling the woman that she wasn't a baby anymore and that she could walk very well on her own. But the lady seemed very worried so Katie took her hand and let the lady lead her away. Katie left her trash on the desk and the lady chatted cheerfully as they walked to the bathroom.

Strangely, the lady wouldn't let her go into the bathroom right away. Instead, she inspected the room before she gave the okay for Katie to use the facilities. There was another little girl already using a stall, so Katie took the one next to hers. The lady waited in front of the stall as Katie closed and locked the door behind her. Katie had to wait to start peeing. She could never go right away when someone was just standing there waiting on her. She began to hum a tuneless song to take her mind off of things.

She let out a sigh of relief when the water finally began to flow. In the stall next to her, the little girl began to make strange strangling noises. Katie frowned, thinking that the girl was throwing up.

"Are you okay in there?" she called. Why hadn't the lady asked that? Surely it was her job to make sure everyone was okay. The little girl didn't answer; she was still making throw-up noises. Katie hopped off the toilet and pulled her pants up. She grasped the door and thought that the metal felt much colder than it did when she first went into the stall.

The door burst open, the aluminum bending and scratching the wall as it banged into the stall. The man from the playground stood in the opening, looking fierce and angry. He lunged at Katie, his big hands grabbing her by the arms. Katie let out a piercing shriek as she struggled to make him let go of her. She fought and bit and kicked, going for anything that she could reach. The man hissed a couple of times in pain but he wouldn't let go. His hands were hurting her and the shock of it ripped a scream from her throat and brought tears to her eyes. He hauled her roughly out of the stall and began to drag her, kicking and screaming, from the bathroom.

Suddenly, the man stopped. His eyes widened with surprise and his hands released their painful grip on her arms. Katie fell backwards onto her butt; her astonishment at suddenly being let go made her go quiet. Her hand landed in something hot and sticky on the floor. Almost against her will, she looked down to see what she had landed in. She saw the office lady before she saw the blood spreading out on the floor. The lady was covered in blood and her blue eyes stared blankly up at the ceiling. Her long blonde hair was streaked red and clumped with the blood she was laying in. Her belly was open and her insides had been pulled out.

Katie was screaming before her mind registered what her eyes had seen. She tried to scramble to her feet, but she kept slipping in the blood. It was all over the floor. She began to sob, afraid that she wouldn't get away, that the man would kill her just as he had killed the office lady. Her whirling mind suddenly thought of the other little girl who had been in the stall next to hers. Where had she gone? Had she been eaten? Or had she managed to escape? She saw little girl clothes piled up in the toilet she'd been in but no little girl.

She was seized by the arm again and flung against the wall. She nearly fell, but she managed to keep her feet despite being stunned. The man turned on his heel and she saw another man standing behind him. He looked exactly like the first man, except that he was very, very angry. The second man's face began to melt, and his eyes grew until they bulged and his teeth grew long and sharp in his mouth. He lunged at the first man and they fell crashing to the floor.

"Run!" screamed the first man as he hit the floor with a thud. "Run!"

Katie was in motion before the man screamed the second time. She pushed herself away from the wall and tore out of the bathroom as fast as her legs would carry her. She was at Chris's classroom before she realized where she was going. She paused with her hand on the door and wondered if Chris would be safer if he stayed in his class with his teacher. But a roar echoed through the halls and that made up her mind. She couldn't tell if the monster's cry meant that it had won or lost but it did mean that it was still alive.

She threw the door open and every face in the room turned toward her with looks of surprise. Katie gestured at Chris, telling him to come to her. He looked at her in confusion and shook his head. The teacher was coming towards her, probably coming to yell at her.

"Come on, Chris!" she cried. "The monsters are here!"

Chris sprang out of his seat and bolted from the door. The teacher reached out to grab him but Chris ducked her grasp and was out the door. Katie grabbed his hand as soon as he reached her and, together, they ran away. Neither had a destination in mind, only that they must get away or hide. They made turns whenever they presented themselves and many times they came to exits leading outside. But Katie refused to leave the building, she remembered the man outside and she was afraid that there were more out there. So they turned and headed deeper into the school.

They stopped to get their bearings and to catch their breath. Katie bent over and rested her hands on her knees and panted. Chris leaned against the wall and shivered. His eyes were wild and glassy as he looked at his sister.

"Is that blood?" he asked pointing at her clothes. Katie's face crumpled as she struggled not to cry.

"Come on," she gasped and took Chris by the hand again. She thought that maybe they could find a closet or storage cabinet to hide in until the monsters went away. Chris suddenly stopped running, digging his heels into the floor and yanking Katie backwards. She let out a yelp as she hit the cold hard floor with her back. Chris struggled in her grip as he simultaneously tried to help her back to her feet and run away. Katie got to get her feet, her head pounding painfully from where it struck the floor and, feeling like she needed to throw up. She was on her knees when a low evil growl reverberated down the hallway and shivered up her spine.

Katie looked over her shoulder, her eyes wide with terror, fully expecting to see her death bearing down on her and her little brother. Instead, she saw something that looked like a man, but clearly wasn't. He had a face, two arms and two legs attached to a body, but that's where the resemblance ended. His face looked melted, the flesh of his cheeks hanging off his bones until the red under flesh of the eyes showed like a basset hound. Its mouth was huge and had long pointed teeth jutting from between the gaping lips. Its shoulders were hunched and the broad back was bent until its long arms nearly dragged on the floor. Its legs moved stiffly as its hips swiveled in an awkward gait.

It advanced slowly at first, but gained speed as it found its rhythm. It reached for them with twisted hands tipped with sharp talons. Chris and Katie let out a terrified shriek. Katie finally got to her feet and Chris frantically pulled on her hand. It laughed in triumph as it saw its prey within its reach and its spit flew in slimy streaks against the walls and floor.

The children ran faster than they'd ever moved in their lives. Chris suddenly turned right, and nearly lost sister and monster alike. Katie managed to turn with him and the monster flew past the turn and crashed into a small trash can. They gained a few seconds' lead and they put on another burst of speed as they saw the classrooms up ahead. But Katie felt her heart sink as she heard the slap of the monster's feet on the tile floor coming closer and closer behind them. She could feel its hot, rancid breath on her neck and the prickly points of its claws pulling on her shirt. They were going to die. They were going to die with their insides pulled out all over the place. She let out a weeping wail and almost gave up as Chris pumped his arms and legs harder. He didn't look back at her. He tucked his head down and kept running.

A hand suddenly shot out and grabbed Chris by the arm. He disappeared with a scream of horror. Katie followed, pivoting on her right ankle and twisting it. She ignored the shooting pain streaking up her leg to her knee and flung herself into the open arms of a young, sweet-faced man. He pulled her into the classroom and kicked the door closed. He drew Katie and Chris further into the room and shouted at the other students to stay away from the door. The monster streaked past howling and then it fell silent with the sound of breaking glass.

An alarm went off, its banging racket shattering the already broken air and adding to Katie's confusion. Her head hurt badly and the back of her neck and shoulders stung and burned. Her shirt felt hot and wet and all the strength drained from her skinny legs. She collapsed onto the floor; her hands gripped the scratchy fabric of the carpet. Chris' arms appeared around her neck and he rested his cheek against hers. His breath was hot against her ear. She couldn't support the weight of both of them and she fell all the way to the floor. She cried out in pain when her back touched the carpet and she knew she was hurt.

The teacher's face appeared above hers, his features wrinkled with concern. His hands took Chris gently by the shoulders and pulled him away from his sister. He screamed at being separated from her but Katie just didn't have it in her to fight to keep him close. The teacher kept Chris at arm's length as he examined Katie, his concern turning to fear at what he saw. Katie wondered at it, but didn't care. She hurt so much and it was all that she could really concentrate on. She heard the ringing of the alarm and the shrieks of her little brother, but it rolled off her like water on a duck's back.

She suddenly didn't hurt so much anymore. She felt relaxed but a little weaker than before. The teacher was shouting urgently at her now, she could see that, but she couldn't hear it. Her vision grew foggy and her mouth felt dry. Her eyes rolled up in her head and all she knew was black.

CHAPTER 20

Maddie walked between Fred and George with George's lacy handkerchief pressed to her nose and mouth. It was heavily burdened with George's cologne and it helped with the effects of the intoxicating spores drifting in the night air. Since her face and neck were still exposed, she still suffered from giddiness and had to concentrate to keep from swooning drunkenly.

She did manage to keep some sort of control over her telepathy. The voices of the city no longer threatened to overwhelm her but she did have some trouble whenever she made eye contact or accidentally brushed up against someone. So, she kept her head down and her eyes locked on the ground and let the men guide her through the obstacles in her path.

And so it was that she found herself standing on a cracked street corner, regarding a large stained building across the street. The place was located on the border between the slums of the poor and the middle-class section of the residential area of the city. Here, what had once been a charming and mildly affluent part of the city was beginning its first sliding steps backward into poverty. The streets were beginning to show signs of disrepair, cracks disturbed the smooth pattern of the raised sidewalks and the first crumpled bits of pot holes had begun to appear along the cobbled pavement of the road. The decorative trash facilities were overflowing with refuse that had grown far beyond the control of the remaining garbage handlers of this part of town. The pretty iron fences outlining the boundaries between properties had peeling paint that revealed bits of rust. Just like all other parts of the city, the yellow grass was thin and sickly, if it grew at all.

Barnum's club was like any of the buildings in its immediate vicinity except that it was a massive structure that consumed most of the block that it squatted upon. The building was a three-story monstrosity that began with a dumpy first floor and rose straight upward until it ended in a sharply-pointed slate roof. A few dirty windows dotted the sides of the upper floors while people moved across the thin drapes and cast shadows upon the opaque glass. It was dirty and the flaking, yellow plaster needed patching in places. Garish graffiti dotted the sides with crude threats and odes as well as childishly scrawled cartoons of figures engaged in lewd and absurd sexual acts.

The front door was a pair of ironbound stone doors painted black with little square windows lit with dim yellow lights. A barker stood in front with a scantily clad girl in each arm. Whenever a passerby came close, the barker would spring into action and began to cheerfully recite his pitch. As the potential customer came ever closer, the barker would all but toss a girl into the man's arms while she cooed and wiggled suggestively against him. More often than not, the invitation was accepted and the man and girl would disappear beyond the black stone doors. As soon as they swung shut, a new girl would appear and cling to the barker's arm, to wait her turn.

The barker was as scantily clad as the women were. He was bare-chested and wore pants so tight that it was easy to see what state of arousal he was in at any given moment. Colorful tattoos graced his bulging arms from wrist to shoulder as cheap rings studded his thick rough fingers. On occasion, a woman would happen by and the barker would throw himself at her and then they would disappear inside. Almost immediately after, another gaudily dressed man would take the vacated post with the girls.

The Agents had their heads together and were quietly discussing how best to approach Barnum. With Maddie still intoxicated by the local fauna, they considered her disabled for the mission and had reduced her to the role of showpiece for the duration. Which was just fine by her. She knew that she didn't know her ass from a hole in the ground on this one and felt perfectly content to just do as she was told. But waiting for the men to make up their minds was a tedious process and she was getting bored. So she began to let her mind wander while the men planned and plotted.

She stared at the surrounding buildings with their stained walls and sagging roofs. Various streetlights were set in intervals along the sidewalks and did very little to light the narrow alleyways between each building. Down the alley behind her, Maddie heard a woman's shriek followed by the cruel laughter of men. She turned towards the sounds as the woman began to beg. The men only laughed harder and their pitiless thoughts drifted down to the Tracker.

Perturbed, Maddie started down the alley. As she walked, she reached behind her belt and pulled the familiar rod and held the smooth cool metal shaft loosely in her hand. Her thumb rested lightly on the switch, her brain tingling as instructions of hand to hand combat with multiple opponents in limited space began to fill her head. It told her what to do if an enemy had a projectile weapon or if he out weighed her or was significantly taller than she. Maddie tried not to struggle against the process as her muscles began to itch and jump when the nanopack began to give them memories along with her brain. She had to pause a second to let her body settle down so that she could move without hopping sporadically about.

Maddie had kept the handkerchief pressed to her face through the entire ordeal until she came upon two figures crouched over a third at the end of the alley. The bigger figures pumped their arms up and down and Maddie could hear the dull thick sounds of flesh striking flesh. The woman cried out and sobbed with each blow while the men congratulated each other on the fine bruises and cuts their fists left upon the woman's body. The scene disgusted Maddie and she couldn't stop the low growl from forming in her throat.

The small sound caught the men's attention and they turned towards her. At first their thoughts darkened irritably that their play had been interrupted but they quickly brightened when they saw the strange woman standing in front of them. At their feet, a small, malnourished woman sobbed through swollen eyes and bleeding lips. Her clothes were dirty rags barely covering her small, withering breasts. She was barely conscious though she struggled hard to regain her feet and get away while her tormentor's backs were turned. Maddie scowled at the men and tossed the handkerchief arrogantly to the ground.

The bigger man had claimed first mounting rights; his pants were open and his genitals hung partially erect as he approached. Maddie allowed herself a glance downward and couldn't help but scoff. The man flushed at her reaction to him and charged her with a snarl.

Maddie struck with a whirl and a flourish, easily dodging the man's clumsy attack and cracked him hard on the back of his head. He fell without a sound in a crumpled heap in the dirt. Maddie stepped over him easily as the second man came to the rescue of his friend. Maddie got a glimpse of his ugly face that was made uglier when she hit him hard on his large bulbous nose. He fell with a shriek of pain and outrage as blood gushed from his prolific appendage. Maddie followed the strike with a crack to the top of his pointed head and stood to the side as he fell unconscious to the dirt.

She waited a moment and felt at their stunned minds to be certain that they still lived before she turned to the weeping woman still struggling against the wall. She kept out of arm's reach as she attempted to get the poor creature's attention. Too often, victims often lashed out blindly when they were still in a panic and Maddie didn't want to go around with a black eye for her trouble.

Two more figures appeared at the entrance of the alley. Maddie stood up to confront them and noticed that these two were more feminine in form. It was likely that these women were the victim's friends, but there was no reason to bet the girl's life on it. Maddie brandished the rod and swayed on her feet. Crap! She had thrown the handkerchief into the dirt and now she was reeling from the effects of the night spores again. The women rushed forward and kicked the men as they passed them. The rapists moaned in pain, but remained prone in the dirt.

"You should not have done that," said the older woman with a hard gravelly voice. The second, younger woman hurried past without looking at Maddie and crouched beside her injured friend and began to comfort the weeping woman. "You should have left well enough alone. A pretty, untouched girl like you will be meat for the wolves if they get their hands on you."

"You're welcome," Maddie growled. The wind picked up suddenly then and brought with it a vaguely sweet smell that left Maddie reeling and feeling squishy between her legs.

"Are you alright?" the old whore asked, taking Maddie roughly by the elbow and jerking her to keep her on her feet. Maddie nodded as she giggled uncontrollably and put out her other arm for support against the wall. The younger whore had the poor wounded girl swaying on her feet. The girl clung to her and looked as if she was going to collapse again at any minute. The old woman gave the pair cold looks before turning back to Maddie.

"Get back in your house, girl. I don't know who taught you to do what you did to those men, but if you know what's good for you, you'll get out of here," the older said harshly. "Those are Barnum's men and they'll be in their rights to make you die screaming for what you did."

Maddie managed a nod despite shaking with mirth and began to stagger away. The older woman gave a heavy sigh and grabbed Maddie's arm again. She pulled her close enough to look Maddie hard in the eye as she pressed a small vial into her hand.

"Best to remember your poor head for the fumes girl," the old whore snapped. "And be sure to use the ointment beneath your nose. Otherwise, you'll find yourself with worse troubles than you suffer now."

With that, she slung the wounded girl's arm over her bony shoulders and the three began to make their way out of the alley. The old woman harangued the other two as they went, even when they paused to hammer kicks into the semi-conscious men. Watching them brought on another fit of the giggles that made it hard for Maddie to walk. She staggered out of the alleyway and tripped over her own feet just before the exit. She sat on her butt in the dirt and laughed uproariously at the sky. She knew that she was completely inebriated and her body yearned for release from the dull ache that had developed uncomfortably in her groin. She feverishly wished that Sam were there to help her with her condition.

Finally, she managed to calm down enough to walk and she staggered towards the place where she had left the Agents. The men regarded her with different expressions of impatience and amusement. Fred was glaring at her like she had kicked his mother down a flight of stairs while George looked ready to burst into laughter. Maddie looked at them both and bent with hilarity.

"Did we have a good time?" George asked in a condescending voice that would have usually pissed her off. But tonight, it was oddly funny in a very sexy sort of way. Maddie made sure to wave her butt around while she giggled helplessly. George snorted a chuckle and looked away.

"I totally kicked ass," she finally gasped as she straightened. Her voice was slurring badly and she found it hard to care. Both men had to put out their hands to keep her from falling down again. The few people walking by gave the three disapproving shakes of their heads as they assumed that their threesome was anything but professional. Maddie laughed at them and called them dirty names.

"Where is my handkerchief?" George asked when she finally finished her outburst.

"It fell in the dirt!" Maddie brayed. "Dirt don't hurt!" She kept chanting it as she leaned into their hands and hopped up and down. Fred was scowling so fiercely that she thought his face might break while George just looked put out. Finally, George pried the vial out of her hand and peered at the clear contents.

"What's this?" he asked.

"Oh, just something an old hooker gave me. I think it helps the air," Maddie chuckled. "She said it goes beneath the nose."

"Well put it on so we can go!" Fred snarled. George gave him a hard look and pulled the tiny cap from the vial. He sniffed it cautiously and grimaced. He took a deeper breath of it and waited. When nothing happened, he spilled a few drops of the greasy liquid onto his finger and jabbed it on Maddie's upper lip.

"Owie!" Maddie laughed. It smelled strongly astringent and she wrinkled her nose. Both men watched her intently as she shifted her weight uncomfortably from foot to foot and loudly announced that she was oh so horny. At that Fred rolled his eyes and slapped her. Hard. At first, Maddie just blinked at him. Then a wicked grin spread across her face and she leered at him.

"Ooh, baby, hit me again! I like it when you play rough!" she crowed. Fred growled and hit her again. This time, the blow rocked her on her feet and her ears rang.

"Hey!"

Her mind was rapidly sobering up and she glared at Fred. "Did you have to hit me so hard?"

"Yes," he said smugly. George ducked his head and fought the smirk on his lips.

"Well, did you have to enjoy it so much?"

"Yes."

Fred let her go with a satisfied gleam in his eye while George chuckled. Maddie harumphed and smoothed her skirts in an effort to regain some dignity. Below her belly button, her body still behaved like a randy teenager but she firmly refused to acknowledge it.

"Let's get this show in the road," she snapped. Her cheek stung horribly but she would be damned if she let Fred see that it bothered her. She began to walk towards the club in a huff but tripped in a pothole and fell on her face. George's laugh rang like church bells in her ears as the men pulled her to her feet.

CHAPTER 21

Maddie was unable to get through the front doors of the club without the barker latching onto her waist. She'd attempted to sneak past without being seen but he had spotted her and let go of the two women he'd been holding as if they were poisonous. He wrapped his long arm around her waist and refused to let go. He beamed down at her when she looked up at him in surprise and revealed his pointed yellow teeth. Maddie shuddered at his display and tried to pull his arm from her body. He still refused to let go and she decided that he was just doing his job. She could always ditch him at the first available opportunity.

Barker wasn't as good looking up close as he was from across the street. The dark street lamps had hidden jaundiced skin and open sores. Dark circles stained the delicate skin beneath his bloodshot eyes. His nose was too big and his jaw was too weak. He tried to give her a look of adulation with dull, glassy brown eyes but could only manage mild interest. His festive hat was frayed at the edges and the fluffy feather was battered and dirty. He stank of acrid smoke and booze, and his personal odor suggested that it had been some time since he last saw soap and water. He staggered and leered at her and she realized with a chortle that he was more stoned than she was. Maddie looked behind her and saw that both Agents were draped in scantily clad girls. Neither of them looked very pleased with their escorts.

Barker took her through the doors which, on closer inspection, had thin black paint peeling from them. The thin, cheap stone threatened to break as they were opened with a dramatic push meant to impress the finely dressed woman and two men. Beyond the doors was a massive cavern of a room that was filled to the rafters with a thick, smoky haze. Maddie's eyes burned and she tried not to breathe too deeply as she was led down a short flight of stairs and into the room. Along with the smoke, the place stank with the unavoidable stench of vomit mixed with cheap booze and cheaper perfume. Two long bars lined the walls to either side of her and were manned by an army of tattered bartenders.

Rough and dangerous looking men leaned against the bar and downed their swill in fast gulps to keep from actually tasting the nasty brew. They each had had their arms around a girl; each one garbed much like the pair draped across Fred and George. Occasionally, one of the men would slobber drunkenly over the girl's face and she would giggle and push at him flirtatiously, in a no-means-yes sort of way.

Rows upon rows of tables crammed the single-room floor and was crowded with gamblers and drinkers and topped with a long-legged girls slowly removing what little clothing they were wearing. The place rang with voices raised in cheers and drunken anger punctuated with the clatter of large dice against the stone tops of the tables. The place was a veritable din of raucous voices and stomping feet.

Most of the customers were men and, any time one of them sat down, a woman sprawled across their bodies as if she were a panting animal in heat and couldn't wait to be taken to bed. Maddie had no doubts that the postures were an act. No woman with any dignity would act like that unless she was getting paid. As if to validate Maddie's assessment of the situation, anytime the men attempted to take these ladies somewhere more private, there would be an immediate conversation having to do with particular acts and what those might cost before the girl was whisked away upstairs or into private little cubbies scattered across the room. The few women customers were as bad as the men. Each woman had a male escort as obvious as the working girls and strippers and seemed happier to provide the same services. Maddie had never seen a male prostitute before but she assumed that they were as thrilled with jobs as their female counterparts.

The obviously dark patches of the room were where most of the private trades occurred. Tall cubicles were scattered here and there where individuals led their rented partners and locked the flimsy doors behind them. The cubicles looked just like the private dining booths at Abiah's inn, save that the chipped latticework was screened for added privacy. There were waiting couches near the cubicles where couples fondled and kissed while they waited their turn for a cheap bed.

It was to one of these couches that the barker attempted to lead Maddie. As soon as she saw his destination, she stopped him with a look and a shake of her head. He silently implored her, flagrantly rubbing his bulging package against her and giving her an anxious look.

"I won't charge a lady like you," he breathed into her ear. Maddie made a face and gagged a little at the smell of his halitosis. He scowled angrily at her and let her go. He glanced at Fred and George and thought better of simply storming off and risking insult. He bowed to her with a sarcastic flourish of his tattered hat and stalked back toward the front door.

Fred and George had shed their escorts and remained where Maddie had stopped the group and crossed their arms over their chests. Maddie rubbed at her body, trying to scrub off the sensation of the barker's crude touch.

"So, now what?" she demanded looking from one man to the other. She was beginning to feel somewhat better, though her brain was still fuzzy and the area below her navel was protesting that the barker wasn't *that* bad. She shifted her weight from foot to foot and tried not to squirm. Fred shrugged and looked at the dirty floor.

"Have you gathered your wits yet, Tracker?" George asked mildly and looked her up and down as if he wasn't sure of the answer.

"I'm beginning to come down, if that's what you're asking," Maddie replied coolly. "But I am a little surprised that it's happening so fast."

Being inside had helped more than she thought it would. Considering the nature of the club, she thought that Barnum would encourage the presence of the night spores, just to keep the ladies up and willing. She wasn't hallucinating as badly anymore. Instead of colorful pixies, she saw a pretty shimmer surrounding everything. She wasn't overwhelmed by hilarity, either, but she was more than willing to see the humor of almost anything offered as a joke.

"It's the nanite package you have. It helps prevent intoxication and shortens the duration of the effects of such substances should you be overwhelmed. It keeps Trackers from being drugged and taken advantage of," George explained. Then he returned to the subject at hand. "Are you ready to take point yet?"

Maddie had to think about it. It took a few minutes because her gears still insisted on turning sluggishly. She was fairly certain that she'd be of some use in a fight but she wasn't sure that she could make decisions that were practical.

"Not really," she said. "But I'm more than happy to follow your lead for now. Just point me and tell me what to do."

The other people were beginning to notice them. They were the only people in the room not looking for sex or a game and were talking softly among themselves. A couple of nearby fellows saw the bulges under Fred and George's coats and began to finger their own weapons. None of them were willing to play hero if they didn't have to. Their lives were short and miserable enough without adding a painful maiming to the long list of things that were likely to kill them. But they weren't willing to be killed wholesale either. So they held themselves at the edge of barely contained violence and waited to see what the three people were planning. George and Fred glanced in acknowledgement of them and then ignored them.

"Shall we find out if our source is correct and see if Barnum is in residence?" George asked.

Maddie shrugged and looked around. She could see no way that they'd be able to even locate someone who knew where Barnum was. Even if she did, she didn't think that anyone here was likely to give away the information freely. Especially since Keung hadn't given them any money with which to bribe a likely stooge. Most of the people here probably didn't know who Barnum was, much less what he did with his time. The few who did blended in with the crowd so well that she couldn't tell them from the normal patrons. Which left only one solution.

She had to take several minutes to gather her thoughts and concentrate enough to keep from being distracted from the lewd and bawdy thoughts of most of the people around her. She sent out her tenuously controlled probe and began her search of the crowd. The people in their immediate vicinity had decided that the trio was harmless and probably discussing a kinky threesome. Further out, the minds she encountered were more concerned with having a good time before returning to their brutal lives. Finally, she found two angry and violent minds that discussed business amidst a sea of individuals who thought only of pleasure.

Maddie turned towards those thoughts and began to weave her way through the crowd, careful not to touch anyone lest she loose the thread. The closer she got to her goal, the more certain she was that these were the men who knew where to find the man she was looking for. Barnum was prominent in their thoughts, and they gave her fleeting images of the luxurious accommodations the man enjoyed.

Fred and George followed closely behind her and made sure none of the wandering hands she passed touched her. They glared dangerously at anyone with rape and assault on their minds. A time or two, they had to physically prevent an errant man from blocking her path as she moved blindly towards one of the privacy cubicles occupying a shadowy corner near the bar.

Maddie made sure that the occupants of the cubicle were the ones she wanted. Two men were inside, one spoke in angry whispers punctuated by the replies of another man. A woman moaned and murmured plaintively but it sounded as if she was being mostly ignored. The men were discussing a future confrontation with a third man who had gotten the better of the pair in more than a few shady deals and criminal acts. They intended to make certain that the third wound up in an unmarked shallow grave far beyond the boundaries of the city. All they had to do was get Barnum's approval of their plan before they put it into action.

That was enough for Maddie. She lifted her fist and banged on the door. The thin stone chipped and cracked under the abuse and threatened to come off its flimsy hinges. The men inside cursed violently while the woman suggested serenity. Maddie gave them a few seconds before banging on the door again. How long could it possibly take for them to lean over and open a damned door?

George gave her a stern look that suggested that she was being impolitic. Maddie returned with wide-eyed innocence and her best smile.

Suddenly, a purple-faced man who filled the narrow entrance and snarled at them in rage flung the door open. The door had come off its hinges in his hand and hung awkwardly in his beefy mitt. He let out a long string of obscenities peppered liberally with spittle that rained down on Maddie like stinky acid rain. Maddie watched him with a bemused expression and silently made bets with herself on when the man was going to drop dead from a stroke.

"I'm sorry, I don't mean to interrupt what is clearly a simple yet brilliant plot to commit murder in the better interest of revenge, but I'm looking for a man named Barnum. I have important business with him and if you would be kind enough to—" Maddie began.

The man stared incredulously down at her then glared daggers at Fred and George.

"Unless you want to lose your whore, you better get the uppity bitch outta my face before I kill her!" Purple-face screamed.

Neither Agent reacted to Purple-face's demands. They remained calm and silent, hands kept politely behind their backs.

"Excuse me," Maddie said haughtily. "But I was being polite. I knocked and everything. I'd greatly appreciate it if you'd just answer my simple question so that I can go ahead and get out of your hair."

"Fuck you!" Purple-face screamed after a short stunned silence. The spit flew from his mouth as he yelled and hit Maddie in the face. Maddie grimaced and wiped her cheek with a finger.

"Fine," she said. "Have it your way."

Then, hoping that the toes of her boots were reinforced with *something*, she stepped back and kicked Purple-face in the balls as hard as she could. Purple-face clutched his privates and dropped to the floor shrieking like a little girl. He writhed as he convulsed into a fetal position, a trick she was certain would cause him a great deal of secondary pain once the agony in his groin eased some. Maddie stepped gingerly over his curled body and into the cubicle. As it turned out, the boot had not been reinforced and she had bruised two of her toes. George and Fred crowded around the door behind her, their guns in their hands and aimed directly at the two remaining people.

The second man had a very surprised looking woman straddling his lap, with one meaty hand still gripping her bare breast through the low cut of her shirt. The woman was bare from the waist down, her long legs emphasized in a pair of thigh high black boots. The man's pants were bunched down around his ankles and it was perfectly clear what the two had been doing before Maddie had knocked on the door.

Maddie pretended not to notice that the people she faced were in the middle of copulation and fought not to gape at their nudity. Meanwhile, her pelvis let her know how much it would like to be engaged in much the same way with a man, any man. Her brain, however, wondered how the man could possibly plot bloody revenge while grinding gonads with the woman.

"Hello, I'm hoping you can help me out and let me know where I can find an Ezra Barnum," Maddie said as sweetly as she could. She knew was being a bit rude, interrupting the pair as she did. The man she kicked was still squealing like a pig on the floor behind her.

"Oh, Master Barnum has his own place on—Ow!" The woman exclaimed as the man she was mounted on hit her full in the mouth. She reeled and nearly toppled off his lap. He caught her by the hips and yanked her back into position.

"Shut up!" he snarled into her shocked face. His eyes had taken on a cruel and drowsy look as he began to thrust hard into her body. The woman gasped and arched her back as she dug her fingers into his shoulders.

"You don't mind waiting while I finish up here, do you? Just make yourself comfortable and I'll be right with you." He said over the woman's shoulder. The woman made small pained noises with each healthy thrust from the man. She might have been enjoying his attentions before Maddie interrupted but she wasn't having fun now. Maddie's expression changed from apologetic cheerfulness to cold impatience. The man turned his attention back to the woman and stared into her mouth.

The man's mind wandered to blood and violence as his body became wracked with pleasure. The woman riding him was weeping quietly, exposing the fine red lines of blood on her lips and teeth. He liked sex and violence and he loved it when the two occurred together. He was young yet and inexperienced, but it wouldn't be long before he began to butcher his women while he rode them. He turned his head and let his flat gaze linger on Maddie's breasts. The look was a threat in itself, suggesting that he would have her next whether she wanted it or not. He thought it would be a simple thing to separate her from her men and to have her as he pleased.

Maddie saw all of this in his mind even though it only took a few seconds for him to think it. She folded her arms over her breasts. The man took it for a sign of her fear of him and it excited him further. He thrust harder into the woman on his lap and made her cry out in pain.

"I think I've just about had enough of this," Maddie growled.

"Indeed," George replied. The muscles in his jaw were clenched as his eyes flared with rage. Fred growled under his breath. Maddie took these responses as agreement to the thoughts she saw in her own head.

"Put one in his knees, would you?"

Two guns fired in loud bursts as the man's kneecaps exploded in a mist of blood, bone and cartilage. The man screamed and released the woman so that he could grip his knees. She scrambled off him and gathered her discarded clothing to her chest. The whore was screaming hysterically and weeping as she cringed in the corner. The shot man was screaming torture and murder at them as he writhed in agony. Angry voices echoed from the great hall behind them.

"You'd better hurry and get what you came for, Tracker. We have company coming," George said through clenched teeth. Maddie turned to the woman and smiled kindly.

"I'm not going to hurt you," she began.

"Barnum keeps his rooms in a bunch of rooms below the club. He does everything in there. He almost never leaves. When he does leave, he always comes back!" the woman shrieked.

The woman spoke so fast that Maddie had a hard time understanding what she'd said. She thanked the woman and gave her a few coins from her pocket before she stepped away from her. She turned to George and Fred where they stood in the narrow entrance. She found that an angry crowd had already gathered around the cubicle. The Agents had both drawn a gun in each hand, and they had them aggressively pointed at the men in front of them. The crowd, in return, had weapons drawn and pointed. Maddie eyed the blocky cylinders and realized that this was the local equivalent of a gun. If things got any further out of hand, she and the men standing between her and the crowd would be cut to pieces in seconds. She thought briefly of using telepathy to alter the mood of the crowd to something more friendly but quickly discarded the idea. The trick required more control and concentration than she currently possessed since her mind was still a bit muddled and her body was driving her to desperate distraction.

"You guys have any ideas?" she asked the men.

"Give up and hope that they won't kill us once they have our weapons?" George suggested softly.

"Probably a safer wager since the Tracker would probably kill us on accident in a fight right now," Fred's mental voice was stronger than George's and the tone had let her know that he was very angry.

"Give 'em up, boys," Maddie said so that everyone could hear her. "We don't have any quarrel with these fine gentlemen."

The Agents handed over their guns without hesitation. Once they were unarmed, the crowd seized all three of them and thrust them roughly into the center of the angry mob. Maddie looked at the mass of angry, drunken faces around her and knew she should be frightened out of her mind. But since she was still goofy from the night spores, the best she could muster was interest. The crowd wasn't necessarily angry because these two particular men had been assaulted. They were pissed because anyone had been assaulted in *this* place. This was their safe haven, where they could gather freely and not fear the violence of their every day lives. They would not tolerate bloodshed here.

Fred and George were wrestled to the ground and had their hands tied behind their backs. Maddie was left on her feet and merely held by the nearest pair of men.

"If we have to rely on the Tracker to get us out of this, we might as well as crawl into our graves now," Fred growled from the floor. George didn't reply but he glared at Fred for his poor attitude. Maddie was jostled and manhandled, but she wasn't tied.

A massive giant of a man pushed into the crowd. He gently shoved people out of his way. The men staggered and danced in the general direction the big man pushed them, as if pretending they had a choice in the matter. He wore an angry expression on his face as he surveyed the crowd and cowed the more rambunctious members of the mob with a single look. Maddie stared up at him, craning her head back to do so. The crowd greeted him with awed murmurs, some hailing him cheerfully while others murmured his name reverently.

Mamun was a man who did not need the excessive flourishes that the other men of Rhasta seemed to covet. He dressed simply in a plain white shirt of linen. He did not add the layers of lace that was so popular among the rest of the men. He didn't wear a hat and his head was covered in very short brown hair that lay flat against his head. Small tattoos peeked just below his hairline and circled his scalp. His black pants were as tight as anyone's but his didn't reveal or exaggerate the contents within. His boots were simple and clean and looked well-worn. None of his clothing boasted the extravagant embroidery or decoration that others wore proudly.

"What's all this, then?" he demanded. Half a dozen people all began shouting at once, trying to be the first to tell Mamun what was going on. Fingers jabbed at Maddie and the Agents as they worked themselves into a frenzy. Mamun lifted his big hand to halt the din of voices. Immediately, the crowd quieted and waited for him to speak. He turned to gaze coldly at the two men lying prone and bloody in the cubicle next to him and the hysterical woman weeping in the corner. His face was contemptuous as he turned back to the crowd and stared down at George.

"What do you say about his?" he demanded.

"I have nothing to say," George said clearly and calmly, despite the fact that his face was being pressed painfully to the stone floor. "I am merely a servant of the Tracker."

Mamun took the news in stride while the crowd gasped in shock and horror. Fred was suddenly lifted to his feet and several hands reached out to straighten and tidy his clothes for him. They frantically pulled at his binds in an effort to free him. Fred glared at Mamun and jerked out of their hands.

"I am not the Tracker either," he snarled.

All eyes turned to Maddie in shock and dismay. She could clearly hear their dumbfounded thoughts. A woman. A weak and stupid woman. She fought the urge to roll her eyes in disgust and stared boldly at Mamun as he regarded her with amusement. His bright, hazel eyes looked her up and down, appraising her form and character. Maddie felt her face go cold as he decided that he wasn't the least impressed.

"Tracker, are you?" he said to her. Maddie, still unable to become excited by the near riot all around her, gave him a small smile and shrugged.

"Have you the Mark?"

Maddie yanked her right hand from the crowd and held it, palm down, so that Mamun could see the ring clearly. He looked blankly at the Mark on her finger and then tried to penetrate her brain through her gray eyes. The crowd held its breath as they waited for the man's verdict. The peace of their last safe haven in the city had been broken and a single arrogant woman had done it. It was a grievous sin and they wanted her and the treasonous men she kept with her punished. It no longer mattered that the woman in question was a powerful figure in their culture; she had lifted a hand to a man in full view of the public and effectively emasculated them both figuratively and literally. Such an act was unforgivable. Under normal circumstances, they wouldn't have hesitated to rip Maddie and the two men to shreds. But with Mamun's intervention, they stopped and waited.

Mamun was a man to be reckoned with in this place. He worked to keep this place of peace and excess safe from the prying eyes and violence of those who worked to take it from them. He protected those who were too weak to protect themselves and he avenged grievous wrongs. He made sure that their families didn't go hungry when times were tough and he worked to make sure that they had jobs when they could not find work on their own. They would, in the end, respect the decision of this man and obey it, even if they didn't like it.

"Their weapons, please," Mamun held out his hand and immediately four pistols were handed over. He tucked them into his belt while he kept his eyes on Maddie. She looked back at him and calmly admired the wide shoulders and the broad, heavy chest. That muscular chest moved into a trim belly and shapely hips which flowed smoothly into long, strong, shapely legs and a high and tight ass.

Realizing where her mind was taking her, Maddie shook her head and kept her eyes stubbornly at his face. It didn't help much; Mamun was handsome in an earthy and masculine sort of way. His hazel eyes were even and brilliant above a fine straight nose and proud cheekbones. His chiseled jaw framed a well-shaped, full mouth that quirked in a smile that told her that he knew exactly what she was thinking about him.

He lifted a hand and made a beckoning gesture over his shoulder with blunt, callused fingers. More large men appeared from the distant stonework as they assumed custody of the crowd's prisoners. The crowd muttered angrily at this but none of the individuals moved to do anything about it.

"We'll take them to the Holding," Mamun announced so that everyone could hear. "This is for Master Barnum to judge and deal with as he sees fit."

The crowd murmured their approval and began to disperse. There was nothing more to see, especially when there were far more entertaining things to pay attention to nearby. Mamun turned to the three in the cubicle, his features showing his extreme disdain.

"Teacha, I suggest you get dressed and go on home before your father discovers what you've been doing and who you've been doing it with," he said. Teacha nodded and began to dress without regard to modesty as she did so. "I don't want to see you hanging around with this kind of trash anymore. You're a good girl, time to start acting like it."

"Yes, Mamun," Teacha murmured, gazing in adoration at the man. She stamped her feet into her boots and hurried from the cubicle. "Thank you Mamun."

Mamun spared no words for the two men still weeping and moaning on the floor. It was likely that they had gotten what they deserved. Mamun knew both of them to be petty thieves and cruel bullies. He'd had to clean up after them a few times for the sake of peace and he was done with it now. If they had any friends left, they could pick the fools off the floor and take care of them. If they had no friends left, well then, he would be just as happy to sweep them out with the rest of the garbage at closing time.

He turned his broad back and began to make his way across the room to the back of the floor. The men holding the Tracker and her Agents followed without a word, making sure to keep a secure hold on their prisoners.

CHAPTER 22

Sam was saw scores of cop cars crowding the school parking lot and dozens of officers roaming the grounds. Two ambulances were parked near the front doors with their lights spinning and flashing. A gurney was being deposited into the back of one of the blocky vehicles as a paramedic spoke with a police officer. Terror filled his belly and chest as he pulled into the first available parking space and yanked Allen from his car seat. He was making his way towards the front doors as fast as he could when a uniformed police man intervened with a lifted hand.

"I'm Sam Johnston," he said frantically to the bland faced cop. "The school called me and told me to get here as soon as possible. They said that there was an incident involving my son and daughter."

The cop opened his mouth to send Sam back to his vehicle when Darlene emerged from the school. She saw Sam right away and she hurried towards him.

"It's okay, Carlos. He's the father of the victims," she said softly as she patted the man on the shoulder. Carlos nodded and wandered away to do whatever he had been doing when he intercepted Sam. Sam's heart nearly stopped when he heard the word 'victims.' The word implied something terrible and life altering. His brain frantically wondered what had happened and if his children had survived it. He was ready to grab the woman and shake her to find out.

Darlene stepped closer to Sam so that he could easily hear her above the noise of the cops and paramedics. Her expression was grim and she looked as if she'd aged twenty years overnight. Sleeplessness darkened the tender flesh under her eyes. She studied his shoes for a moment as she thought of a way to tell her brother-in-law what had happened to his children. When she finally looked up at him, he looked half maddened by panic and worry. Sam stared intently into her eyes and tried to decide if it were tears that made her eyes shine feverishly.

"There's been a violent incident involving Katie and Chris," she began holding up a hand to keep Sam from interrupting her. She had to get this out, to tell him what exactly he would be dealing with so that he would have the time to freak out before he saw the children. Allen squirmed in his arms as his little head swiveled this way and that as he tried to look at everything at once.

"They're going to be fine. They're traumatized by what happened, but they'll heal," she said quickly to put his mind at ease. Sam was beginning to look as if he was going to collapse in the grass if she didn't hurry this up. "At recess, Katie noticed a man staring at her and told one of the playground monitors. The monitor confronted the man and when she asked him to leave the premises, he threatened Katie. The three monitors on the scene followed school procedures and got the kids inside. They separated Katie from the other children and took her to the front office. They sent security to make sure that the man had left school grounds.

"While they did that, a secretary took Katie to the bathroom when she asked to go. She was attacked and killed while Katie was in the stall. Katie didn't see the actual murder, thank god, but she did trip over the body. Then the killer attacked her. Katie has stated that it was the man from the playground that had rescued her.

"She described the killer as a monster. She said that a deformed and ugly creature had chased her and Chris through the school and tried to kill them both. A teacher pulled both of them into his classroom and the perpetrator crashed through the emergency exit just as the first units arrived. He discovered that the back of Katie's neck and shoulders had been cut up pretty badly. The paramedics are waiting to take her to the hospital now. Chris escaped the incident without a scratch. They're both in the nurse's office right now."

Sam moved towards the school the second that Darlene told him where his children were. His mind was spinning. Who was the man that tried to kill his child? Who had saved her? Why would anyone want to hurt Katie and Chris? They were just ordinary children. They had never hurt anyone. At what point had Chris gotten involved and why?

He decided that none of it was important when he suddenly thought of the creature that had tried to get into his house two nights ago. He wondered if that monster was the same one that Katie had described to her aunt.

A woman stood up as he entered the building. She was wringing her hands and her face was swollen from crying. She hunched nervously as she regarded him fearfully.

"Are you Katherine and Christopher's dad?" she asked tentatively. She looked anxious when Sam said yes, perhaps she afraid that he was going to start screaming at her. He didn't doubt that she was going to be hearing a lot of screaming parents when word about the murder got out.

"I need to see some identification," she said apologetically. Sam nodded and fished into his back pocket. He wasn't going to argue with the woman. After what had happened, the school had *better* ask for identification. Sam presented her with his driver's license and social security card. She stared at them for a moment and then handed them back. She came out from around the desk and escorted him down the hall behind her. The nurse's office was the second door on the left in a long corridor lined with dark doors. She opened the door for him and stepped aside to let him through.

A tidy desk sat in the center of the room. It had a computer on it as well as the small toys that were soothing to sick and injured children and were the tools of the school nurse's trade. Cabinets and drawers lined the office and a row of chairs lined an empty wall adorned only with a closed door. Chris sat in one of the chairs and clutched a stuffed orange cat to his chest and held a can of soda. He stared bleakly at the floor while he kicked his legs in agitation. A plump woman with a dark ponytail sat in the chair next to him and rubbed his back and hummed a soothing tune. She looked like a school nurse if the cartoon-patterned scrubs were anything to go by.

"Mr. Johnston!" the nurse exclaimed as he stepped through the door. Chris' head came up and he threw the soda and cat to the floor as he jumped out of his chair.

"Daddy!" the boy shouted as he threw his arms around Sam's legs and buried his face into his father's thigh. Sam stroked his hair while the boy shook with silent tears.

"He's had a terrible scare," Nurse said sympathetically. The woman looked shaken as she knelt and cleaned the soda from the floor with a trembling hand. "But he's trying to be brave. All he's done since he was brought to me was worry about you and his sister and baby brother and talk about how he needs to kill the monsters that come to his house."

Sam flinched at the last part. Chris hadn't said anything about what had happened that night. He had simply picked up where he had left off as if nothing had happened. Sam had simply assumed that Chris was a resilient child and had gotten over the incident without a qualm.

"How's Katie doing?" he asked softly, bending over and lifting his son into his other arm. Chris wrapped his arms around his father's neck and wept into his shoulder. Allen looked at his brother from Sam's other arm and asked him if he was okay in his little baby voice.

"I think she'll be okay. She's in shock and she'll probably need some stitches, but I think she'll be okay in the end." The nurse gestured to the door, indicating where Katie was. "The paramedics are with her now, and they're getting her ready to go to the hospital. Katie asked them to wait until you got here before they took her away. She was afraid that you'd be too worried."

Sam went straight to the door without another word, trying to avoid another explanation from the nervous and long-winded nurse. Katie was already laying strapped to a gurney with two paramedics fussing over her. Her shirt and jeans were soaked in dried blood and her neck still oozed with the red fluid. Her blond hair hung loose and limp around her face and was stiff with blood.

"Daddy!" Katie called softly with relief when she saw her father. Chris turned and looked at his sister and burst into tears. Katie cried with him as the paramedic tried to console her.

"How are you feeling?" Sam asked as he bounced his boys in his arms.

"I was so scared," she wept, covering her face with her delicate hands. "I thought the monster was going to kill me and Chris."

Sam watched his daughter cry and thought that his heart would break. He didn't know what to say or do, so all he did was gaze with worry and love in his eyes.

"Where would you like your daughter to be treated?" a paramedic asked softly, putting a comforting hand on Sam's arm. Sam blinked away tears and looked at the man. He gave them the name of the local hospital where all three of his children had been born. The paramedic nodded with approval and gestured to his partner to get going.

Sam followed Katie out of the school and watched as she was loaded into an ambulance. The press had finally gotten word of the day's events and was converging on the school. Cops were moving to intercept them and keep them from impeding their investigation and what remained of the normal rhythms of the school. Sam rushed to his van and hastily put the boys in their car seats. He got the vehicle started and drove after the ambulance as fast as he could.

Sam was still waiting at Katie's bedside when Darlene walked into the room. The early afternoon had crawled into early evening as they sat in the emergency room. Katie's injuries had been treated quickly enough but the doctors couldn't decide what to do with her next or how they were going to do it. The medical staff had heard what had happened, of course, and they treated Katie and her father with all the consideration imaginable. But the consideration took a lot of time.

Darlene looked more frazzled and fatigued than she had at the school. Her clothes were rumpled and she had what looked like blood at the edge of her shirtsleeve. She moved to the other side of Katie's bed and sat in the chair placed there without a word. Chris and Allen hadn't noticed her arrival; their attention was all on the cartoons being played on the television bolted high on the wall. Sam gave her a weak smile of greeting, indicating that he didn't have the energy to talk. But Darlene had something on her mind and, like her sister, couldn't rest until she had put it to words.

"How's Katie doing?" she began, gazing down at the little girl's sleeping form.

"They sedated her when she got hysterical a couple of hours ago. She's still sleeping it off," Sam replied dully, hoping that this was all Darlene had to say. "She got thirty stitches in her neck and shoulders. They want to keep her overnight for observation."

"I told you more than I'm allowed to," Darlene said. "They're trying to keep this case under wraps so that we don't have any copycat's false confessions. I'd appreciate it if you didn't talk to the press about it."

"I don't want to talk to the press at all," Sam muttered, wishing that the woman would just shut up. Darlene fell silent and she stared at Katie, then at Chris, with a troubled look on her face.

"I think the attack at the school is connected to the murder case I've been working on," she said suddenly. "I think a man that had killed ten people so far is responsible for the attack on Katie and Chris."

Sam gave her a hard look, then glanced at the boys. They were staring at the television as if they could somehow will themselves into the program. They hadn't heard a word their aunt had said. Sam didn't want to hear this. He wanted to believe that what happened was a one-time occurrence and would never happen again regardless of whether the cops caught the bastard. The last thing he wanted to hear was that his children were the targets of some psycho serial killer and that he might come back for them.

"What makes you think that the cases are related?" he asked carefully. Darlene rubbed her face with her hands and scratched her neck. It was a nervous habit she had from childhood that she could never overcome.

"My killer likes to write a word at each of his crime scenes," Darlene said. "It's a strange reference to a person that he somehow got fixated on. The same word, Tracker, was carved into the chest of the woman killed today. I'm hoping that Katie heard something that might explain the fixation."

"I'll keep my ears open," Sam replied.

"I'd like to question her myself when she wakes up," Darlene said. Sam sat back in his chair and glared at her.

"No," he growled. "Katie has been through enough without you making her hold on to it. You questioned her while she was at the school. She gave you a description of the man who attacked her. That should be enough."

But it wasn't enough and, deep down, Sam knew it. Katie had told him what had attacked her and he knew that they'd be back. The rational voice in his head told him that he was being a fool, that what they had seen and experienced could be scientifically explained. He wanted to deny the supernatural elements that had suddenly entered his life and shook it to the core. But he couldn't. He knew what he saw and he couldn't deny any of it. He felt helpless and worthless and there was nothing he could do about it.

Darlene watched him grow angrier as he stared at her. She bowed her head and sighed.

"Sam, Katie could be our best chance to catch this guy and putting him out of circulation forever."

"It's not a man and you know it," Sam growled. "Or have you forgotten what happened to you the night you slept on my couch?"

Darlene scowled and looked away. "I haven't forgotten."

"They came back and tried to get into the house. I saw it with my own eyes. I don't know what it was, but I can say it wasn't a normal human being. Katie described the monster at school and it was exactly like what she saw at the house. If this one is carving people up, then maybe you should consider the possibility that you might never catch your killer and that maybe you should have some cops protect my kids."

Darlene stared in horror at Sam. She understood the ordeal the man had endured over the last few days and she felt bad for him. If she had known that things were this bad, she would have talked to her lieutenant about putting some units on him for protection. But there were problems with even that.

"What do you want me to do, Sam?" she demanded. "Tell my commanding officer that demons are killing whole families and that we might be better off calling a priest? Or maybe calling in a freak with a tazer he calls a ghost detector? Or, better yet, maybe I should tell him to hand out silver bullets and holy water to the whole force?"

Sam let her have her quiet tirade knowing how absurd it sounded. He raked his fingers through his thin hair.

"I don't know what to do," he whispered.

Darlene was silent for a long time. She had no comforting words to offer. She wanted to tell him to take the kids and get the hell out of town. She wanted to tell him to buy a gun. But she didn't know if any of that would do him any good. So she changed the subject.

"When will Maddie get here?" she asked.

"She doesn't know what happened." Sam moaned. He saw Darlene's stricken face and kept talking. "I left three messages on her cell and she hasn't called me back yet. I don't know if she'll ever come."

"What are you going to do?" Darlene asked, shocked by her sister's behavior. She couldn't believe that Maddie would ignore a phone call from Sam, no matter what she was doing. Her sister loved this man and had often said that her world revolved around him. Maddie's eyes lit up whenever she talked about him and she smiled wistfully whenever she thought about him. Something was going on with her sister, Darlene was certain of it. But she didn't say so to Sam, he already had enough to deal with.

"My mom is coming to get the boys. She'll be keeping them until Katie gets out of the hospital. The doctors say that she'll probably leave tomorrow afternoon. I'm going to stay with Katie until then. After that, I don't know. I don't think the school will take the kids back until this is cleared up, and I really don't blame them. I'm sure I'll think of something. If I don't, Maddie will know what to do when she gets home. She's getting three months off as soon as she returns."

Sam was babbling; he was so tired and upset. He was coming dangerously close to his breaking point. It was all that he could do just to deal with what was in front of him. He didn't even want to think about the future. Darlene murmured that they would get the bastard who did this and then everything would return to normal. Sam accepted it with a nod. He would endure for now, but only because he had no other choice.

CHAPTER 23

He paced his public room like a ferocious caged thing, growling and baring his teeth and gnashing them at the air. He waited in frustration for word that the changeling he had sent to scout the area where two of his brethren had disappeared had returned. He expected to receive word at any moment that the Tracker's heir had been located and destroyed. If the death of her favored offspring did not bring the Tracker to his doorstep, nothing would. Then his plans would fall effortlessly into place and He would obtain the status he deserved.

The discovery of the Tracker's lair had been an accidental thing. As his changelings and grunts scoured the land for suitable victims, they had stumbled across the bit of land which the Tracker made her home. As always, since the time of William, Agents were watching the family closely and had killed the first changeling to stumble across the human den. The corpse had been located by a whining timid who had spent the entire trip among the humans urinating like a nervous Chihuahua. The grunt that had accompanied it eventually got fed up with it and killed it. Luckily, the thing had just enough intelligence to tell someone where the first corpse had been located.

At first, he simply assumed that the death had been a result of a misadventure. Then, just to be sure, he sent another changeling to follow the first one's trail. It also failed to return the following morning. Another scouting trip revealed the second changeling was still lying in some shrubbery at the house. The kill had been fresh and the Agent hadn't been able to hide the body properly yet. A third changeling in disguise watched the house and counted nearly ten Agents coming and going in the following twenty-four hours. It was all the proof He needed.

In the following days, the changelings reported that they only saw a single adult male dwelling in the house with a single daughter and two sons. Six grunts that never returned from a hunting trip on Iza confirmed that the Tracker was currently off world. After that, it was a simple leap in logic to assume that they were looking for a woman. He rubbed his hands in glee and hoped that she was beautiful. If her husband was anything to go on, though, it wasn't likely. The man was fat and beginning to loose his hair. Not the sort of males those beautiful human females generally gravitated toward. Not that it mattered. The things he had planned for her would send him into the heights of such ecstasy that he wouldn't know what she looked like after the first few seconds. But it would be much more satisfying if she began lovely.

He was ready to break down his own door and demand answers when the timid crawled through. It shuffled along with its shoulders hunched protectively around its body as if it expected to be beaten at any moment.

"Well? What has happened?" He demanded impatiently. The timid shrieked and clutched the door behind it. It stared at him with its terrified eyes bulging out of its skull. He watched with morbid fascination, waiting for the thing's eyes to pop out of its head.

"The changeling stalked and attacked the girl as you ordered," the timid screamed. "In the process it killed an unrelated adult female and engaged in battle with a veteran Agent. After it crippled the Agent, it gave chase to the girl who had been joined by a young boy. It pursued the two, until another adult male pulled the children into a room. At that time, the police were arriving and the changeling was forced to flee. It is certain that it bloodied the girl, but was unable to say how severely."

"She isn't dead?" He snarled. He had wanted to display the child's body in a way that would flaunt the Keeper's failure in his face.

"No, Master!" the timid cried, cringing.

He trembled with fury; his fists clenched so tightly that his nails gouged his palms. He growled and shrieked his frustration. No doubt the child had seen the changeling. And the changeling had chased her though a public place. The girl would talk, she was a female after all, and there would be many other humans to corroborate her story now. The police force would have written down every word the child uttered as if it were gospel and eventually the tales would reach the religious leaders. The men of god always believed. And they always took action. It was just a matter of time before the police realized that the child wasn't delirious with terror and the two groups would eventually join forces. In the past, such alliances had proven fatal. Nothing was so dangerous as a pissed off zealot with a weapon. There had to be a way to keep the two groups from joining forces.

Then a devious idea came upon him. Her grinned so broadly that his small ears began to ache. He took a moment to preen in the delicious glow of his own brilliance. He turned to the timid and found that it had fainted from its terror. He frowned at the pile of filthy rags slumped on the floor. Luckily, he was feeling charitable so he let it lay there unmolested. He called a second timid into his presence. It arrived quickly and shook so badly that dust rose up around it and flakes of dirt pattered onto his clean floor. He paid it no mind as he gathered the trembling thing into his arm.

As it fought for consciousness, he drew it further into his room and began to tell it of his plan. He would have policemen systematically killed. Any religious men who spoke of hunting demons would die. He would bring the Tracker to him and destroy all of her heirs. It would be a glory of human bodies and human blood. The lair would feast for years on what he was about to do.

CHAPTER 24

Arnold didn't leave the hospital until her niece was securely placed in a private room. Her father fussed over her while the children's Nana gathered up Allen and Chris. Nana had kissed Katie sweetly on her forehead and took the boys home. Arnold had called work and asked for a couple of volunteers to come and see to it that Katie wasn't disturbed while she recovered and tried to sleep. A couple of guys stopped by wearing their street clothes. This wasn't an assignment they would get paid for and therefore they stayed out of uniform. Carlos was his usual charming self. He took a couple of minutes to tease and joke with the little girl. Katie managed to muster a smile for him but she was too tired and frightened for the laugh he was fishing for. Kyle, Carlos' partner stood silently by, pretended that he wasn't there and that there wasn't a little girl sitting in a hospital bed. Kyle was a bit over sensitive when it came to kids, which was a big reason why he was still a traffic cop by choice.

It wasn't long after Katie arrived at the hospital that the press arrived there as well. They sat out in the parking lot, forbidden to enter the facility after the doctors realized that they were getting in the way of paramedics bringing people in and would keep walk-ins from even getting to the door. So they sat in the parking lot and waited for something interesting to happen. It looked as if Katie would be something of a celebrity for awhile.

Arnold walked out of the hospital with her head down in hopes that she would be mistaken for another anonymous visitor. But today was not her day and she had been recognized from the school and from the Escobar crime scene. The reporters descended on her like vultures on carrion and jabbed their microphones into her face. She pushed and ducked away from the reporters and kept her mouth firmly clamped shut no matter how lewd or odd the shouted question. A few reporters stood their ground in an attempt to keep her firmly pinned in their midst. But a dirty look and a flash of her handcuffs quickly changed their minds.

She finally broke through the herd and rushed for her faded car. A few stragglers, hoping to scoop their competition, followed and called her name. They shouted more questions about the recent murders of two whole families and asked if the killings were somehow related to the attack at the local elementary school. Arnold ignored them as she got into her car and slammed the door on their faces. Before this day she never understood why celebrities bitched about the media. Why couldn't they just accept the hounding reporters as a normal hazard of the job? But now she knew the monkeys to be the filth-flinging annoyances that they were and she hadn't even been dealing with them for an entire day. This was not good. She started her car and honked the horn to get the parasites to move along, wondering how Sam was going to deal with this mess.

She managed to pull out of the parking lot and out onto the street without incident. When she was halted at a traffic light, she took the opportunity to call Maddie and find out what the hell her sister thought she was doing. She didn't have her work number, Sam had refused to give it out saying that he wasn't even supposed to have it and he didn't want Maddie to get into trouble. Even so Maddie always kept her personal phone with her, so Arnold called that. She thumbed the speed dial on her faded keypad and listened to the shrill ring as she waited for her sister to pick up.

"Yes?" a deep male voice answered. Startled, Arnold checked the window of her phone to make sure she hadn't accidentally dialed the wrong number.

"Is Maddie there?" she asked hesitantly.

"Might I ask who is calling?" he was cool, arrogant and she didn't like this unknown man answering her sister's phone.

"This is her sister, Darlene," she snapped. "Who the hell are you?"

"I apologize, but she is unavailable at the moment. Might I take a message?"

"Yeah, tell my sister that her daughter had been attacked at school and to get her ass home," Arnold snarled. She was almost certain that this guy was Maddie's mysterious and rigid boss. Was he so bad that he didn't even let her answer her phone while she was at work? Arnold ground her teeth while the man fell silent.

"Is the child well?" he asked finally. There was no emotion in his voice. He was calm and collected in a way that stated to the world that he just didn't give a shit. Arnold fumed as she decided whether or not to tell the guy to mind his own business.

"No, she's not. She's frightened and hurt and needs her mother."

"I will relay the message at the next possible moment. Have a good evening, Ms. Arnold, and be assured that no further harm will come to the children."

Arnold's mouth dropped open to demand some answers to the man's cryptic comments when he hung up. She tried calling back, but he refused to answer the phone.

Instead, she got Maddie's cheerful greeting, followed by jokes about leaving messages before a beep. Arnold repeated her message into her sister's voicemail and tossed her phone in frustration into the seat next to her. She continued to guide the car to the police station. She'd been given permission to go home but, after today, she wouldn't get any rest. She might as well work. Her thoughts wandered to what Sam had said about the strange creatures at his house and Katie's description of the man who had attacked her at school. She remembered the doctor mentioning that he would have thought that an animal had caused the girl's injuries if the child hadn't insisted otherwise. The medical examiner had said much the same thing about the wounds on all of the bodies. He said that he would have insisted that animals had attacked the families if it weren't for the gruesome writing found next to the victims.

Katie had described her attacker as looking like the man on the playground at first, but then had changed when the other man had come to her rescue. His flesh had melted until it hung on his bones and his arms and legs didn't look right for a person. She didn't have the experience or the vocabulary to describe the limbs adequately, so she simply said that he looked as if he'd been born wrong. He still looked like he had at first, but uglier and more deformed. Katie had been vehement about it, to the point that she burst into angry tears when her aunt suggested that she might have been too afraid to know what she saw.

Then Arnold thought about the pictures of deformed men that Shorn had shown to her and Cooper during their interview with him. The pictures had shown men with skin that looked too big for their frames and so hung loosely around their nude bodies. They were twisted and deformed and looked as if "they'd been born wrong." Arnold made a frustrated and enraged noise and pulled a U-turn at a traffic light. She called Cooper as she drove for Cassville Road and informed him of her thoughts and what she was doing. He sighed and told her to keep him posted. She knew what he was thinking. Shorn was a crackpot and a dead-end lead. But her niece had been attacked today and he would let her do almost anything that would make her feel better. And she might feel much better if she got another look at those pictures.

She was at his front door before she knew it and Shorn appeared before her as if by magic. His face was animated as she asked to see his pictures one more time and he hurried off to get them. It wasn't until he was gone that she realized that he was wearing striped pajamas. She checked her watch and saw that it was eight o'clock at night. She stuck her hands in her coat pockets and waited. Shorn clearly didn't mind being disturbed.

She heard shooing noises coming from the back of the house and a woman emerged. She was an over-processed bottle-blonde with black roots hugging her scalp and too much make-up over scarred and wrinkled skin. She smoked a cigarette as she flounced her way towards the front door. She paused to examine Arnold as she passed and eyed her angrily.

"You a new girl?" the woman demanded.

"Excuse me?" Arnold asked.

"You new? Shorn here calls me every weekend and lately he ain't had me at all. I'm thinkin' some new girl got his business," she woman snapped. Arnold gaped as the other woman sized her up. The woman was a prostitute! Arnold nearly laughed out loud until she got what the woman was implying.

"Are you asking me if I'm Dr. Shorn's new whore?" she asked incredulously. The whore gave her a flat look then raised her eyebrow. She gestured with her cigarette at Arnold's clothes.

"If the shoe fits, honey," she drawled.

Arnold looked down at herself. She was wearing stylish black slacks and a blue business shirt. Her shoes had high heels on them but they made her legs look longer and she thought that the toes were cute. Surely she wasn't wearing hooker shoes! She gawked at the old whore and then had to suppress the urge to laugh.

"I'm a cop," she said as icily as she could manage. The whore scowled and took another drag on her cigarette. In the house beyond, Shorn was rummaging loudly. Arnold reached into her coat pocket and pulled out her badge. The woman paled when she saw it and started moving for the front door at top speed.

"Wait a minute," Arnold said. The prostitute froze, her hand holding the doorknob in a death grip. Arnold let her see the grin she'd been hiding and pulled out her notebook. "Can I ask you some questions?"

"Like what?" she asked suspiciously.

"Your name, to start," Arnold tried to keep it friendly, since people did not answer questions from hostile people.

"I'm Leona," she replied cautiously. Arnold kept her pen still and continued to smile.

"How long have you been seeing Dr. Shorn?" she asked. At that, Leona got the hint that Arnold had no intention of taking her in. Arnold was perfectly willing to spend the rest of the conversation pretending that the other woman was simply Shorn's girlfriend. She took her hand off the knob and visibly relaxed.

"A couple of years. We usually see each other on weekends. He keeps pretty busy with his research during the week."

"What is it that Dr. Shorn is researching?"

"Some Tracker nonsense. He goes on and on about some people called Distari, and how they're trying to kill us all for experiments and how the only person that can stop them is this Tracker person. He's pretty obsessed about it."

Arnold jotted this down.

"Has he ever said or shown you anything that explains why he is so interested in the subject?"

Leona looked at Arnold with open amusement. She took a drag from her cigarette and let it out slowly.

"He's shown me some pictures of deformed people. Nothing special, though. They look like those old pictures of the holocaust or those Japanese people after they dropped the bomb on them. He says that they've been hunting people ever since we arrived on this planet."

Arnold let that one go. She didn't want to get into a conversation with a hooker about whether or not she believed that humans were alien immigrants to Earth. She did take a few notes regarding the possible paranoid mental state exhibited by Shorn.

"Has Dr. Shorn ever said or done anything with you to make you believe that he has ever harmed anyone in any way?"

Leona burst into laughter at that.

"Hell, no!" she exclaimed. "Are you kidding me? That man is just plain nice! I never heard him say a bad thing about anyone much less do anything that might hurt somebody. He won't even step on a spider. He just picks it up and throws it out the door."

Arnold smiled and waited for Leona to stop her guffawing.

"But you know," Leona said taking a last puff from her cigarette and looking for a place to put it out. "About a year ago, he said that he found out who the Tracker person was. Said it was some old guy just emigrated here from Germany. He wanted to meet him but Shorn told me he got eaten by those Distari guys. Awhile later he gave me a necklace he bought off the Internet. He said it belonged to the dead guy and that it would protect me. I thought it was pretty, so I took it."

"Do you have it with you now?"

By way of reply, Leona fished around in her deflated cleavage and pulled out a small medallion on a thin gold chain. She held it out to Arnold but didn't take it off. Like Leona said, it was pretty and she didn't want to part with it. Arnold stepped forward and held the delicate thing gently on her fingers. It was a thin disc of hammered gold, etched in silver and embossed with brass in a series of graceful lines drawn in an elaborate knot. Tiny balls had been welded at compass points in the knot and lacquered white. A fifth ball had been placed in the center and lacquered blue. The pattern looked oddly familiar to Arnold. It was as if it was something she looked at everyday, but never really noticed until now. Its source tickled at her brain, threatening to enlighten her if only it could struggle out of the darkness.

"He called it the Tracker's Mark," she explained while Arnold admired the trinket. "Says it's the way the Trackers have been identified over the centuries. He says that only the people associated with the Tracker wear the symbol and the Tracker has to protect them."

Leona gave a shrug and tucked the necklace back into her bosom when Arnold let it go.

"You know, he saw what happened to those people who got killed across the street," she said. "It scared him pretty bad. He thought that maybe that family got killed because the Distari made a mistake. He's been thinking that they are going to come and kill him."

"Why would these things want him dead?"

"Cuz he's looking for the Tracker. He says that all he has to do is find out who inherited all the German's stuff and that person is the new Tracker."

Arnold heard Shorn's footsteps coming towards them from the back of the house. She flipped her notebook closed and stuck it back in her pocket. She fished a battered card out of her purse and handed it to Leona.

"If you think of anything else, could you give me a call?" she asked. Leona gave her a look, but slipped the card into her own small pocketbook.

"Did he really see those people get killed?" she asked fearfully.

Arnold didn't answer. She gave the woman a sympathetic look. Leona looked worried about Shorn beyond what a jaded whore should. Arnold had never believed in the hooker with a heart of gold myth. But Leona was human and she had said that the man was nice to her. Maybe he had been very nice to her and she'd fallen for it. Arnold thought it was a shame.

Arnold knew that she was on the verge of a break in the case. Shorn had something to do with it, of that she was almost certain. Of all the people the Anderson's knew, only this old man had any familiarity with the word Tracker. Leona managed to get out just as Shorn arrived holding his box of photographs. He grinned broadly, his watery eyes lit up with anticipation. He grabbed a handful of pictures and offered them to Arnold.

She thumbed through them and took note of the distinctive features of the deformed people. Many of the images were of men with awkward proportions and had oversized skins that hung off their bones. Other pictures were of hunched man-beasts that snarled at the camera with long teeth and had overly long and muscled arms. One or two of the pictures were of small, frightened-looking old men dressed in tatters and coated in filth.

It was the pictures of the loose skinned men that interested her. They looked a great deal like what Katie had described.

"Where did you take these pictures?" she asked. Shorn blinked in surprise, as if he hadn't expected the question. Maybe he hadn't. He didn't look like a guy who lived in reality very often.

"Uh, some of them are ones that were given to me by other witnesses. Some of them I took during my travels. The places vary," he said.

"Have you found your Tracker yet?" Arnold asked as nonchalantly as she could. Shorn stared at her like he was trying to remember something. Arnold said nothing and pretended not to watch him struggle.

"Not yet," he murmured. "Gustav Haughmein had requested in his will that the records regarding his estate be sealed and his heir's identity kept a secret. I don't know why, the Tracker is supposed to have great power. Surely his heir would be someone invincible."

Arnold had stopped listening. Instead she was busy feeling the blood in her veins stop flowing and turn to ice. She knew the name. A year ago, Maddie had been named the sole heir of an obscure and dead relative. She had inherited a little money, some old clothes and odd knick-knacks. She shook it off. It had to be an odd coincidence.

"Are you okay, detective?" Shorn asked. His big bony hand rested on her shoulder. She looked up and noticed a tattoo on the side of the old man's neck. It was the same pattern as Leona's necklace. Arnold flinched and pulled away.

"I'm fine, thank you. I came here wondering if you had remembered anything else about the night the Anderson's were killed?"

Shorn looked at her, his eyes steady and calculating. She felt her skin crawl as he somehow changed from a goofy eccentric to a sharp-minded predator.

"I know that they're trying to draw the Tracker out," he said evenly. "Why else would they spell his name in their guts?"

"How did you know about that?" Arnold asked calmly.

"The news. The press reported it earlier when they talked about that poor girl getting attacked at school," his voice had changed to sorrow and concern, but his eyes stayed hard. "Is she okay? The Distari didn't hurt her did they?"

Arnold cursed silently. Someone was talking to the press. There was going to be hell to pay tomorrow. And now the nuts would be coming out of the woodwork and making false confessions and giving fake leads. Not that it mattered. She looked into Shorn's serious gaze and became certain that she had her suspect right here.

"What makes you think that these Distari creatures had anything to do with it?" Arnold challenged.

"They interviewed witnesses. They all described a Distari. The pictures are in your hand."

"Do you keep any large pets?" she asked suddenly, remembering what the ER doctor and the medical examiner said about animal attacks. Shorn frowned at that.

"No, ma'am. I live alone," he said softly.

"Do you mind if I take a look around the premises? The Anderson's were killed right across the street, and it's possible that some crucial piece of evidence landed in your yard as they fled the scene," she said carefully. Or you killed the Anderson's and there's some crucial piece of evidence in your house, she thought. But I have to ask because I don't have a warrant. And she wanted to look around before the man had a chance to hide anything.

Shorn's breath caught and his eyes took on the look of realization. His features grew cold and stony as his gaze flared with anger.

"I'm afraid I must ask you to leave, Detective Arnold," he said politely through clenched teeth. "You see, my lady friend only stepped out to go to the gas station and I expect her back any minute. She will be unhappy with me if I put her off any longer."

Arnold nodded at the lie. The hooker was long gone by now. But she had to accept the excuse and go on her way. She still had the photographs clutched in her hand. She hoped that it was enough to get her a search warrant by morning. She turned to the door and left the house as fast as she could before Shorn remembered his pictures and realized that they were about to be used against him.

CHAPTER 25

Maddie found herself alone in what looked like a classic medieval dungeon. The walls were built from roughly hewn and poorly fitted blocks of stone. The floors were not covered over, instead it was made from the very dirt it was carved from and there were scattered bits of hay and trash lying along walls and in the corners. Torches were set in brackets, and the sputtering flames sent smoke up the walls and ceiling, and it stained everything a sickly black. Everything was coated in dried bodily fluids and excrement, filling the air with the stink of death and bodily fluids. Maddie had already vomited several times from exposure to the reeking air, and the contents of her stomach only added to the dismal wretchedness of the place. She sat huddled on a filthy pile of straw in a corner as far away from the pool of her last three meals as she could get. She watched the thick black bars covering the cavernous opening of her cell like her salvation lay just beyond.

She had been separated from Fred and George almost from the moment her foot touched the stained dirt of the dungeon floor. Mamun gave her a regretful look as he stopped in front of an empty cell and told his men to take the Agents further into the dungeon. Both Agents gave Maddie intent looks, making it clear that it was up to her to get them out of this situation. Mamun made no move to follow his men and shifted his attention to stare boldly into Maddie's eyes.

"I apologize for this, but Master Barnum will want to ask your men a few questions," he said softly. Maddie didn't respond. Her mind was racing, and grasping for any idea in her distracted brain that would lead to a plan of escape. On the outside, Maddie kept her expression chilly and stared boldly back at the towering man. She knew exactly what "asking a few questions" meant and she was fairly certain that none of it would involve polite conversation. Finally, an idea occurred to her, but she wasn't sure it was a good one. She'd never attempted it before and, in her current state, she was worried that the result would come back to bite her in the ass. But she had no other ideas and she was getting desperate.

She sent out small quiet thoughts and touched Mamun's mind. She moved sluggishly around the rough and complicated paths of his consciousness until she found the place that she wanted. She altered his perceptions and judgements in what she hoped was in subtle ways, firmly persuading the man that she was the most remarkable and beautiful woman that he'd ever encountered. She quietly convinced him that she was a woman who was right and pure, and that he should do anything required to make her safe and happy, at any cost. She jumped out of her trance when his callused hand touched her cheek and the thick pad of his thumb caressed her lips.

Maddie remained stiff and cold at his touch, letting him see her displeasure, wondering if she was committing mental rape. She decided that it didn't matter, what was a little of enforced infatuation in the face of the lives and well-being of her friends? Mamun would eventually recover; no harm, no foul.

"If I don't get my Agents back, I will come for you and see to it personally that you burn for it," she said in an icy voice. Mamun smiled indulgently at her. He didn't believe for a second that a woman of her obvious virtues would ever do anything violent or vindictive. But he understood her rage and could not find any fault with it. He would be just as angry if he were in her place.

"Do not fear for your men. They will be returned to you as soon as I can manage it," he said gently. He meant what he said, but carefully left out what state of health Fred and George would be returned to her. He was very uncertain if he could get to them before they came to any harm. He cringed with dread at what he imagined would be her reaction to any physical injury her men would come to.

His face grew sad as he studied her eyes. His hand had not moved from her cheek and she didn't do anything to move away from his touch. She needed him to believe that he could have her if he did as she asked and allowing him to touch her reinforced the idea.

On impulse, he cradled her face in both hands and kissed her softly on her mouth. Maddie's eyes widened in astonishment as her brain stuttered cold in shock. His lips were surprisingly soft caressing her mouth, his tongue teasing her lips without forcing its way through. Regrettably, her body thrilled at his sudden attention and she very nearly threw her arms around his neck and kissed him back. She barely managed to remain stone-faced and kept her lips pressed tightly together in a cold firm line.

She wanted to tell him to stop, but she was afraid that if she opened her mouth to speak, he would take it as an invitation and deepen the kiss. She couldn't push him away either. Mamun had taken advantage of her momentary astonishment to drop his hands from her face and wrap his arms tightly around her. He crushed her against his hard, broad chest and trapped her hands between them. Maddie was much stronger than she'd been before she became the Tracker, but it didn't mean that her strength was superhuman. There were still plenty of people who were stronger than she and, by the feel of his powerful body, it was likely that Mamun could overpower her in a heartbeat. If he decided he could take what he wanted, there wasn't a lot that she could do to stop him.

She stiffened in his arms and pressed her trapped arms against his embrace but Mamun wasn't taking the hint to back off. Past experiences taught him that all women were vulnerable to his charms and the woman he was currently holding would be no different. Perhaps, since she was so good and pure, she would quietly protest it for a time but in the end she would become as infatuated with him as he was with her.

He dragged his mouth from her lips and he left a path of lingering kisses across her cheek and along her neck. His hot breath scalded her flesh and she couldn't help but make small noises, thanks to her morally bankrupt body.

He lifted his face from her throat and gazed down at her with hazel eyes gone smokey with lust. He smiled in satisfaction; he had heard the same sounds from multitudes of other women and he knew the voice of passionate longing when he heard it. He kissed her again, this time sliding his tongue between her lips and teeth. He explored her mouth slowly, relishing the taste and texture of her and swearing silently to himself that he would do anything it took to possess this woman. His hands slid down her back and gripped her butt in his big, strong hands. He ground his hips into her belly, letting her feel the pressure building in his body.

Maddie thought suddenly of Sam and it occurred to her that she was doing something that he would leave her over regardless of the circumstances. She turned her head away from the kiss. Mamun took the movement as a demand for him to pay attention to other places and he began to gently suck and caress the tender spot behind her jaw. His hands kneaded her butt and pressed her hips ever more tightly against him. Maddie cleared her throat to gain control of herself. The sound brought Mamun's head up and he gazed into her eyes, looking very certain of what would take place next. Maddie crushed that certainty like a bug beneath her boot.

"Don't you think that there are more romantic places to do this sort of thing than in a dirty dungeon?" she asked as calmly as she could in a voice gone suddenly hoarse. Mamun looked abashed and he released her as if her skin burned him.

"Forgive me, lady. I…I am not myself," he said. He shook his head in an effort to clear it.

"No one is themselves today," Maddie said shakily, trying to get her own shit together while soothing the big man's hurt ego. She shifted her weight from foot to foot, noticing with dismay that her panties were feeling decidedly squishy.

He moved past her, and was careful to rub his body against her so that she could feel the hard lines of his well-shaped form. Maddie chuckled at his antics, almost feeling bad for his discomfort and for leading him on. Mamun levered the iron bars covering the cavernous opening of the cell. He looked regretfully at her as he gestured for her to enter the cell.

"Despite my wishes otherwise," Mamun said, "For now I must follow Barnum's orders. You'll be safe here for the moment. I'll return as soon as I retrieve your friends."

Maddie stepped into the reeking cell and turned to face him through the bars. Mamun reached through the bars and stroked her cheek softly with the backs of his fingers.

"I will get them back, I swear it," he said. Maddie gave him an encouraging smile and took his hand from her cheek and patted it.

"Thank you, Mamun," she said. Mamun smiled broadly when she said his name. His filed pointed teeth gleamed in the dim light, ruining his looks entirely for Maddie. She kept her face neutral while she cringed inside. She retreated to the thick blackness of the cell. Mamun turned and left the dungeon, striding confidently with his head and shoulders back as his massive arms swung.

Meanwhile, Maddie looked for a semi-clean place to sit and tried not to breathe too deeply. Eventually, the smell of fear and gore did get to her and she was forced to scramble back and forth across her cell to throw up. Soon, her stomach was completely empty and she was reduced to dry heaves. Her head pounded with sharp unbearable pain behind her eyes and at her temples. She crawled to the cleanest corner of her cell and curled up on the dirt there and rested her head on the floor.

Shortly after Maddie crawled into her corner, she began to hear the screams. The sounds of rage and agony echoed from deeper inside the dungeon and echoed fiercely against the walls. Beyond that the voices were angry and pained, Maddie couldn't tell who it was or even if they were male or female. She huddled against the dungeon walls with her hands clapped over her ears and prayed that it wasn't Fred and George doing the screaming.

After what felt like an eternity of having to listen to the terrible cries, Mamun rushed past her cell followed by a group of other very large men. He didn't even glance her way as he passed with a deep scowl turning his handsome face into a cruel mask. He made sharp, incoherent noises that the men following seemed to understand, nodding as they stepped quickly to flank and then pass him.

Maddie read the anger and frustration coloring their thoughts. The events leading to this moment had been filled with one tedious obstacle after another. They were at their limit with the brutality produced by these dungeons for much of their lives and they were eager to finally see some small revenge. Maddie managed to scramble to the bars on her hands and knees, pressing her face to the cool metal. She watched the men make their way down the corridor until they disappeared around the corner and was gone.

Men shouted and Maddie could make out names, vague threats and insults. She heard the crash of metal striking one another and then the floor. There were more shouts and insults and then silence. Maddie scrambled from the bars as heavy footsteps approached her, dragging something heavy along with them.

Mamun and his men appeared and came to a stop in front of her cell. They were angrier than when they had first gone by and their livid faces showed it. Mamun and another man had blood on their faces, which they swiped at uselessly with their hands. Two other men held George, his lean form was held limply between them with his head slumped painfully forward so that she could not see his face. Fred stood behind them, his features held carefully blank but his eyes burned with a fierce rage that frightened Maddie. There was blood splashed across the front of his shirt and the lace at his wrists was stiff and flaky. His skin was pale and clammy and only when Maddie looked closely she could see the slight tremble in his hands.

Mamun levered the door open and the two men carrying George brought him in the cell. A third man hurried to get in front of them and spread a thick clean blanket onto the center of the floor. They lowered George gently onto the blanket and he moaned as they settled him face down and arranged his limbs.

Maddie rushed to his side, her headache momentarily forgotten as she began to check the severity of his wounds. The men retreated to give her room and stood away while she pulled blood-soaked bits of charred and shredded cloth.

"Forgive me, lady," Mamun murmured regretfully. "I did all I could, but still I could not reach them in time."

Maddie turned towards him with a biting remark and the look she saw stopped her. He was angry, that was clear on his face, but there was also a terrible shame there, too. She took a moment to be sure that George would continue to breath for another few minutes and she stood up to face Mamun. The men that had accompanied him flinched and stepped back as she went to Mamun and looked into his face. She glanced at each one, feeling their shame and disdain though she couldn't understand why they felt that way.

She reached up and placed a comforting hand on his chest. Mamun's skin was hot beneath her cool touch and she had to concentrate to keep from being distracted by the smooth muscles straining under the white shirt.

"Mamun, I do not blame you for the injuries done to my men. That blame lay fully on those who did this to them. I know you did everything you could and for that I'm grateful. Thank you." She said gently.

Mamun's expression softened then, and he took her hand from his chest and held it firmly in his own. He stared directly into her eyes and seemed to search for something there. He must have found it because he wrapped her tightly in her arms and kissed her soundly. He released her abruptly and she stared panting and weak-kneed. He gave her a smug smile and bowed over her hand.

"I shall send a man with medical supplies so that you may treat your men's injuries without delay." One of Mamun's men took this as his cue to leave and he jogged out of the cell without a word. "I fear that I must leave you here for the time being. Things will be dangerous soon and you will be safest behind bars."

He turned and left the cell trailing men behind him. Maddie turned back to Fred and George the second the bars clanged closed. George's eyes were closed and his face had gone slack. He had sunk deep into unconsciousness. Fred sat next to him with a wry look in his eyes.

"You're good," he said with his lips twitching.

"What are you talking about?" she snapped, as she knelt beside him.

"You're not nearly pretty enough for men like Mamun to throw themselves at you feet. You brain-jacked that guy and he didn't even notice."

Maddie flinched and squirmed uncomfortably. "I know, I'm an evil bitch and I really shouldn't have done it. I just couldn't think straight and I was scared. I couldn't think of any other way out of this."

"You did just fine, Tracker. We all do things we do not like in order to get the job done. You needed an ally and so you made one. I cannot fault you for it."

Maddie gave Fred a grateful look even while she wondered if the man was dying. She felt his face with her hands to check if he was feverish. He pulled away from her hands and grasped her firmly by the wrists. He stared at her intently with one thought clear in his mind, *"Don't touch me."*

Astonished by the taste of anguish in his thoughts, Maddie finally really *looked* at him. Fred was among the most attractive of the Center's Agents, a fact that the torturers had not missed. The left side of his face was swollen and deeply bruised and there was a ragged cut stretching from his ear to his jaw. He held his back stiff against the wall and he sat more on his hip than directly on his bottom. He had his long legs stretched out in front of him and they were splayed as if it pained him to sit normally. His entire body shook as he dropped her wrists and looked away. From the blanket, George lifted his head and peered at them with black and swollen eyes.

"I'm sorry," he said in a trembling voice. "I tried to stop them. But there were just too many of them."

Fred shook his head and dismissed George's apology with a stiff shrug. He kept his eyes on the floor as his skin began to flush from head to toe. Both of the men's minds were like raw, open wounds. Maddie didn't try to read their thoughts; it was as if their memories and feelings were thrust upon her whether any of them liked it or not.

She saw four brutish men advance on Fred while two others held him with his arms pinned behind his back. Fred struggled as hard as he could against the men who struggled harder to contain him. The four men advanced on him and grinned lecherously and thought that there was one sure way to break a man quickly and that this man was very pretty. They looked at his blunt teeth bared in a snarl and assumed that he had more feminine passions and desires. They laughed at the thought that they would break Fred and make him enjoy it.

The first man reached out and ripped the ridiculous lace from his collar and pressed it to his face and grinned evilly at him. Fred snarled and, using the men holding him as a brace, lifted his legs and kicked two men hard in the face with the high heels of his shoes. Blood exploded from their noses and mouths as teeth were knocked from their gums and their palates were split. The pair went down while their companions screamed their rage and drew daggers from their belts. They advanced on him, their cruel purpose more solidly in their minds with a few extras added for good measure. Fred thought frantically that he would rather die than endure the torment these men had planned. He struggled violently against the men holding him and watched as the others came towards him.

But his captors held tight and one even managed to pull a metal tool from a rack on the wall beside him. It gleamed in the dull light as it was lifted to the zenith of the man's stroke and brought down hard on the side of Fred's face. The tool had a sharp edge and it sliced across his cheek and into his jaw. Fred grunted and fell to his knees as he blinked against the lights that danced in front of his eyes, the pain throbbing in his face. He was struck again, this time in the back of his skull and he fell forward in his captor's hands and vomited explosively. Somewhere, George was shouting angrily. His cries were punctuated with the thick heavy sounds of flesh being struck.

Fred's limp body was hauled roughly up and thrown face down on something flat and coarse. A man grasped him painfully by his hair and pounded his face into the flat surface until he nearly lost consciousness. Rough hands tugged at his pants and he heard the fabric rip and felt cold air move across his bare buttocks and groin. George was screaming and the men were laughing. Fred gathered enough of his wits to begin his struggle anew. He managed to get an elbow into a gut and he heard the satisfying crunch of an instep being destroyed with a well-placed stomp. A hand reached around and grasped his scrotum, squeezing. Fred arched his back in agony and screamed.

He heard a woman giggle and the soft rustle of skirts. She spoke in a slurred and incoherent voice and was given soft laughing orders by the other men. He could smell her as she approached on unstable feet. She nearly fell and put a cool hand on his butt to stop herself from tumbling. She sniggered as the men made encouraging sounds.

Fred waited for the torture to begin with his eyes clamped shut and his teeth clenched tightly together. He was prepared for the bone crushing agony, the searing pain and the smell of his own burning flesh. He was ready to fight for his life under the bruising weight of suffocating water. The woman giggled again and he felt something hot and wet engulf his penis. He gasped as he felt sucking, gentle at first and with increased pressure as it moved down to the base of his manhood. The sensation felt good, which shocked him into immobility and the mouth began to eagerly slide up and down his shaft. He felt her moan while a mild and pleasurable vibration tore a groan from his throat. He clenched his teeth harder to stop making any further sounds as his penis grew long and erect in the whore's mouth. She made delighted sounds and her delicate fingers stroked the inside of his thighs and his testicles. Against his will, he could feel the pressure building and he had to fight to keep from thrusting as hard as he could into the wet pleasure along his body.

At the height of his reluctant ecstasy, callused hands parted the cheeks of his buttocks and then he felt a sharp stabbing pain that pierced the length of his body. Fred screamed in agony even as the whore brought him over into an orgasm, forcing his body into convulsions that wracked him over and over. He could hear men laughing and George screaming with rage.

Maddie slammed her mind closed with a sobbing cry. Tears poured down her cheeks and blessedly obscured her vision of the man huddled miserably in front of her. He was angry at what had been done to him and felt ashamed at what he thought he had allowed to happen. The worst part was the pleasure he had felt during the terrible attack. He would never forget it and he loathed himself all the more for it.

"Are you okay?" Maddie knew it was a stupid question but she didn't know what else to say. Of course he wasn't okay. He might never be okay ever again. Maddie wanted to throw her arms around him and comfort him. Of course, she couldn't do that, the very thought of being touched made Fred want to vomit. He might fly into a hysterical rage if she came too close to him. She needed him to hold it together, at least long enough for them to get out of here.

Fred had ignored the idiotic question. He had sunk far into a quiet and pleasant place in his mind where he seemed content to stay until he was needed again. Maddie watched him helplessly for a moment then turned back to George. He had lost consciousness again and she fussed over his prone body and tried not to pay attention to the pounding migraine that insisted on trying to blind her.

She was trembling and nauseous when one of Mamun's men appeared carrying a steaming pitcher and bowl. He handed them through the bars to Fred then passed a thick, folded package over. Fred accepted all of it without a word and brought them to Maddie. The man didn't wait to see what was done with the things he brought. The moment that he was relieved of his burdens, he was out of sight. He had known what had happened to Fred and he was ashamed to be near him. Maddie fought the urge to shout insults after the asshole as Fred set out the pitcher and bowl and unwrapped the package to reveal a neat mass of bandages.

Maddie poured the hot contents of the pitcher into the bowl and smelled the scent of medicinal herbs as the steam bathed her face. Fred had already retreated to his corner so Maddie decided to leave him alone and tend to George while the Agent was still out cold. She wiped away the blood from the tattered wounds of his back, marveling that the burns, cuts, and bruises were not as bad as she had first thought. The score marks were shallow and the places where hot irons had been applied to his body no longer had the charred look about them and were merely blistered.

By the time Maddie had finished washing George's back and was unrolling the bandages, the wounds were almost healed and scarring up. She stared with open-mouthed fascination as a long cut knitted itself and faded away without a mark. Her astonishment must have reached Fred because he shifted in his dark corner and spoke.

"The nanopacks assist with the healing of the damage done to our bodies. They speed healing and recovery from a few weeks to just a couple of hours. Both of us will be healthy in just a little while."

Maddie finished with George and moved to Fred. He let her look at him, even though he remained adamantly hands off. The swelling had gone down considerably and the deep purple bruises had faded to greenish yellow. Instead of bathing Fred's face for him, Maddie offered Fred a fresh cloth soaked with fresh water from the pitcher. Fred took it without expression and scrubbed at his face. Maddie turned away to give him his privacy and settled down next to George. Her head was in agony and her stomach threatened to expel the bile boiling in her guts. Her skin flared with a hot blush that left her panting for breath.

"Are you alright?" Fred asked from his corner. "I can smell the heat coming off of you like you're on fire."

"Just a hot flash," Maddie muttered miserably.

"Aren't you a little young for that?" he asked. His voice was low and neutral, like he didn't really care. Maybe he did, maybe he didn't. Maddie didn't really care either. She was too miserable to think about it.

"Not young enough," she replied. "I'm in my thirties, plenty old enough for hot flashes."

Fred nodded and accepted this. He fell silent as he finished cleaning himself and settled back into his corner. He sank bitterly into his head and did not notice when Maddie fell over onto the floor next to George.

CHAPTER 26

Keung sat in his office and waited. He was deep in thought and stared vacantly out of the glass partition between his office and the Control Room without truly seeing what was happening. The events of the last two days had been troubling to say the least and, in the end, he was forced to contact the Quarter for official orders. So, while he waited for a reply, he sat and brooded and fumed.

Outwardly, he appeared as calm as he always did. His stoic expression and impeccable clothing remained unchanged as he lounged in his plush leather chair and rested his steepled fingers against his lips.

Inwardly, he was boiling with anger. The Tracker's family was under attack and the Distari were acting boldly and without concern of discovery. It made him nervous to see a sudden change in their behavior, and he pondered the solutions as he thought of the problems. He knew better than anyone that the attack on the children had not been a serious one. If the Distari had truly wanted the children dead, there wouldn't have been anyone left alive to say what had happened. With the murders of the Andersons and the Escobars, there was no doubt in Keung's mind that the Distari were attempting to flush the Tracker out. Why they were choosing to do so now was not as troubling as the fact that they had discovered the identity of the Tracker. That had not occurred since the time of William Demonsbane.

On occasion, Sherman poked his head into the office with papers that needed Keung's review and signature before they went into the Library. Keung reviewed the paperwork, barely seeing what he was reading, and scrawled his signature on the bottom before sending the young man on his way.

Finally, just when Keung was running out of patience and was about to make crucial decisions on his own, the wishes of the Quarter be damned, the air in his office began to thicken. Keung drew long, deep, laboring breaths as it became more difficult to draw the thick air into his lungs. A dark figure, neither short nor tall, fat nor thin, male or female appeared before his desk. The figure's limbs were defined by soft light as well as the slender torso, the long neck and the slightly oversized head. The Quarter's features and the details of his clothing remained shrouded in darkness so nothing about the individual could be identified.

Keung was able to breathe more easily as the figure solidified, and he moved to close the blinds over the glass partition and smooth the nonexistent wrinkles from his suit. He assumed the proper subservient attitude as the figure came to its final solidity. This was no mere projection, The Quarter were coming to him in person to discuss the things he had just hinted at in his report. Keung made a small sigh of relief when the air thinned back out and returned to normal.

The Quarter moved, lifting his face and regarding him with a tilt if his head. His arms, which had been stiff at his sides during the journey, were now clasped calmly behind his back. He stood at parade rest, projecting a sense of ease and discipline.

"We received your troubling reports regarding the Tracker's heirs. We are wondering how such a thing could have happened during the watch of such a responsible and capable Keeper."

Keung flinched a little at the implied insult. His first priority was to safeguard the Tracker's safety, that of her family and the secret of the Quarter. An attack on the Tracker's family was perceived as a threat to everything the Center wanted to accomplish.

"The Distari have grown bolder, sir. The logical conclusion for their recent activities is that they have grown desperate in their own efforts to attain their goals and seek to use the Tracker's family to tip the balance in their favor."

"It does not answer the question of the Tracker's safety. How is it that the Tracker's heirs have been identified for the first time since the time of William? Such a thing is unforgivable, Keeper. Part of our contract with the Tracker is to guarantee the safety of the Tracker's family and peace of mind. Should that contract be violated, she would be within her rights to take whatever action she deemed necessary against all she perceived as a threat. I, for one, would not like to be seen as a threat by an angry Tracker. Would you?"

"No, sir, I would not," Keung replied. He doubted that they were under any real threat from the current Tracker. As she was now, she couldn't do much with her rage except stammer incoherently and stamp her foot at people. Perhaps one day she may become a formidable figure but, for now, she still strongly resembled the silly and bored housewife that she had once been. Still, he did not enjoy the hours of shrieking and the long bitchfests she could unleash when she was upset. He assumed that her hysterics were much worse and he would go to great lengths to avoid the experience.

"I request permission to bring the Tracker's family into the safety of the Center. To do so would free up the manpower I need to locate and eliminate the lair that currently threatens the heirs."

"Denied. Simply reinforce the current complement of Agents guarding the family."

"Sir, the family lives in a relatively isolated neighborhood. We cannot even rely on the local police force to assist us in case of the worst. They are simply too far away. There are many flaws in security in the home itself to protect them adequately. Bringing them into the Center's fold would guarantee their safety."

"No, Keeper. Find the flaws and correct them. Bringing the family into the Center would jeopardize the secrecy we need to move as freely within the five galaxies as we do. This is intolerable." The Quarter snapped irritably.

"Sir, the marriage is falling apart. Allowing the family to know some of the secrets would salvage the relationship and keep the family intact.

Allowing the Tracker to maintain contact and knowledge of her heirs' location and well-being has always been a goal as well."

"Do not presume to remind us what our goals are and have always been. You overstep your bounds. The Tracker's personal life has always been and always will be her responsibility and her problem. If she cannot maintain her family, it is because of her own doing. Do not further press this issue, Keeper."

Keung sighed in frustration, knowing that the Quarter had said all they would about the matter and would refuse to compromise on the issue, no matter how logical it was. Even more illogically, he knew he would follow the order.

"As always, we watch the events in the areas in which Trackers make their home. We do not like what you have reported there as well as the things we have seen. How is it that a single Distari lair has eluded you for so long?"

Keung had no answer for that. To be truthful, he had not known that they were in the north Georgia town. It had been so long since he had to think about the Distari, that he had not expected them to suddenly appear, much less identify the family. He remained silent, embarrassed of his oversight and unable to defend it.

"Are you aware of the murders in the region?"

"I am. No doubt the cases will go cold and eventually forgotten, as they always are."

"The Tracker's sister works to catch the killers. She is already too close to the Tracker and the Tracker is a careless woman. Should Ms. Arnold ask her sister the wrong questions, the Tracker could end centuries of careful secrecy."

"I understand." Keung didn't understand. What was he supposed to do? Kill the woman? Kidnap her? Laying a false trail would require manpower he didn't have, and it might blow up in his face anyway. Darlene Arnold was a clever woman; he didn't expect her to remain fooled about anything for very long.

"If you have trouble locating the Lair, release Shorn and allow him to sniff it out for you. He has a talent for locating Distari."

"Of course," Keung replied. Shorn was one of the very few citizens of this planet who firmly believed in the existence of the Tracker and Distari. But unlike all the other paranoid and half-crazy individuals who followed the local legends, Alcott Shorn had spent the last twenty years gathering evidence to prove what he knew to be true. The problem was that during an inspection of the man's home, the Agents had found that the man had collected some very compelling evidence to back up his claims. The Center left him alone, mostly because he was considered a harmless crackpot by most of the world and because the man had an uncanny knack for finding useful artifacts and Distari lairs.

Keung nodded silently by way of reply. The Quarter abruptly left without another word with a cold whoosh of air. Keung collapsed in his chair and smoothed his mussed hair and took calming breaths. Then he called Sherman into his office and began to relay the orders he'd been given.

*　　　*　　　*

Sherman sat behind the Tracker's desk, contemplating the telephone perched on the corner of the gleaming surface. What he was thinking about doing was against every oath he'd taken when he entered the Center. But he couldn't help but listen to the conversation between Keung and the representative from the Quarter. The Keeper had made some very valid points on the Tracker's behalf. But Keung could do nothing about the problems. Of all the people employed by the Center, the Keeper was the most closely watched. As a simple assistant and gopher, Sherman held the least of the Quarter's interest. So it was left to him to do the things that Keung could not do.

The only problem was that he was held under the same shackles of the nanopack that everyone else was. They were programmed to detect any acts of treason or violation of the iron laws. If he did or said anything that went against the laws, he would suffer painfully for it or even killed. He did not want that to happen more than anything. It was all very well and good to act secretly on the Tracker's behalf but it was quite another to die miserably while he did it. He would have to be very cautious with his thoughts and words to avoid that miserable fate.

The decision made, he grasped the phone in his sweaty hand and cleared his mind. He punched in the numbers that would connect him to the Tracker's home and waited for the husband to answer. It took four rings for the Tracker's husband to answer the phone.

"Hello?"

The man's voice startled Sherman. He had expected a lot of things from the sort of man that would be wedded to the Tracker. But a melodious speaking voice had not been one of them. A mental picture of a very pretty man popped into his head and he thrust it hurriedly away.

"Samuel?" he asked, just to be certain of the voice's identity. The Tracker had two brothers and her father was still living and any of them could be visiting the house. He could not simply begin talking to the wrong person. It was one thing to blurt out Center secrets to the husband but it was wholly another to speak of them to siblings who would most likely have nothing to do with it.

"This is he. May I ask who is calling?"

"Look within your home, husband," Sherman said cryptically. His spine began to tingle and he felt his bowels loosen.

"I beg your pardon?"

"Look within your home for the answers you seek."

"Who is this?" the husband was angry now, his melodious voice had become harsh and hard.

146

"The lives of your children depend upon it." Sherman nearly shouted the last sentence and slammed the phone down while Sam was still sputtering in anger. Sherman's arm was convulsing painfully. His bowels had evacuated themselves and his back muscles were screaming in agony. He pushed back from the desk and fled from the office. He cradled his agonized arm as he ran for his room. People jumped out of his way, casting startled and alarmed looks after him. His nose had begun to bleed profusely and he was getting blood on his shirt and leaving drops of it on the floor. He hit his bedroom door and he slammed the door shut behind him and collapsed onto his bed, moaning in agony.

CHAPTER 27

Sam hung up the phone and stared at it as if it had come to life in his hand and bitten him. The call he'd just received had been the creepiest of his life and it made his skin crawl. He was locked into frightening and foreboding thoughts when Katie's small high voice lifted from the broad kitchen entryway.

"Daddy? What's wrong?"

He tore his eyes from the phone and stared at her like she had suggested that the sky was green. She stared back with a frightened look on her face and fiddled nervously with her shirt. Katie hadn't slept well since that terrible day at school when she'd been forced to run for her life. Even in the hospital she had to be sedated so that she would sleep and still she woke screaming in the night. Now that she was home, the nightmares were worse. She slept only when the fatigue overwhelmed her and she just couldn't stay awake anymore. Her fair skin was gray and her blue eyes were rimmed with red with dark shadows underneath.

Chris appeared beside her, his eyes looking as haunted as his sister's did. He was sleeping in fits and spent his days playing lethargically by himself and saying nothing. Neither child had been back to school since it happened and the merest suggestion of their return sent them both into hysterics.

"Is Momma coming home?" Chris asked, speaking the first words he'd uttered that day. Sam looked away from them without answering. His thoughts went back to the strange phone call and what he should do about it. The caller ID had listed the number as unknown and dialing star 69 had simply told him that the number was unlisted. He could ignore the call as a crank; there had certainly been enough of those since the story about Katie broke in the news. He could report the call to the police, but it seemed unlikely that they could do anything about it beyond tapping his phones and waiting for the guy to call back. Or he could simply search the house for any signs of anything out of the ordinary.

He stared at the kitchen and found everything exactly as he kept it. He wandered out into the living room and everything looked normal. He checked the kids' bedroom and bathrooms and found those to be perfectly normal too. He even looked under the beds dug through the closets. Again, he didn't find anything out of the ordinary. But the strange voice in his head kept repeating itself, urging him to keep looking. Which was how he found himself standing in front of a locked door at the foot of his basement stairs. Maddie had appropriated the space after she had first taken her job and closed it off to the rest of the family. No one went in there. Maddie even avoided the place as often as she could. He had no idea where she kept the keys and hadn't even bothered to look. He gripped the screwdriver tightly in his hand and looked down at the knob.

He set to work on it, prying the knobs from the door and jamming it into the mechanism and levering the latch out of the doorframe. The door swung open easily and Sam stood up to stare into the dark room within.

"Daddy? What are you doing? Mommy says no one can go in there," Katie said from the stairs. She startled him and made him jump half a foot in the air. His jump frightened her and she jerked and nearly fell down the stairs.

"Katie!" Sam shouted his heart pounding in his chest. "Mind your own business! Go back upstairs and find something to do!"

Katie gave him a hurt look as she ran back up the stairs. Sam turned back to the doorway and entered the dark office and flipped on the lights. The dark room became bright so abruptly that it stung his eyes. Sam squinted until his eyes adjusted to the change and he was able to see the rooms clearly. He gaped at Maddie's office in pure astonishment. The room was severely kept with nothing to indicate who might occupy the place. Everything looked functional and uncomfortable as if Maddie found no rest or refuge in the place and never wanted to.

The racks that lined the walls held weapons of every sort and shape imaginable. There were guns, some obviously antiques and some modern, while others looked as if they came from a science fiction comic. There were swords, many of which looked ancient in style and design. She had sturdy bows with elaborate arrows, staffs made from wood or metal, staves, pikes and other things he couldn't recognize. There was furniture shoved into corners along with pieces of neatly stacked and oddly designed armor as well as weird costumes hanging from hooks.

In the room's only empty corner sat a battered desk with Maddie's computer on it. He went through the drawers and found the bits of the chocolates Maddie favored as well as an assortment of pens and notepads. There were some disks held in a case but Sam left them alone when he couldn't figure out how to turn the computer on. He stepped back and looked at it all and tried to comprehend what his wife was doing when she was away from home. By the looks of things, it appeared that she had become a gunrunner or an illegal antique dealer, or some sort strange of combination of both.

He felt sick to his stomach as he began to berate himself for missing something this crucial. After all, she was making more money than he thought she could possibly make in a research job. She left town for long periods of time and she never talked about her work. How could he be so blind? How could she do this to them? If the cops searched the house now, they would no doubt arrest Maddie for possession of an illegal weapon. Hell, the room was a veritable arsenal that would pull his wife a life sentence.

Next to the desk was a narrow doorway. He tried the knob and found that the door was unlocked. He opened it, hoping that whatever he found in there would explain clearly what Maddie was doing and that all of it was harmless and perfectly legal. He was confronted by a narrow room lined with shelves and packed with books, scrolls and stacks of paper loosely bound with string. There were hooks hanging from the shelves from which hung medallions of assorted sizes and attached to gold and silver chains. Sam pulled one off the hook and stared at the tangle of twisted metal set with diamonds. All of the medallions were of the same design and there were a dozen of them.

He hung the medallion back on its hook and pulled a book from the shelf nearest to him. The book contained strange writing in an angular calligraphy. None of the words written in thick, red ink made any sense to him. The pages weren't made of paper but from some sort of smooth thick material that didn't crease when the page was folded. Shaking his head, Sam replaced the thick leather bound volume and pulled a scroll from a stack on another shelf.

He opened it gently since the tightly rolled paper was thin and looked very delicate despite the fact that it was clearly new. The scroll contained an ink drawing so well-rendered that it looked as if the picture had been woven into the thin paper. The colors were vibrant and each detail was perfect. He opened the scroll completely, spreading his arms wide to do so. He nearly dropped the thing when he realized what he was looking at.

It was a drawing of the beasts that had been stalking his family. In this picture the monster was displayed in a diagram, detailing every inch of it inside and out. The organs had been drawn so that the insides were displayed in detail with tiny strange writing accompanying each diagram. In the border of the drawing was a word written in black bold lettering, declaring itself and forcing the eye towards it: Distari.

With shaking hands, Sam carefully rolled the scroll up and returned it to its place on the shelf. His spinning thoughts rapidly drew the only conclusion he could make in the face of the evidence in Maddie's office. She was involved in something illegal and she had drawn these beasts to her family. Worse yet, she had known that these things were hunting them and she hadn't said a word about it to her husband. He couldn't imagine why she would do such a thing.

Rage was the only word for the burning sensation filling his chest. It was so intense that he was panting from it. His fists were clenched at his sides and he didn't notice that his nails were biting deeply into his palms. His body shook with the force of his rage and it was some time before he gained enough control of himself to move without falling.

He rushed up the stairs and went in search of the phone. Katie and Chris gave him frightened looks when they saw his fierce expression. He didn't want them to hear the things he was about to say to their mother. He snapped his fingers and ordered them to their rooms. They scrambled to do as they were told, knowing that now would be a terrible moment to make the slightest protest.

Sam nearly broke the phone as he dialed Maddie's personal work number. He seethed as he waited for her to pick up.

CHAPTER 28

It had taken the press no time at all to connect the murders of the two families to the attack at the local elementary school. They dutifully reported the speculations of anyone with a half a brain and willing to get in front of the cameras, which further fueled the rising hysteria. For the first few hours, only local news media were making their reports but the bigger conglomerates soon caught on and began to descend on the small north Georgia town. Within twenty-four hours, the story was being aired on every news channel in the country as well as the few international channels. The entire event was rapidly spiraling out of control, causing no end of trouble for local law enforcement.

The woman who had died for the Johnston children was given a hero's memorial to which the entire town attended. The press covered that, too, obtaining comments and interviews from the frightened locals in attendance. The Johnston children had attended the event as well but their father had whisked them away before the cameras could focus on them.

The press had found a leak in the police's ranks and managed to milk a few gruesome details of the carnage of the murder scenes. The details grew with the telling and soon it was hard to tell the difference between fact and fiction. Meanwhile the station's one man press department was going crazy trying to field the flood of calls coming from reporters who were asking for information and interviews for their stories.

The entire community had gone into a panic. They were locking their doors for the first time in decades and making sure their windows were tightly secured. They were afraid to send their children to school and more calls poured into the station's phone lines and bogged the system down with hundreds of leads and frightened complaints. Police personnel were being stretched thinly in the force's attempts to meet the hysterical demands of their community. Patrolmen, down to those who ordinarily worked traffic detail, were reassigned to help calm panicked citizens and to examine potential crime scenes. Higher-ranking officers and every detective were set to track down every tip and lead that poured through the phones. Most of the information was the false, hysterical imaginings of frightened people and the very few legitimate leads were too vague to be of any use.

Since the explosion of bad publicity had begun, the men who felt most of the sting were those who led the department and gave the orders. More than anyone, they were desperate to catch their killer but they were extremely wary of rushing the investigation faster than it could go. They were painfully aware that the world would be scrutinizing their every move, ready to leap like rabid dogs on any mistake the detectives made on the case. The ensuing criticism and scandal would most likely cost many jobs. Which was why it took several hours for Arnold to convince her superiors to request a search warrant for Alcott Shorn's house. Thankfully, Cooper had gone to bat for her despite the fact that he thought that the man was just a harmless crackpot. But, historically, harmless crackpots have turned out to be some of the most notorious killers, so her partner had backed her up. It was their only lead so far, so he stood strongly beside her while she lay out all the evidence she had. They examined the weird pictures provided by the suspect himself and the bizarre statement given by Shorn's "girlfriend."

By the time they finally agreed that the current evidence justified a search warrant, it was too late to contact a judge to get it. Arnold started to put on the pressure to wake someone up but the lieutenant decided that Shorn was not a flight risk and that the request could wait until first thing in the morning when the judges were awake.

Disgusted by her superior's reluctance to make a decision quickly enough to be acted upon in a prompt manner, Arnold fumed her way to car. She planned to order the most gluttonous pizza possible and eat herself into a stupor the moment she got home. Her waistline wouldn't thank her for it but, as stress-relieving habits went, compulsive eating wasn't really all that bad.

A group of uniformed officers were leaning against their marked cars and gossiping in the parking lot. They spoke and laughed loudly, their conversation peppered by the squawking of the dispatcher coming from their radios. Their day had been as hard as hers had and no doubt they were exhausted. But the constant infusion of stress and bad coffee was combining forces to keep them over-stimulated and wide-awake.

Suddenly, the dispatcher shouted an urgent all units call for a possible murder in progress. She gave out the address and time of call before saying, "I think this might be our guy!"

The men started moving the second she'd made the call an all units but they moved faster when they realized how close the address was to their location and they nearly ran when the dispatch made the final declaration. Arnold knew that it was all she needed to hear. She jumped into her car and raced out of the parking lot and followed the speeding patrol cars with their flashing lights and their sirens wailing into the deep autumn darkness

It took only minutes for them to reach the house. By the time Arnold slammed on her brakes and leaped from her car, the adrenaline was pumping furiously through her body and she was fervently praying to God that they reach the family in time. She didn't know if she could face the deaths of another group of innocents.

They could hear the terrified screams of agony coming from the house as they ran to the front door with their hands on their weapons. The shrieks lasted for long, agonizing seconds as they hit the door and the sturdy wood stopped them cold. Arnold stepped back to let the men work and prayed that the screaming would continue. The cries meant that they were still alive and, so long as they screamed, no matter how horrible it sounded, it meant that they were still alive. And while they were still alive, there was still hope.

Officers Dewitt and Carroll began to kick frantically at the door in an effort to break it down. Frantic and impatient, Reid picked up a rocking chair from the small porch and lifted it over his head. He sent it crashing through the picture window in a shower of glass. Fielding was through the shattered window in a flash, his gun and flashlight drawn and ready. Arnold watched him go and thought that things were already going terribly wrong, that they were not doing things with safety and procedure in mind as they were supposed to. But she said nothing. Like the men beside her, she was desperate to get to the screaming family beyond the door.

Fielding opened the front door to let the rest of them pass into the house. So far, the scene lacked the total destruction displayed by all the other murder scenes before this. The house was dark and, wherever the flashlight beams touched, there were splashes of bright fresh blood. Reid took point followed by Dewitt, Carroll, Fielding and, finally, Arnold. None of them spoke as they rushed to the back of the house where the screams originated. Animal shrieks had added their voices to the cacophony of death and terror and echoed off the brittle drywall. A man's dismembered arm lay in the middle of the short hall. The officers stepped over it in their haste, barely checking the empty rooms they passed in their eagerness to get their killer.

Arnold's heart was in her throat as she concentrated more on covering the men's backs rather than the screaming coming from the next room. There was a stench of more than just blood and death in the air but of something more foreign and evil. The smell burnt her nose and turned her stomach and she knew it was something that would haunt her dreams for the rest of her life. Her heart was pounding so hard that her head began to ache. She kept thinking that, in their haste, they were doing something wrong, that there was something that they were forgetting or overlooking.

Dewitt kicked the flimsy bedroom door open and began screaming police presence and that everyone one should get down on the floor. But his voice faltered and then stopped mid-sentence. The screaming had reduced itself to terrified whimpers and small sounds of pain. There were four sharp intakes of breath and Reid cried out in shock and horror. Arnold turned and looked over the men's shoulders and stared in horror at the mad scene that assaulted her brain.

A young mother and her two children huddled together on a mattress set on the floor. She clutched her two sons protectively against her body while her hands covered their eyes to keep them from seeing what was happening. The father lay on the floor at the opposite end of the bed, his brown eyes staring vacantly and his blood pouring from his body and pooling on the threadbare carpet.

Bending over the man's body was a creature so big, twisted and distorted that it could barely be called human. It pulled a bloody muzzle-like face from the gaping wound in the father's abdomen and snarled in a red spray at them. There were three more of the things in the room with the first, these ones more deformed and animalistic than the one eating at the man.

Two were crouched at the foot of the bed and were paused in the process of slowly advancing on the woman and children. A third one crouched, waiting in a corner, its terrible face twisted into a leering grin. Four sets of monstrous eyes turned and looked at the cops filling the doorway. Their victims didn't seem to notice that help had arrived. They continued to stare in horror at the creatures that had attacked them. Time seemed to stand still as the two groups regarded each other.

Then the deformed monsters moved in an explosion of blood and time. Men screamed and fired their weapons as the beasts moved almost too fast for them to see. Gunfire erupted as the first of the monsters slammed into the small crowd confronting it and burrowed in hungrily with teeth and claws. The bullets did little to stop them. They paused briefly whenever small holes erupted in their bodies but they shook it off and came on anyway.

Dewitt went down first, screaming in terror as the beast rode him to the floor, gnawing at his throat. The other four retreated immediately as predator and prey collapsed together in the doorway, blocking the path of the others. No one wanted to leave the family to the mercy of the monsters, so they stopped as a group a few feet from the short hall and opened fire upon the beasts as they clamored over the pair locked in a deadly embrace. The woman and children began to scream again, their shrieks shattering what little remained of the sanity inside these walls.

The monsters galloped on all fours like animals at the officers. Reid was screaming and uselessly emptying his gun at monsters that barely noticed. Fielding was screaming frantically into his radio, calling for back-up while Carroll and Arnold continued to hold their guns aimed and waited for their deaths to come to them.

The monsters cleared the hall with two short lurches and struck with lightening speed. Reid fell clutching his throat, making a gurgling scream as blood sprayed against the wall. Fielding's face disintegrated in a flash of claws and flesh. Carroll fell under a massive ball of teeth and twisted flesh, screaming and fighting all the way to the floor.

Arnold stumbled away from the mass of screaming and bleeding bodies, unable to believe her luck that she was still unscathed. She gripped her gun with both hands and searched for a target. The flashlights had been lost somewhere in the retreat and in the darkness it was hard to tell what was human and what was monster. She found a target that looked misshapen and shot it without thinking. The bullet struck the monster's head, sending blood and brains across the room. The monster slumped on top a still-struggling Carroll and stopped moving. She turned her gun to the next deformed monster and took careful aim.

She suddenly flailed helplessly as she spun uncontrollably, first in one direction and then another. She couldn't breathe and the cold rawness of her throat was replaced by the hot metallic taste of blood. She gasped, struggling to draw breath into her lungs only to choke on the thick liquid beginning to fill the vital organs. Her eyes bulged in her head and she spun around again She had dropped her gun somehow and found herself staring stupidly down at it. Her head snapped back on her shoulders, bringing with it an overpowering agony and she found that her legs could no longer hold her up.

The screaming intensified as she slowly collapsed on the floor. Blood filled her eyes and painted her vision red until everything faded and grew and became blackness.

CHAPTER 29

Maddie was only dimly aware of the voices talking urgently around her. She simply lay where she had landed when she collapsed, her cheek resting in whatever filth she had fallen in. Her nose told her that it was something particularly foul but she couldn't bring herself to care. Caring would have required her to move and she wasn't the least bit interested in moving a muscle. Her eyes were tightly closed despite the shuffling going on around the dungeon. Not because she wasn't interested in what was happening around her, but because she didn't have the strength to lift her eyelids. A large, warm hand rested gently on her back and added more heat to the scalding temperature of her skin and began to carefully shake her. Every motion he made sent a spasm of agony through her body. She whimpered as her skull began to scream and every joint in her body awoke to pain.

"She's awake," a man said softly over her head.

"Is it safe to move her?" A face leaned close to her cheek, his breath hot on her burning face. The hand moved from her back to her throat and rested lightly on her pulse.

"She's tougher than she looks. She just needs to get out of this hole."

Maddie would have cringed at the thought of moving around but it would have hurt too much to do it. Two pairs of hands grasped her by her arms and shoulders, lifting her carefully from the filthy floor. She cried out as her body wracked with pain that left her shuddering from head to foot.

"She's convulsing."

Strong arms wrapped around her body and held her tight until she finally stopped trembling. Maddie hardly noticed. Her stomach had declared open war on her and she didn't have the strength to fight it. She bent slightly forward at the waist and vomited violently, woe to anyone standing in front of her. She heard swearing and the shuffling of boots in the dirt as she brought up bile and stomach acid on whoever was standing in front of her. She couldn't bring herself to care, though, as she simply took a deep painful breath and sagged into the arms that held her.

There was a heated debate which Maddie ignored. Abruptly she was urged forward with a firm poke in the ribs that nearly sent her retching again. She took the required step forward just to make it stop. She whined in protest, wanting only to lie back down in the funk on the floor. She was poked again and she walked forward. Soon she was in full-stride and hating every minute of it. She kept her head down and her eyes closed as she walked. She only changed directions when someone pulled on her arm and stopped when someone tugged on her shoulder. She had no idea where she was, no clue of where she was going. And, frankly, she didn't care.

She was pulled to a stop and someone jammed a hat down on her head. She wept openly from the slight weight and pressure of the garment against her scalp. She heard a heavy scraping noise of something massive being dragged against stone. It shattered her eardrums and sent shock waves of agony through her head and down her neck. She would have fallen from it but a strong arm wrapped itself firmly around her waist and kept her on her feet.

She was thrust out into sunlight so bright that it lit the insides of her eyeballs a bright orange. She was pushed into walking forward. She reeled at the movement and the cacophony of sound coming from the city around her. The crowd jostled her relentlessly and she stumbled over cracks and obstacles left in her path.

Just as Maddie's knees were about to buckle from the pain and her confounded senses, she was pulled into a dark cool place. She cried in relief, her tears leaving cool paths down her scorching cheeks. It felt so good that she cried more, sobbing hysterically and making a mess. The hat was pulled from her head and she was settled almost comfortably into a chair. A feminine voice joined the masculine chatter and scolded them softly. Cool slender hands touched Maddie's forehead and murmured in astonishment. There was a further discussion between the female voice and one of the men. An arm hooked itself under her knees and another gathered her around her shoulders and cradled her like a child, as there was talk of a fever and someone suffering from brain damage. Maddie wished that the voices would just shut-up and let her lie down somewhere.

She panted with relief as the voices finally fell silent and she was carried up a short flight of stairs. She was set down on something flat and soft while a cool damp cloth was placed across her forehead. She lay there complacently while someone tugged at her clothing. There was more urgent whispering as people moved around her filling things with water and set things down on tables. She ignored it all and let herself sink into sweet, painless oblivion at long last.

When she awoke, she was dressed in a loose sleeveless sleeping gown. She was clean and her skin felt cool. Her hair lay loose and sweetly fragrant across the enormous pillow. She was tucked comfortably between smooth sheets and a single thin, soft blanket. The open window beside her revealed that night had fallen once more. The room was draped in darkness save for a single oil lamp glowing weakly on a small table in a far corner of the room.

She stretched, happily noting that the pain in her joints was gone and her migraine had mellowed to a dull ache in the back of her head. She turned in the bed and saw the large hump of a man sleeping beside her. At first she smiled, thinking in her sleepy mind that Keung had finally sent Sam to her side to comfort her. But the longer she stared at the broad back, the more she saw that the heavy muscles, the defined arm resting along the slim waist and narrow hips resembled nothing of her husband. With a gasp she sat bolt upright in the bed. She stared wide-eyed at Mamun sleeping peacefully next to her in the bed. His dark head rested on a large pillow similar to hers with a big arm curled underneath it. Appalled by the man's nerve that he thought he could get away with sharing her bed, Maddie twisted on the mattress and planted a cold foot against the small of his back. Mamun's eyes flew open the second her foot touched his skin and he was in the process of turning and grasping for her ankle when she gave him a powerful shove. Mamun fell out of the bed with a surprised yelp and a dull thud. His tousled head came up over the edge of the bed and glared at her as she gathered the bedding up and clutched it to her chest.

"What is wrong with you?" Mamun demanded. Maddie gave him a scathing look as she struggled out of the bed to put the massive piece of furniture more completely between them.

"What do you think you're doing in my bed?" Maddie retorted.

"I was sleeping!" Mamun snapped. He got to his feet using the mattress to pull himself up. He was shirtless which revealed his impressive and, Maddie had to admit lovely chest and rippling belly exposed over a pair of very loose pants.

"Couldn't you have found another bed to sleep in?" Maddie asked. "This is an inn. I'm fairly certain that there was someplace else you could have slept."

"I could have, yes. But since George went to his bed the second we entered your rooms and Fred went whoring, it was decided that I should be the one to look after your safety and health."

"Well, thank you for putting yourself out like that," Maddie sneered. "But as you can see, I'm perfectly healthy and quite safe. You can go now." She pointed at the door, leaving the man with no doubt about what she wanted him to do. Mamun gave her a look that should have left her cowed but didn't and gathered up his belongings scattered all over the room. Maddie watched him suspiciously, giving him the sensation that she thought he was going to jump upon her in a rut and rape her. Mamun rolled his eyes and left, slamming the door behind him.

Once he was gone, Maddie went in search of clothes. She found hers cleaned and folded neatly next to the dim lamp. She dressed slowly, afraid that any sudden movement might bring back the migraine. As she pulled her shirt over her head, she began to get small glimpses of memory from the day's events. She remembered Fred and George's ordeal and she remembered tending their wounds. She couldn't quite remember at which point she had become ill but she did recall being awakened from her stupor and being held in strong comforting arms.

She flinched when she remembered how she had used her powers and her own feminine whiles to enlist Mamun's help. She groaned in disgust at her own actions and prayed that she had not done any lasting harm to the man. In the past, she had always disdained women who used manipulation tactics on men to get what they wanted. In a single act of hypocrisy, she had stooped to their level and had jacked Mamun's mind and forced him to do her bidding. She hadn't even bothered to open her mouth and ask him to help her. He had turned out to be a fairly decent guy. He might have helped her if she had asked and now she'd never know for certain.

She could feel his resentment and confusion from the other side of the door. She remembered the short make-out session they'd shared in the dank dungeon and felt her face flush with embarrassment. The man had every right to be pissed at her. She'd been running hot and cold with him since he set eyes on her and it wasn't right. With her hand on the doorknob, she decided that, while she wasn't about to tell him that she had screwed with his head, she would be unfailingly nice to him and stick with it.

At the thought of Mamun, she felt a familiar ache below her belly button. She paused at exiting the room and realized that the window was fully open to the night. She hurried to it and closed it tightly. The small vial of clear liquid that the prostitute had given her in gratitude sat on a small table near the bed. She scooped it up and dabbed the content under each nostril, breathing deeply of the sharp astringent scent as it filled her nose. The scent did little to ease the ache but it did stop it from becoming overwhelming. Maddie decided that it was good enough and she finally left her bedroom.

As she entered the small meeting room, Maddie saw that George was awake and dressed. He sat hunched over a plate of food in one corner. A quick peek into his mind revealed no signs of the pain and trauma from his ordeal of the night before. He was actually in a good mood and his thought process was as sharp as ever. Mamun was at the single tiny window, fully dressed and glaring out at the street below. He kept his back to the room, his anger radiating clearly from his body. George thought that the whole thing was endlessly amusing and he was laughing silently.

"Where's Fred?" Maddie asked, sternly ignoring George's mental laughter.

"He's out coping. Don't worry, he'll be back safe and sound very soon."

"Does Keung know what happened to him?" Maddie asked.

"We will make a full report of the events upon our return," George replied calmly, his hilarity fading.

Maddie hadn't asked where Fred was or what he was doing. Given what the man had just been through, she was surprised that he was coping as well as he was. He would do what he had to in order to deal with what had been done to him. She wasn't one to criticize him. But as soon as they got home, they would get him some real help.

"Make up with Mamun before his head explodes," George said sternly, pulling her from her thoughts. *"You've already jacked his mind, there's no point in torturing the poor man as well."*

Maddie didn't argue with George but did immediately do as he told her. She ducked her head and approached Mamun as he stubbornly continued to ignore her. She stood right beside him until he finally looked at her with suspicion. He crossed his arms and waited silently for her to speak.

"I'm sorry I was rude," she murmured, fiddling guiltily with the lace on her shirt. "You were just trying to help me and I acted like a bitch. I'm hoping that you'll look beyond my poor behavior and accept my apology."

Mamun smiled a little and lifted Maddie's chin with his coarse fingertips. Maddie thought irritably that no one had done such a condescending thing to her since she was a small child but she kept her mouth shut about it. Mamun wasn't trying to antagonize her so she put up with it.

"It'll be okay, Tracker. I just don't understand how it is that you would allow me to kiss you but refuse me the comfort of sleeping at your side," he said. Maddie's face reddened and she could hear George's mental chuckle in her head. She fought the urge to glare at him for laughing at her embarrassment and concentrated on answering Mamun. She struggled for a plausible answer as she opened her mouth to speak.

Suddenly, a loud, sharp ring tore through the room, making both her and Mamun jump. She began to frantically search through the deep pockets of her skirt while the phone continued to ring and George glared at her from his chair. Mamun had taken several startled steps away from her, eyeing her as if he expected her to pull something horrifying from her pocket. Fred came in then, his face wearing a dark scowl as he closed the door behind him.

"Hurry up and answer the damn thing," he growled. "I can hear the ringing out in the hall."

Maddie hit the talk button and pressed it to her ear as Mamun was asking what the tiny machine did. George fielded the other man's questions and quickly ushered him out into the hall. Fred took George's chair and sat down, giving Maddie a murderous stare that she turned her back on.

"What the hell have you been doing?" Sam snarled into the phone without buildup or even a greeting. Maddie's brain stuttered a moment and she shook her head to clear it and deal with what was happening in front of her.

"What are you talking about?" she asked trying to keep her voice low. George came back in without Mamun and glaring angrily. Maddie scowled back and shook her head at him.

"I'm talking about the small arsenal and antiques you've got stashed in your office," Sam was almost screaming he was so enraged. Maddie flinched and pulled the phone from her ear. Her headache was returning with a vengeance.

"What were you doing in my office?" she demanded, refusing to answer his question. What was she supposed to tell him? The truth? There was no way he would believe it. Secretly, she was elated. Finally something had happened that would allow her to come clean with him. She just couldn't do it over the phone. She would need to be face to face with him to make sure he believed every word she said.

"Fuck your office, Maddie!" Sam snarled. "What have you been doing to make your money? And don't tell me you've been doing research, we both know that's bullshit."

Maddie bit her lip, desperately trying to think of something to say.

"I don't know what to tell you," she finally said quietly. She could feel the Agents' eyes boring into the back of her skull.

"Why don't you just tell me the truth?" Sam said. "For the last year, I've put up with your secrets and lies. You've been putting our family in danger and you never said a word about it. You're involved in illegal activities and you told me nothing. You brought weapons into our home and you said nothing!"

Maddie stood there, stunned. She could understand why her husband was angry and she certainly couldn't blame him. She just hadn't realized that he would be so angry. She had pictured this moment as somewhat calmer and that she would be face to face with him, not listening to him vent his spleen over the phone. She didn't know how to calm him down so she did the only thing that came instinctively to her. She said something stupid.

"Oh, come on, Sam. I think the danger part is a bit of an exaggeration," she scoffed. Sam responded with a long, profound silence. She would have thought that he had hung up on her except that she could hear his angry breathing.

"Don't bother coming home," he growled. "I've had enough. I cannot, will not do this anymore. It doesn't even matter if you quit your job now. I'm filing for divorce as soon as I can and I'm keeping the kids and the house. Do whatever you want, just don't come back."

Maddie's jaw dropped in astonishment. Of all the things she ever imagined Sam saying to her, divorce had never been a word she thought he'd use. She babbled almost incoherently, struggling to put sense to what he was saying to her and why he was saying it. Sam sighed and began to angrily recount the events of the last week at home. Maddie fell into horrified silence as he told her about the monsters skulking around their home, the attack on Katie and Chris at school and the cryptic phone call to the house which led him to her office earlier that day.

"Look, don't do anything, Sam. Let me get to the bottom of this. I'm coming home as soon as I can," Maddie said quickly as he finished talking. Rage as dark and hot as Sam's was boiling in her chest. Her head hurt and it pounded in time with the roiling in her guts.

"No, Maddie," Sam insisted. "It's too late. Don't bother coming home — I'm changing the locks. I'll have my lawyer contact you and work out visitation with the kids when you get back."

A touch of panic had taken the edge off the anger in his voice. Maddie heard it and latched tightly to it.

"Sam, don't do this. Wait for me to come home and we'll work this out. We always work it out," Maddie said frantically.

"No, Maddie. Not this time. I've had enough. I will not raise my children like this. This is what has to happen. My lawyer will call you."

Then Sam cut the line, unwilling to talk to her any longer. Maddie stared at the phone in her hand with a stunned look on her face. She tore her eyes from it and gazed hopelessly at the Agents standing at the opposite side of the room from her. George looked at her with eyes filled with sadness while Fred kept his stricken gaze on the floor. Maddie shook as she stood up and faced them. The rage was growing at the sight of them until her flesh burned from the heat of it.

"Did you know about this?" she hissed. "Did you know about what was happening to my family?"

The two men exchanged looks and shook their heads at her in confusion.

"We are on a mission, Tracker. We do not receive updates on the events at home while we are away. You know this," George said softly.

"No, I don't!" Maddie shrieked. "I don't know anything! No one will say a word to me about anything!"

Her hands flailed uselessly at her sides until her fingers brushed against something on a table. Maddie snatched it up without looking at it and flung it as hard as she could at the two men. They ducked as glass shattered over their heads. Maddie had lost it. She began to snatch everything she could get to and lift and threw it at the men in front of her. They ducked and dodged the missiles she flung at them. Her head pounded and her skin scorched but she barely noticed it. She continued to vent her rage on the room and the men within it. Mamun's head appeared through the door and was immediately pulled back when Maddie sent a water pitcher sailing towards it. He slammed the door and locked it.

"Tracker! Tracker!" George was shouting at her, trying to distract her. Fred circled carefully to take a position behind her. Maddie spun with a smooth, round object in her hand and flung it at Fred. It hit him on his head and he went down.

"Madeline!" George yelled. Startled by the odd use of her name, she turned back to George in time to see him sailing through the air at her. She screamed as his body slammed into hers and tackled her to the floor. Maddie stopped fighting and lay under him, weeping bitterly into the stone floor beneath her. George soothed her hair and whispered comforting words in her ear. Maddie jerked out from underneath him and glared at Fred as he groaned on the floor. An ugly bruise was rapidly spreading across his forehead with an angry lump at its center.

Maddie found her phone where she had flung it against the door. She picked it up and began dialing the Center. Mamun stuck his head back in cautiously and gave her a frightened look. Maddie ignored him and went to the window. Mamun entered and looked at the devastation around him.

"What happened?" he asked in awe.

"The Tracker is enduring a personal crisis," George replied simply, helping Fred off the floor. The room was in shambles, the furniture in a crumbling ruin and scorch marks peppered the walls. George and Fred avoided the big man's gaze and collapsed into two of the room's remaining chairs.

Maddie ignored the mutterings of the men as she waited for a tech to connect her with Keung. The Keeper answered the line with his usual cold monotone.

"I'm resigning my post," she snapped. "Get me home."

Keung let out an irritated sigh. "No," came the simple heartless reply.

"What do you mean, no?" Maddie demanded.

"I mean, no. You will stay where you are and complete the task set before you," Keung replied. Maddie fumed for a few seconds, considering her argument.

"Did you know what was happening to my family?" she asked.

"I know what is going on, yes,"

"Why didn't you tell me?"

"You have your mission. That is all you need to be concentrating on. The well-being of your heirs is my problem until your return." Keung replied.

"Well, you're doing a fucking shit job of it," Maddie snarled. "My daughter has stitches in her neck! I don't call that taking care of her well being."

"She's still alive."

"Fuck you, Keung. Take me home."

"Very well. But before I send the Threshold for you, tell me, how do you intend to protect your family from the Distari who hunt them?" Keung snapped, finally becoming angry enough to let it show.

"Distari?" Maddie got a rerun of the bloody and monstrous images she'd gotten just after she'd arrived on Iza.

"The Distari. They who have declared a blood feud against you and every Tracker since William of Lundren. Tell me, how do you intend to preserve your children's lives?"

Maddie blinked against William's memories. She saw though his eyes as he faced down a hideous creature clutching a small boy in its long claws.

"I have my skills," she growled.

"No, you don't. The nano pack you carry will be removed from your body and your mind cleaned of all memories associated with your time as Tracker. A painful procedure, I promise you. The weapons and records stored at your home as well as the protection of the Agents will be removed. But your resignation will not call off the Distari threat. They will still come for you and your children. And you will have no defense against them. With your resignation, you and your family will surely die. Tell me, Madeline, do you still wish to tender your resignation and return to your family?"

"How can I believe anything you say?" Maddie asked. "How can I trust you to take care of my family when I can't? My marriage is ending because of the things you've asked of me. How can I continue to do as you tell me?"

"Your children still live, Madeline. As long as you continue to serve, they will remain so."

"You've taken my family hostage."

Keung was silent. It stretched out between them until it was heavy with guilt and grief.

"I'm sorry but I have no choice in this," he said softly. "And I am sorry for what you have sacrificed."

Maddie didn't acknowledge his words. Her fist clenched so tightly that her nails dug into her palm. She thought for a way around Keung's words. The memories swirling in her head told her the truth of his words. But then, those very images could be false, fake memories created for the Center's purposes. How could she tell the difference? Did she take the risk and return home and possibly suffer the cruel fate suggested by the terrible visions in front of her? Or did she stay put and do as she was told like a good puppy? In the end, she went with what was safest. Any way she looked at the situation, the only course of action that guaranteed the lives of those she loved most was to remain the Tracker and let her marriage go.

"I will stay and complete my mission," she said quietly in a trembling voice.

"Very good, Tracker. Come home soon," Keung replied. The heat had left his voice and he cut the line. Maddie took a moment to scrub the tears leaking from her eyes before she turned to face the men. They stared back at her, silently waiting for her to speak.

"Let's get this over with. I want to go home," Maddie said hoarsely.

CHAPTER 30

The emergency room doctors had been astonished by Arnold's injuries. When she had been rushed through the doors, she had been covered in blood and was fading in and out of consciousness. She muttered incoherently and had to be sedated when she grew hysterical. Peeling back her tattered and bloody clothes, the doctors had discovered several deep gashes on the side of her rib cage and deep, ugly bruises spreading from under her right arm reaching down to her right mid-thigh. An x-ray revealed that several of her ribs had been cracked. After giving her eighty stitches and binding her ribs tightly, they began to push through the paperwork to admit her.

Arnold remained on the ER bed for a time, contemplating the events of the night and the fact that she had been very lucky, even though she didn't feel that way. Dewitt and Reid had both been killed and Fielding was currently in surgery to repair the damage done to his face. Thinking of the man brought back the terrible memory of seeing the flesh suddenly stripped from his face and leaving naked bone and bulging eyes behind.

The young mother and her two boys had managed to avoid serious injury but the trauma of the terrible night would no doubt require a lifetime of therapy just to sleep. Carroll had fared better than anyone else as he had walked into the emergency room with only a few deep cuts and bruises and had walked out a couple of hours later. No doubt he was at home drinking heavily and trying to forget what had happened.

It had taken some insisting but Arnold managed to hobble painfully out of the hospital, only after being presented by a paper that absolved the hospital of any responsibility if she should die. Arnold had signed it gladly; she hated hospitals and its smell of blood and antiseptic. The nurses did force her to walk out on her own though they watched her closely to be sure she didn't fall over. They hovered like vultures, ready to swoop down and whisk her away at the first sign of weakness. Arnold managed to get out the door but the process had been excruciating.

Cooper had driven her home. He made it clear that he disapproved of her decision to go home against doctor's advice. She ignored the lecture that ate up the time it took for him to drive to her house. She had staggered through her front door and collapsed exhausted into bed without showering or changing her clothes. The painkillers the doctors had given her did more than numb the pain. They had laid her out so that she fell into a deep dreamless sleep.

She woke in the late hours of the morning. Checking the time, she managed to pull herself out of bed, cursing the pain and heading straight for the shower. The sheets were spotted with blood and she grimaced at it and turned away. The shower was hot and soothing against her bruised flesh but stung her where the stitches were set. She was forced to move slowly and carefully to avoid pulling at her wound or jarring her ribs.

She was outside and standing stupidly in her driveway when she finally remembered that her car was still at the crime scene. Exasperated with herself, she dug her cell phone from her purse and called Cooper. Her partner gave her a lecture about pushing herself too hard and being reckless and ordered her back to bed. Then he hung up. She was about to call Sam for a ride when her cell phone rang. The number displayed in the window was unfamiliar but she answered anyway. There was no telling what it might be about. With any luck, it was the call that would lead her straight to the beasts that had killed two of her comrades the night before.

"Hey, Arnold, it's Charles Carroll," came an uncertain but amiable voice. "How are you feeling? I heard you were home already though no one's happy about it. Are you up and about yet or are you still in bed? I don't want to disturb you if you're still recovering."

Everything he said came out in a hyperactive rush, as if he needed Ritalin or was suffering from an anxiety attack. Arnold would have laughed at him if it didn't hurt like hell just to breathe.

"Have you heard about Fielding yet?" she asked, avoiding his questions.

"He made it through surgery but he's still in critical condition. His wife is with him but I think one of the girls from dispatch has the kids," Carroll replied. "Look, can you leave the house? I was wondering if you'd like to talk."

"You'll have to come get me. My car is still at the scene," Arnold replied, trying to sound completely pain-free.

"Sure, gimme directions."

Arnold gave him directions to her house to which Carroll reported that he would arrive in fifteen minutes. He pulled into her driveway in ten. He drove a sleek, shiny machine that screamed 'bachelor.' It was tricked-out in all the flashy and usual ways from the fancy rims to the gleaming paint job in a way that proclaimed the driver was both available and desperate.

Arnold approached the door gingerly and pulled it open with a groan. Carroll grinned at her as she sat down and carefully put on her seatbelt.

"I got a call from this guy named Shorn. He dropped your name a couple of times and asked me a lot of questions about what happened," Carroll said casually. "I told him that it was a case in progress and that I was not at liberty to discuss it. I thought maybe that you might want to go talk to him."

"Sure, but I gotta go to the station first. I have to get a couple of things done before we go talk to him," Arnold replied. Carroll shrugged and made a noncommittal noise. He fell silent as he steered towards downtown. Arnold watched him stew in his own thoughts. There was discoloration under his eyes as if he hadn't slept in many days and his boyish face sagged wearily. His large dark eyes were tight and blood shot, as he watched the traffic along the roads. He noticed her watching him and gave her an awkward grin and a falsely cheerful wink. Arnold quickly turned away and stared out the window until he pulled into the station's parking lot.

Arnold was out of the car almost before Carroll had turned the engine off. He had to jog to catch up with her as she headed into the police station. He hurried to beat her to the door and grinned as he held it open for her. She gave him a perplexed look for his sheepish expression then suppressed the urge to roll her eyes. The patrolman was developing a crush on her and she didn't want to be bothered with it. For the time being, she would simply ignore it until she was prepared to deal with the man.

Arnold was halfway to her desk when Cooper intercepted her by simply standing in her path. She gave him an irritable look that stated that she was not willing to put up with another lecture from him. She squared her shoulders and straightened her posture to hide her obvious pain. Her right side protested the position and she fought the urge to bend over the agony in her right side.

"The GBI want to talk to you in the interrogation room," Cooper said flatly. "We had told them that they had to wait until you were well enough to come in on your own but it clearly looks as if you're doing just fine."

He scowled sternly at her while his voice dripped with angry sarcasm. He wasn't going to lecture her, thank god, but he was going to torture her for her rush out of her sick bed.

"What is the GBI doing here?" she demanded angrily, ignoring his tone.

"After last night's fiasco, the Chief decided that we weren't equipped to deal with the homicides. They called the GBI to assist us in the case. The guys showed up this morning and just took everything over. They've already taken all of our case files and are squatting in Marshal's office since he's retiring next month."

Arnold shook her head in anger and disgust, shifting her weight from foot to foot.

"So where do we stand on the case now?" she asked.

"We aren't on the case," he growled. "They've completely taken over. I'm assigned to another case and you are now on medical leave until a doctor and a shrink clear you for duty."

Arnold gaped in shock and outrage. She wanted to grab Cooper and shake him until he told her how this happened. This was her case! She had stared at the mutilated bodies. She had examined the blood spatters and interviewed the witnesses. She had gazed into the eyes of the dead children and promised them justice. These guys had no idea what they were dealing with and would no doubt get themselves and others killed.

"This is bullshit," she snarled. "I've seen the bastards that have been doing this! They don't have a clue as to what they're dealing with!"

"You saw them?" Cooper asked. "Can you identify them? How many were there? What did they look like?"

"I saw them," Arnold said carefully, not wanting to give too much away. Cooper hadn't been there. If she started spouting tales of monsters and demons attacking cops, he was going to think that she was going crazy. She knew that she would think the same thing if she hadn't faced the beasts herself. Obviously, Carroll had been vague on the subject as well or Cooper wouldn't be so excited right now. "Why? What did Carroll say?"

Cooper rolled his eyes and snorted rudely. "He didn't say a damn thing. He just told us that it was too dark and things happened too fast for him to be clear about anything. Now everyone's all hot and bothered to talk to you. You better get going. Someone's probably told them that you're here by now and they'll be waiting."

Arnold walked stiffly to the interrogation room and rested her hand on the knob, staring through the long narrow window. A man in a stiff blue suit sat at a small table with a notepad with two cups of coffee sitting in front of him. He tapped his pen impatiently against the table and glanced at his watch. With a sigh, Arnold twisted the knob and pushed the door open.

The GBI agent looked at her with a cold, hostile gaze that didn't warm at all with the stiff smile on his thin lips. He greeted her by calling her by her first and last name and by telling her his name: Kyle D'Angelo. He offered her his hand to shake and kept his grip loose in that way that men did whenever they shook hands with a woman and thought they might hurt her. Arnold eyed him angrily, unkindly thinking that he wasn't close to being strong enough to bruise her hand even if he wanted to. Arnold gave him a weak smile as he invited her to sit in the uncomfortable chair with a vague gesture.

The interview dragged on for two hours. D'Angelo grilled her like a suspect, asking her questions about the details of the night and asking her more questions designed to find some flaw in her story. She did hold back from him and the man was smart enough to realize it but he couldn't get her to say anything that would prove it. She was vague when he asked for a description of the perps, saying only that there had been four of them, large males, but that the house had been too dark to see anything else.

She didn't know D'Angelo and that made her suspicious of him. But as the interview drew on, she developed the opinion that he possessed no imagination, was anal retentive and rigid enough to do everything by the book. No doubt that if she told him everything she had seen and experienced, the man would try to have her psychologically evaluated and maybe committed. He spoke in a forceful voice that said that he was easily provoked and probably had frequent bursts of temper. His face grew flushed with anger as she grew more vague and she knew that she was about to see an example of the man's temperament.

"What are you hiding?" he snapped near the end of the interview. Arnold gave him her best startled and innocent face.

"What do you mean?" she asked. "Why would I hide anything from you? I want to find this killer just as badly as you do."

D'Angelo scowled at her and took a deep breath in a poor attempt to remain calm. Arnold watched him go through relaxation exercises and nearly burst out laughing. The man was a mess! No wonder he had completely taken over. He needed to solve this case for more than just to stop the senseless slaughter. He needed to solve this to save his job and make a name for himself. She shook her head at him and decided that she really needed to head this guy off. He would pin this on some poor innocent rather than walk away with it unsolved.

"I don't know about that," D'Angelo growled. "I think you want this case for yourself. You want the glory and the fame and you can't stand that someone more qualified than you has taken over."

Arnold leaned back in her chair and crossed her arms and stared coldly at him. Moving had hurt and she was forced to sit very still and stare while the pain wracked through her body. The man was accusing her of the very thing he was doing and it pissed her off to no end.

"Are you done with me yet?" she snapped. A snarled curled his lip as he waved her away. She got up, her body spasming with pain as she moved. A sweat had broken out on her forehead by the time she walked the few steps to the door.

"Do you have anything that might have missed being filed?" D'Angelo asked in a tone that implied that she was purposely withholding evidence. She shot him a cold look over her shoulder and pulled the door open.

"No. Everything I had you have now," she growled. With that, she turned and stalked out of the room and let the door slam shut. She silently cursed the idiot as she walked tenderly to the lieutenant's desk to confirm her medical leave and then went back to her desk.

Cooper and Carroll were speaking heatedly in low tones. They fell silent when they saw her approach; Cooper crossed his arms in frustration while Carroll looked embarrassed and angry. Arnold stopped between the two men, looking first at Carroll before leveling Cooper with a scathing look. The men took a step back, more to get out of her way than because they were angry with each other.

"Who wants to take me to my car?" she growled, ignoring the tension passing like electricity between the men.

"I'll go," Carroll volunteered eagerly as Cooper opened his mouth to speak.

"Let me know how the search warrant on Shorn goes," she told Cooper as she checked her watch. Carroll was already gone, making a beeline for the door.

"I canceled the warrant," Cooper replied smoothly. "We both know that the old man had nothing to do with the homicides and the evidence you brought to justify a search was weak, at best. I felt it was in the department's best interest not to be sued for invasion of privacy and harassment."

Arnold nodded in defeat and turned away. Cooper's hand came down gently on her shoulder and held her back.

"Go home and heal," he pleaded. Arnold gave him a long flat look before she jerked away and continued out the station doors.

CHAPTER 31

Things were falling apart in a way that Keung had never seen before. He was used to dealing with any number of crises. He was more than equipped to make life or death decisions and manipulating entire cultures to fit his needs and agendas. But those sorts of problems were generally short-term issues that rarely affected him personally. This was a long-term problem involving emotions and the fates of a family in his care. The Tracker's husband had changed the locks on her home and was contacting a lawyer.

Keung was secretly pleased with the sudden availability that the Tracker would soon be enjoying. Without the bonds of marriage and family, the Tracker would be free to do anything at any moment and that made his life somewhat easier. But a brief conversation with Elcia made him realize that the fallout from this personal crisis would be difficult to deal with. Whenever most men had such problems, he may speak to one or two special individuals about it but then sink eyeballs deep into his work and would never share the problem with his boss. Elcia had made it clear what type of woman the Tracker was and what kind of trouble she would cause once she got home. She had been a sheltered housewife and mother of three small children before she began her service. She had had no reason to learn to mask her emotions or to hold them down to a dull roar. No doubt, she would be a mess during her divorce and long after it was finished. She would talk about it at length and would be searching for a shoulder or two to cry on. Anyone in her line of sight would be an acceptable shoulder and Keung feared that he would be caught in a series of opportunities for the Tracker to latch onto him and cry.

Not that he didn't feel bad for the woman. He could certainly understand her pain. He just didn't know how to deal with an emotionally raw woman. The last time a woman had come to him with her heart broken, she had wound up in bed with him simply because he didn't know what else to do to shut her up. Since he had no desire to share a bed with the Tracker, he was eager to avoid any emotional situation with her. In the meantime, he had housekeeping set up a suite of rooms and put them at the Tracker's disposal.

He wondered how unpredictable the Tracker's husband would become as events unfolded. The man was angry and anger had a tendency to blossom into vindictive acts. Reports stated that he had broken into his wife's office but they did not say what Samuel had discovered or what assumptions he had made. He could expose the Center anytime he felt like it and that made him very dangerous.

When the question of what had finally triggered the Tracker's husband into abandoning his marriage, an Agent suggested that someone had called Samuel and informed him of his wife's identity. An examination of the Center's phone records had revealed a call from the Tracker's office to her home. Then Andre reported Sherman's sudden illness and potentially long stay in the medical quarters. The two events had been too much of a coincidence and several Agents had walked away from the meeting promising pain on the young man. No doubt the Quarter knew about the security breach and would have something to say about it.

Keung ground his teeth angrily and wondered how he was going to keep Sherman's ass out of the fire. Not that the fool deserved any assistance. More than one person had made it clear that they felt that the boy should be allowed to face his punishment alone and undefended. But this was not the first case of insubordination Keung had dealt with and he had learned through bitter experience to understand the reasons for the disobedience before the Quarter got involved. He would, at the very least, hear Sherman out before he decided what to do about him. It was what he would do for any of the people who served under him.

"Keung, the Quarter is in Medical," came Andre's low soft mental voice in his head. A wash of panic followed the words, making it clear that things were not happy for the doctor. *"They want to talk to Sherman."*

Keung moved faster, doing everything but moving through the floors of the Center at a dead run. The people who encountered him in the halls scurried out of his way or took the risk of being knocked over and left sprawling, unnoticed. Keung barely saw any of them as he hurried along.

He burst into the Medical quarters, his green eyes blazing with nervous energy as he scanned the receiving room, looking for signs of trouble. Andre appeared almost out of nowhere though Keung knew he had been in plain view the whole time. Andre had a talent for going unnoticed whenever he wanted to. The doctor was pale and trembling though he was trying to hide it.

"They're already with the boy," Andre said quietly. "They would not allow anyone to remain in the room with them."

Keung nodded and moved forward without breaking his stride. A few steps of his long legs took him to Sherman's room. Even outside the door he could feel the familiar chill and the abrupt change in air pressure that always occurred whenever the Quarter came calling. If he concentrated, he could feel Sherman's terror and the Quarter's quiet rage through the shields locked around the room. He took a deep soothing breath and went inside, tearing the shields to shreds as he did so.

Two dark figures turned towards him as he coolly took in the room and came to a stop at a respectful distance from the figures. The figures were dark, but not as shadowy as they were whenever they came one at a time. It was as if whatever powered their disguise was straining at its limits. He saw vague outlines of their features, his heart pounding as he realized what the presence of two members of the Quarter meant. The Quarter felt threatened by Sherman's actions and meant to take action against the perceived danger.

"We did not send for you, Keeper," the two voices admonished coldly. Keung cleared his voice and glanced at Sherman's sweating and terrified face. His large eyes pleaded with him to do something, anything, to help him. Briefly, Keung wondered what the Tracker would do if she knew

what was happening and why. No doubt she would coldly leave Sherman to his fate. Considering what Sherman's actions had cost her, Keung was tempted to do the same. Still, Sherman had served well and it was the Keeper's duty to protect all his people, even if it was from each other.

The Quarter had fallen into an expectant silence and waited for Keung to do or say something to explain his unwanted presence. Keung shifted his weight and stared back at them.

"Sherman is one of those I keep, sir," Keung said finally. "It is my duty to bear witness to his life and defend him in his time of need."

The Quarter didn't respond, instead they looked to one another as if conversing silently. Keung could almost hear their hushed voices as they decided what he meant. Sherman huddled in his bed, his eyes flitting fearfully from one dark face to another.

"So you are claiming responsibility for this one's actions?" they asked. A cruel tone sang in their voices as they faced Keung fully. He couldn't be sure but they seemed pleased by his subtle admission of guilt. He squared his shoulders and braced himself for what might be coming. Silently he promised to make Sherman pay dearly for the shit storm he had stirred up.

One of the dark figures approached Keung slowly; one glided forward while the other remained beside the bed. Keung let his neutral gaze rest on the figure's face. It was a bold move, one that he had never dared before. His fists clenched at his sides and he concentrated on the sensation of his nails biting into his palms and not on the panic threatening to explode through his chest.

Suddenly, he felt a compulsive need to kneel at the figure's feet and grovel tearfully for forgiveness. He wanted to kiss their shoes and worship them until they forgave him for his transgression. He fought the compulsion, closing his eyes against the fear and took deep, calming breaths. His brain struggled to jabber incoherently in a mad panic but he shoved the wailing voice deep into his subconscious and locked it away. He realized then that the Quarter was trying to manipulate his mind and bend him to their will. It was a cheap, cruel trick and he resented it. He struggled against the compulsion, glaring hotly into the face of the man in front of him. Keung had given everything else for the Quarter but his dignity he would keep.

The realization stopped the panic cold and, with a snarl, Keung thrust them from his mind by sheer force of will. Both figures staggered at the push. They regained their balance quickly and pretended that Keung had not just done as he had. They buzzed with discussion again then turned back to Keung and Sherman.

"Keep these orders in your memory, for we will not repeat ourselves," the Quarter began ominously. *"When you leave these facilities, you will withdraw your search for the Distari lair. Then you will give orders to remove Agents from the Tracker's family. It is our understanding that Samuel Johnston is making attempts to sever his ties to his wife and therefore has foregone the benefits due to the Tracker's spouse. Also,*

remove protection from two of her children as well. We do not care which two must do without, we leave that decision up to you."

Keung's blood froze as his jaw dropped in an uncharacteristic display of emotion. The Quarter had just effectively ordered the assassination of the Tracker's family. Nothing like this had ever occurred before and it stopped Keung's mind dead. He stammered and gaped for several moments before his protests could finally organize themselves coherently. The Quarter seemed smugly satisfied with his reaction and they stepped back. The beginnings of a tingling pain began in the small of his back and jolted him out of his horror.

"We are sworn to safeguard the Tracker's family in acknowledgement of her life of sacrifice and service. I cannot, in good conscience, do as you have just ordered me," Keung said with more force than he felt. Inside, his guts twisted and boiled with fear and desperation.

"The discoveries made by the Tracker's spouse and his consequent actions are a threat to our security. Such things cannot be tolerated and must be eliminated."

"But the children! They are innocent and completely unaware of what is going on around them."

"They are surplus and not needed. Only one child is needed to safeguard the bloodline and will be much easier for the Tracker to care for while completing her service. They represent an unnecessary use of manpower. You will do as you are told, Keeper. Or we will take further action against your person and, if necessary, against your descendants."

"But if the Tracker manages to retain her marriage?" Keung asked frantically. He ignored the outright threat. Keung did not have any children as far as he knew. He began to plot ways to approach Samuel and convince him to remain legally married to the Tracker, even as he realized that the move would only spook the man and make things worse.

"Then, of course, the Tracker's family will maintain their protected status."

Keung had to contact the Tracker and tell her what was happening. He was prepared to give her almost everything she asked for to maintain the integrity of her family. Perhaps she could convince her husband to remain legally married even if they did not continue to live together.

The figures moved in closer to Sherman and Keung, seeming to grow larger and menacing. Keung faced them boldly, his eyes flashing with his growing fury even as his expression remained blank and hard. Sherman whimpered and shrank into his bed. The pain began for both of them, starting in the small of their backs and working its way up their spine. Sherman began screaming immediately, his eyes bulging and his mouth gaping. Keung held out longer but as the pain intensified and the blood began to trickle and flow, he fell to his knees and began to release his agony. The dark figures of the Quarter stood over them and watched intently as they writhed.

Outside in the receiving room, Andre heard the screams and sent the most nervous of his staff away while he prepared to pick up whatever pieces remained when the Quarter was finished.

CHAPTER 32

Mamun took a minute to spread an extra coat of lotion on his face and neck before stepping out into the night. The wind was nonexistent which meant that the night spores would be thick. He had his feathered hat on and was pulling on his gloves when Abiah approached him. She was wearing her wide-brimmed hat but, since night had fallen, the veil was pulled neatly back and artfully pinned to the brim. Mamun looked upon the small woman's cheerful face, noticing that she was a lovely creature with her thick, black hair and plump, rosy mouth. She smiled at him and batted her long dark lashes. Her front lower teeth were properly filed into points and she used them to bite her upper lip coquettishly.

Ordinarily, he would have snatched up a tasty tart like her the second she showed the slightest interest in him. And Abiah was very tasty, indeed. She was rounded and curved in all the right places and she had large dark eyes with a thick rim of black lashes. But his thoughts were consumed with the images of another woman, one that was currently in her room alternating between violent cursing and heart breaking sobs. He wondered what had happened to throw her into such a riot of emotion. One moment she was babbling into a slender box and the next she was in a clear rage and destroying her room.

The Tracker's wrath had been truly frightening. As she continued to vent her rage against the two men she kept with her, the room had grown stifling hot as small fires exploded to life and then quickly died. George had ordered him out of their presence and Mamun had not argued. To be honest, he had wanted to stay and comfort the Tracker with whatever had set her off but the strange occurrences had spooked him badly and left him feeling out of his depth. In the end, all he could do was flee and hope for the best.

"How is the Tracker faring?" Abiah asked, her wide eyes gleaming with concern. "I feared greatly for her well-being when you brought her in this morning."

"She is much recovered, thank you," Mamun replied staring at Abiah's shapely bosom more out of habit than actual lust. Abiah noticed the direction of his gaze and squared her shoulders so that her breasts thrust out just a little further for him to admire. Mamun hardly noticed the gesture. He suddenly realized the state of the Tracker's suite and knew that when the little innkeeper saw the damages, she was going to be pissed. Wanting to do something useful for the Tracker, Mamun reached into his pocket and withdrew a few small gold coins and offered them to Abiah.

"The Tracker had a mishap and it has left your rooms in an unfortunate state of disrepair," he explained as he pressed the coins into the startled woman's hand. "This should cover the cost of the damage."

"Don't worry about the costs," Abiah said sweetly giving him the coins back. "The Tracker and her people pay very well for every privilege." She had put an emphasis on the last two words in a way that implied that trashing her rooms was a frequent privilege that the Tracker had regularly engaged in. Mamun put the coins back into his pocket with an inward sigh of relief. The gold was the allowance that his true master afforded him to cover both his personal and professional expenses. He had offered Abiah a great deal of money he couldn't really afford to lose.

He took a few more moments to exchange pleasantries with Abiah before politely tipping his hat to her and stepping out into the full night. He stood on the raised stone walk for a few minutes, looking one way, then another. The young women of the city strode cheerfully along the walks, some arm in arm with each other or with some fresh faced youth while others walked purposefully with baskets over their arms for their shopping. He watched them go by as their long, full skirts brushed the ground and their upper lips gleamed with fragrant liniments.

Across the street, a half-naked whore cast lustful eyes at him and beckoned to him with a long-fingered hand wrapped in a crimson scarf trimmed in purple. Mamun grinned and went to her even as the Tracker's pretty face popped into his mind's eye. She smiled at him as he crossed the street and took a deep breath and let it out so that her barely concealed breasts nearly fell out of her dress. He stopped when they were nearly touching, his mouth curving in an easy smile while the whore continued to breathe deeply of the night air. Standing this close, he could see that Banita was doing without the protective liniment.

She smiled seductively at him while her hands caressed his broad chest over the smooth cloth of his shirt, then under it. He touched the smoothness of her cheek and he leaned down for a kiss. She jerked back flirtatiously but shook her head.

"You know better than that, Mamun," she purred, pulling her hands out from under his shirt and turning her back on him. She flounced down a nearby alley, casting come-hither looks over her shoulder as she went.

Mamun followed quickly, ducking into the alley way on Banita's heels. He found her in the deep shadows and he reached for her, his fingers hooking into the threadbare fabric of her second-hand skirt. She squeaked with delight as he pulled her to him and rubbed her hips suggestively against him. She made whimpering noises as his hands gripped her bottom tight and squeezed. He bent and buried his face in her neck and tasted the salty flesh of her pulse. Banita panted with excitement, her breath coming hot and quick against his cheek and ear. She lifted a long leg and wrapped it around his hip and rubbed her sensitive bits against him. He sucked air between his teeth, caught off guard by the erotic movement and thrilling in the excitement of it.

"The General wants a meeting with you on Market Street. He wishes you to make your report regarding the Tracker's progress," she panted and flicked his earlobe with her tongue. Mamun moaned and ground his hips into her.

"When?" he asked. He turned his face just slightly and nibbled her neck. Banita laughed and clung to him.

"Oh, an hour. You have time to linger if you want. My treat," she purred. Mamun considered the offer. The last day and night had been an exercise in restraint. Every moment he spent with the Tracker, he wanted to pull her into a private spot and peel her clothes from her body and gaze at her sweet nudity. He pictured himself lifting her up and riding her until she screamed with ecstasy. He could see her face flushed with orgasm, her head thrown back and her body arched beneath him.

Banita giggled and began to tug at the ties holding his trousers closed. With a start, Mamun stepped back and put the woman at arm's length. His back hit the wall and stopped him from going any further. Banita took the move as a suggestion of preference rather than a rejection. Her seductive smile grew broader as she lifted her skirt to show him what was hidden beneath.

"Thank you for your kind offer," Mamun said, trying to sound regretful. He chose his words carefully; he had heard plenty of stories about what Banita did when she thought she had been slighted. All of the rumors had been bloody. "I have become familiar with a woman of some renown and I fear that if I dallied here with you, she would learn of it and refuse me."

The whore looked at him with a wry expression of disbelief and her hands on her hips. She threw her head back and laughed a harsh braying sound.

"No need to be so pretty about it," she scoffed. "You could have simply said no. I have customers enough to keep my ego soothed."

She laughed harshly again and flounced out of the alley, turned the corner and disappeared. Mamun let out a sigh of relief. He took a moment to adjust himself more comfortably in his trousers before stepping back out into the street. He checked the road to be sure that no one had been watching him and he began to walk.

He reached the market well before the appointed time. While he waited, he glanced through the various trinkets and pretties on display, thinking that perhaps a gift would improve the Tracker's disposition. But he quickly gave the idea up. What could a man possibly give a woman like the Tracker? None of the usual things seemed appropriate and the things he thought might go over well were far out of his price range.

"I never thought of you as a romantic," a man said in a harsh, worn-out voice. Mamun put a glittering brooch back on the thick velvet it was displayed on and turned to face the grizzled man.

"I think all men could be moved to romance if the right woman strikes his fancy," Mamun replied, ruining his casual tone by flushing with embarrassment.

"And how hard has the Tracker struck you?" the General laughed. "I had not heard that she was beautiful but, then, our king does not yet consider such things."

Mamun flushed harder, horrified that the object of his affection was so obvious. He did take a moment to think on the Tracker's appearance. Truth be told, she was not the usual type of woman that he found attractive. She was cute rather than beautiful and she struck him as someone's mother rather than a woman who could be found in a man's bed with any regularity.

"She's a remarkable woman," he said finally, wondering what it was about the Tracker that he found so irresistible. Perhaps it was a sign that he was finally ready to marry. His mother would be pleased. The General's lips quirked in poorly disguised amusement.

"Give her up. Almost all Trackers are wedded. You might be able to convince her to spread her legs for you and knowing you she most likely will, but you will not be able to keep her. The Trackers are loyal to hearth and home and will not be tied down by the likes of us."

Mamun shook his head, refusing to believe the advice the older man was giving him. He recalled the passionate moment he had spent with her in Barnum's dungeon. Granted, places of torture did not generally send him into the throes of lust but he still had found himself trying to wrap the woman around his body. It all felt peculiar.

"How goes it with the Tracker? Has she yet succeeded in locating and eliminating the criminals?" the General asked. As he spoke he began to walk, as if the pair were a rich man out with his servant. Despite their relaxed postures, both men were tense, searching the surrounding crowd for spies and assassins. Anyone who looked in their direction or passed too closely were given sharp looks and, if they didn't immediately back off, were put on a mental list for further investigation. Everyone backed off.

"She made something of a scene last night going after Barnum. A pair of his lackeys was maimed and Barnum had her escorted to the dungeons as a result. Her men were briefly tortured. I managed to get them out quickly and all three seem healthy enough now. But one of the men suffered humiliation and I'm concerned that he will not be able to restrain himself for very long."

The General acknowledged the information with a nod. "The Agents who serve the Tracker are very disciplined men and are renowned for their ability to do their work without flaw. However, if the man goes into a murderous rampage, he'll likely save us a lot of trouble in the end. Don't worry too much about it. Has anyone become suspicious of you?"

Mamun shook his head. "No sir. No one has questioned my identity, not even the Tracker."

The General grunted a laugh. "That's a first. The last Tracker was a very difficult man to fool. He always knew who was who and what was happening. In my experience, the man had never made a mistake nor was he ever caught off guard. Perhaps the fact that she is a woman makes her vulnerable and she is not meant for work that is clearly meant for men."

"I think it is because she is inexperienced. The men follow her around as if she were a child. Always guiding her, always teaching her." Mamun said a little defensively. He flinched at his own tone while the General gave him a wry look. But he let the comment go.

"Have you been protecting her as ordered?" he asked.

"She's still alive," Mamun retorted, trying to cover his embarrassment. His orders from the King had been very clear. He was to see to the needs and well-being of the Tracker even if it meant sharing her bed. He had certainly done that, though not in that most pleasurable of capacities. And the Tracker had not been pleased about it. The memory of earlier still left him chagrined.

"What does she intend to do next?"

"Exactly as she was requested. Locate and capture Barnum and Cass and deliver them to King Kadar. How or when she intends to do so is not known to me."

The General grunted at this and thought a moment. "Your orders remain the same, Captain. I'll have runners follow you at a discreet distance from here on out. Signal if you need reinforcements or when the Tracker has achieved her objectives. His majesty wishes to enter the city as soon as she has taken Barnum and Cass so that she may present them to him in full view of the public."

Mamun bowed his head and turned away without another word. The General continued his steady walk until he disappeared into the market crowd. Mamun didn't look back as he gently pushed his way through the throng.

He had stopped to get his bearings when his eye was drawn to a familiar face. Huddled amongst the laughing and chattering faces were Fred. The man stared at him with a cold, angry countenance on his pale face. Mamun swallowed a gasp and blinked in surprise. When he looked again, the man was gone. Mamun stared hard where the Agent had been, wondering if he'd really seen Fred standing there. He looked around, trying to find the man he had seen. Seeing no one, he sighed and started on his way back to the inn.

CHAPTER 33

He was playing with a wonderful new toy. It was a lovely thing, with long, yellow corn silk hair springing from its scalp and down its back. It had large blue eyes that grew larger whenever He came near it. It was just a passing fancy, a little something that would keep him amused while he waited for his plans to come into fruition.

It was a stupid thing really, always making useless gestures and never knowing just when to shut-up and succumb. But then, if it had just lay down and let him kill it, it wouldn't be so entertaining. It had a wonderful tendency to weep and babble incoherently while it squirmed and pressed its body into the rough stone walls until its flesh grew purple and bloody.

He crouched in front of it in order to get a better look at the large, round glands perched securely on its chest. He reached out with a finger and poked it, marveling that it was much softer than it looked. He grasped it in his hand and the toy wept hysterically and pushed frantically at him. The fire made its yellow hair turn to a color that reminded him of blood. He thought about cutting her head to see the blood flow and study how the liquid stained the long, soft strands. It stared at him with bulging eyes and it cringed in terror.

It made no further sounds until he smiled at it with open joy. The toy stared back at him with horror for a moment, then began to shriek. The wailing went on for a long time, sending thrills of pleasure up and down his spine and making him laugh. This one was very strong. Most humans lost consciousness or went jabbering mad within moments of gazing upon his long, gleaming teeth bared in a smile.

Abruptly, a soft, timid knock on his chamber door interrupted his play.

"Come!" he snarled impatiently. A trembling hand appeared around the door, followed by the rest of the stinking, shaking timid.

"Milord, the changeling and its grunts has returned from the feast," The timid said in a quavering and whining voice. He eyed it and wondered how it could remain on its feet when it was shaking so badly.

"So soon? Was the prey dissatisfying?" he asked as if he cared.

"The changeling has reported that five armed humans interrupted them. But Distari did manage to kill three adult males and maim a fourth. Unfortunately, two adult females, two young males and a single adult male have survived relatively intact. The changeling wants to know what your orders are regarding the incident." It trembled and cried while it spoke, increasing the flow of mucus and tears that seemed to pour out of it at all times.

He reached out and stroked his toy's hair as he thought about what to do. The toy trembled and wept under his touch which drove him to distraction. He shook himself to come back to the matter at hand and concentrated harder. What to do? For the first time, there were survivors and survivors told stories. If it were just one then there was very little threat of danger. But in this case, there were several individuals who could corroborate each other's stories. Such a thing could prove disastrous if the humans became hysterical and went hunting for the beasts that frightened them.

The survivors had to be eliminated before they could spread panic among the human population. Of course, the changeling who had left them alive would be sent to do the job, not that such a thing would be considered a chore by the creature. They enjoyed the slaughter and would return pleased and well fed. The slaughter would keep the lair settled and content.

He laughed as he gave his orders to the timid and rubbed his hands greedily together. The words fell into an incoherent muttering and laughing. The timid screamed in terror and ran for its very life. He was too busy preening in the glory of his own genius to notice that the timid had left the door open. Nor did he see the girl with the corn silk hair get shakily to her feet and begin to move silently along the wall. She watched him with wild eyes as she moved and kept her back pressed against the wall. He was still laughing when she squeezed through the open door and disappeared into the lair.

* * *

The girl with the corn silk hair ran through the deserted streets of historic downtown. Held deep in the throes of terror, she was unaware of the freezing early December wind and that she was completely nude. She opened her eyes wide in a desperate attempt to penetrate the velvety darkness that lined the road.

She didn't see the dark shops that lined the streets and the bare skeletal trees that clustered on every street corner and lined the sidewalks. Instead, she saw the dark wet twists and turns of the underground abyss from which she had just emerged. She still saw the monsters with their horrible teeth and claws, their rotting flesh and gleaming eyes. Her numb, abused body still remembered the leathery texture of their skin upon her smooth, white flesh. She was forced to stop and vomit whenever the sensation became too intense.

She ran as hard as she could and the soles of her feet bruised and split so that she left wet red footprints on the cement behind her. She ran beneath a dim, orange streetlight just as a battered pickup truck passed her going in the opposite direction. The brakes shrieked as the truck came to a stop and the figures within rubbernecked in astonishment. The truck's raw brakes startled the girl into stopping and she stared wide-eyed as two figures emerged from the cab. One was small and squat and it stood near the truck gawking at her while another, much larger figure rushed around the front of the vehicle.

"Sweetie! Honey! Come here, baby!" the squat figure called in a high, sweet voice. The girl stared in disbelief before she let out a blood-curdling scream and ran away. The woman turned frantic eyes to her husband as he dug a tiny cell phone out of his pants pocket. He gestured his wife to silence as he called the police and told them about the naked girl running down Main Street.

The girl stool in a pool of yellow light with her arms wrapped tightly around her body. She had finally realized what the freezing wind was doing to her and she searched for a place to hide and get warm. There were tight, dark places between the buildings that looked promising enough but then she remembered that the things she was running from liked small, dark places.

She heard the hard tap of heels on pavement and it dragged her attention from the cold to the feminine figure coming towards her. She cringed as a woman stepped into the light. She wore blue jeans tight enough that they looked painted on with a faded halter top and a short faded blue jean jacket, unflattering to her thin, sagging body. Her face was boney and worn with cheap make-up caked on her skin to cover the discoloration and blemishes. Her brassy blond hair was pulled into a pretty clip and fell in glistening waves down her shoulders and back.

"What are you doing?" the woman snapped harshly. She eyed Corn silk warily and pulled a cigarette from a pack in her pocket. Ordinarily, Leona avoided crazy naked people whenever she could. Usually the appearance of such people meant that there was going to be trouble. But the nude girl in front of her didn't feel at all like the hard, used and discarded girls she was familiar with. This girl was very pretty, toned and well-fed. She had fresh cuts and bruises all over her body. The girl belonged to someone and, judging by the expensive cut of her matted hair, there was a very good chance there would be a generous reward for the her return.

Besides all that, this was a small rural town. Naked, battered girls simply did not run loose on these streets. If they did exist in this wholesome town, they stayed safely out of sight behind closed doors. The presence of a hapless victim in this place could mean that there was something truly dangerous on the loose and, in her line of work, she could use all the information she could get on any predators in the area.

Corn silk didn't answer the question. She stared with wild eyes at Leona and wondered if she dared ask the woman for a warm, safe place to stay. She didn't look like one of the things that had grabbed her. The monster that had snatched her had looked like her best friend at first. Then it had followed her to an isolated place and her skin had melted from her face and all her joints had turned in all the wrong directions. It had lunged at her and grabbed her before she could scream.

The next moments had been a swirl of terror and flashes of images that would haunt her forever. She was taken down into the underground through a series of stinking tunnels and antechambers. There had been hoards of the beasts, all of them cavorting and leaping in the packed spaces. They howled and scrabbled for her when they saw she was in their midst. The one who had taken her had snarled at them and continued to drag her along until it delivered it to its master.

That one had been by far worse than the scores of others she had glimpsed before. He had looked human at first, normal, sane, handsome even. But he had locked his strange bulging eyes on her and smiled that freakish smile. She stared in horror at those orbs filled with twisted thoughts and the very white smile that nearly bisected his impossible face. She took a shuddering breath and began to scream. It was several hours before she could stop and only then because she had grown hoarse.

The woman in front of her seemed nothing like what she had experienced. She was old and ugly and... human. She stared impatiently at Corn silk while she sucked on her cigarette and tapped her foot.

"What's your name?" she asked suddenly. Her voice was dry and growling. Corn silk eyed her warily, still unsure of the woman and her intentions.

"Emma," she replied hesitantly.

"I'm Leona," she turned at the sound of sirens echoing in the distance and felt the urgency of the situation. Soon the cops would be here and they would take Emma away. If that happened, she could say goodbye to the reward the girl would bring. Leona had to stash the girl fast before she lost her.

"You wanna come with me? I know a place nearby. It's not much but it's warm and it has showers," Leona said. Emma stared fearfully at the distant flashes of red and blue coming towards them. Somehow Leona seemed safer than the unknown driving down the street did. The aging prostitute seemed unlikely to be one of those monsters in disguise.

"Okay," she said desperately and rubbed her arms. Leona put her arm around the bruised and naked girl. Alcott's house was just a couple of blocks away. The old man was tenderhearted and would probably take the girl in without question. He'd take good care of her, too, and make sure that she was cleaned and fed without abusing her further. Plus, he was better at getting information out of people than anyone that she ever met. Emma huddled into Leona's warmth, ignoring the stink of cigarettes and sex and praying that she hadn't made a terrible mistake.

CHAPTER 34

Maddie had managed to calm down by the time Fred returned to the room. She was arming herself and muttering darkly about men, marriage and work. George was packing their things neatly in their bags and setting them by the door. Fred barely spared a glance for the Tracker as he closed the door behind him but he watched the Master Agent intently for signs of what was going on. Fred hadn't been willing to spend any time in a small room with a heavily-armed and highly-skilled hysterical woman and so he had decided to scout the area and get a feel of the city. He had managed to get the impression that the local population was in a festive mood before he spotted Mamun leaving the inn. The man had felt suspicious while he made his way across the street and ducked into a narrow alley. Fred began to follow him immediately, merely to see what was going on.

"Sir, I followed Mamun into the marketplace," Fred said quietly. George straightened and looked at him. George looked tired and irritable, an odd expression for the normally amiable Master Agent. Fred supposed that the expression came from dealing with a volatile crazy woman alone for too long. Fred pushed the thought firmly away with a cautious glance towards the Tracker. She was glaring at him as if she had heard his thoughts. Fred flinched and sighed and thought that she probably had.

"He met with an older man that was clearly an authority figure of some sort and they spoke together at length. They were nervous in posture and feared discovery. Unfortunately, there was a large crowd of revelers in the immediate vicinity and I could not discern their thoughts or their words. Mamun saw me when his meeting ended and he reacted with fear," Fred said.

George sighed and rubbed his aching eyes. He was tired and irritable from spending too much time with a woman who lacked the discipline to keep from projecting her nasty moods onto others. He wanted to rail at the universe, not listen to his Agent explain that they had a spy. The Tracker approached the men with a dark scowl on her face and her arms crossed over her chest.

"What did Mamun do?" she asked.

"He is a spy," George growled. Maddie's scowl grew darker and she snorted angrily.

"Who does he work for?" she asked. Then she suddenly held up her hand and shook her head. "Never mind, I don't want to know. Regardless of what he's told anyone, we still have to complete the mission and the sooner we get it done, the better. We just assume that Mamun is working for either Cass or Barnum or worse, both and that they know everything that we're doing and when we plan to do it."

Fred turned away shaking his head and muttering angrily while George reached out and grasped Maddie by the shoulders. His fingers dug into her with a bruising grip. Maddie growled an "Ow!" just as George began to speak.

"Tracker," he began, clenching his teeth in an effort to keep his voice even and calm. "Who Mamun is working for and what he has told them does matter. I don't think it would do anyone any good if we got our asses blown off because we didn't find out what the enemy knows. We must call the Keeper and notify him of the situation and await the analysis of the most recent data and get new orders before we go in."

He watched the Tracker think about this, his teeth clenching tighter as her anger and frustration poured into him. Good grief! The woman needed to learn how to control herself so that she kept her moods from influencing others. Her anger and despair set him seething and ready to kill the next thing that moved.

"How long will that take?" she asked.

"It could be a couple of days before the data is properly analyzed and Keung has new orders for us," George replied. Somewhere behind them Fred snarled and kicked something hard enough to break. The Tracker's anger flared and George pulled away from her with a hiss. The woman was hot! He could smell the intense heat boiling from her skin from where he stood. She glared at him with eyes gone glassy and feverish.

"No, I can't wait a couple of days for new orders. I need to get home. We get the mission done tonight," she snarled. "Where's my hat?"

George stared in disgust as she turned away and began to search through the room. He noticed that her movements were staggered and she had a hard time staying on her feet without bumping into the furniture. She swore and buried her fingers in her hair, rubbing at her scalp and neck.

"Tracker, I think it would be best if we waited. You are not well. Something is wrong with you and you need to be in bed and resting," George protested. Fred had stopped his quiet cursing and stared intently at Maddie.

"I feel fine," she growled. "I just have a headache."

"Tracker, I must insist—" he began.

"Who gives the orders on the field?" Maddie snarled as she rounded on him. "Which of us is responsible for completing the mission?"

George stiffened and glared down at her with his hands clenched at his sides. The relentless chore of a woman had picked a hell of a time to grow a backbone and pull rank on him. Her lip curled in a snarl as she squared her shoulders and prepared to face him down. He made a quick estimation of his chances of winning a screaming match with the harpy and immediately gave up on the idea. The Tracker could easily out-shriek him anytime she wanted to. She was very well versed in the arts of women's manipulations and she utilized her high, nasal voice to full ear-rupturing effect. In fact, the Tracker had done it so well on past missions that he had been willing to do anything just to shut her up. He thought about just hitting her. In a real fight, he could take her easily. But he doubted that Keung would let him get away with kicking the hell out of the Tracker, even if it was to knock some sense into her thick skull. He often wondered why her husband complained about her frequent absences.

"You hold the superior rank," George relented finally. Maddie gave him an angry nod of satisfaction.

"We go tonight. We hit Barnum's club first, grab some DNA, beat the crap out of him and leave him were Kadar could find him. After that, we come back here, shake Cass's whereabouts out of Abiah and take that guy out the same way as Barnum. From there, we go home," she said.

"I've never heard a more ridiculous plan in my life," George sneered. He had had enough of the brainless twit and he was finally losing his temper. "You do realize that we're all going to die, don't you?"

"Well, that's your problem now, isn't it?" she shot back. "I'm sure you'll think of away to keep us alive. That is your job."

The door to the suite suddenly opened and Mamun stepped into the room to be confronted by three hostile stares. He stayed by the door, leaving his hand on the knob while his other hand wandered to rest on his gun. He glanced at Fred and wondered what the man had told the others.

"What do you think you're doing here?" The Tracker snarled coldly.

"I have come to assist you as promised," he replied hesitantly, feeling his heart sink in dread. She took three long strides across the room and went up on her toes to put her face closer to his. She bared her teeth at him and snarled. He stared back at her flushed face and saw the dark circles smudging the flesh beneath her eyes. She swayed slightly on her feet, coming close enough for him to feel the feverish heat pouring off her body. His fingers twitched compulsively with the need to scoop her up in his arms and carry her to the bed where she could lay down and get some rest.

"Really? Because I was under the impression that you're a spy who's giving information of my activities to my enemies," Maddie said. Mamun shook his head in denial, unsure of any other way to respond to the absurd statement. He had been reporting her plans to his superior officers who had deep personal interest in the success of her task. He would not consider any of them the Tracker's enemies. His eyes went back to Fred who returned the look boldly. The man had mistaken the encounter in the market and had told the others his assumptions.

He heard the unmistakable sounds of guns clearing holsters and cocked and saw that the Agents had moved to get a clear shot at him. He tensed up, waiting for them to draw down on him and kill him.

"Who are you?" she asked.

"I am your friend," he replied. Behind her, Fred and George raised their guns and took aim at his chest. Mamun gave them a hard blank look and struggled to keep his hand away from his own weapon. The Tracker seemed to consider his answer, her head cocked slightly to the side as she thought about whether or not she liked him well enough to let him live.

Mamun had imagined his death many times since the day he began his training as a soldier and had his teeth filed in the traditional way of fighting men. He had seen his death on the battlefield, falling valiantly to an overwhelming enemy and giving his life to his king and country. If he was very lucky, he would die a very old man in his bed, surrounded by multitudes of grandchildren. But never had he imagined that he might be gunned down in an inn room on the orders of a woman. It seemed stupid and undignified.

"Do you want me to shoot him?" Fred said hungrily. He stared at Mamun with bloodthirsty eyes as his gun tilted to aim at Mamun's head. The Tracker turned to eye him warily, letting the fear build in Mamun's chest until his heart hammered against his ribs painfully. The Tracker and George stepped back so that Fred could advance on him with a bloodthirsty look on his face.

Maddie watched Mamun stand his ground as Fred stalked towards him with the gun trained on his chest. Mamun made no move to either defend himself or get away. He fully expected to die here and all he could regret was that he wasn't on the battlefield. Maddie stopped Fred with a thought while George whispered softly into her head,

"We need to know what he has said and to whom. If he isn't a spy for Cass or Barnum, we could use him in your insane plan."

Maddie thought about that. Sure, Mamun would be handy in the coming evening, if he wasn't betraying them. They could tie Mamun down and torture him until he told them everything but that would take a long time and Mamun would be useless afterward. That left only one other option. It was quicker and, at worst, would leave him disoriented for only a short time if Maddie didn't accidentally kill him. She had to admit that she didn't really know what she was doing when it came to ferreting out information directly from someone's mind.

She let out a cleansing breath as she tried to remember everything that George had tried to teach her regarding her abilities. It was difficult and she had to take time to gather her fraying wits and concentrate on what she was doing. Her head was pounding so badly that she could barely see across the room. Her stomach rolled in agony and her body burned with a terrible fire. Her insides felt like they were about to explode.

"Any time now, Tracker," George's soft mental voice brought her back to herself and gave her something to focus on.

"Move, Fred," she said testily and sent a spear of power into Mamun as Fred stepped aside. Mamun jerked as if punched from the psychic impact and reeled from the disorientation of Maddie's invasion. He would have collapsed if Fred hadn't caught him and lowered him to the floor. Quickly, Fred pulled Mamun's twitching body further into the room and closed the door to hide them from any prying eyes. He kept his gun out and trained on the prone man, just in case he did something unexpected.

Maddie hadn't meant to see as deeply into Mamun's mind as she had. But she was simply too ill and undisciplined to get the information she wanted and get out. Her head swam with a lifetime of Mamun's memories and experiences and she very nearly fell. She saw his mother's weary face hovering over his with a tender look. She laughed at his three sisters' antics as they played at their dolls in the family room. She felt the wind on her face as Mamun played with other small boys in the pleasant, middle-class neighborhood he grew up in. She saw his father, at first a strong and protective presence in his son's mind, grow slowly more violent with addiction as he became old and bitter before his time.

She heard the quiet tears of his mother and Mamun's own relief as his father was stretched out on the coals to burn after he died. Mamun was ashamed to be glad his father had died even though he had tormented his mother and sisters for so many years. It was that shame that drove him to leave school before he had finished and start working odd jobs around the city in order to feed and clothe them. Maddie felt the embarrassment and glee of his first sexual experience and then the joy of his first love.

As a young man with his mouth still raw from the rites of manhood and his heart aching with the rejection of his sweetheart, Mamun had joined the army in a desperate effort to keep his family from starving from the crushing poverty his father's death had left them.

He worked his way diligently through the ranks; his heroics brought victory to his country and saw men screaming their lives away on the battlefields the old King chose on his path of conquest. The defeats were agonizing things, though blessedly few, while their retreats were always shielded by the men Mamun led.

Finally, after just ten years, he was given the rank of Captain. His mother had laughed with pride when he showed her his badge of rank and the eldest of his sisters was finally able to marry thanks to the dowry his improved salary afforded her.

Just a few weeks past, a messenger arrived at his tent and ordered him to the King's presence. Kadar always kept his movement and location a closely guarded secret so it was a surprise when Mamun was led over a hill to a massive tent just a few hundred yards beyond his own camp. The tent was a grand place, the cut of the waterproof felt and the placement of the tent poles positioned so that it resembled the royal palace at the capitol. Mamun was brought to a wide flap guarded by two men in shining breastplates and ushered inside.

A frail old man shuffled up to him as he entered the tent and gestured for him to follow. Mamun did so, his eyes staring at the splendor of the rare, polished wood and stone furnishings around him. His broken and filthy boots tread on thick carpets and he could smell the savory aromas of good meat on the fire. Dim gaslight gave everything a warm friendly glow, allowing the royal household to move in and out of the light wherever they went. Mamun marveled at their finery, even those who were clearly servants or slaves were dressed in the most exquisite fabrics and leather.

Then the old man stopped at the edge of a thin, darkly-colored veil and told Mamun in a wheezing voice to stay put until someone came for him. Mamun replied with a bow, not knowing how else to address a man of uncertain rank. The old man's eyes danced and his lips twitched as he turned and faded into the darkness. A soldier dressed in the King's royal colors appeared from behind the filmy veil and escorted him inside.

Mamun crossed the boundaries and could barely make out the throne on its pedestal and a massive bed carved from shining marble and hung with thick curtains. Across the curtained area stood a large wooden table with several aging men bent over it. They spoke in hushed voices and never looked up, as if what they were studying would disappear if they looked away from it. Two figures suddenly stepped away from it to stand in a bright pool of yellow light. They were dressed in the inoffensive and bland clothing of bodyguards and they bristled with weapons of every type. They wore the rank badges of royal bodyguards gleaming on their breasts. The bodyguards stood silently for a few seconds then stepped aside to reveal a smaller, more delicate figure.

The figure stepped forward into the light. It was a solemn-faced boy of no more than eleven wearing a heavy robe of crimson and blue and a thin gold circlet over his dark curls. Mamun could only gape in astonishment as the boy lifted his small hand and offered him the signet of a fox to kiss. The bodyguard chuckled as Mamun dropped to one knee to kiss the ring dutifully, feeling confused and not a little disgruntled to be bowing to a child young enough to be his own son. He bent over it, unnerved by how small the King's hand felt in his own.

"I have heard of your many great deeds, Captain," Kadar said in a high child's voice. He looked into that soft innocent face and saw a spark of intense intelligence hiding in the large, dark eyes. The King was one of those strange genius children who noticed and understood everything they heard and saw. Because of his unique understanding, Kadar projected an image of maturity beyond his tender years and often came up with strategies seasoned veterans never considered. It was an unsettling thing to be confronted with such an individual and Mamun wondered how long it would take for the boy's impressive intellect to drive him mad.

"I am flattered that the tales of one such as I has reached such royal ears," Mamun responded with the proper tones a lowborn peasant used when speaking to his social betters. The King grinned in the way of children, giving lie to the rigid somber image that he first projected. The King actually looked ecstatic to be standing there looking at Mamun.

"Your majesty," one of the bodyguards said softly with a gentle smile. "You have a meeting with an ambassador in a few minutes."

Kadar reddened and looked away and pulled his hand from Mamun's. "Yes, of course. Come, Captain, I have a very important task for you."

The boy walked back to the large table, expecting Mamun to follow him. Mamun got to his feet and went after the boy when the bodyguards gestured for him to do so. The King stepped up to the table and allowed one of the grizzled generals still standing there to help him onto a tall stool so he could see the maps spread across the surface. Kadar settled his robes more comfortably as he sighed with annoyance. A General fixed Mamun with a critical eye and gave him a nod of approval. Mamun looked around the room, feeling the eyes of every man boring into his skull. Everyone he saw was giving him looks of approval as if he had done something impressive.

Kadar beamed as Mamun approached the table and nearly jumped up and down in place. Mamun watched the boy's excitement, not knowing what to think about the unwarranted enthusiasm. The various generals and advisors smiled wryly at the King's antics as he turned to the papers and maps scattered across the table.

"My task for you is very secret and very important," Kadar began, the childishness melting away from his young face and was replaced by more adult-like seriousness. "I have not told any of my advisors or Generals about it. Only your commanding officers, you and I will know where you are and what you are doing."

Mamun glanced at the men around the table and wondered who the hell these guys were. If they weren't advisors or generals, then what were they doing here? The men raised their brows and smiled mockingly. They took several steps away from the table and turned their backs. Mamun frowned at them, still wondering who these fools were.

"How might I serve you?" Mamun asked turning his attention back to Kadar.

"I have sent for the Tracker," Kadar boasted proudly. "He is coming to complete a task I have set for him in the capitol city of Rhasta. There he will capture the criminals Barnum and Cass and present them to me at a ceremony when I take the city. It will, of course, be a grand display of the power I wield. When the people see this, the word of my influence and power will spread to the other kingdoms and they will not dare to oppose me any longer."

Mamun stared in open-mouthed astonishment at the boy's pure arrogance. Did he really believe that he could command a figure like the Tracker? By all accounts, the Tracker was a creature that worked to his own ends without regard or favor to one country over another. There were tales of kings and priests who died messy and painful deaths because they attempted to enslave a Tracker. Yet, this child dared to do so and then bragged about it. Kadar looked at him expectantly as if waiting for the older man to be impressed. Mamun looked at the table and pretended to examine a map to hide the horrified expression contorting his face.

"What is it precisely that your majesty would like me to do?" Mamun murmured fearfully. He was fairly certain that he wasn't going to like his orders.

"I wish for you to greet the Tracker and assist him in this task. I also wish that you would report his movements and alert me when he has taken the criminals so that I may accept them as a symbol of my sovereignty from the Tracker's own hands."

Kadar grinned at his own brilliance. Mamun just felt ill at the idea. He dared not criticize the king for his mad plot; kings have killed for lesser things and it was likely that no one knew what drove this boy to murder.

Mamun found himself saying, "Yes, your majesty."

Maddie pulled away from Mamun's mind and did her best to keep from throwing up as she came more into her own body. She was swaying on her feet while George pressed a steadying hand on her back. Mamun was sitting on the floor moaning and rocking back and forth with his arms hanging limp at his sides. Maddie shuddered and sat down in a chair behind her and put her head in her hands. Happily, her migraine had decreased to a dull throb at the top of her head that made her giddy with relief.

"That was just plain mean," George said sardonically as he gently touched her face.

"What the hell do you mean by that?" Maddie snapped, pulling her head back and slapping at his hands. She wasn't burning up anymore, her skin felt cool and her breathing came easier. A small errant breeze trickled through the cracks of the window shutters and ran over her skin. She shivered and the goosebumps rose on her skin. It felt pleasant to suddenly be so cool.

"You could have been gentler with Mamun," George replied. "He fell over when you hit him and nearly went into convulsions. Remember to take it easier the next time."

"I don't think there will be a next time," Maddie said, suddenly remembering the more intimate of Mamun's memories and blushing so hard that she felt dizzy.

"So what did you get?"

"Mamun is a Captain in Kadar's army," Maddie said. "He was sent to report our progress to Kadar. The little bastard is trying to use us as intimidation tactics in his war."

George barked a sarcastic laugh. "Well, we all know how well you like to cooperate with kings."

Maddie gave him a dirty look then snorted a laugh, too. If Kadar thought he was going to boss her around, the little brat had another thing coming. She had half a mind to just bend him over her knee and spank him in front of the city.

Mamun was coming to. He clutched his head and groaned in anguish. Fred was still crouched next to him and he turned to George and Maddie.

"Is he a spy or not?" he asked irritably. Maddie grinned and shook her head. A vague plan was forming in her head, one that involved Captain Mamun presenting the prisoners to Kadar just to let the little brat know that she wasn't going to be used for political gain. People would assume that Mamun had done the work and she didn't have a problem with that. After her look into Mamun's thoughts and memories, she liked him a whole lot better than she had before. And she didn't mind if he took credit for what she did. Besides, he would be coming along tonight, so he would deserve all the credit he got. George was right, her plan was a little slap-dash and they could use the extra man.

Mamun lifted his head from his hands and peered at her with tight bleary eyes.

"What did you do to me?" he asked in a ragged voice. Maddie shrugged uncomfortably and went to kneel down next to him. The dizziness had passed quickly and she was thinking better and moving straighter. She looked him in his beautiful eyes and smiled sheepishly.

"I'm sorry," she said. Mamun glared at her and climbed painfully to his feet. Fred had stepped back to stand next to George.

"You going to be okay?" she asked.

"Yeah," he growled leaning heavily against the wall and blinking in an effort to get the room to stop spinning. Maddie caught Fred and George exchanging looks out of the corner of her eye. She narrowed her eyes suspiciously at them and put her hands on her hips.

"What?" she demanded.

"You have put the Captain through quite a bit," George began with a gleam in his eye. *"It would be quite understandable if he became uncooperative. Perhaps you should do something to make it up to him and soothe his ego a bit."*

"What would you suggest I do?" Maddie snapped back. George smirked and shrugged but said nothing. He went to stand next to Mamun and the pair began to speak softly to one another. Maddie tried to eavesdrop but George firmly brought his shields up without even looking at her. Maddie harrumphed and walked into her bedroom in a huff. She still needed to get her things together if she intended to get home at the end of the night and the Agents left her to do her own packing. It was an arrangement Maddie was happy with since there were several girlie things she kept in her bags. Stuff like tampons and underwear were none of their business and she would rather that they never put eyes on it.

She had most of her things tucked neatly into the bag when Mamun tapped at her bedroom door. She grimaced and sighed. His thoughts boiled with anger and anxiety that he was struggling to push aside so that he could speak reasonably with her. She did feel guilty about what she had done which was why she didn't just tell him to wait until she was done.

"Come on in," she called, scooping up the last of her underwear and jamming it in the bag. Mamun entered and softly closed the door behind him. Outside, Fred and George were thinking so determinedly of ammunition and weapon distribution that it made Maddie suspicious. She narrowed her eyes at Mamun and wondered what the men were up to. Mamun gave her a look that told her he had very little patience for anymore of her clumsy tricks so she didn't even bother to skim his mind to find out what he wanted. She shrugged to herself, silently saying that everyone deserved the privacy of their own minds. That went doubly for Mamun since she had just destroyed the crap out of his personal space.

"You could have just asked me," he said suddenly. Maddie gave him a blank look that told him that she didn't know what he was talking about. "Instead of ripping into my head. You could have just asked me."

"I had to know the truth." She replied. "I don't know you very well and I had reason to be distrustful of your motives. You were behaving suspiciously and I have to do what's necessary to guarantee the safety of my men."

It was a load of crap and Maddie knew it. More often than not, the Agents were the ones who made sure she didn't get hurt but she had to say something to Mamun that he would understand. He had access to Barnum's club and he probably knew enough of the right people that he could get her close enough to the target to get the job done quickly.

"You could have just trusted me," he said lamely. Even to him that last part sounded dumb. It occurred to him that in her shoes, he wouldn't have hesitated to do as she had. What was worse, he wouldn't have felt the least bit guilty about doing so. The Tracker was looking at him with a regretful look on her face instead of the haughty one she was trying for. Maddie choked back a few retorts regarding men and trust and just managed to fake a smile.

"Well, I'm very sorry it happened this way," she said as sweetly as she could manage through clenched teeth. "Is there anyway I can make it up to you?"

Maddie held the smile until her cheeks ached. She gave him her best innocent look and waited for him to shrug and tell her that an apology was all he wanted and that he was ready to go. Instead, his lips curled in a leering smirk and he moved around the bed to stand closer to her.

Maddie blinked up at him in wide-eyed surprise. He was giving her a look of unbridled lust as he leaned into her. Maddie leaned away, trying to figure out what was wrong with the man. Was he really coming on to her? It was not an experience she was used to and didn't want to embarrass herself by making stupid assumptions. She wondered what could have possibly possessed the man to fixate on her. He was very attractive and she knew from his own memories that he usually had a herd of lovely girls jumping up and down at the chance to make him happy. Those types of guys never took an interest in her.

Then she remembered that she'd brain jacked the man and she did feel stupid. She felt his breath on her cheek and thought about telling him what she'd done. But she got rid of that idea real quick. If she confessed with toying with his mind to get him to do what she wanted, especially since he was going to do it anyway, there was a very good chance that he was going to be really pissed. She could only imagine what she'd have to do to apologize for that. Besides, the effects of the brain-jacking had to have worn off by now.

He stepped even closer until his body was just a dirty thought away and he touched her cheek softly with the tips of his fingers. It occurred to her that Mamun was just screwing with her head to watch her squirm. She gave him a mocking look and prepared to call his bluff. His eyes took on a heated drowsy look, a look that was very similar to the one Sam used to have when he was hinting around for sex. His body heat spilled off him and flowed like silk over her skin. She shivered at the sensation and took a sharp breath through her slightly parted lips.

He smiled at her response and settled his weight more solidly on his feet. Women had swooned in his arms before and he didn't want to drop the Tracker when her knees buckled. The disorientation of the mental invasion had worn off and now his brain was flooding with endorphins, overcompensating in its attempts to restore normalcy. He was feeling *really* good and wanted more.

He saw the Tracker giving him a hard look from between his hands. Her fingers were soft where they grasped his and pried his hands away.

"I have never swooned in my life and it is very unlikely that you'll ever be able to make me do so," she growled. Mamun pulled back in surprise. She had read his mind. Unnerved, Mamun watched as she stepped back and went back to tying her bag securely closed. He grew frustrated at the opportunity that was about to slip away.

Maddie fastened the hooks of her bag in place as she thought. Mamun was still standing too close and staring at her. His attentions had sent an electrical sensation across her skin and her heart was still pounding with excitement. She was in a dangerous situation. She was a married woman and she shouldn't be alone with this man. She shouldn't have put the thought that he could have her in his head in the first place. What would Sam think? What would he do if he knew?

With those last thoughts, her head came up in indignation. What could Sam possibly do? He'd already told her that he was divorcing her. For all she knew, he was drawing up the papers at this very moment. And for what? Because he couldn't handle her job. It seemed like a bullshit excuse not to get things worked out. She had put up with the insane demands Sam's career had made on them for ten years. But after a single year since she got a job, Sam was going to bail on her. She decided that if she was going to get divorced, then she was damn well going to do something to deserve it.

She turned to Mamun and this time she leaned into him, tilting her face up for him to kiss. He looked at her like he thought she was a crazy person but he managed to shake it off. Good things were happening and he wasn't about to put the brakes on because the woman was being contrary. Women were always contrary. He wanted her and her sudden change of mind seemed more good fortune than he could expect.

He grabbed her and pulled her tight against him before Maddie could change her mind again. He wrapped his arms tightly around her and crushed her against his body. Maddie let out a startled gasp as she clutched at the front of his shirt with her fists. The entire length of her body was molded into his so that she had to cling to him to stay on her feet. She stared into his eyes and realized that it had been a very long time since she'd been held tightly like this and it felt so good.

Mamun's fingers brushed the side of her breasts as his hands traced her ribcage and drew a ragged gasp from her. She slid her hands across his broad chest, feeling the hard ripple of his muscles under the smooth fabric. Mamun smiled a little and bent down, his lips parted to kiss her. Maddie rose up on her toes to meet him halfway, her hands sliding to grasp his arms and steady her. His mouth was soft and firm, the sweet texture of his lips like velvet.

He took his time caressing her lips with his, drawing her lower lip gently between his sharp teeth and holding it there. She made a soft sound in her throat and wrapped her arms around his neck and dug her fingers into his thick hair. His lips guided her mouth open and he deepened the kiss, his tongue sliding past her teeth to stroke her tongue. Maddie caressed his tongue with hers, examining the soft texture of his mouth and thrilling in the sensation of his pointed teeth against her lips.

His hands wandered up her back and stroked her hair before grabbing it firmly and drawing a sharp gasp from her. He moaned in pleasure as his free hand moved to the front of her body and cupped her breast. His thumb moved across her blouse and began to tease her nipple until it rose and grew hard. She arched her back slightly and encouraged him to do more. His hand released her hair, grasping her butt and pulling her hips up until her pelvis was pressed tightly against his. She could feel the hard length of him press against the tight fabric of his trousers. Eagerly, Maddie moved her body against his, drawing another moan from Mamun as he gripped her tighter.

He broke the kiss and dragged his mouth across her cheek and to her earlobe. She panted breathlessly as his tongue flicked out and touched her ear in a wet caress. Both hands were gripping her bottom hard now, kneading her rounded flesh with his big hands. She moved with the rhythm of his hands, her pelvis rubbing eagerly against him as he brought her tight to his hips and relaxed in an imitation of the act to come. His mouth moved down her throat. He nibbled at the side of her neck and licked at the spot aggressively when he bit her too hard.

He lifted his head and kissed her again, hard. His tongue moved in and out of her mouth, sucking just enough to keep the kiss from turning messy and stealing the breath from her. He straightened without letting go of her ass, which put her head higher than his as he used his hands to angle the most tender part of her hips even with the tip of his hard body. Maddie let out a small cry of pleasure into his mouth as she grew more aggressive which each gentle push of her hips. She deepened the kiss beyond what she had thought possible. She wrapped her legs around his waist and pushed against him. She felt his eagerness pressing hot and hard against his pants and prodding happily between her legs. He staggered a little off balance when she shifted her weight and he took the half step forward to the bed until he banged his knees against it.

She pushed her bag off of the bed as she was lowered down on it. Mamun pushed her further across the mattress, rubbing his hips between her legs and forcing another cry of pleasure from her. He never broke the kiss as he lay the full length of his body on top of hers. Maddie marveled at how well his form fit her own, how perfectly he moved with her and how good his hard body felt under her hands and between her thighs.

He leaned a little to the side so that his hand could pull her blouse from the waistband of her skirt. He went back to caressing her throat with his mouth as his hand worked its way up the front of her body, his fingers deliciously stroking every inch of skin that he touched. Finally, his hand covered her breast, his thumb stroking her nipple until it grew hard against the satin of her bra. She gasped and arched her back against his hand, all but begging him to keep going. He pulled her shirt up over her breasts, studying her bra with a curious look on his face.

"It unclasps in the back," she whispered against the top of his head. He looked into her face and kissed her, both hands going underneath her back to fumble with the hooks. She arched her spine to give him more room to move. He finally pulled the straps apart with a frustrated grunt and pushed the garment away from her chest. He was breathing hard as his mouth covered her breast and began to suck at her tender flesh. She made a small cry of pleasure and grasped his hair and held him against her.

He pushed her skirt up with his hands while he drew away from her breast and stretched her nipple taught. The rosy flesh sent thrills of pleasure through her body, deepening the arch of her back and spreading her legs wide. He let her go and she collapsed back on the bed as he licked a wet, hot trail across the mound of her breast to bury his face in her cleavage. His mouth licked and kissed the place between her breasts while his hands stroked her legs, first on the smooth outer sides of her hips then moving to the more sensitive parts along her inner thighs. Maddie spread her legs wider, making eager noises and pulling his face back to hers for a kiss. His fingers slipped into her panties and found her wet, hot, tight and pulsating around his hand. He moved his fingers in and out of her, stroking the slick walls of her body and searching for that sensitive spot that would persuade her to abandon her senses and make love to him. She lifted her hips in rhythm with him, panting and crying out with every stroke of his fingers. It was good, so good, and she yearned to release the pressure she could feel building between her legs.

She made a protesting noise when he pulled his fingers from her and began to tug at the buttons at the back of her skirt. He swore softly and pulled something from her waistband. She saw it and it took a second for her to realize that it was the all purpose rod that she took with her everywhere. Mamun tossed it aside and went back to pulling at her clothes and running his tongue slowly around her nipples.

Maddie moaned and arched against him. His mouth felt so good, and she gasped as her skirt loosened and his fingers slid under her panties and found her opening again. He used his fingers to explore her further, shifting his weight easily as he gave her breasts on last exquisite flick of his tongue and began to make his way down her body. She tried to relax back into the moment, into the pleasure and intimacy Mamun was offering. But something nagged at the back of her mind, telling her to quit messing around and get back to work. She shook her head and tried to drive the annoying voice from her head. She almost hoped that Mamun would simply rip her clothes off and sink his body deep into hers. Once he was inside her, driving his long hard cock in and out of her, she would be well beyond the point of telling him no and she could simply relax and enjoy the orgasm.

She stared dreamily up at the ceiling and her pleasure-fogged mind began to come into focus. Out of nowhere, she felt smug satisfaction coming from George in the other room. He knew that Mamun was seducing her and was certain that the sex would keep her preoccupied until he could get new orders from Keung. It had been an easy thing to convince Mamun to do. The man had been desperate for the experience of the Tracker's legs around his waist and, as far as the Agent was concerned, the good Captain was more than welcome. George's thought jerked Maddie completely away from all thoughts of sex just as Mamun drove two fingers deep and hard into her body. She gasped as a small orgasm took her; it spread her legs wide again and made her grind her hips against his hand. Mamun gazed at her face with his eyes shining and certain of the next act.

"Stop," she gasped, pushing Mamun away from her breasts and pulling herself off of his hands. Mamun stared at her from the edge of the bed and panted with a look of confusion on his face.

"What's wrong?" he asked as he moved to bring his face even with hers. "Did I hurt you?"

"No," Maddie said and moved further away from him. She got off the bed and stood against the wall to get her legs to stop trembling. "Did George put you up to this?"

Mamun scowled at her. "Do you think I'm such a whore that I would share a bed with any woman I was aimed at?"

He was offended and she couldn't blame him. She would have been pissed at the question, too. But George was relaxing in the sitting room, feeling confident that he wouldn't be going out tonight. The Agent had something to do with Mamun's attempt to get her into bed and it pissed her off. Mamun was sitting on the edge of the bed with his shirt unlaced and the top of his pants open. Maddie stared at the tanned flesh peeking out from around his clothes and felt a shiver of pleasure that it all still looked eager to slide into her. She wanted more than anything to let him do what he wanted but she couldn't shake the idea that this was all planned and staged.

"No, I don't think you're a whore. I'm just wondering what you and George talked about before you came in here," she growled. Mamun opened his mouth to answer than closed it with a snap. He frowned in concentration but couldn't remember what he and the Agent had talked about. He knew that they had had a conversation but he just couldn't remember what it was about. Maddie snorted and threw her hands up in disgust.

"I thought so," she growled. "First I jack you, now George. You're going to go batty with all the people jerking you around."

"Jacked? What is jacked?" Mamun asked. Maddie looked at him and bit her lip as she realized that she had said too much. She had to think fast. She didn't need the man to get pissed off and fly off the handle. What if she still wanted to go to bed with him when the mission was over and Mamun hadn't been manipulated into going with her? What if there was enough time to do it? He wouldn't take her to bed if he were pissed with her. And she wanted all of her options available.

"Just a slang word we use at home meaning that you'd been talked into something without knowing what it was," she said. She crossed her fingers behind her back for luck and watched Mamun's expression turn to suspicion. Finally, he shook his head and let it go.

"I will say this and then I will forget about it for now," Mamun growled and stood up off the bed. "I know you think something bad has happened to me and you don't want to tell me what it is. Which means it's something that will anger me rather than injure me. I will continue to assist you because I promised to do so. But later you will tell me what you think happened."

Maddie chewed her lip in that way she knew was irresistibly charming. She stood close to Mamun and let her fingers glide erotically across his chest. "I'll tell you but only after you throw me down and ravage me until I beg for mercy."

Mamun gave her a smile that said he was looking forward to that moment. But his eyes told her that he wasn't buying her delay tactic at all. He was going to take her to bed, he was certain of that, but she was also going to tell him what he wanted to know. He began to pull his clothes together as the Tracker headed out the door and began to angrily scold George. Mamun bent to tuck his pants into his boots and let out a laugh when he saw her panties still lying on the floor.

CHAPTER 35

Sam watched his children over an orange crush as they ate their hot dogs and greasy french fries and sucked at their own thick orange drinks. Allen ate cheerfully and with gusto, cramming the limp fries into his mouth as fast as he could. He laughed and clapped his hands but only because he was too young to understand what was going on. Chris didn't truly understand what was happening either but his sister had been nice enough to explain as much of it as she could to him, so he had a good enough idea to be depressed about it. He and Katie ate slowly and somberly, keeping their eyes on the table as they choked down their food. Sam smiled sadly and tried to think of something reassuring to say.

"It's not like you guys will never see Mommy again," he said gently. "She loves you very much and she'll visit as much as she can."

Katie and Chris lifted their dull eyes at him and said nothing. Katie's eyes began to well with tears as Chris scowled angrily at his father as if he thought he was lying to him. Sam didn't think he was lying by promising that Maddie could see the kids whenever she could, nor did the promise interfere with his strong desire to keep the woman out of their lives as much as possible. Maddie's job kept her away and he felt it was unlikely that she would be able to visit the kids more than two or three times a year.

The last few days had been very difficult for them. Since the attack at the school, Sam had kept his kids as close to him as possible. They stayed in the house and they didn't go to school. Not that the school had complained. Katie and Chris's teachers sent their work to them along with the teaching instructions and a note hoping that they're doing well.

Because he wasn't willing to leave the children alone, even with a sitter, he took them with him when he went to see the lawyer. Chris hadn't thought anything of it at first, since he and Allen were just happy to get out of the house. Katie had read the sign on the door and turned accusing eyes to her father. Her very young face grew stony as she stopped in her tracks and refused to go in.

"Why does the lawyer have divorce written on his door?" she asked suspiciously.

Sam took a deep breath and tried to think of a way to explain things to her that would not make her hysterical. Chris and Allen were distracted by a nearby holly tree and began to run around it, laughing. Sam glanced at them to make sure they weren't straying too far and turned back to Katie. She stared daggers into his head and crossed her arms.

"Because he's a divorce lawyer," he said carefully.

"He helps people get divorced, right?" she demanded. She didn't ask like she didn't know but as if she did and wanted him to tell her what they were doing here.

"Yes," he said.

"Are you and Mommy getting a divorce?" her voice had dropped low and fearful.

Sam didn't want to tell her now. The look on her face said that she was bracing herself for her world to fall apart. She trembled and hugged herself with her thin arms wrapped around her belly. He thought about simply lying to her but that would probably make things worse later when the paper work was signed and filed and he had to tell her everything.

"Yes, baby, Mommy and I are going to get a divorce," he said and took her by her small shoulders. Tears welled up in her big eyes and coursed down her soft cheeks.

"Is that why Mommy has been gone? Because you made her move out?" she asked.

"No, Mommy has been gone because she's out of town for work," Sam explained. "She would be with you right now if she could."

"Then why are you guys getting a divorce?"

Several answers popped into Sam's mind but none of them were things he could say to an eight-year-old girl about her mother.

"It's just the way things have worked out, sweetheart. Mommy and I still love each other but things have changed in a way that make it impossible for us to be married anymore." It sounded lame even to him and his daughter gave him a frown that said that she thought he just might be retarded.

"Did you get a girlfriend?" she asked.

"No!" Sam was more surprised by the question than offended. He hadn't expected his daughter to know about such a thing.

"Does Mommy have a boyfriend?"

Sam had to think about that. He really didn't know what the hell Maddie was doing and he preferred to think that if she didn't have time for him, then she didn't have time for a lover. "No, Mommy doesn't have a boyfriend."

"Then why?"

"I promise to tell you one day when you're older and can understand things better," he replied. Katie rolled her eyes and turned her back on him. She knew what that phrase meant. It meant that Daddy knew exactly what his reasons were but was too embarrassed about them to tell her. It made her mad when she was treated like she was stupid.

Sam yelled for the boys to come back from the tree and they went into the office. The receptionist was happy to watch the kids while Sam went to speak with the lawyer. Mr. O'Reilly explained that while a trial separation was not required by law to receive a divorce, he preferred it before he filed any paperwork. He had had many clients change their minds in the middle of the proceedings which wasted a lot of time and money. To which, Sam explained in as vague of terms as possible that he believed that his wife was involved in illegal activities that could pose a danger to the children. O'Reilly perked up at that as he smelled something interesting in what were usually mundane proceedings.

"So you'll be filing for sole custody of the children?" he asked. He got up and began to thumb through a filing cabinet in the corner. Sam watched him and felt guilt stab at his chest. He squirmed a little in his chair and wiped his sweaty palms on his pants.

"Yes, but probably with visitation rights of some sort. The kids are pretty attached to her."

"This is a state that tends to favor the mother in custody battles," O'Reilly warned.

"I don't think that my wife will be fighting for custody," Sam replied, feeling depressed as well as guilty.

"Do you have proof of your wife's activities? She might try for custody in the end," he asked.

"Yeah, but I don't think that I'll have it for much longer. I'm sure someone will come by to clean out her office soon," Sam replied. He didn't say that it would probably happen while he was out of the house. Hell, he didn't even remember seeing any of the stuff in the office come into the house in the first place.

O'Reilly sighed. "I'm afraid that it won't be considered theft until the divorce is finalized."

It went on like that for another hour. Sam told the lawyer about the attack at the school and how he believed that it was connected to Maddie's work. O'Reilly asked if Sam had called the police about the things he'd found in the office yet, and then told him to document everything. After that, everything wound down and Sam signed a document stating that O'Reilly would represent him. As Sam went into the reception area, he saw Katie sitting in a chair and glaring at a lollipop as if it had done something offensive. She didn't speak or even look at him as he led all three out of the door.

Katie sat whispering to Chris as Sam began to drive towards Atlanta. He felt guilty and wanted to take the kids somewhere in hopes of lifting Katie's spirits. By the time they entered the city, Chris was crying silently with his small hands over his face and Katie was casting dirty looks at the back of her father's head.

Allen was finished eating and Katie and Chris had given up eating to stare angrily at their food. Sam gave them a few moments longer before he decided that it was time to go. He smiled broadly at them in an attempt to make them feel better. Both of them glared hatefully back at him.

"Do you want to go to the museum? Or maybe the aquarium?" Sam asked jovially and ignored their angry looks.

"You made Mommy go away!" Chris cried suddenly, pounding his fists on the table. Katie broke into a new wave of tears.

Sam sighed, not knowing what else to do or say. So he gathered up the remains of their meal and threw it away. Katie and Chris were quiet as he led them out into the parking garage. Allen finally picked up on the mood and began to whimper in sympathy.

The van was in the far corner of the small parking garage, crammed under a bridge. The sun was making its long descent towards the horizon, making the shadows of the place seem longer and deeper. Sam stopped and looked around as he held Allen by the hand while Katie and Chris clung fearfully to his legs. There was something off about the garage, something that hadn't been there when they'd arrived. It wasn't anything that he could see; it was just an unidentifiable sense of fear. He saw a man lurking near the exit to the street. He couldn't see the man clearly but he was wearing a dark suit so that he blended into the shadows behind him. Only the pale square of his face betrayed his presence to the family. He made eye contact with Sam and nodded once and turned away. Sam frowned after him and pulled his children closer. Katie had seen the man as well and she stared suspiciously at him as Sam pushed her roughly towards the vehicle.

Sam hurried to the van while telling himself that his unfounded fear was based on the creepy man in the shadows. He pressed the button on his key chain which unlocked the vehicle's doors and lit the interior.

Twilight was falling fast, plunging the garage into darkness and making the surrounding building glow with a bright orange light. The garage felt creepier in the lengthening darkness and the fearful atmosphere intensified. Sam's skin crawled and the hair on the back of his neck stood up on end. The children felt it as well and, as he scooped Allen up, the boy trembled and whimpered fearfully. Chris ran for the van on his own, pumping his short legs in his rush to get to safety. Katie moved closer to her father, her head swiveling on her skinny neck in her attempt to look everywhere at once.

A low growl began in the darkness, so low and soft that, at first, Sam thought it was just traffic passing overhead. But as it went on and on, it grew louder and fiercer. Sam realized that it wasn't anything he'd ever experienced before and he froze in his tracks. His blood curdled and it took everything he had to not start weeping uncontrollably. Allen squealed and clung to his neck while Katie began to hyperventilate. He looked down at her and saw her wild eyes shining in her white face.

"They're here," she whispered. "They're going to kill us."

Sam's heart almost stopped when large round spots of light blinked open in the dozens of dark places all over the parking garage. Light managed to flash through the garage as a passing vehicle drove by with its lights on. Headlights flashed across the glowing lights and gleamed on horribly twisted and bent bodies. The growling grew more angry and intense until it became a chorus of threatening noises. Sam stared at them with wide eyes, afraid to move and afraid not to. Katie was weeping and Chris was jerking frantically on the door handles of the van.

"What are you waiting for? RUN!" a man's voice very nearly screamed. Sam broke into a hard run, grasping Katie by her shirt and dragging her along behind him. She screamed when she lost her balance and fell. Her feet scraped along the pavement and bled when her shoes came off her feet. The van was only a few feet away; he would be able to reach it in seconds. He could see Chris screaming as the door suddenly opened and the boy fell backwards to the ground.

A terrible scream broke the stream of growling as a mass of twisted bodies exploded from the darkness. They charged them on all fours, their toothy mouths drooling and snarling. Their yellow eyes burned with evil light as they streaked towards their prey. Sam looked back at the van, closer than ever, but he feared that he wouldn't make it. Chris was back on his feet and struggling into the vehicle, screaming for all he was worth.

He made it to the van and slid to a halt, nearly falling and dropping Allen. He nearly tore his own shirt off in his effort to get the baby into the van. Allen hit the seat face down and was still struggling upright when Sam grabbed Katie and threw her bodily onto the seat next to him. He jumped in after them and slammed the door shut just as something huge and hard slammed into the side of the vehicle.

The van rocked with the impact and the glass in the side window became a spider web of cracks. The children screamed in terror as more bodies struck the van, causing more damage to the windows and denting the metal. Sam climbed into the driver's seat and fumbled in his pockets for the keys. The van was rocking violently and he could hear the animal roars surrounding them. He didn't dare to look up. If he did, he would see the monsters fighting to get at them and he would be frozen with terror while his children were slaughtered.

Sam pulled his keys free of his pocket just as one of the beasts threw itself onto the hood. He screamed as he stared into its eyes through the windshield. It snarled at him and lifted a massive deformed hand. It punched through the glass, showering him with thick, gummy shards and scrabbled to get a grip on him. Sam pressed his back into the seat and struggled to get the key into the ignition. Behind them, the back window shattered and fell away as more of the monsters crowded into the window until they got stuck. Katie and Chris climbed beneath the seats, dragging Allen along with them.

Cruel hiccupping laughter tore through Sam's head as the van was rocked more violently. The tires were lifted off the ground and slammed back to the earth with bone-jarring force. The children were begging him to save them, to get them away. They were begging for their young lives and wailing.

Explosions echoed all around them, followed by the angry shouts of human voices. The monster on the hood stopped trying to reach Sam and turned towards the sounds and bared its teeth in a vicious growl. Suddenly, it spasmed and fell before it slid slowly off the hood and left a thick trail of oily blood behind it. The beasts struggling to get through the back window suddenly disappeared from view. Sam finally managed to jam the key into the ignition and he turned it.

The engine roared to life as Sam threw the van into reverse and turned in his seat. Three pairs of yellow eyes peaked at him from over the rear window frame. There were banging thuds as more of the monsters moved across the roof. More explosions erupted from the outside and he saw heavy bodies fall past the windows.

"Stay down!" Sam screamed at the children and jammed his foot onto the gas. The van lurched into motion. The beasts at the sides leaped away as the van slammed into the three monsters crouched behind the vehicle. The trunk door buckled inward as two of the beasts fell under the shattered bumper and the third jumped out of the way. Sam shoved the van into drive and hit the gas. The tires squealed and smoked for a second then the entire vehicle jerked as they sped forward. Sam went for the nearest opening to the street, not caring if any traffic was coming his way. He caught a glimpse of a man as he shot out of the garage and out into the street.

Horns blared and tires shrieked as the oncoming traffic slammed to a halt to avoid hitting the battered van that suddenly appeared in their midst. He kept his foot jammed onto the gas as he twisted the steering wheel and just barely avoided driving on the sidewalk and running into other cars. He raced for the freeway as he struggled to swallow enough of his heart so he could speak.

His chest burned and when he touched it, he gaped when his fingers came back bloody. Cold wind blew through the shattered windshield and into Sam. He couldn't hear his children over the roar of the winter wind and the roar of nearby traffic.

"Katherine! Christopher! Allen!" Sam screamed over his shoulder, his voice sounding panicked. He kept the corner of his eye on the road in front of him as he tried to look for his children. Had they been snatched? Where were they? Why weren't they answering him?

"We're here!" Katie answered, her voice shrill with hysteria. "We're all here!"

"Are you guys okay?" he asked. He looked for a place to pull over in case she said no although he really didn't want to.

"Yes, Daddy, we're okay!" Katie shouted to his immense relief. "What happened to the man who saved us?"

Sam managed to glance back at her. Her face was ashen and she was trembling slightly with shock and cold. Faintly, he could hear Chris and Allen crying with fear. Had there been a man? He remembered seeing a man before they were attacked and he remembered hearing him shout, but he didn't remember seeing the man after that.

"I don't know. I'm sure he's okay though," he replied. "He had a gun so I'm sure he killed all the monsters."

He hoped that the pale man was okay, but he had no intention of going back to determine the man's fate.

"Daddy, you're bleeding!" Katie's voice cracked with terror as her hands flew out to touch him. Sam shrugged her hands away.

"I'm okay, just a few scratches," he said smiling and trying to reassure his daughter. "We're safe now, everything will be okay."

"No it won't. We'll never be safe again. They'll just keep coming over and over until they kill us." Her voice was choked with tears. She began to weep in heartbreaking despair. Sam didn't know what to say to make her feel better. He was too terrified that she might be right.

CHAPTER 36

Carroll was making dinner with his gun lying within easy reach on the counter next to him. It was his usual habit to simply go out for his evening meals, but tonight the darkness felt too oppressive. He wouldn't admit it to himself but he didn't want to step out of the safety of his house without a light to pierce the cloaking darkness and reveal the things that lurked there. He had spent the last of the daylight convincing himself that he just wasn't ready to talk about what happened yet. The nightmares were still too new, too real, and he just wanted time for the terror to grow more worn and threadbare before he began to talk.

He poured the pasta and boiling water into a colander sitting in the sink. As he did, his eyes wandered to the gun and he fought the urge to pick it up and hold it in his hand for comfort. He couldn't help but remember that what had been in that house had gotten away. They were still out there, hunting more families and lying in wait for those that got away. Carroll shook the thought away. He was certain that he and his fellow officers had not been the monsters' intended target and it seemed illogical that he was significant enough to them that he would attract further attention. But then, nothing about what he experienced was logical.

Since the Portmans had been the obvious targets, they were now in protective custody. The lieutenant had worried that the surviving family was still in danger and had sent them far away to be watched around the clock by heavily-armed veteran cops.

Earlier, he had called the hospital to find out how Fielding was doing. He had been informed that the officer was in a coma, but stable. He asked after Arnold next and had been told that she had been released just a few hours after she had entered the emergency room. He had seen her gaping wounds and the puddle of blood that had formed beneath her. He had seen the paramedics leaning over her and working frantically through the blinding red and blue lights. She'd been taken away on a gurney, half-conscious and moaning. He had sat up to watch her leave, pressing his hand to his burning chest, stunned to still be alive.

He heard the keening of Mrs. Portman from the bedroom and he saw the crumpled and mangled bodies of Dewitt and Reid. He looked around for Fielding and found him laying inches from him, the white bones of his fleshless face gleaming in the emergency lights. Carroll had turned his head to vomit which brought more pain to his upper chest and shoulders.

The paramedics turned their attention to him as more cops appeared to search the house and persuade Mrs. Portman and her children to come out of the bedroom. Forensics set up their equipment while the people from the coroner's office began to examine the bodies. Carroll let the medic press him back to the floor and stared hopelessly at the ceiling. Beside him, he heard a deputy coroner gasp, "My God! He's still alive!" The paramedic abruptly abandoned Carroll as he turned to Fielding and the horror of his face. Unable to look anymore, Carroll struggled to his feet and staggered out of the house to sit in the weedy front yard.

After that, the night was a blur of doctors and nurses who stitched up the cuts in his chest and administered painkillers. Detective Cooper and an agent from the Georgia Bureau of Investigations showed up and somberly took his statement of the nights events.

Later the next day, he had picked Arnold up at her home and took her down to the station. She had looked pale and moved in stiff gestures and steps. Cooper intercepted them as soon as they entered the building while Arnold was pulled away by the Agent from the GBI. Cooper had been relentless in his line of questioning. He hadn't believed Carroll's account of the events of the previous night despite the fact that Mrs. Portman had corroborated the story and that Arnold was repeating the facts to the GBI. The detective had implied that the junior officer had been telling lies or hallucinating. At first, Carroll had remained calm and patient. He reminded himself that if he had been in Cooper's place, he wouldn't have believed the story either. But Cooper became increasingly hostile as the time wore on and Carroll had nearly run out of patience. Finally, Arnold had reappeared in a snit and she and Cooper exchanged angry words he was careful not to over hear. Then she limped out in a huff and he took her to the impound lot to pick up her car. She took herself home which left him with nothing else to do but go home and stew.

He got a phone call telling him that he was being put on medical leave until his stitches healed up and the psychiatrist the city kept on retainer cleared him for active duty. He had his first appointment in two days. That bothered him, too. He didn't know what he was going to say to the man that didn't make him sound crazy. So he refused to think about it.

He put the cooked pasta on a plate and drowned it in the tomato sauce he had simmering on the stove. He tucked his gun into his hip holster, grabbed a beer and took his dinner into the living room to eat. He settled comfortably into his favorite chair and turned on the TV, careful to avoid any channel that might be covering the bloody crimes of the last couple weeks.

The gruesome murders of two whole families and Mr. Portman plus the attack of the two Johnston kids at their school had drawn international media attention. The case was sensational; there was no doubt about it. The reporters didn't even have to add anything to make it camera-worthy. They filmed everything and got in everyone's way. Several complaints of trespassing, blocking traffic and vandalism had come in when the reporters had become too bloodthirsty.

Only the most vicious threats the brass could legally make had kept the victim's identities from leaking to the press. No one wanted the media to become more of a nuisance than they already were and no one wanted the media camped out on their front yards. To compensate for the lack of information, the reporters were interviewing anyone who would stand still for the cameras. The locals were happy to be interviewed. The well-groomed reporters with their microphones and chunky cameras felt glamorous to the blue-collar population. But, since most of them knew at east one cop personally, none of the interviewed had anything bad to say about the police force. They were confident that the killers would be caught and that life would continue as before. They were frightened by the deaths but they all firmly believed that if they prayed hard enough, it wouldn't happen to them.

Most of the interviews had been taken out of context or edited to make better television. The police force looked inept, the local citizens appeared either hysterical or woefully undereducated and inbred. The media portrayal of the whole mess was the reason why the GBI had stepped in. Carroll thought that it wouldn't be long before the Feds took over and everything was taken from the department's control.

Carroll ate his meal and stared at the TV, neither tasting his food nor really concentrating on the movie flashing across the screen. He allowed his brain to shut down and take a break from his worries. It felt good to just turn off and coast along on autopilot for once. The beer began to kick in and he felt his body relax. He set his empty plate aside and settled more comfortably into his recliner.

He drank his beer and let his eyes droop and become unfocused. Eventually, the beer bottle was empty and warm in his loose grip. He jerked himself out of a doze and dragged his body out of the chair and into the kitchen. He got another beer out of the refrigerator as he threw the empty one into the trash. He twisted the top off the bottle and tossed it into the sink as he wandered back into his living room. Just as he was moving around the couch, he looked up and saw something in his sliding glass door that made him freeze in his tracks and set his brains spinning in terror.

A pair of glowing, disembodied yellow orbs glared hungrily at him from the other side of the glass door. Carroll's blood froze in his veins as his heart hammered in his chest in its terrified effort to force the blood through his cold arteries. He stared wildly at the yellow eyes as he waited for them to become something his screaming brain told him was impossible. Nausea rose in his throat and his fingers grew numb. The monster came into focus as it stared at him and smiled, revealing its rows of long, gleaming black teeth.

It was mostly hidden by the blanket of the night, only its disembodied head and torso floated cruelly at his door. Long fingers like terrible ebony claws appeared beside its face and tapped at the glass. It ran its tongue back and forth across the glass, leaving trails of thick brown saliva smeared and dripping down the door. Unable to move or even breathe, Carroll watched in fascinated horror. His brain was screaming at him, jabbering at him to do something, anything, but his body refused to move. He felt himself held tightly in the thing's evil thrall and there was nothing he could do about it.

Suddenly, the beer bottle slipped from his numb fingers and shattered with a loud crack on the floor between his feet. Beer splashed over his shoes and stained his pants legs. The sound acted as a gunshot at a dog race. It jolted Carroll out of his stupor and he pulled his gun from its holster. The beast hunched and leaped through the door in a spray of gummy glass and began to streak towards him. Time slowed down as he took aim with a two handed grip. He saw the thing bearing down on him, and he knew that it was moving faster than any human and that it would be seconds before it crossed the living room and began to tear him apart.

He fired two shots into the thing that looked like his death. It flinched but didn't slow. Carroll was still firing shots as fast as his finger could pull the trigger when the monster slammed into him. It rode him all the way to the floor and tore into his chest and stomach and ripped his life away in just a few short seconds.

*   *   *

It hung in the darkest of shadows and took its time making the minute adjustments it needed to avoid detection by the humans. It would be entering a place full of harsh lights and human crowds and it feared that in such circumstances it would be spotted for what it was. It had even bathed an activity that the humans engaged in that it felt was useless, at best. The soap and water stripped it of its identifying odor and the lubricants that helped him change shape without pain. It felt dried out and naked.

It had all the details now, even to the last wrinkle of the simulated clothing formed from its own skin. It stepped awkwardly into the light and squinted painfully at it. It felt ridiculously unbalanced standing as it did on two skinny legs and narrow feet. It much preferred the feel of four solid limbs supporting his body to the precarious posture he held now.

Its first few steps were unsteady and it nearly fell. Passing humans gave it odd looks and one actually touched him with a steady hand.

"Are you okay?" the human asked, as its brow crinkled hideously.

It stared at the human male, the rich stink of it filling its nostrils. It felt the lean meat rippling along its arm and it fought the urge to tear into the creature and feast upon it. This human was not food. He had been very specific about which humans were to be eaten and which ones were not. This human was to be left alone. So it bared its teeth in an imitation of a social gesture and nodded. The expression frightened the creature. Its skin grew white and its eyes bulged. The male nodded nervously and hurried away.

It could taste the human's fear and it relished the exquisite flavor. It continued down the shining white hallways, coming across the occasional human as it walked. They knew instinctively that it was a predatory creature that meant them harm but in the manner of these "modern" creatures, they pretended not to notice that it was there. They avoided its gaze as if it didn't exist or they bared their teeth at it as if trying to placate it. It leered at the ones who smiled and laughed when they flinched and moved faster.

It moved through the rooms and corridors easily. The shiny, white, level floors let him move quickly through the stark pastel halls. It paced each floor of the building, sticking its head into each darkened room looking for its intended target. It had already tried to sniff the human out but the harsh scents of antiseptics mixed with copious amounts of body fluids masked the scent of its prey.

The humans were growing suspicious and hostile by the time it located the male it was looking for. The human looked like a strange dead insect where it lay in the narrow bed. Tubes and wires stuck out of its body and along its arms. The male's head was wrapped like a mummy in bandages, leaving only a little opening for him to breathe. Small spots of blood dotted the whited gauze and its flesh was slack where it hung loosely from its bones. It stared at the sickly thing and its lips curled in disgust. That was certainly not good food to eat. It looked fragile and gamy. Only the thoughts of what He would do to it made it step into the room.

It closed the door securely and blocked it with a chair. The room was dark and, aside from the hissing noises coming from the machines, it was quiet. Satisfied that it would not be disturbed for the few minutes the task would take to complete, it glared down at the human lying in the bed. It grimaced in disgust again and reached for it.

A few minutes later, it left the room and walked rapidly for the box that would take it to the bottom floor to its escape. It heard the shrill, hysterical screaming of a female and couldn't hold in the grin. The human had tasted as bad as it had expected but the resulting terror of the other humans made it all worth while. It did nothing to hide the blood staining its chest and stomach. It did not matter. The humans he passed were too busy running towards the frantic, terrified screams and paid no attention to the creature they passed. Eventually, it was forced to change its shape to cover the blood as humans wearing uniforms and bearing weapons filled the hallway. It ducked into the moving box and found itself alone with a small, plump female dressed in bright clothing. Her small, polite smile twisted into a look of horror as it shifted into something more familiar and mobile.

It turned its head slowly toward the little female and smiled as her mouth gaped soundlessly at it. Killing the unconscious male had been dissatisfying and had left a bitter taste in its mouth. It looked at the female and considered how she would taste. She looked so plump, so tender and so delicious. She would be the perfect chaser to satisfy its blood lust and wash the bitter taste from its mouth. It advanced slowly on her, knowing that she couldn't get away from it in the tiny room. Its jaws dripped with saliva and its claws ached to rend her tender flesh. She let out a small squeak that nearly sent the beast ripping through her.

But the elevator stopped moving with a slight jolt and the metal doors slid open. Two males in white coats stared in open-mouthed horror at the unexpected sight of the beast towering over the plump little female. One of them let out a loud scream and ran away. The other just stood there, frozen in terror. It gave the frightened female a last snarl before it leaped through the ceiling hatch and disappeared. The little female collapsed in a heap on the floor in a dead faint.

CHAPTER 37

Arnold picked up her car and went straight home. She dropped her purse on the floor and collapsed on the couch. It took a tremendous effort to just kick her shoes off her feet and leave them lying on the floor. She lay there limply and panted from the sharp pain that stabbed her side and from the choking despair that threatened to overwhelm her. She gagged on the lump that formed in her throat as hot tears slid down her cheeks.

She curled up tight on the cushions and wept bitterly while her mind replayed the horrors of the night before. Men were dead, men that she had worked with, played with and gossiped with. Dewitt had been there when she had learned that her husband had been unfaithful and Reid had thrown a party for her when the divorce went was final. Fielding had been happy to go out drinking with her those first few weeks afterward and listened patiently as she bitched miserably about the futility of marriage.

Dewitt had a daughter who had just started college and was pre-med. Reid had gotten married six months ago when his girlfriend had turned up pregnant. She hadn't given birth yet and now their unborn child would grow up without a father. The thought of Reid's baby dragged more tears from her and made her cries so painful that her chest felt as if was going to cave in. Why had the case been taken from her? She needed that case. It was for more than just to keep her from wallowing in the emotional cesspool developing inside her. She needed revenge but she was helpless to do anything but weep impotently on her couch. She cried until she fell asleep with her arms wrapped tightly around her body and her legs tucked against her chest.

She woke up hours later, her body stiff and aching. Her face was swollen from crying and her wound felt like they were on fire. She straightened carefully as her body protested every bend of joint and flex of her muscles. She took deep, even breaths and tried to work through the pain. Finally, she managed to drag herself from the couch and she staggered to the bedroom. Her head was developing a dull throb at the back of her skull which promised to become a fairly serious migraine soon.

She sat on the edge of the bed and began to peel her wrinkled and stale clothes from her body. She flinched when her shirt caught on her bruised flesh and she looked at her ribs and saw that the bandage was saturated with blood. The blood had dried a bit and the thick fluid was crusty and tacky around the gauze.

Arnold sighed wearily at it and finished taking her clothes off. A hot shower cleaned the wounds although the warm water made her stitches sting. On the plus side, the water soothed the pain in her joints and eased her developing headache. She stepped from the shower still fatigued and went through the agony of wiping the water from her body with a soft towel. She was still wet in places when she let the towel drop unnoticed to the floor.

She stared at her body in the mirror and at the gruesome stitches crisscrossing her side. Deep, ugly bruises covered half her body from armpit to mid-thigh and made her skin swollen and painful. She had to close her eyes to force herself to look away from the awful damage. She kept her eyes down as she reached for clean bandages and made her way back to the edge of the bed.

The despair became overwhelming again and, by the time she had finished bandaging her wounds, she was weeping. She fell back against the mattress and gave in to the tears until she fell asleep from exhaustion. At first her sleep was like the heavy press of a mountain rather than the velvety relief she so desperately craved. Then she began to dream terrible, bloody dreams filled with the beasts she had barely escaped as they slaughtered Dewitt and Reid over and over again. The dream shifted and she was forced to watch as demons ate her niece and nephews. Their blood sprayed her face and she squeezed her eyes closed as their piercing screams rang in her ears.

And she woke, jerking upright in her bed. Her eyes were wild and her breath rasped in her raw throat as she struggled not to vomit. Her ribs screamed at her and forced her to bend forward and she hugged her sides. The phone was ringing incessantly at her bedside table. Night had fallen and the streetlights cast a sickly glow through the room. She had slept the day away. The nightmares still lingered in her mind and made her blood curdle with terror. Finally, her brain registered the shrill sounds of the phone and she managed to untangle the blankets from around her legs so she could reach the phone.

"Hello?" she gasped.

"Darlene?" Cooper's voice sounded raw and frightened. He used her first name which meant something was really wrong. She wracked her brain, trying to think of what could possibly make his voice sound that way. She knew that he and his wife were having trouble — had she left him? Had something happened to his kids? Or was he still just really pissed at her?

"What's going on?" she asked settling in to listen to another lecture which was the best of all the possible options.

"Are you alone?" he demanded.

"Of course. What is wrong with you?" she asked.

"You need to come in. Now." Cooper sounded frantic. The nightmare was fading as her brain came more awake and she focused on the conversation.

"Why? What's going on?"

Cooper sighed like he had repeated the story too many times already and telling it one more time would break him. Arnold waited patiently for him to speak, not wanting to rush him but also not wanting to leave the house without a good reason. She was tired and her body ached and her mood was such that she was as likely to burst into tears for the smallest thing.

"Carroll and Fielding are dead," Cooper said, his voice thick with grief. "Mrs. Portman and her two sons were attacked. The mother was killed and the boys were badly mutilated. It isn't known if they'll make it or not."

"My God," Arnold gasped in shock. As of this moment, Arnold was the only cop who had been in the house that was left alive. It left her breathless. Her eyes darted to the deep shadows of her room, looking for monsters in every corner. Her ears heard every small sound and examined each one for a hint of her impending doom.

"You need to come in," Cooper repeated. "Are you able to drive yourself or do you want me to come and get you?"

"I'll drive myself. I just need to clean up and get dressed," Arnold wasn't about to argue with him. She could do that later as soon as she found out exactly what happened and figured out what she was going to do about it.

"Hurry up. I'm going to send a car if you don't get here in a reasonable amount of time," he warned.

"I'll call when I leave the house," she promised. Cooper's idea of a reasonable amount of time was a bit extreme and guaranteed that he would try to send the entire force out after her.

Cooper hung up without saying goodbye and Arnold paid no attention to it. She dressed as fast as she could and wrapped her hair into a messy ponytail to hide that it was a snarled mess. Her stitches had begun to bleed again in her haste, and all she did was wipe the blood from her skin with a bit of toilet paper and throw a shirt on over the rest. Her pain pills and bandages were stuffed into her purse with her cell phone and some cash and she hurried out the door.

She made sure her gun was within easy reach on her belt once she had eased herself into the car. She had her key in the ignition when her cell phone went off and made her jump so badly that she ripped a stitch. It continued to sing its merry tune while she squirmed in her seat and made muffled pain noises. She dug the cell phone out of her purse and hit the talk button.

"Detective Arnold?" came an anxious male voice before she could say anything.

"Who is this?" she asked as she turned the key in the ignition.

"It's Alcott Shorn, detective. Please I need a few minutes of your time."

"What can I do for you, Mr. Shorn?" Arnold put her car into reverse and pulled out of her driveway without looking. Luckily, there wasn't anyone coming. She stayed on the phone in hopes that Shorn was going to give her something useful to work with rather than blabbering on about things that might have happened a thousand years ago.

"There's someone here you must speak with," Shorn said. "The poor girl has been through something truly terrible and I believe she may have some very important information regarding your case."

"What does she have, Mr. Shorn?" Arnold made it out of her street and waited for traffic to clear so that she could turn left.

"I think she might know where the Distari lair is. How soon can you get here?" he sounded frightened. Arnold turned left and began to thread through traffic.

"I'll be there as soon as I can," she said tersely and hung up in the middle of Shorn's heartfelt thank you. At the red light she called Cooper and told him where she was going. If she hadn't, the man probably would send out ten cars rampaging through the county until she was found.

"I thought you were coming straight in," he said crossly.

"I'm interviewing a potential witness, Coop. I don't think I'm going to be cut down in their house," she replied hotly.

"Fielding was killed in his hospital bed with a half a dozen doctors and nurses within earshot. Carroll was in his apartment when his killer smashed through his sliding glass door and ate him. I don't mean that it tore him up and spread him out, I mean it ate him. We found a corpse and plenty of blood but we can't find most of his internal organs. The only explanation I have for what I saw is that the man was eaten. Mrs. Portman was killed and her sons mutilated right under the noses of four cops. Don't assume that you'll be safe just because you're with people. You need to get your ass in here so that we can protect you."

Arnold sighed irritably. She got what he was telling her and it scared her. But she suddenly had access to someone who might be able to tell her where to find these monsters and how to destroy them. She didn't want to give that up, not when more people were almost certainly going to die.

"I'm armed," She told him. "I can defend myself."

"Carroll was armed. And he wasn't as injured as you are." Cooper retorted.

Arnold turned onto Cassville Road and flicked on her high beams. The dark streets were lined with older subdivisions that lacked modern streetlights.

"Why don't you come in and I'll send out Hatcher to pick up your witness and bring them to you at the station to be interviewed," he offered.

"No, Cooper. My witness may be suffering from post-traumatic stress disorder and a stressful environment might make her shut down. I'll call you and check in every half-hour, okay? Besides, I'm almost there," Arnold said. She hung up before Cooper could argue anymore. He called her right back, but she ignored him. Two more left turns and she was pulling into Shorn's driveway. She made sure that her gun was loose in the holster and dropped her cell phone into her purse.

Shorn had the front door open before she had mounted the porch steps. He was dressed in a faded T-shirt and pajama pants covered by a dingy bathrobe. His white hair was in its familiar state of disarray and his thick glasses were propped crookedly on his large nose. He watched her come towards him with his face flushed with high anxiety as he wrung his hands nervously.

"Thank you for coming so quickly," he said. "Miss Emma is becoming quite unstable. I'm worried that her hysteria will become permanent." His voice was quivering with worry and his grimy eyes blinked rapidly at her from behind his glasses.

"Miss Emma?" she made it an open question, leaving the man free to answer anyway he wanted.

"She was brought to me nude and quite battered. Her hands and feet were the most badly injured, as if she had to claw her way out of wherever she'd been. Her mind is … bent. She is silent most of the time but then she starts talking and can't seem to quiet herself. It makes sense if you know what you're listening to. But if you don't, it all sounds like gibberish. She is quite suspicious of anyone who comes near her. She's terrified that they'll turn into monsters and drag her back to where she came from. She weeps a lot and will not allow me to call her family or a doctor," The old man sounded like he was overwrought with the girl's plight. Arnold gave him a gentle pat on his arm and a reassuring smile.

"Why don't you let me in so I can speak with Miss Emma," she said.

Shorn nodded miserably and stepped back to let the detective inside his home.

CHAPTER 38

Keung was going through the first batch of files about the Quarter that Elcia had sent up from the library. Most of what sat on his desk was centuries old, mostly repeated through oral tradition and in the cryptic languages from long lost civilizations on distant planets. The files mostly told tales of a benevolent society of advisors who were omnipotent and sought only justice and prosperity for the people they sent the Tracker to. The tales matched everything Keung had known to be true about the Quarter; at least what he thought he had known up until the last few days.

The Quarter's most recent orders to abandon all but one of the Tracker's children were contrary to everything he had ever seen or heard of his masters. The Quarter had always honored the contract they kept with the Tracker to the letter. When a man or, in this case, a woman was bestowed with the title and duties of Tracker, she was guaranteed the safety and well-being of her family. It granted the peace of mind that most Trackers could not do without and allowed them to do their work quickly and efficiently. Besides which, maintaining the integrity of future generations was beneficial to the goals the Quarter was trying meet. Trackers were always taken from the same family and the Center had always gone to great lengths to ensure the family line to make sure that there was always an heir and that the transition from one Tracker to the next moved smoothly.

Obviously, not all Trackers succeeded in producing children. When a Tracker failed to do so, the future heirs were chosen from the offspring of a sibling. In extreme cases, like that of Gustav Haughmein and the current Tracker, the line of inheritance had been in question. Haughmein had been a homosexual and the only child born of a long line of only children. Since he had not sired children, his genealogy was carefully traced to locate a relative who had the most ancestry taken from Trackers. The current Tracker was descended from no less than four Trackers including the prolific William Demonshane. Her children were descended from five, since their father was a descendant of an ancient Tracker who had died centuries before the early medieval William.

The genetic heritage of the Tracker's children meant that they were humans closest to being pure bloods on this planet full of nomads. They were unique for that reason and that reason alone should have guaranteed the Quarter's protection. They held the potential to be as powerful as the first of the Trackers and should be carefully guided and protected.

Keung's mind came around to the Quarter's order to abandon two of the children and, for the first time in years, he scowled. He heard a frightened squeak and he looked up to see one of Elcia's assistants standing just inside his office door. She clutched a stack of books and papers to her fragile chest and stared with wide, scared eyes and her mouth had formed into a little "o" shape.

"What do you want, Sanja?" Keung asked, forcing his expression back to cold neutrality. Sanja jumped and hurried to him and dropped the stack on the edge of his desk.

"Elcia wants to know what you need all this stuff for," she asked in a trembling voice. She stared at the floor, too frightened to meet the Keeper's gaze.

"Tell her that I'm just ascertaining behavioral trends. There's nothing to worry about," he replied. The stack teetered precariously on the edge of his desk and he put out a hand to steady it. Sanja nodded and ran from the office.

An hour later, Andre was darkening his doorway, holding a clipboard and giving him a stern look. Keung glanced at him then settled in to ignore the man. Andre rarely left the medical quarters and having the doctor in his office meant that the man was about to be an annoyance.

"How are you feeling?" Andre asked.

"Fine," Keung replied without looking up.

"Your scans revealed severe swelling in all of your joints and some nasty lacerations in your respiratory system. If I didn't know any better, I'd say you're sick and in a great deal of pain," Andre's voice was thick with sarcasm.

Keung didn't respond. He flipped the book in front of him closed and made the binding crack as he tossed the ancient volume aside. Elcia would have a fit if she knew how he was handling the literature.

"I have to say, I was very surprised when I went into the infirmary to check on your progress and found your bed empty," Andre persisted.

"How is Sherman doing?" Keung asked only because Andre expected him to ask and not because he really cared. At that moment he didn't care if the little bastard was writhing in agony so long as he didn't die. As soon as Sherman recovered, Keung was going to strangle him to death.

"He's stable but still whining like a little girl. He's not as tough as some of my other patients," Andre gave him a look that Keung ignored. "How's your pain?"

"Fine," he lied. His joints still screamed with pain whenever he moved. It took all his effort to keep from breaking into a sweat. Andre narrowed his eyes as he smelled the lie.

"Do you want some pain relievers?"

"Have Captain come straight into my office when he gets in," Keung said without looking up. Andre sighed and gritted his teeth and left. He knew a dismissal when he heard one.

Captain was already halfway across the Control Room when Andre spotted him. The grizzled veteran's mouth was bent into a scowl and his eyes flashed with anger. He stalked towards Keung's office and paid no attention to the staff he bumped into and sent scurrying in his wake.

"Keung said to go right in," Andre muttered unnecessarily. Captain just growled at him as he brushed past. He was planning to go straight in regardless of whether or not Keung wanted him to. Andre put his head down and kept walking. The Tracker was due back soon and, if the past was any indication of habit, she was likely to return with casualties in tow. He needed to get surgery and triage ready to accept patients.

Captain went into Keung's office and slammed the door closed behind him. He stalked up to the desk with an angry look on his scarred face. Keung blandly looked from the long scroll spread out across his desk.

"So which of the children do you want me to allow to die horrible deaths?" Captain snarled through clenched teeth. Keung regarded him coolly and leaned back in his chair.

"You've received the order then?" he said.

"Straight from the Quarter's mouth to my own ears. I don't think I have to tell you that their surprise visit left the Agents in a state of compulsive activity. They've broken down and cleaned every piece of equipment we have three times." Captain snapped. "Since when does the Quarter break the chain of command and tell us what to do themselves?"

It was a good question and Keung didn't have an answer. He could only act as if the Quarter frequently behaved this way. He looked at Captain and saw that the man was angry with more than just the Quarter's breach of protocol. Keung waited patiently for the man to continue.

"The Distari have identified the Tracker's family. The heirs came into the city for a meal and were attacked in a parking garage downtown. An Agent tailing the family was able to intervene until the family was able to escape. The Agent is being treated for the injuries he sustained in the line of duty," Captain crossed his arms and glared down at Keung. The Keeper had gone very still. His eyes and lips had tightened ever so slightly. Captain knew the look even though he hadn't seen it in decades. The man was on the verge of exploding.

"So, do you want me to follow the Quarter's orders or do you have a better idea?"

"You realize that question is the very reason why the Quarter broke the chain of command," Keung said with an evil smirk. Captain cocked his head and regarded him curiously. "You aren't carrying out their orders immediately and without question. You are asking me what I want you to do."

A small, satisfied smile played at Keung's lips. He liked that his people regarded him higher than the Quarter.

"What are your orders, sir?" Captain said simply.

"We follow the orders we were given. The eldest son will do as the sole heir. Put Agents in a mile perimeter around the heir's home and see to it that nothing gets by," Keung said. He pulled the scroll towards him and began to read.

"Sir, I don't have the man power for that. With the hunt going on—"

"Pull the men from the detail. The Quarter has canceled the search for the lair so we have the manpower to guard Christopher. We can put a man on the hunt some other time," Keung said to his desk. "However, I'm afraid that with the current sate of affairs, the Center will not be able to reinforce you immediately should you enter into a conflict with the Distari. I think it would be best if you took the field with the men and supervise them in person. I believe I can trust you to make the right decisions in a crisis."

Captain left the office feeling pleased. He'd just been given free reign to do as he pleased. He would protect all of the Tracker's heirs and, if the opportunity presented itself, he would destroy the lair. He walked quickly for the elevators and made plans to gather his forces and see if Bob would let them play with the fun toys.

CHAPTER 39

Maddie found herself back in Barnum's club and trying to look like she had every right to be there and that she had no plans to cause any trouble whatsoever. She kept her hands clasped demurely behind her back and her breasts thrust out so that none of the men currently leering at her noticed the Tracker's Mark on her finger. At her side, Mamun wrapped a protective arm around her shoulders as he swapped dirty jokes with an old woman. Maddie scanned the smokey room and looked for any sign of Fred and George. Of course she did not see them. The Agents were skilled at disappearing whenever they wanted. And they would remain hidden until Mamun and Maddie found their way into Barnum's personal chambers.

The plan had been a simple one. Mamun would enter the club in his usual capacity as local hero and club employee. It was his night off so he would bring Maddie along as his date. Mamun would talk some of the bodyguards and toughs into letting him take Maddie down to Barnum's private rooms and thereby sufficiently impress her enough to get into her panties. From there, they would be joined by the Agents and they would move to get to Barnum, capture him and leave him in an easy place for retrieval after they nabbed Cass.

Of course, the only problem with the plan was that Maddie had made such a stink during her previous visit to the club that she would most likely be recognized and promptly evicted. So Maddie had spent a half an hour in front of a mirror applying the make-up she always kept with her but rarely used. She lined her eyes with black mascara and eye liner. Dark smokey shadows and colors were applied elaborately to her lids and she managed to darken her complexion with base and powders. Lip liner and lipstick made her lips seem fuller and a quick press of brown eyeliner to her cheek gave her a mole she hadn't had previously. A few barrettes and a pony tail holder gave her a loose hairstyle and emphasized the natural curl of her hair. She emerged from the bathroom certain that she looked like a porn star. Too expensive to be a common hooker but too flamboyant to be taken seriously as a permanent companion.

Mamun's eyes had grown wide while George took one look and let out a hulking gut laugh. Even Fred allowed a smile to quirk on his lips as his eyes climbed up and down her face and form. Maddie scowled as Mamun and George hooted and cat-called their approval of her disguise and off they went.

Maddie simpered at a leering bouncer and pressed herself tighter to Mamun's side. The man let out a raucous laugh and Mamun moved them deeper into the club. He steered her towards one of the massive bars where he was met with cheerful greetings and raunchy cat-calls. Mamun responded to these with hard slaps on the backs of the men and flirtatious kisses on the cheeks of the few women. Curious glances were shot at Maddie followed by knowing exchanges of whispers as people speculated on what she was and who she was to Mamun. Maddie allowed herself the luxury of skimming the gossips' minds. Most of the people assumed that she was simply some random hussy that had caught Mamun's eye. She was something to be used to relieve some physical needs for a short time and then discarded. Two of the men were already making plans to scoop her up as soon as Mamun threw her away.

Maddie blushed at the lewd images in the men's minds and fought the urge to dive under a table. She decided that ignorance was bliss and shut her shields tight. The bartender winked at her like she was a common floozy and put a drink on a napkin in front of her. She managed a weak smile and pretended to sip at the strong-smelling concoction. Mamun was a few moments longer talking to the bartender and the other customers.

A strange man sidled up to her at the bar while Mamun's back was turned and began to aggressively flirt with her. She cringed away from him, unable to hide her disgust at the rank smells of his breath and body. He described how he would treat her in lewd terms and ignored her obvious contempt. Maddie was seconds away from belting the guy when Mamun noticed the man's unwanted attentions. He swept her roughly into his arms and kissed her until her knees buckled.

"Barnum is in residence tonight and one of these guys is going to point us in the right direction," he whispered intimately into her ear once he'd broken the kiss. "Try not to beat anyone up until you absolutely have to."

Maddie snorted rudely and poked him in the ribs hard enough to make him grunt. He gripped her ass hard enough to hurt and smiled merrily. She gave him a dirty look as Mamun laughed and let her go. He put his hand on her waist and moved them both away from the bar. Another man moved away from the bar and waved at them to follow him.

"It's very difficult to take you seriously when you look like that," Mamun grinned as he fought the urge to cop another feel. Maddie growled and poked him again. They threaded their way through the crowd, Mamun acting like a single man out to blow off the stress of the week while Maddie was the cheap date he was using for that purpose. Finally they reached the far end of the massive common room where they came face to face with a large man dressed stiffly in dark blue and eye-jarring red. He stood just beside a bit of wall with a brass knob sticking out of it. Their guide stepped up and spoke to the guard who glared at Mamun and then nodded.

Maddie concentrated on trying to look vapid as Mamun stepped forward and spoke with the men. They took their time, speaking in friendly, muted voices and ending with a handshake. Finally, Mamun stepped away and gestured to her while the man twisted the knob and opened the wall. The door pivoted on thick stone pins to reveal a long, dark corridor that disappeared far beyond the wall. Maddie blinked at it and wondered how far it went.

"Try to look impressed," Mamun whispered in her ear as he led her into the shadowy doorway. The man smiled knowingly at her as they passed him and pursed his lips suggestively at her. Remembering to stay in character, Maddie giggled vacantly and clung to Mamun's biceps.

"Oooh, Mamun!" she simpered sarcastically so that only he could hear her. "You're sooo cool and dangerous!"

The door closed behind them and left them standing in the dark.

"Javis just let me know that Barnum is having a bad day," Mamun said. "Which means that he's more paranoid than usual and he's more likely to kill someone for no good reason. He'll probably have close to ten nasty men guarding him."

The headache was beginning to build again and she pressed the heels of her palms against her temples in an effort to squash it. "Shit."

"Just so you know, Barnum has been hearing voices for a couple of years now, has become obsessive over strange things and he's always been a sexual sadist." Mamun said. "You'll need to be very, very careful about what you say and do."

Maddie grimaced and groaned as she kicked uselessly at the floor. She muttered and swore under her breath as she let Mamun guide her further down the passageway. The door opened again and, as they turned toward it, they saw two men silhouetted against the smoke-filled common room. They dragged a third body through the portal and quickly closed it behind them. Fred and George quietly took their places behind Maddie.

"It looks as if our information was a little off, guys," Maddie said as they continued on their way. She noticed that the floor of the corridor wasn't level, but that it sloped downward into the earth. *"It seems that Barnum is off his gourd and is having a bad day."*

"How reliable is your information?" George asked irritably. *"Abiah didn't say anything about Barnum's mental stat, and she's always been very thorough."*

Of course my information's faulty, Maddie thought, bristling at the comment. I'm just the Tracker, not some inn floozy who can shake her ass and smile pretty! It was a bitchy and vindictive thought, she knew that, but she felt that she deserved more credit than a gossipy innkeeper got.

"Hey, Mamun," Maddie hissed. "How do you know that Barnum's a nut job?"

Mamun paused to be sure he knew what the Tracker was asking before he spoke. "He gutted a bartender last week when he got a drink recipe wrong and Barnum thought he was trying to poison him. The man screamed for two days before he finally died. Barnum watched it all and laughed. Why?"

The why sounded irritable so Maddie told him the truth. "George just wanted to know how you knew that."

"I was there," he growled.

George snorted in disgust and shook his head. His brain boiled with irritation. He had a hard time believing that the woman had made such a potentially fatal omission. Homicidally crazy people were more dangerous than most and the fact that Barnum was one of those was much needed information. It just didn't seem like something Abiah would miss. He liked Abiah enough to think seriously about it when she asked him to go to bed with her. Of course, he had refused since he was on duty.

The corridor twisted downward, each turn coming at ninety-degree angles, so that the passageway turned in upon itself, first going left, then going right a few feet later. The deeper they went, the darker it became as they went beyond the weak light shining through the cracks in the doorframe behind them. They were nearly blind as they made a turn and were confronted by the yellow light of a bulb hanging bare from the ceiling. Finally, after an eternity of walking downward with their way lit by naked bulbs at infrequent intervals, they came to a wooden door bound in battered, rusting iron. The wood was old and badly warped so that it was splintering at some places and big gaps showing through the wood.

Mamun took a deep breath and knocked on the door, careful to strike only the metal holding the fragile wood together. The light beyond flashed as a man moved back and forth behind it. He paused and Maddie saw that he had pressed his face to the door to stare between the gaps in the planks.

"What do you want?" asked a rough and angry voice.

"It's Mamun. Open the door."

The man paused and a moment later the door opened. The splintering wood made a hideous scraping noise on the stone floor and set Maddie's teeth on edge. Mamun put his hand on the small of her back and pushed her inside as her head pounded with renewed force.

"I don't know the doorman," Mamun said softly.

"So what?" Maddie snapped.

"So, the only time Barnum changes his guard is when he's killed all the others," he growled.

"Shit," Maddie snarled. Behind her, George and Fred discreetly loosened their guns in their holsters under their coats.

The room they had stepped into was a vast space with clean white walls and a gray canvas tarp stretched across every inch of the floor. At the far end of the room was a tall chair carved completely from white marble that glowed in the dim light. The chair sat on a small platform draped excessively in delicate white fabric that fell in crumpled waves and curls onto the floor. There were more wooden doors, one for each of the four walls of the room. They were solidly made and cleanly varnished with crystal knobs that sparkled like precious jewels.

"What's with the doors?" she asked softly.

"Wood is precious here. Only the very rich and powerful own objects made from the material," Mamun replied misunderstanding the question.

"No I mean, why are there so many doors in the room? Are some of them closets?" she asked.

"They are positioned so that men can enter the room at a moment's notice. Each door leads to a different section of the compound."

"There's a compound?"

Mamun looked at her as if she had lost her mind or that she might be stupid. He did not say anything; he just shook his head and looked away. Of course there was a compound. She was the Tracker and should known to scout out her enemy's territory before she confronted him in it. Maddie couldn't help but pick up on the thought and felt herself blush in embarrassment and felt very dumb. The man had made a very good point. No wonder George thought they were all going to die.

"Something's wrong with all of this," Maddie said, suddenly noticing the suspicious black and brown stains scattered across the canvas. The little group kept moving further into the room but Maddie just couldn't tear her eyes from the stains. There was something familiar about them, something she should know off the top of her head. It nagged at her and her head threatened to explode with it.

"Those are blood stains," George said with growing alarm. *"I think we're expected—"*

His words were cut off abruptly as what felt like an invisible blade stabbed into Maddie's brain. Her eyes bulged and she staggered as her mind let out a roar of agony. Mamun's hands caught her and held her as George and Fred's guns cleared their holsters and aimed them outward. Men in pastel-colored suits burst from each of the four doors and seemed to fill the room around them.

Maddie straightened with an effort and felt a gun being pressed into her hand. She grasped it as she reached behind her back and pulled the rod from her belt. A flip of the switch and a long gleaming blade emerged from the end. Mamun glared dangerously at the men surrounding them and held his blocky weapon in his big hands.

"Try not to shoot me please," George said with a tone of high humor.

"Then don't stand in front of me," Maddie replied with her own slightly panicked teasing.

Maddie stared at the men surrounding them with their own weapons drawn and aimed and realized that she could not sense a single thought from them. Her head was pounding so badly that she thought she might throw up. She struggled to hold her own weapons steady and stared into the faces of grim men with eager eyes.

"Okay? Now what?" Maddie asked through clenched teeth. She stared at the fuzzy forest of weapons before her and tried to estimate her chances of surviving a pitched battle. She did nothing but her finger caressed the trigger of her gun. She blinked against the pain as her brain suddenly tried to escape through her forehead. Her stomach lurched violently and she swallowed convulsively to keep from vomiting.

"You guys head blind, too?" Maddie asked, making a conscious effort o speak English.

"Stone cold, Tracker," George replied while Fred grunted confirmation.

"Shit," Maddie glared at the men who suddenly reminded her of the trendy hit men from a bad 1980s crime drama. One of them met her gaze and actually winked lasciviously at her. Maddie nearly shot him in the face.

The men moved back, making an opening in their ranks leading to the tall chair on its platform. A big fat man emerged slowly from the door positioned behind the chair, carrying a heavy metal club in his beefy hands. He was one of the biggest men Maddie had ever seen; he was damn near seven feet tall if he was an inch, with every centimeter of his body covered in a thick, sickly layer of fat. His neck was wider than his head and the thick folds of flesh poured over his collar and settled on his shoulders and chest. He wore a black shirt thick with ruffles and appeared as if it should have cut the circulation from his shiny, bald head. Maddie eyed him warily, noticing the intense helter-skelter look in his dark, beady eyes.

Barnum approached them, smacking one end of the club into the palm of his hand so that it made a thick, meaty sound when it hit his flesh. He walked straight up to Mamun and sneered right into his face. His thick glistening lips curled in gleeful satisfaction that revealed a row of tiny pointed teeth. Mamun let his blocky weapon press into the heavy folds of fat around Barnum's gut and let his face go blank as the massive man let out a barking laugh.

"Did you really think that I wouldn't notice your arrival, Tracker?" Barnum jeered. "Did you really believe that one such as yourself could possibly be over looked by one such as I?"

Maddie blinked and had to do a double-take at the priggish fat man. The fool actually thought that Mamun was the Tracker! Maddie exchanged glances with Fred and George, letting them see her astonishment. They shook their heads, telling her to remain quiet and let the man think what he wanted. Meanwhile, they would stall for time until someone came up with some sort of plan.

Mamun glared and bared his teeth at Barnum. "Stand down, Ezra Barnum, and submit to the will of the Tracker!"

Everyone gaped at the man's audacity, even Maddie, who wondered frantically what the asshole thought he was doing. She looked back at George, who shrugged to tell her that he didn't know what the hell was going on either. Barnum let out a loud, braying laugh that went on and on until Maddie thought her head would explode. His men echoed the sound, their own voices carrying an edge of hysteria in them. They were frightened but the trick was to determine what it was they were scared of: Barnum or the Tracker? Some of the men were trembling while others had broken out in prodigious flop sweat.

"I most certainly will not and there is nothing you can do to make me," Barnum giggled and pointed his club into Mamun's face. He turned his attention to Maddie and the Agents. His tongue slipped between his thick lips like a pink slug and ran it around his mouth as his eyes dragged up and down Maddie's face and body. Maddie stared coolly back, hiding the intense revulsion he provoked in her.

"I see that you bring bodyguards and a woman. I cannot fault you for that. I also will not travel without one of my whores to tend my needs and a pair of men to watch my door while I ride her." Barnum said.

He moved to pass close to her and bent his head to let his cheek brush the top of her head and drew a deep breath.

"You smell pretty," Barnum whispered loud enough for all to hear. "Don't worry, my dear, I'm not going to kill you right away. You and I are going to have a great deal of fun together before you die. If you please me very well, then you will live longer."

Maddie took a deep breath and held it. It took every ounce of self-control not to shoot the man then and there. She knew that if she did, there was a very good chance that his men would kill her anyway. Instead, she concentrated on the terrible headache. Barnum left a wet kiss on her temple and moved on. Maddie could not repress the shudder that suddenly wracked her body. She wanted to throw up so very much. Barnum glanced at the Agents and a broad smile split his face. He stepped into Fred gave him a mocking stare.

"The men said that you were tight and firm and just as pretty as a girl. I am pleased to see that they described you so accurately." He laughed into his face. Fred's face darkened and he began to flush dangerously. George shot Maddie an alarmed look and began to edge away from the other Agent while still holding his guns out. The goons standing closest to George noticed his movements and took a nervous step back. Everyone but Barnum felt the dangerous rage boiling off Fred and was eager to get out of the way before the man exploded.

"Which did you enjoy more? Using the whore or being the whore?" Barnum said, as he let his club trail lightly and suggestively down Fred's body. The Agent's face was livid as the club came to a rest near his groin. It was the last insult and Fred erupted in a force of violence so fierce that it took everyone by surprise.

George slammed into Maddie and took her to the floor as Fred's fingers convulsed and the barrel of his gun burst into tiny explosions that fired bullets one right after the other without a pause between them. The heads of a pair of goons exploded in a gush of blood and tissue. Bullets cut the air over George and Maddie's bodies as the bodyguards returned fire without a second thought. George pulled his body over hers to keep her shielded from the death exploding all around them. Maddie clung to him and kept her eyes squeezed shut. Men screamed in terror and pain and their sounds were quickly drowned out by the ear-shattering recoil of more gunfire. Thick liquid and wet globs spattered the exposed parts of her body.

Suddenly, the gunfire ended in a roar of silence. The screaming continued, singing in time to the thick sounds of flesh striking flesh, the crack of shattering bones and the wet noises of soft body cavities being opened up. The screams began to quiet and she could hear Barnum shrieking orders to his surviving men. Fred was roaring and growling like a rabid animal. She heard doors bang open and the sounds of footsteps echoing away.

George cautiously lifted his head and looked around. After a moment, he lifted his body from Maddie and sat back on his heels. Maddie sat up and groaned in pain. She felt the back of her head and found a knot forming on her skull. Her head pounded worse than ever. Behind her, Mamun let out a low whistle and she found herself looking around in shock.

The room was littered with bodies. She stared at all of them and thought that there couldn't have possibly been that many men in the room when Fred lost his mind. Many were riddled with holes of various sizes. Most were ordinary bullet-hole size but some were the size of Fred's fist. Arms and legs lay scattered about like trash and heads were stacked in a loose pile off to one side. The floor was covered in a huge puddle of blood that was inches deep and making its creeping way towards the pristine chair and platform.

Maddie gagged as she pulled her hand from something too thick to be blood and quickly got to her feet. George still had his guns out and he was scanning the room as Mamun struggled up. His eyes were so wide that the whites showed all around the irises. He looked at the carnage on the floor and shook his head to rid his hair of the chunks of gore.

"What just happened?" he asked dully.

"Barnum pissed Fred off," George replied as if things like what just happened occurred every day.

"Where is Fred?" Maddie asked. The stink was beginning to get to her. No one ever talks about what death smells like. She'd always imagined that it smelled something like rotten meat or dirty pennies but this smelled like a butcher shop housed in a dirty toilet. Unable to hold it any longer, she bent over and vomited noisily onto the floor. She braced her red-coated hands on her knees to keep from falling back into the gore.

"He's probably going after Barnum," George replied ignoring her as he checked his guns to make sure the barrels were clear. "You okay?"

Maddie thought he was talking to her until Mamun answered. "I'll be fine. It's just a flesh wound."

Maddie looked up at him. His white shirt had turned red and clung wetly to his chest and belly. The left shoulder of his shirt was a ragged mess, and the flesh beneath it was slashed and gouged. His arm hung limply at his side and looked a little skewed. Mamun moved easily as he bent and picked up his weapon one handed and shook the blood from it. The shoulder looked bad and she looked around for something to bind it with. But anything that could be used for a bandage was saturated with blood. She looked down at herself and saw that at least one of her sleeves was still moderately clean. She grasped it tightly and pulled it free and off her arm.

She held it out to Mamun and murmured about binding his wound. Her brain was tingling with a download of emergency medical information and it made her eyes cross and her head spin. Mamun was looking at her with a mix of surprise and embarrassment. He stepped away from her as she got closer and shook his head.

"That's okay, I'm all right," he protested. He was blushing so hard that she thought that he might pass out.

"Shut up and hold still," she growled. He did as he was told though he kept his eyes diverted away from her. She scowled at him in annoyance and wondered what he was so embarrassed about. "What is wrong with you?"

"I'm sorry, Tracker. It's just that your arm is exposed and, well…" his voice trailed off. Maddie barked a laugh despite her aching head.

"You've seen my boobs and had your hand up my skirt but it's my arms that are pornographic?" she chuckled. Mamun gave her a weak grin. Maddie tied up the shoulder, making sure it was wrapped and tied so that it kept his arm from moving too much. She stepped back to admire her handiwork and nodded in satisfaction. She went looking for her weapons and found them nearby. She used her skirt to wipe the gore from them, and then tucked the gun into her belt. She kept the rod with the blade extended in her hand.

"Shouldn't we go catch Fred before he kills Barnum?" Maddie asked. George nodded and gave her a small smile as he cocked his head and listened intently.

"I hear screaming," George said and disappeared into a doorway near the platform.

CHAPTER 40

The house was lit brighter than daylight. Every lamp, light fixture and flashlight Shorn owned was on and set in such a way that not a single shadow remained in the place. Even the refrigerator door was left open so that the tiny bulb could do what it could to chase back the darkness. The furniture and books and papers that had once been scattered all over the place was now shoved against the walls and stacked neatly into place. There could be no doubt that nothing hid behind the strange piles.

Shorn closed and locked the door as soon as Arnold entered the house and moved past her without speaking. He led her to a door set just off the kitchen. The old man put his face to the wood and knocked softly. There was a muffled sound as if whoever was on the other side was throwing things around.

"Come in." The voice calling them was soft and feminine with the sweet lilt of deep southern coloring the tone. It made Arnold think of those southern belles who started out as pampered princesses and ended up hypersensitive socialites and manipulating matriarchs. However, this girl's voice was raw, as if it had been cruelly stripped of the soft velvety element that made these types of women what they were.

Shorn slowly turned the knob and opened the door just enough to put his head inside. He spoke softly and gently and was answered by that sweet southern. Shorn pulled his head out of the door and gave Arnold a slightly frustrated look.

"Just one moment please, detective. Miss Emma is afraid to receive visitors and I must reassure her that you do not intend to hurt her," he said.

Arnold gave him a weak smile and nodded for him to go ahead. Shorn disappeared beyond the door and left her standing in the kitchen by herself. After a moment, she began to wonder if the visit was worth pissing Cooper off for.

The bedroom door opened slowly and revealed a young woman wrapped in a bulky terry cloth robe. She was a small delicate thing who seemed almost lost in the oversized garment and the men's slippers that were too big for her tiny feet. She had a thick wealth of golden hair that shone in the bright light of the room. Her blue eyes were huge in her delicate, heart-shaped face and the tired bruising below her eyes lent a tragic aura to her already-considerable beauty. Arnold stared at her, thinking that this girl looked exactly like some fairy tale princess that was always kidnapped by the evil dragon.

"You must be Emma," Arnold said kindly. Emma sunk deeper into the robe and gave her wide frightened eyes.

"Who are you?"

"This is Detective Arnold. Don't you remember? I told you that she was coming by to talk to you about what happened," Shorn took Emma's small hand in his big ones and gave it a comforting pat. Arnold smiled at the girl, letting the expression warm her eyes. She knelt on the floor in front of her to make herself seem more approachable.

"You can call me Darlene," she said. Emma just gave her a blank look as if she didn't quite understand which language was being spoken to her.

"I don't want to go home," Emma snapped like a petulant child. "I won't go home and face them after what happened. I can't do it."

Arnold smiled and wondered what Emma's family must be like if the girl was so unwilling to return to them after the ordeal she had been through. She gave the girl's knee a kindly pat and noticed that her fingertips were swollen and cut and the palms of her hands were raw. Emma noticed Arnold's attention, and her eyes became cold.

"I don't need you to feel sorry for me," she snarled.

"I'm sorry." Arnold said sincerely and without excuse. Emma could easily decide that she didn't like Arnold well enough to tell her a thing and there was nothing Arnold could do about it. Beyond a few cuts and bruises and Shorn's say so, she had no evidence that a crime had been committed. So she put on her friendly cop face and waited for Emma to make up her mind. She hoped that the girl would hurry up, though. Cooper was going to shit his pants if she didn't call him soon.

"They can change their shape when they want to. They can look like anyone you know," Emma began, speaking so softly that Arnold had to strain her ears to hear her. "That's how they got me. That's why no one has ever seen them kill people and how they can get away. It looked like my friend and then it dragged me away. They dragged me underground and kept me there and tortured me. I don't know how long they had me or how they could let me escape."

Her voice trailed off as she sank back into the horrible memory of her ordeal. Her eyes glazed over and she trembled violently. Arnold shook her gently to bring her back and squeezed her hand reassuringly. Emma blinked rapidly and focused her eyes on Arnold's face.

"It was the master who had me. He tortured me. He would touch me and poke me. But the worst was how he looked. He was more human-looking than the others and that was what made it so bad. He could change from a normal looking man and into something ugly and terrible just by smiling. He would get into my face and stare at me and it scared me so bad that I couldn't look away. And he would laugh and laugh until I fainted. He liked to tell me over and over what he was going to do to me and how much he would enjoy it."

Emma's eyes filled with great shining tears and spilled down her smooth cheeks. She was growing hysterical just from the memories. She struggled to breathe through the sobs and she wiped uselessly at her nose. Even sobbing messily, Emma was beautiful. Shorn made comforting noises and rubbed circles into her back like he was comforting a child. Emma took a few deep shuddering breaths before she spoke again.

"Can you tell me where they took you?" Arnold asked.

"No," Emma said bowing her head. "All I remember is being downtown shopping and then I went with my friends to have something to eat at the square. Then everything was dark and I was being dragged across dirt and some rocks."

"My lady friend told me that she found Emma near Main Street and Tennessee Avenue last night," Shorn explained to Arnold. Arnold pulled a notebook and pen from her purse and began to jot the street names down. Emma watched with a spark of hope beginning to light up her face.

"You believe me?" she asked shakily.

"Detective Arnold has faced the Distari before, Miss Emma," Shorn told the girl. Emma stared with eyes filled with awe. A smile pulled at her full-sculpted mouth. Arnold patted her hand again and leveled a look at Shorn.

"It was on the news," he said. "Not the Distari part, of course, but that you and other officers were killed or injured defending that family. I could tell what happened."

Arnold shook her head and continued to take notes.

"They're going to kill some more people," Emma said in a rush. "They're going to kill some cops that got away from them and a family that belongs to someone called Tracker. A husband and some kids. They know where the family is and they're waiting for her to come back so that they can get her in a trap."

"Her?" Arnold asked. Flashes of the strange terrifying sensations she had experienced first at her sister's house then again just before she was attacked at the Portman house tingled along her spine. Katie's descriptions of the things that had attacked her whispered through her brain. It was trying to tell her something that she wanted badly to ignore. She took all of it, shoved it deep and squashed it flat. She kept her face as neutral as possible as she waited for Emma to elaborate.

"They always referred to the Tracker as a woman. They never said her name or the names of the people in her family. They talked like they lived nearby and that they weren't going anywhere."

Arnold had looked away to hide the sudden look of shock on her face as the blood froze in her veins. She had to stop writing to hide the trembling in her hands. What Emma had described made it sound as if she had been held by the very same group that Arnold had encountered. She had to clear her voice several times in order to speak. Her throat was dry and felt like it was trying to close off.

Arnold studied the girl. There was something just a little off about Emma. She knew a lot and had survived beasts that had easily slaughtered armed men for just seeing them. She had been in their home and yet she still breathed. Arnold's first reaction had been to take the girl in and put her under protective custody. It seemed clear to her that Emma would be killed once this Tracker's family had been eliminated.

But the what ifs snuck into her head. What if Emma wasn't what she seemed? What if she was one of these Distari creatures in disguise? What if she was bait for this Tracker woman? What if she was exactly what she appeared to be? Shorn watched Arnold and saw the fear and uncertainty play across her features. He frowned, thinking things over and suddenly seeming to understand Arnold's predicament.

He gave Emma a big smile and patted her hand. Emma had gone back to weeping fiercely. Her thick golden hair fell around her face and gave her a place to hide.

"You've done very well my dear," he said gently and kissed her cheek. Emma did not move. She had returned to whatever hell Shorn had pulled her out of and could not see anything else. Shorn stood up, gesturing for Arnold to do the same. She followed him out of the bedroom and waited while he closed the door softly behind them. The girl's heart-wrenching sobs could still be heard, though the door and walls muffled it somewhat.

"You think that Emma is lying, at least in some small way," Shorn said quietly. Arnold sighed and shrugged. What could she say?

"Don't worry. The same thought had occurred to me as well. Why don't you just leave her with me? If the Distari wanted me dead, they would have killed me twenty years ago. I'm certain I'll be quite safe."

Arnold hesitated. It seemed unreasonable that she leave a pair of civilians in potential danger, no matter how confident they were of their safety. Besides which, Emma was a witness and she needed to file a formal statement and her family needed to be notified of her whereabouts.

"I'll see to it that she's available to you at any time," Shorn said as if reading her mind. "And I'll call you if she says anything else. I promise that she'll be safe here. I've had safety precautions in place for years just in case I was attacked. Everything will be okay."

Shorn squeezed her shoulder and smiled. His eyes were bright with excitement. Arnold gaped at the old man. He was actually enjoying himself! Arnold felt mildly appalled at that. People were dying horribly and this old fool was having a good time. Arnold let it go with a shake of her head. Shorn mistook the expression as a protest.

"If you take her to the police station, she'll only repeat the same story. They will not believe her and nothing will be achieved. If you stand up for her, they'll think you're mad and send you away. Do you want that?" he looked triumphant when she gave him a dirty look. Then she shook her head again, this time in defeat.

"Can you give me a clue to the Trackers identity?" she asked finally. Deep in her mind, a voice whispered that she already knew the answer to that question. But she stubbornly ignored it as Shorn gave the question some thought.

"As I have told you before, most of my research is concerning the Distari. I run across stories about the Tracker from time to time but I didn't keep most of the literature. All I know is what I told you and your partner. Although there is something that the stories always say that might be of use to you."

He turned and went into the living room where he began to rifle through the neat stacks of papers and books. He finally came up with a tattered volume in his hand. The title and the author's name had been rubbed away with time and the edges of the cloth cover were frayed. He opened the book and revealed thick pages that had long gone yellow and soft at the edges. He thumbed through it quickly, like he knew exactly what he was looking for and where to find it. He grunted in satisfaction and held the book out to show her what was on the page.

"This is the Tracker's Mark. It is the only way the Tracker and her associates can be identified," Shorn said. "Although the stories say that the associates rarely display the Mark openly, the Tracker wears it at all times."

Arnold looked at the black and white engraving that took up the right page of the book in Shorn's hands. The delicate and exquisitely detailed drawing depicted a mass of intertwining lines and whorls that wove in and out of the pattern without end. The artist had drawn five bright stars, four set at points of a compass among the elegant pattern of twists and turns. A fifth bright spot sat in the middle of it all and had been drawn a little bit larger than the others. The image nagged at her brain. It was so familiar to her but she couldn't quite place it. It was like a song that had only been heard while the mind was occupied with something else. It was heard and registered somewhat but did not notice enough to be able to know the tune when it was heard again.

"You've seen the Mark?" Shorn asked excitedly. Arnold frowned and opened her mouth to speak but then her throat nearly closed as the realization suddenly hit her like a kick in the guts.

She knew where she had seen the Mark. A simpler but no less stunning version of the same thing had graced her sister's finger every day since she had received that strange inheritance from the random German cousin. It was soon after his estate began to arrive in crates that Maddie had started her job. Arnold's heart pounded in her chest until she thought she was going to have a heart attack. Her brain reeled like a trapped bird and all the frantic movement centered on a single thought: What the hell was Maddie doing and who was she doing it for?

Emma's warning screamed through her brain and her pounding heart nearly stopped. Maddie was doing something that had caused these monsters to go after the children. Arnold was fairly certain that her sister had no idea what was happening or else she would be home protecting them. She bolted for the door without saying a word. She seethed with growing rage as she got into her car and sped away towards her sister's house. She swore that the next time she saw her, she was going to shoot Maddie in the ass for being so damn stupid.

CHAPTER 41

The timids were frenetic with panic as they rushed in small, dirty groups that raised thick clouds of stinking filth. They were sobbing in terror as they went wandering in broad circles that nearly took up the massive antechamber. Every few moments, one of the group would collapse in a dead faint and the strange bits of bone and rock they compulsively carried would roll from their limp hands. Seconds later, another timid would gather up the fallen bits and resume wandering.

Their incessant movement annoyed the changelings and grunts and they snarled and swiped at them with their claws. Occasionally, the claws would strike a timid that had wandered too closely and great gashes would appear in their rags and blood would dribble into the dirt. The timid would scream in agony and terror and hurry to rejoin the herd. He found it all amusing as hell. He grinned as he watched the flurry of chaos and filthy rags as it moved in a large circle.

He simply sat upon his throne and watched, the bored expression on his weird face fading into a grin of anticipation. He had been in a stupor of boredom ever since the girl with the yellow hair had escaped. She had done a great deal to keep him entertained and he missed her. Of course, the timid that had allowed her to escape had been most severely punished. Its remains hung in gory tatters from the ceiling at the center of the antechamber, mounted as a warning to any who failed to follow orders. Perhaps it was the corpse swinging over head that had sent the timids into such a snit.

One of the grunts hit a timid solidly and sent the frail and pathetic thing flying. It hit the floor with a wet smack and sprawled bonelessly. It did not move and made no sounds, which meant that it was dead. The other timids shrieked in terror and they scattered and ran in whatever direction they were already pointed. They hit the ring of grunts and changelings that had gathered around them and they broke on the mass of stinking bodies like an ocean wave upon rocks. The grunts barked with laughter while the changelings growled.

The stink of fear filled the larger Distari like an intoxicant, triggering the hunting mechanism in their brains and the whole room exploded into blood and violence. The bigger and stronger creatures tore into the timids who would only cower and squeal as they were snatched from the floor and shook about like a dog with a prize toy. Some were lifted high into the air and flung about while others were simply pulled apart into unrecognizable bit of ragged flesh. A few managed to avoid serious harm by either playing possum or disappearing into the crowd when the grunts became distracted with the feast.

He sighed impatiently and stood up so that all could see him. If He allowed this to continue much longer, there wouldn't be any timids left. Not that the idea particularly bothered him. But the timids were the only creatures clever enough to complete the meticulous tasks that were often necessary to his comfort. Changelings were intelligent as far as lesser Distari go but they lacked the finesse to do anything well but kill. The grunts were little more than mindless animals. They lived for the feed and were only good for random cruelties and mass slaughter. It was time to put an end to the fun and find out what had upset the timids so much.

The herd had fallen silent after a few moments. He moved from the throne and they melted away from his advance as he made his way to a huddle of surviving timids. They wept and shivered as he towered over them and reveled in their terror like a man starved for food. Finally he sighed in satisfaction and regarded the filthy pile of flesh at his feet.

"What has occurred that caused you to engage in such foolish endeavors and excite the blood lust of the entire lair?" He snapped.

"He's coming!" came the squeaked reply from somewhere inside the pile of stinking rags and open sores. He cocked his head curiously and gave them a gentle smile, which of course, only made them wail. One fell away from the huddle in a faint. A grunt snatched it with the tips of its claws and tore it apart while its fellows fought over the bloody pieces.

He ignored all of that while he contemplated the answer. Did they mean that the Keeper was coming? That would be odd, considering that only one Keeper had dared to confront a lair and that fool had been eaten almost five hundred years ago. Was it an Agent? That seemed more likely, since Agents were a constant nuisance and were frequently found lurking around lairs waiting to kill Distari.

"Who?" He made his voice rough and cruel just to let the pathetic things at his feet know that his patience could grow very thin very fast. The huddle began to tremble until a thin cloud of dirt rose from their bodies. The hid their faces in their hands and wept miserably.

"The Master is coming!" the hysterical reply was shrieked for all to hear. "The Master is coming and we must prepare!"

He felt the blood drain away from his body and settle heavily into his feet. How could this happen? His time to deal with the Tracker and her heirs was not up yet! His face contorted with a rage that made everything in the room flinch.

The fact that only the timids had gotten advanced warning of the Master's arrival meant only one thing. Panic began to take hold as he suddenly felt his life being counted in minutes. But, instead of immediately killing everything in reach as he was wont to do when he was upset, he spun on his heels and hurried to his personal suite.

It was too soon. Far too soon. The Tracker was still off planet and out of his reach. His lair was not strong enough to go chasing after her through the five galaxies. His plans were in a fiery ruin. The Master was coming and had not given Him advanced warning. It meant that The Master meant his demise. Someone had discovered his plans and had betrayed them to those who would be most threatened by them.

He had to clasp his hands behind his back to keep them from shaking. He entered his suite and sat in the chair before the fireplace. He let the heat of the raging inferno held inside the cold stone bathe his skin and force his muscles to relax. He stared into the blue and orange flames and felt his eyes glaze over as he let go of his visual focus. He needed to think, to lay down new plans and figure out how to salvage the situation. He had some time; the timids had said that the Master was coming, not that he was already here. He had some time left to save him, and he intended to use it very wisely.

It didn't take him long to come up with a solution to all his problems. His face split into an evil grin and his breathing slowed until it became slower and deeper. He sent out a thread of command and brought a changeling to his presence. The changeling crawled along its belly towards him, prostrating itself and whining submissively. He let it snivel while he thought of just the right phrasing so that the thing could understand his orders.

"Gather together a crowd of grunts and go to the Tracker's family. Kill them so that there is no doubt about who had slaughtered them. I want her to come to us enraged and crippled with grief. I want her here, where we can surround her and tear her apart so that the Master may bathe in the glory of her screams."

The changeling smiled from its place on the floor. It understood His orders and could feel the glee coming from Him. It ducked its head and simpered away. A few feet from the door, it grew daring and rose up fully on its feet, and ran from the suite to gather its fellows for the hunt.

CHAPTER 42

They pounded down a hallway that sloped ever downward into the earth. Screams of agony and death echoed against the walls louder and louder the further they went. The men ranged far ahead of Maddie, their longer legs and heavier muscles eating the distances almost effortlessly. Too soon, she was forced to slow down and stop to catch her breath and pull herself together. Her head pounded terribly and her skin burned in agony. She pressed her head against the stone walls and let the coolness of the rock soothe her. The men jogged back to her with anxiety on their faces. For the moment, the screams had died down though they could still hear Fred roaring his bloodlust in search of more victims.

"What are you doing?" George demanded angrily. Maddie looked up at him and squinted. Her headache was so bad that she was having trouble focusing on him. Mamun put a hand on her shoulder and she flinched and whimpered in pain.

"I just need to catch my breath," she whispered. "Keep going, I'll catch up."

She was beginning to regret her decision not to stay at the inn and wait for orders. Her head hurt so much and she longed to lower her body into icy water. She was too sick to be out chasing criminals. George was right; she was going to get them all killed. But it was too late to change her mind now; she could hear Fred laughing maniacally from somewhere ahead.

"I told you that you weren't well enough for this," George growled. "You insisted on it, Tracker. Get up and do your job as you have commanded us. And you'll do well to think before you act next time."

Maddie nodded. She didn't want to argue with George, not because he was wrong but because she didn't have the energy to do so. Maddie closed her eyes and wrapped her arms around her body as the shudders wracked her.

"What happened back there?" she asked just to keep from moaning and whining like a baby. "I'm completely head blind."

"Barnum's a psychic." George replied coldly, as if she should know this already. Maybe she should have. "We encounter it from time to time. Usually they aren't a problem. They avoid us and we leave them alone. Sometimes they go a little crazy when they can't cope and they pull shit like this."

"How?" Maddie asked. She began to slowly force her body straight and steady on her feet.

"It depends on the environment, which is why there are so few natural psychics on your home world. On certain planets, the people have evolved so that a small percentage of the population can mentally manipulate electromagnetic fields. In our case, Barnum screwed with the electrical fields around our bodies and made our nanopacks go haywire. It looks as if the physical attributes we gained from the technology are still intact, but our mental skills have been shut down. It's temporary. If we don't go back online once Barnum has been eliminated, then the Doc can fix us once we get home."

Maddie pushed away from the wall and stood with shaky knees.

"Let's go."

Just then several men began to scream. The sound was fainter, which meant that Fred had moved further down the corridor. Gunfire followed it and then there was more screaming and shouting. George and Mamun turned toward the sounds with their hands going to their weapons. George let out a low curse and the men took off, running as fast as they could go. Maddie hurried after them. She struggled to keep up and wondered if it was possible to vomit while running full tilt.

They came upon the scattered and dismembered bodies very quickly after that. They were forced to slow down and pick their way through the bits and pieces of men and the slick pools of blood they left on the floor. Maddie gaped at a body that was riddled with gory fist-sized holes. She tore her eyes away from it and hurried to catch up to the men.

She lost Mamun and George as the bodies grew thicker on the ground and she had to tiptoe through them to keep from tripping. They lay in awkward positions across the floor. Some sat propped against the walls in macabre poses of death, their empty eyes forever held in expressions of pain and horror. Maddie stared at it, wondering what was going on inside Fred's mind that he could do such things. She could certainly understand what had triggered his rage and she couldn't blame him for it. But these were the violent acts of someone who was deeply disturbed.

She followed the sounds of ferocious battle. She could hear George and Mamun's voices joining the fray along with the crash of gunfire. She put up the blade and tucked the rod back into her belt. She took the gun out and held it in two hands and kept it pointed at the ceiling. George had waited for the last minute to give her a gun for a good reason. Maddie was a nervous shooter which meant that she had a tendency to pull the trigger anytime she was surprised. That tendency had gotten a good many Agents shot during her first few weeks as Tracker until George had taken the guns away from her in disgust. She was getting better about it through rigorous training and drills but the men still had a tendency to flinch and duck whenever she held a gun in her hands.

She made her way carefully and made sure that her finger remained relaxed on the trigger and that her gun was pointed up so that she didn't shoot herself. She could hear George and Mamun shouting angrily amidst the echo of gunfire. Maddie hurried up and wiped sweat from her forehead with a sleeve that was stiff and tacky with blood. She approached a door that was open a crack and pressed her back against the wall.

Maddie took a deep breath and held it. She wished feverishly that she had the telepathy back so that she could find out what was going on. She steeled herself to go through and join the fray. Her brain tingled and nearly drove her to her knees. Armed combat instructions downloaded into her memory centers and her joints spasmed painfully as muscle memory was added to back up the information in her brain.

She used her foot to kick the door open as soon as the tingling in her body stopped. She poked her head around the door jamb and took a quick look around. The room beyond was too dark for her to see anything clearly. Something had happened and the fighting had stopped. She squatted and hunched to make herself as small a target as possible while still remaining somewhat mobile.

She bolted through the door without a thought. It remained dark and silent as she hurried blindly through the room in hopes of finding one of the men.

"Tracker!" George hissed from her left. Maddie changed direction without slowing and just barely managed to not fall down. George touched her elbow when she got close enough and she stopped.

George murmured an apology as he took his hand away. His fingers had been merely warm but, with the scalding heat filling her pours, that small heat had burned her arm terribly. George moved to get her attention in the dark and turned to Mamun. They spoke softly together for a moment. Mamun shook his head and shrugged. Maddie didn't pay much attention to the pair. Her eyes were focused on the smaller figure hunched between the men. Maddie reached out and touched the figure and it moaned. She recognized Fred's voice and she leaned unsteadily towards him. Her hand grasped the table they were using for cover as she leaned as close as she could.

"Fred, are you okay?" she whispered. She wanted to reach out and feel that he was alive but she was afraid that touching him would give her more pain.

"Don't call me Fred. How many times do I have to tell you that I hate that?" the Agent snarled.

"Are you okay?" Maddie asked, ignoring him.

"I'm fine!"

George snapped his fingers between their faces to get their attention.

"Barnum went out that door over there," he pointed to a door just to their right. "Fred and I will stay here and cover you from behind while you and Mamun go after him. Be quick, I don't think that Barnum plans to stay in the area much longer."

Maddie nodded and turned to the door and made a run for it with Mamun on her heels. They took a moment to open the door and peer through it and make sure that the hallway beyond was empty. They eased into the corridor and as Mamun led the way, rushed down the hall. While moving, Maddie traded her gun for the rod and extended the blades at both ends. She didn't want to trip in the odd light of the weak bulbs overhead and accidentally shoot Mamun in the back. Mamun moved stiffly and his arm swung uselessly at his side. It seemed as if the shoulder wound hurt him worse than it had before. Mamun paused at a closed door; this one made of stone, and regarded her with pain-filled and feverish eyes.

"How long do you think it will take Fred and George to join us?" Mamun looked a little gray and his face was clammy with sweat. He was panting as if he'd just finished a hard run rather that a quick jog.

"Hasn't the bleeding slowed down yet?" Maddie hissed. Her head was pounding and her skin flared hotly and all she could think was that if this guy passed out from blood loss, she wasn't going to drag his ass around.

Mamun glanced at the wound and moved the shoulder slightly. He flinched and grimaced. "It's not bleeding so bad."

Maddie sighed in disgust and answered his question. "I wouldn't expect to see them any time soon. They'll meet us on the way back, though. Fred was looking a bit rough."

She took a moment to gather her wits as she swayed on her feet. Mamun steadied her with a quick hand but said nothing.

"Let's go," Maddie said. "I don't want Barnum to get away. You have more combat experience; you take point."

Mamun pushed away from the wall and raised his blocky gun. He took the knob in his hand as Maddie moved out of his way. The knob turned easily and the door moved silently as he opened it. Maddie peered into the brightest room she'd seen since she arrived on the planet.

Mamun stepped through the door and Maddie followed. She found herself in a massive underground warehouse that was easily twice as big as the social club above it. Tied bundles and oversized barrels sat stacked against the walls and were crammed onto shelves. The shelves were lined up in neat, narrow rows and hung with tall ladders. The floor was rough-hewn and made from dark stone and there was a broad double door at the far end of the complex.

"This is Barnum's secret warehouse. Everything that enters the city winds up in here or in another like it across town owned by Cass. The big doors lead out of the city and empties near the river. There's a fortune in goods and contraband in here."

Maddie stared, looking for any sign of Barnum. But the warehouse was silent and not even a stray breeze made its way through the place. They kept walking, moving slowly so that they could spot potential trouble. They began by combing the aisles with their weapons held out in front of them.

Maddie stopped dead as a high-pitched laugh echoed through her head. It was a crazy sound, full of mirth and murder. Mamun spun in place and searched for the source of the hideous sound. He hadn't grasped what Barnum was yet and didn't understand what telepathy meant. So the things that happened in his head would be very real for him. It made him potentially dangerous to Maddie and she took a step away to put some distance between them.

"What's happening?" he demanded. He stared at her with eyes gone wild with terror.

Maddie gave him a hard, flat look. "Barnum's screwing with our heads."

Barnum began to taunt them, chanting "Tracker" over and over again. He suddenly stopped and burst into manic giggles that sent shivers up and down their spines.

"I'm going to kill you and paint my walls with your blood!" Barnum sang merrily. He continued along this vein, describing in graphic detail exactly how he would butcher their bodies and use the parts. Maddie looked around, hoping to spot the holes where the bastard would hide. Barnum was a huge man; there weren't many places he could go. Maddie touched Mamun's arm and he jumped. He watched as Maddie gestured out a plan, staring at her with wild, panicked eyes. He was afraid and struggling to keep it together.

Barnum was still whispering to them in their minds as they split up to search the warehouse. It was difficult to ignore him as his voice grew into a painful thing that echoed through their bodies. She had to find Barnum. She was at her wits end with the raving lunatic. She was sick and tired and she just wanted to go home.

Barnum had picked up on Mamun's fear and Maddie's frustration and began to laugh at them again. He stopped making sense. He scoffed gibberish into their heads. Rage and a desperate need for blood coated the nonsense syllables.

Suddenly, footsteps echoed along the long rows of shelves. A man let out an enraged scream. The sound of metal striking metal rang out and echoed through out the warehouse.

Maddie turned toward the sound and began to walk quickly toward it. The clanging split her skull and she had a deep wish to be dead. Mamun appeared just in front of her as she emerged from an aisle of shelves and she followed him towards the noise. Barnum had stopped talking to them telepathically; instead, he was screaming in time with each shattering strike. The footsteps sounded closer and a man in a blind panic appeared as if from nowhere and ran towards them. They stopped and held their weapons aimed as the man passed them and disappeared.

Mamun started forward again, holding his injured arm tight against his body. Maddie held her blades ready. Holding it away from her body and keeping her distance from Mamun so that she could swing it freely without stabbing herself or her comrade.

They came upon a pair of badly battered corpses sitting in a large pool of blood. Red fluid and bits of flesh and bone streaked the walls near them. They simply stepped over the corpses without looking at them. Maddie's headache roared in her skull. Her skin had cooled a little in the chill air of the underground warehouse and she gave thanks for that small relief.

Barnum was laughing hideously while he continued to bang on the shelves in the warehouse. Distorted images of mutilated bodies, visions of screaming, blood-drenched women and gasping, weeping children rolled through their minds and blocked their vision. Mamun let out a small cry through clenched teeth while Maddie shuddered through it. Mamun began to move faster, flinching and shuddering with each new image of horror. It had to stop; he was desperate to make it stop. He would do anything, *anything* to make it stop. Behind him, Maddie did her best to ignore the images as her stomach lurched. She had to jog to keep up with Mamun and she kept her eyes locked on the space just above his shoulder.

They turned a corner and found Barnum laughing and banging a long metal rod against an empty shelf. He turned and glared at them as they slowly approached. He growled like an animal and bared his teeth. Blood dribbled from his mouth and over his chin. Mamun shuddered as the images wracked his brain. He aimed his gun at Barnum's head and stopped moving forward only when the Tracker touched his arm.

Maddie moved to stand beside Mamun and she stared at Barnum. The big man had gone so mad that he suddenly seemed like less of a threat so long as they stayed out of his reach. But she could still feel the murderous rage he was projecting into her mind and knew that the man would soon go on a rampage. Barnum was dangerous, not just to his enemies but to everyone he encountered. His gift had turned him into a rabid animal and he needed to be put down.

Maddie frowned with pity at the pathetic creature. Whatever he had been just an hour before was lost. There was nothing recognizable as human in that bloated body anymore and he had come to a brutal end of a terrible life.

"Kill him," she said hoarsely.

Mamun didn't hesitate. He pulled the trigger with a sharp bang and a hole suddenly blossomed in Barnum's forehead. Barnum's eyelids fluttered as he reeled and dropped to the floor. Feeling sick, Maddie pulled a glass sample tube from a large pouch on her belt. She knelt next to the massive twitching body and held the tube under the bleeding hole. Blood dribbled into the tube and, once it was half full, she capped it and put it back into the pouch.

Mamun was sitting on the floor, resting his head against a shelf behind him. He was ashen now and his closed eyes had dark, terrible circles beneath them. Maddie moved to stand next to him.

"Is that it?" he asked. He opened his eyes and stared at her, his bright orbs glassy with pain and anguish.

"For now, I suppose," Maddie replied. She could sense Fred and George coming towards them. George was cursing violently as he all but carried a half-conscious Fred towards them.

"Go on back to the inn. We'll meet you there," Maddie told him as gently as she could. *"We've taken care of Barnum and we'll go after Cass once everyone has had a chance to recover."*

"Understood," George replied then went back to cursing. Maddie turned back to Mamun.

"We need to stash Barnum where Kadar can find him before we head back," she said.

"Why?" he asked dully.

"Kadar wants his prize, doesn't he? Now get up and help me," Maddie retorted.

Mamun sighed and struggled to his feet.

CHAPTER 43

Keung sat staring at the monitor on his desk. He watched the movements of the Tracker's family through the windows of the house where they had taken refuge. They were living with Samuel's family now, which made his life somewhat easier. The Distari had proven themselves to be capable of locating the Tracker's family but Keung was confident that they would remain safely hidden for the time being so long as they did not return home. Still, Captain had put thirty Agents around the family home in hopes that the Distari would reveal themselves. Captain planned to follow the beasts back to the lair and exterminate them where they slept. Another four Agents kept watch on the family as well, just to be sure that nothing else happened to them.

He turned the monitor off with the gentle touch of a button and stood up. He took the time to smooth his suit properly over his torso before he left his office. He stepped into the Control Room and saw that it was in its usual state of organized chaos.

"How is the mission progressing?" Keung asked as he mounted the observation platform. The technicians who spent all of their time monitoring the steady stream of information that came into the Center flicked switches on their consoles. A stream of words began to march across the center screen. The words were written in code and they moved much faster than Keung could keep up with.

"The Tracker is currently engaged in a confrontation with one of the crime lords that she was sent to capture," the tech reported. "Her metabolism and heart rate are escalating dangerously and her body temperature is rising far beyond normal."

"Run a diagnostic check through the Tracker's nanopack and find out what's wrong. Then try and fix it through remote," Keung snapped. There was a flurry of tapping noises as the tech sent the order to the satellites.

Suddenly, a spasm wracked Keung's back that bowed him and drove him to his knees. Shrieks of agony rang through the room as men fell writhing from their chairs. Keung struggled to his feet and looked around. Every person in the Control Room was down and screaming. Blood appeared at their ears and in their noses as they clutched at their oozing heads. Keung felt a tickle along his neck and he slapped at it. He looked stupidly at the blood on his hand and tried to blink away the red that filled his vision.

He swayed on his feet and tried to get his bearings right. The room was spinning violently and the screaming had risen to a cacophony of agony. A second spasm of pain, this time in his head, sent him reeling and vomiting uncontrollably. He pulled up gasping for breath and wondered what was going on. The cries of agony and pleas for mercy exploded into his head as his mental shield broke down and left him raw and exposed to everything. Keung struggled for control and grasped the console in front of him in an effort to regain his grip of reality.

Six Agents burst into the Control Room and threaded through the convulsing bodies. Andre and three nurses followed closely behind them. They had blood on their faces and in their hair. Keung watched them coming towards him and wondered how the medical staff managed to get hurt. Andre scowled as he peered into Keung's eyes and pulled at the tender flesh beneath his eyes. Keung cried out in pain and jerked away from the offending touch. Andre dug into the pockets of his lab coat and came up with an injection gun.

"Time for an upgrade," Andre said and jammed the gun against the side of Keung's neck. He pulled the trigger and Keung felt a sharp pain. He screamed and fell back, clutching at Andre to keep from falling off the platform. Andre pulled his hands away and lowered him to the floor. He made sure that Keung would go no further and he stood.

An Agent appeared at Andre's side and whispered into his ear. The Agent's face was streaked with red and blood bubbled out of his mouth as he spoke. Andre nodded to him and turned back to Keung. He knelt back down and grasped him firmly by the wrist and consulted his watch.

"Are you feeling better yet?" Andre demanded. Keung took a moment to think about it before answering. The convulsing pain was fading and the carnival of agonized sounds was quieting. Keung stared in astonishment at the blood staining the white lab coat and the unnatural scarlet in the whites of the doctor's eyes.

Keung got shakily to his feet and automatically straightened his clothes. He took in the scene around him as five Agents and three nurses were moving from person to person. They pressed injection guns to any exposed flesh they could find and moved on. In moments, the injections of new nano systems took effect and men began to calm down and sit up.

"Report," Keung growled in a raw voice. An Agent stepped to his side and spoke in a low voice as if speaking pained him.

"Sir, a Master came into the area. We believe that the method they use to travel interfered with the nanopacks. Doc is administrating next year's upgrades to cancel out the effects." The Agent said.

"What about the men in the field? Has there been any word of them?" Keung demanded. He straightened as a bit more of the nausea faded away. The Agent stiffened and looked away. He took a moment to gather his thoughts.

"We've been unable to make contact, sir."

Keung began to move towards his office as soon as the words were out of the Agent's mouth. He stepped over the men who were still lying prone on the floor. The Agent followed closely behind and had to struggle to keep up with the much taller man.

Keung hit the office door and nearly wrenched it from its hinges when he opened it. He hurried to his desk and swung the monitor around and turned it on. The screen displayed the Tracker's home from an awkward angle. The camera was lying on the ground like it had been knocked off its mount. Keung tapped on the desk and the shot changed to a broader shot.

The yard was drenched in the orange light of the setting sun. Long shadows crawled across the grass and pooled at the foundation of the house. Keung tapped the desk again and the shot narrowed to focus on the front living room window. He could see Samuel and the children moving around inside. The father was carrying a pile of clothes in his arms and speaking to Katherine. The family was back in residence. When had that happened? How long had they been there? Keung forced the questions out of his head and struggled to focus on the problem at hand. A Distari Master with enough technology to disrupt the Center's nanopacks was within thirty miles of the Tracker's house. The timing was too good to be coincidence.

"Recall the Tracker and get the cars ready! Gather up any of the surviving Agents and make contact with Captain. Tell him to converge on the Tracker's home and prepare for battle!"

CHAPTER 44

The Master strode into the darkness of the antechamber, bringing with him the almost physical feel of darkness. He was shrouded in it, wearing a cloak that draped his body so that his figure was nearly indistinguishable. He was accompanied by two elites, a pair of arrogant lackeys who chose to nibble at the scraps of glory from the Master rather than take the responsibility of a lair on their own.

The elite glared down their noses at Him, their lips curled up in condescending sneers. They followed precisely in the Master's footsteps with their backs rigid and their arms stiff. He greeted the group surrounded by minions of his own and made sure that there was a respectful expression on his face. He bowed his head to hide the contempt he knew was gleaming in his eyes as he bent and kissed the Master's ring.

A smooth chuckle oozed from underneath the cowl as He bent over the hand. He did not dare to challenge the Master by peering up into the cowl. He had no interest in risking his hide in a duel, not when he could lure the Tracker into doing his dirty work for him. At any moment now, he expected to see the changeling come through the door and tell him that the Tracker's family had been eliminated and that the woman was one her way. She would, of course, be in a murderous rage and a Master would be the perfect target to beat her vengeance upon.

"Do I draw such loathing from you that it is a burden to greet me with all due respect?" there was a note of amusement in the Master's silky voice. He shivered under the cool dulcet tones and he phrased his words very carefully.

"It is not loathing that forces me to treat you with disrespect. It is simply the incredible awe you inspire to all in the lair."

The Master let out a weary sigh as if His painful incompetence was a terrible burden. "Very well, show me to my rooms."

He bowed over his hand again and stood with as much grace as he could muster. He turned and moved through the antechamber and set an easy pace. Too slow and he implied that he was stronger than the Master, which would result in a duel to prove the Master's incredible strength. Going too fast was a challenge to the Master's authority and would result in a messy and painful death.

He gave the Master his own suite of rooms. There weren't any other spaces in the lair that wouldn't offend the cantankerous creature. He would sleep in an empty chamber elsewhere. The loss of the rooms didn't bother him, though. It was very likely that the entire lair would be destroyed in the coming battle and he will lose them anyway. In the end, his efforts would be rewarded when he was promoted to master and was living in the luxury he'd always dreamed of.

The Master surveyed the suite from the darkness of his cowl. His lackeys sneered and insulted the accommodations under their breath until the Master spoke.

"Where is the entertainment to keep me from growing bored?" he asked. The Master was referring to a harem of squealing human girls, all of whom would be pleasing to the eye and thrilling to the touch. He sighed with irritation at the Master's foolish lusts.

"It is impossible for me to maintain entertainment here," He said. "The surrounding human population is very small and they recognize the loss of the individuals very quickly. It would not take long for the humans to find us in their midst after that. If I searched beyond my territory, I would be accused of poaching and a war I cannot win would begin."

"Do not presume to tell me how to deal with the humans and competing lairs," the Master snarled. "I am better aware of the world than you and your backwater hovel."

He bowed his head and said nothing. He had discreetly reminded a Master of the laws and gotten away with it. He had challenged the Master's intelligence and remained alive. Best not to poke the Master's rabid temper and risk a fatal tantrum. He glared angrily at the Master's feet and hungered for his bloody end.

"I suppose you are wondering why I have come to your lair," the Master began.

"I do not presume to ask such bold questions of my betters," He replied to the floor.

"Of course not," the Master laughed. "I came because you are very near your deadline. My spies tell me that you have located the Tracker's heirs and have just sent your creatures to eliminate them. I have come to ensure that you make no mistakes."

He had to struggle not to glare directly into the Master's face. The pompous fool had come to steal his glory! There was a distant explosion that shook the room and made small stones and dirt shower down on them. He heard the howls of death of the grunts and changelings from somewhere in the far distance. He lifted his gaze from the floor and grinned at the stricken elites flanking the stiff Master.

"You will not have long to wait," He said and smothered the laughter that bubbled in his throat. "The Tracker herself is on her way and you will be able to personally witness her doom."

CHAPTER 45

Sam took the kids with him to the house to get the things they needed for an extended stay with his parents. The night before had been a long, rough one. The kids wanted the things that comforted them best with them when they slept. They needed clothes and toiletries and Sam wanted to get a couple of the guns he had seen in Maddie's office. He just hoped that her office hadn't been cleaned out yet.

His parents had offered to keep the kids while he went to the house but Sam had simply shaken his head and told them that he preferred to keep the kids with him. Truth was, he was afraid that if he left the children with them, they would be attacked and maybe they wouldn't survive. So far he'd been lucky. None of the children had been seriously injured. He didn't want to involve his parents anymore than he absolutely had to. At the moment, he was considering leaving town as soon as he had the kids packed.

He did borrow his Dad's pickup truck. It was designed to haul stuff by the ton and certainly looked sturdy enough to survive another assault. He put Allen's car seat in the back of the extended cab and felt confident that if the shit hit the fan again, he could defend his children with a simple press of the gas.

Half and hour later, they had driven north on I-75 and were on the road leading home. Not that it felt like home anymore. Instead, it felt like a tomb. The children were afraid to go in and had begged to stay in the truck. Sam held the front door open and gave them a look that told them that they'd better get a move on or there'd be hell to pay. They moved reluctantly, dragging their feet until Sam yelled at them to hurry it up. Then they jumped and scurried through the door. Sam scanned the yard and the neighbor's property and checked to be sure that there was nothing out there to attack them. He felt exposed and vulnerable in the dying sunlight. His heart hammered in his chest as he stepped into the house and locked the door behind him.

He left Katie to keep an eye on her brothers while he went directly down the basement stairs to Maddie's office. The door was still exactly as he had left it and it opened easily in his hand. He flipped the light on and went straight to the gun rack and stared at the weapons and wondered which one was going to give him the least amount of trouble. There were plenty of weapons that he did not recognize and didn't understand how to use. Some he couldn't even tell which end was which.

A pair of handguns looked familiar but had a few attachments that looked rather exotic. He took one down and examined it. He turned it in his hands and was careful to keep his fingers away from anything that might be a trigger. He could cock it but he couldn't see how he would load it or chamber a round. Baffled, he stared at a little meter in the grip that glowed blue. A small yellow button was located near what appeared to be the trigger guard. Hopeful that the safety was on, Sam pointed the gun away from his body and pressed the button.

Something heavy dropped from the grip and landed between his feet with a thud. He looked at the gun and found that the meter had turned red. He picked up the cylinder and looked at it. It looked like a drill battery. It had four copper contact points at one end and the rest of it was encased in thick, black plastic. He shoved it into the hole at the bottom and the meter turned back to blue. He grunted, pleased and astonished that it was battery powered. It didn't shoot bullets. He wondered what it did shoot and decided that he didn't really want to know. He put it back and found something more conventional in Maddie's arsenal. He jammed it into his pants and took down another exactly like it.

He found a pretty standard-looking gun that looked like any hunting rifle he had seen displayed in gun stores. The long bullets that went with it sat on a low shelf nearby. He slung the rifle over his shoulder by its strap attached to it. He grabbed the box of bullets and filled his pockets with them and loaded the rifle. He made sure that the safeties were on before he went back upstairs.

He passed through the living room and saw that Katie had put on a cartoon for her brothers. They sat watching the TV and stuffing their faces with Maddie's chocolate stash. He went around the stairs toward the master bedroom. He put the guns on the bed and dove into the closet. He fished out every piece of luggage they owned. Then he went from room to room and gathered everything he thought they would need for the next few weeks. He piled the clothes and toys on the bed and began to sort and organize everything.

"Daddy!" Katie's shriek echoed through the house. Sam dropped what he was doing and grabbed blindly for a gun. One of the handguns filled his palm and he ran for the living room.

The children were clustered around the picture window with their wide eyes staring out into the yard. Katie turned to Sam as he came into the room, her face pale with terror.

"Daddy," she cried hoarsely. "They're coming, Daddy! They're coming!" Her voice rose to a hysterical shriek with each word she spoke. She stood frozen while her brothers backed away from the window with tears in their eyes. Sam rushed to the window and looked out.

They came like one creature, flowing and moving in what seemed like a synchronized dance of blood and death. There were so many of them moving freely and openly in the twilight that terror rose like bile in his throat. There were so many of them, more than he ever imagined possible. He staggered from the window as if he'd been struck. Frozen and helpless by the sight of so many of them coming for them, his mind shut down and refused to deal with what his eyes were telling him.

"Daddy! Daddy!" Chris and Katie were pulling on his arms while they begged for him to move. Allen was sitting on the floor with his face hidden in his hands and he was screaming. Something hit the front door with enough force that the wood splintered and bowed. Sam jumped and snapped out of his terrified stupor. He shoved the children behind him and ran to the front door and turned the deadbolt. He was panting, and his mouth was dry and his throat burned with panic. His hand sweated around the grip of the gun and he nearly dropped it.

He spun when he heard an eerie whining coming from the kitchen. Monsters were clustered around the sliding glass door. They grinned at them and licked the glass eagerly. In the mellow glow of evening sun, they were somehow more horrible, as if the light exposed them in all their hideous and deadly glory. The monsters on the back porch stared at them greedily, their eyes gleaming and they pulled back their thick rubbery lips in a sneer.

Suddenly, his mind snapped clear as it flushed with adrenaline and his brain kicked on his fight or flight mechanism. His children were screaming and helpless with terror. He saw everything with sharp clarity. He could see every drop of saliva dripping from those horrible teeth, the dirt and blood crusting their claws. He thought that the doors might hold, but it wouldn't take them long too simply smash through the window.

"Upstairs!" Sam yelled, and hauled Allen to his feet. He shoved Katie towards the stairs with his foot. "Get upstairs!"

Katie and Chris ran for the stairs while Sam followed behind carrying Allen. The doors in the kitchen exploded in a crash of wood and glass. Katie let out a scream while Chris put his head down and ran faster. Sam turned and saw the monsters begin to stalk through the shattered door. They laughed that strange high hiccupping laugh. Sam raised the gun and aimed it carefully. They saw it and stopped and their eyes narrowed and they hunched their bodies defensively. Sam thumbed the safety off and pulled the trigger.

The barrel of what he had thought was a semiautomatic pistol released a narrow beam of fiery heat and struck the beast closest to him. It bore a scorching hole through its thick torso before bursting in an explosion of blood and chunks out of the other side. The beast shuddered and wailed before it fell twitching to the floor. Sam stared in astonishment at the damage the gun inflicted. What the hell was Maddie involved in?

He fired two more shots into the mass of bodies hunched together just inside the door. They scattered and the shots hit the outside deck and burnt smoking holes into the varnished wood. Sam spun on his heel and tore towards the stairs and his children. The picture window exploded next, showering him and Allen with sharp glass. He threw his hand up to protect his small son's face and he felt a piece of glass cut his cheek near his eye.

Hot blood trickled down his cheek as he raced up the stairs and ran into the spare bedroom after Katie and Chris. The beasts had pounded up the stairs after him, screaming and growling with anticipation. Sam slammed the door shut in time for something heavy to slam into it. The door shuddered but held. Sam thanked Maddie for insisting on the expensive mahogany doors and threw Allen onto the bed. Katie rushed forward and locked the knob as Sam grasped one of the plush sitting chairs. The monsters pounded on the door and Sam shouted at Katie to get out of the way while he jammed the chair under the knob. There was no way that the door was going to hold but Sam intended to make it hold for as long as possible. He pushed the dresser against the door and grabbed the end table and stacked it on top of it. It still wouldn't hold long enough for him to figure out a way to get out of the house. So he decided to get into the one part of the house he was certain these things couldn't reach.

The attic was accessed through a folding ladder in the ceiling of the walk-in closet. If he could get the kids up there and close the entryway, the access door would be flush with the ceiling and the monsters couldn't get their massive fingers into the cracks to open the door. Since there were no windows, there was no other way for them to get in there until he could call for help. The door rattled as more heavy bodies slammed into it. The wood was beginning to splinter and the end table toppled off the dresser.

Sam pulled the string and the ladder fell down with a clatter. Sam quickly unfolded the steps and braced them firmly against the floor. The children were howling with terror as the monsters got ever closer to getting through the door. Sam grabbed Allen and carried him halfway up the ladder before he simply chucked him hard enough to sail into the attic and land on the thin wooden floor. Allen howled in pain and surprise as Sam stretched out for the next child.

He grabbed Katie and hauled her up to the ladder just ahead of him. He smacked her legs to get her to move faster as she scrambled clumsily up the steps and disappeared into the attic. He heard her coo to her little brother. He turned and grabbed Chris just as the door made a loud cracking noise. He heard the laughter change into triumphant hooting. They were through the door already. He tucked Chris under his arm and climbed the ladder as fast as he could. The dresser shot across the room and slammed into the opposite wall just as Sam set Chris down. The bedroom door exploded inward as he struggled to pull the ladder up. One of the monsters glared at him from the floor. Sam's eyes widened and he had just enough time to pull back as the monster leaped high in the air and snapped at his face.

He yelled and shuffled backwards on feet and hands. He gave up any idea of getting the ladder up and resigned himself to simply making their stand here. The beast was up the ladder and into the attic, snarling and slavering as it advanced slowly on them. The children shrieked and fled to the furthest corner of the attic.

Sam faced the beast stalking towards him and pulled the gun from where he had jammed it into his waistband. The aimed it at the thing's head while his hand shook violently. The beast roared as he fired into that terrible face. The head exploded in a burst of thick mush and red mist. Sam scrambled deeper into the attic to position himself more solidly between the children and the next monster he knew would come through the attic door. He held the gun in both sweaty hands and waited for death to come.

CHAPTER 46

Arnold raced through the darkening streets at dangerous speeds as she headed for her sister's house. She dug into her purse and searched blindly with her fingers for her cell phone. Growling with frustration, she upended her purse onto the seat and snatched her phone. The phone rang in her hand and she hit the talk button.

"Darlene? Where are you?" Cooper was pissed.

"The witness was viable and stated that the Johnston family was the killer's next target. I'm on my way there to take the family into protective custody." She barked. She slammed on the brakes and barely avoided slamming into a slow moving vehicle making its way down the narrow tree lined streets of Grassdale Road. Her headlights reflected off the skeletal winter branches that intertwined overhead to make the road a claustrophobic tunnel.

"What?" Cooper squawked.

"My sister is involved in something that caught these things' attention and now they've targeted her family," Arnold lay on her horn to prompt the car in front of her to move faster. The car remained stubbornly at its current speed.

"What the hell is your sister doing?" he demanded.

"I don't know but I'm going to shoot her until she tells me. I'll call you when I get there."

"Do you want back-up?"

Arnold caught something out of the corner of her eye just at the edge of her vision. She turned her head towards it in time to see it again. A bent and twisted body streaked across lawns and driveways. The monsters moved ahead of her down the road and crossed Highway 41 and kept going. Dear God! She thought frantically. They're going after them now!

"Yes!" she all but screamed. "Send back-up! The killer is going after them now! I just spotted one on Grassdale going east towards Peoples Valley! They're moving fast and I'm in pursuit!"

She gave Cooper her sister's address and the perps' descriptions and hung up the phone. She growled through her teeth and pressed the gas to the floor and swerved around the car in front of her. She raced into the falling night, praying with every fiber of her being that she made it to Sam and the kids in time.

She came to a screeching halt in their driveway and came within centimeters of hitting a huge red truck parked in front of the house. Arnold leaped from her car and ignored the terrible pain in her side. She pulled her gun as she ran for the shattered front door. Screams rang through the house followed by the hideous growling and laughter she'd become so terribly familiar with.

She paused at the front door just long enough to make sure that the foyer was clear. She heard the terrified, high-pitched shrieks of the children and Sam's enraged roar. Katie shrieked for her Daddy as an explosion shook the house. Arnold glanced upstairs and realized that was where the noises were coming from. She threw caution to the wind and ran up the stairs as fast as she could. Her boots crunched on broken glass and bits of wood and drywall. Back-up would arrive any minute. She only had to hold out until then.

She hit the second floor landing with her gun up and aimed. The house was dark. Sparks showered out of a light fixture in the middle of the hall and brought small flashes of illumination to the shadowy hallway. She turned to her right and saw a cluster of twisted bodies trying to squeeze themselves through a small hole in a door. They hooted and growled as they struggled with each other. One would break through and a moment later another of the explosions would shake the walls.

She fired into the mass, releasing two bullets that struck their targets. Two of the monsters crumpled to the floor and kicked violently in death throes. She heard a growl to the left and she turned in time to see another of the monsters bearing down on her. It leaped the last foot, its claws extended and its maw wide. She fired two more shots into its mouth and ducked as it soared over her head. It slammed into the beasts still clustered around the door and they howled in rage. She heard rapid thumping coming up the stairs behind her and she spun and put two more bullets in the pair rushing up the stairs behind her.

She screamed as something hard slammed into her and drove the air from her lungs. A monster dug its teeth into her shoulder as it rode her to the floor. She screamed and rammed the barrel of her gun into its face. She pulled the trigger three times and watched as its head disintegrate. She gagged and choked as she fought to push the thing off of her. Its dead weight was crushing her and she was frantic to get it off before more of them came to kill her.

She managed to roll it off and get to her knees when she was hit in the back and driven face first to the floor. Something sharp dug hideously into her flesh. She grunted and screamed helplessly, as it ripped apart her ribs and dug into more vital things. The pain that had crippled her at first was suddenly gone. She felt light-headed and wondered at the strange chewing sounds above her head. She could hear a shrill noise and it was getting on her nerves. She realized that it was her voice and that she couldn't stop it. Pain renewed itself along her buttocks and legs and she screamed. She was growing light-headed and the edges of her vision were fading. She realized what was happening then.

They were eating her alive.

CHAPTER 47

Mamun laid on the couch with an arm thrown over his eyes and his shirt thrown in the trash. Most of his shoulder and chest had been cleaned and bandaged. Maddie sat slumped in the chair next to him, cannon-balling one glass of water after another and chowing down the painkillers.

Fred and George had arrived at the inn just a few seconds after Mamun and Maddie and they had gone directly into their room and hadn't come out. Fred had been covered in so much blood that they couldn't tell how much of it was his or someone else's. A quick examination revealed that he'd been shot twice, once in the side and once in his arm. Beneath the blood, his face was covered in deep ugly bruises and there were deep gashes and cuts all over his body. For a normal person, these injuries would be crippling if not fatal but, with all the nano-enhancements the Agents and the Tracker carried, Fred would eventually be okay.

Fred was still muttering angrily as George cleaned him up. George had grinned at the Tracker and told her that he would be fine. Then they disappeared into their room and left Maddie to tend to Mamun's wounds.

His shoulder hadn't been as bad as it had looked at first. Maddie had dug deep into the first aid kits they always brought along on missions and managed to gather everything that she needed. She took a moment to let the nanopack download the medical information she needed then set to work. She gave him the full treatment, anesthetic, stitches and potent painkillers. Now he lay on the couch in a happy stupor and waited for something else to happen.

"How's the headache?"

Maddie looked up to see George standing over her. He was clean and a bandage peaked over the blood-crusted ruffle of his collar. He gave her a weak grin through the exhaustion that pulled at his face.

"No better," Maddie replied. "But Mamun is in a very happy place. Have you found Abiah yet?"

She patted Mamun on the head and he chuckled dreamily.

"No, the inn's manager said that she's out in the city on some personal business," George replied. "I did go over the information she gave us on Cass. I managed to determine that most of it is pure unadulterated bullshit. Which is weird since everything she gave us on Barnum was accurate. Except, of course, his homicidal insanity and psychic powers."

"So what? You think she's hiding something?" Maddie asked and rubbed her eyes.

"I don't know. But I think we should be on guard until we find out what she thought she was doing. It could be that Abiah is a traitor. Or it could be that she just doesn't have as reliable sources for Cass as she did for Barnum. Either way, I'm recommending that you confront her as soon as you can."

Maddie moaned and rubbed her head. She didn't want to confront Abiah. Confronting her meant that she would have to jack her head the way she had Mamun's. She was already nauseous and aching. She certainly didn't want to add to it.

"Did the manager say when she'd be back?" she asked.

"He expects her to return shortly."

"Will it be safe to assume that you, at least, will be backing me up? Fred's still a little crazy and I just gave Mamun a butt load of pain relievers. I'm willing to bet that he'll be a bit stoned for awhile."

"I will go with you," George chuckled. "But I did have to sedate Fred. He'll need more attention when we get home."

"He'll be okay then?"

"I think he'll recover from his injuries, eventually," George replied quietly. Maddie fell silent and rubbed at a spot on her head that was pounding harder than the rest of her skull.

"You know, it's strange. I thought the nanopacks were supposed to keep me from getting sick," she said.

"I believe that you're developing a secondary gift," George said. "It's quite common for Trackers with halfway decent strength to do so. Judging from your symptoms and the scorch marks on the walls, I'm sure that it will no doubt prove to be explosive."

"When?" she asked.

"I think it will manifest very soon. Once it does finally emerge, we'll deal with it."

"Fine," Maddie stood up and picked up her belt and began to put it back on. She saw the gun in a holster on it and felt proud of herself. She had a gun for several hours and she had yet to shoot someone she wasn't supposed to. "I'm going down to the common room to wait for Abiah. You wanna come with?"

George stood up with a weary sigh and buckled his holster around his hips. He put the blood-splattered coat on over it to hide the guns. Mamun's eyes blinked open and he stirred. He rolled off the couch and staggered to his bag sitting in the corner. He pulled a clean shirt out and pulled it over his head. He tucked it into his pants awkwardly with one hand and picked up his gun.

"Maybe you should stay and rest," Maddie suggested. He looked worse than when they first got back. There were dark circles under his eyes and his skin had a gray tinge to it. He gave her a cold look and said nothing. He continued going about the process of getting ready to go. Maddie shrugged and walked out the door to go to the common room. If the man wanted to go out and hurt himself more than he already was, it was up to him. He was veteran soldier and he knew his limits and could deal with it if he over-extended himself.

Maddie sat at an empty table in the women's section of the common room. She made certain to sit so that she could see everyone who came in or went out the inn's doors. George and Mamun followed a few minutes later and sat down as nonchalantly as their injuries would let them. The waitress gave them all odd looks as she saw George's blood spattered clothes and the bruises that covered all three faces but said nothing as they gave food and drink orders. She returned quickly, bringing fruit juice for Maddie and George and a strongly bitter-smelling concoction for Mamun. He immediately began to gulp down the stuff while Maddie and George ignored theirs.

As they watched the door, the atmosphere in the inn grew decidedly tenser. The barmaids moved brusquely and avoided eye contact and conversation. The customers ate their meals quickly and disappeared. The bartender jumped every time someone spoke to him and the bouncer fingered his bludgeon nervously. Everyone's minds buzzed with fear. They knew what was happening and they were determinedly *not* thinking about it.

Fidgety from the rising stress in the room, Maddie glanced at the kitchen in time to see four men appear. The men had noticed them as well and they grinned evilly. The drugged haze disappeared from Mamun's eyes and George straightened a little in his chair and loosened his guns. They watched intently as the men shambled up to them.

The men were rough-looking and heavily-muscled. They wore grungy clothes speckled with bits of food on the crumpled ruffle collars. Their faces were shiny and clean and their dark hair was slicked back against their scalps. Maddie picked at her salad and pretended to disregard them as unimportant.

"Get ready for a fight," George said pushing his plate away. Mamun did the same and leaned back casually in his chair. He put his hands behind his head and stared nonchalantly at the men as they came to a stop at their table. The movement exposed the weapon at his hip. The men paused at the clear warning of violence and then sneered at it.

"These are fetches," Mamun said casually as if the men weren't standing right there. The men seemed to take offense at the term and they scowled at him. "I've seen them lurking around the inn off and on since I got here. They scare the customers and harass the barmaids. They're useless scum."

"Would they know where to find Cass?" George asked.

"Without a doubt," Mamun answered still staring calmly at the four men. The inn's door opened and Maddie got a whiff of their heavy cologne mixed with ripe B.O. Maddie grimaced and thought that there was a good chance that none of the men had seen soap in a year. One of them leaned over and stared into her face. She leaned away from him as far as she could.

"What's the matter? Do I offend you?" he sneered. "Not to worry, you'll like me well enough when the fun begins."

Maddie narrowed her eyes at him but, for once, she had nothing to say. Her head hurt too much for her to think of a snappy comeback.

"There's supposed to be four of you," said the tallest of the bunch. "Where's the pretty fellow?"

No one answered. Mamun and George looked at him as if he'd spoken a foreign language and smiled humorlessly. The tall fetch shrugged and pulled a club from his coat.

"It don't matter. We'll find him. Cass wants a word with you," he said with a smirk.

Suddenly, the other three men had weapons in their hands and were staring at them with glee. No one moved as they tried to decide whether or not they wanted to take these four on right then and there.

"This is a lot easier that chasing Cass down on our own," George said dryly. He held his hands away so that one of the smelly fetches could disarm him. *"I have to say, though, I do like it much better when the bad guys come to us."*

"I like it even better when there are no bad guys," Maddie retorted. The man pulled her weapons free of her belt and tucked them into his own. Then he took special joy in running his hands along her body, taking care to squeeze the softer and more appealing parts of her anatomy. Mamun handed over his gun and a big knife he'd been carrying in his boot without a word. He was looking from Maddie to George as he waited for them to give any indication of what they intended to do. Instead, the pair were exchanging wry looks and snorting at each other. The Tracker grunted and rolled her eyes as one of the fetches gripped a handful of her ass and pressed the front of his hips against her. Mamun fought the urge to strangle the bastard as he glared death into the man's face. The man laughed at him.

To Maddie's surprise, the men didn't lead them out of the inn. Instead, they led them up the stairs used exclusively by men. Surprised servants jumped out of the way as the small crowd made their way up. One man noticed Maddie in the center of the group and growled insults at her. She didn't hear him; her ears were ringing too painfully to pay attention. She stared at the fetch in front of her and wondered if she could brain jack more than one man at once.

They were led down hallways that had gone suddenly silent. The walls were lined with doors that led to occupled rooms and yet there were no sounds coming from them. It was as if everyone had known what was going to happen and no one wanted to get caught in the crossfire. They reached another flight of stairs, this time they were narrow and steep. It led into a trap door set into a part of the inn she hadn't noticed from the street.

The fetches banged the trap door open and continued up the stairs and through the floor above them. They entered a room that stretched the length and width of the inn. Curtains were hung where the pointed roof dipped down, giving the place the illusion of rooms. Scantily clad servants ducked around the curtains and rushed across the sparsely furnished areas, carrying gilded trays and delicate glassware. There was a group that bent over the floor and it appeared that their sole purpose was to clean and maintain the thick, colorful rugs spread across the floor. Fragrant candles and lanterns lit the entire place with a warm and cozy light and there were more servants making sure that those were kept lit. While pretty, the effect of the entire room made Maddie feel claustrophobic and she had to take a deep breath to settle her fraying nerves. The perfumed oils and wax used to light the place smelled delicate and exotic and made her nausea worse.

They were led through the room where there were servants waiting to move the curtains aside for them whenever they came close enough. They stopped in the center of the floor just before a deep pit sunk a few feet into the stone floor. The fetches pointed their weapons to the floor and removed their feathered hats from their greasy heads and bowed reverently. The pit was piled deep with cushions of cream and scarlet satin as well as soft, thick blankets. Nude bodies writhed and moaned along the soft luxury of the pit. They were so tangled together that Maddie had a hard time telling who was male and who was female. She counted feet and determined that there were at least ten people in there and, by the ratio of hairy toes to the hairless ones, she realized that the women greatly outnumbered the men. Someone screamed in ecstasy and the writhing became more frenzied. Maddie wrinkled her nose and blushed. She had suddenly realized that she was witnessing an orgy. Bleh!

"We have brought the Tracker and her bodyguards as ordered, milord," said one of the fetches.

"Go away now."

Maddie looked down directly at her feet. A single feminine figure sat against the edge of the pit, watching the orgy and sipping a deep red liquid from a delicate glass. She stared at the long, dark hair flowing down white shoulders and shapely arms. The voice was familiar but she didn't dare to put a name to it.

The fetches stepped back and disappeared, leaving Maddie and the men alone with the delicate woman and the raging orgy. She didn't try anything daring, though; since she was fairly certain that there were bodyguards hidden somewhere and they would jump out and kill her if she looked to do something violent.

The woman turned and stared coolly up at them with large, liquid brown eyes and a mocking smile on her full lips. She sat up so that she could stare at her prisoners and, in so doing, showed that she was wearing a very sheer nightgown over her small and curved frame. Maddie could see Abiah's dark nipples and a mole over one breast through the material. Maddie rolled her eyes at the woman's estimation of her own sex appeal.

"I understand that Ezra Barnum is dead," Abiah said pleasantly as she stood up in the knee-deep cushions. "I'm sure that if my husband could speak, he would thank you for your services."

Maddie glanced back to the pit where a tall man was coming up for air amongst a cluster of moaning women. He did things with them that made them cry out and arch their backs. One woman spread her legs wider and offered herself to him. The man grinned and one of his hands disappeared into her. The woman screamed in delight and began to grind her hips into his limb. Maddie was so put off that she let out an involuntary "Yuck!"

Abiah glanced back at the pit and let out a derisive snort. "My husband is a man of large appetites."

"No shit," Maddie growled. Abiah laughed and climbed out of the pit, her hips and legs moving gracefully in a way that reminded Maddie of sex. Maddie frowned and folded her arms. *"What is she up to? This can't be for my benefit."* She said quietly to George.

But there was no answer from George. Maddie glanced at him and saw that his face had gone slack with lust and his eyes were locked on Abiah's sensual body. Maddie gawked in astonishment then looked over at Mamun. He didn't look as far-gone as George did but, from the way he watched the woman, Maddie could tell that he was definitely interested. Maddie poked at George who grunted but didn't move. Mamun gave her an annoyed look when she jabbed him in the ribs. She shot daggers at him with her eyes.

Oh, for crying out loud, Abiah is psychic too, Maddie thought as Mamun turned his attention back to the woman. But instead of being crazy and brutal, Abiah specialized in something subtler. Like so many women in a rigid and male-dominated culture, she was using her sexuality as a weapon. Not that Maddie could fault her for it, she'd been doing the same thing herself ever since she stepped foot into Barnum's dungeons. It was just that the choice of weapons and her mental abilities were entirely too effective for Maddie's taste. George and Mamun were completely incapacitated.

Abiah was gliding towards a servant holding a delicate pink robe out for her, moving slowly and lazily so that the men could appreciate every movement of her shapely body. She slid into the rode, every flex of muscle and turn of wrist and ankle made an art of motion, more precise and graceful than a dancer's choreographed movements.

"I do have a task for you," Abiah said smiling seductively.

"Oh, is that right?" Maddie sneered. The bitch was working her last nerve. Abiah smiled and glided up to the taller woman and stopped just before their noses touched. Abiah lifted her long delicate hand and began to trace a line across Maddie's throat and down her chest between her cleavage. Maddie removed her hand firmly and scowled.

"You're wasting your time," Maddie growled. Abiah laughed seductively.

"Not entirely," she replied smoothly and moved to George. The Agent bent eagerly and kissed Abiah firmly on the mouth as his hands roamed along her body. Abiah moaned and pressed her body against his before she pulled away. George groaned and let her go reluctantly.

Abiah gave Maddie a smug look and moved to a servant holding out a silver tray. She rifled through a few sheaves of paper and lay them back down.

"I have a few other things to do for you to do," Abiah repeated. Maddie glared but didn't answer. "As I'm sure you know, King Kadar has his eye on my city. The army here is sadly weak and, if it comes down to a fight, the city will fall. Because Kadar does not share power and his policies regarding those in my profession are rather extreme, I would be forced to go underground. I would lose some freedoms and my income would dwindle. That would be very inconvenient.

"When you present Barnum's corpse to the king, I want you to cut Kadar's throat."

Maddie scoffed so hard she choked. "Who the hell do you think you're dealing with?" she demanded.

"It doesn't matter now, does it?" Abiah replied. "You'll do as I ask and then you'll do more. If you do not...well, there are ways to convince you to my way of thinking."

Maddie could clearly hear what Abiah meant. She had a firm hold on Mamun and George. They would do anything Abiah asked, even cut their own throats. And they would do it with a stupid smile on their faces. Maddie shrugged.

"So what? They're just men, I can always find more," she replied nonchalantly. Maddie was hoping that if Abiah thought that Maddie didn't care about the men, then she wouldn't hold them hostage.

That caught Abiah off guard. Her eyes narrowed and Maddie could feel the little woman probe at her mind. She tightened her shields and held her ground. Abiah wasn't nearly as strong as Barnum or the Tracker, so she couldn't get into Maddie's head. But she was by far subtler, which made it difficult for Maddie to determine how she held both of the men at once.

"Very well, then. Mamun," Abiah gestured to the Captain with a graceful gesture of her hand and Mamun came rushing forward. He smiled down at her and waited eagerly for her to tell him how best to please her. "Do you have a knife?"

"No, the men took it from me in the common room," he replied sadly. He looked disappointed and almost ready to cry.

"Don't worry, I have one here," Abiah replied kindly and stroked his cheek. Mamun's face brightened at her touch. A servant hurried forward and presented them with a sheathed dagger with an ornate hilt. Abiah took it and held it out to Mamun. She glanced at Maddie out of the corner of her eye, and let the Tracker know that she was going to call her bluff.

"I'm afraid that your chest doesn't have enough holes in it," Abiah pouted. "I was wondering if you'd be a dear and remedy that for me."

Mamun frowned at her. "Holes?" he asked in confusion. "What do you mean?"

Abiah unsheathed the dagger and pressed it into his hand. "Could you? Please?"

Maddie rolled her eyes. This was the dumbest thing she'd ever seen. No one was going to stab themselves to death just on her say so no matter what Abiah could manipulate their minds. Mamun grasped the blade and began to unbutton his shirt. He looked worried as he did it. Maddie stared hard at him, willing him to think for himself and decide that this was a very bad idea. He pressed the blade to his chest until a drop of blood gathered on the blade and trickled down his bandages. He frowned uncertainly at Abiah as if he was unsure of what he really wanted to do. Abiah was staring intently at his chest, her small pink tongue caressing her lower lip. Finally, he took a deep breath and the blade slid deep into his chest. He screamed and pulled it free. Abiah laughed and Maddie jumped and started forward.

"Stop!" Abiah held up a forceful hand to Maddie. "Stop or I shall make him do it until he dies. But what do you care? They're just men. You can always find more."

Her sneer was what had finally tipped the scales. Hot rage flared in Maddie's mind until it blinded her and burnt away everything and left behind only the purest hatred. Instinctively she was aware of Mamun falling to the floor and that George was kneeling at Abiah's feet with the same knife in his hand. The blade was at his throat and he was smiling happily into the woman's face. Maddie shook with her own rage until it burned her skin and melted her bones.

She screamed her fury, feeling the terrible heat pour out of her body and spread across the room. Abiah stared at her in surprise before her face suddenly began to blister. She screamed and tried to shield her face with her hands but it was futile. Her thick waves of ebony hair burst into flames. She fell shrieking to the floor and writhed in terrible agony. More voices followed, rising in a horrible clamor to the heavens.

Maddie blinked and suddenly the heat was gone. All she felt was blessed coolness. The headache was gone and she nearly wept with relief. She took deep, panting breaths and nearly choked on the thick smoke that was filling the room. Tears poured from her eyes as she looked around in a stupor. More people writhed on the floor with their bodies engulfed in flames. The pit behind her was a bonfire of shrieking death and the smell of roasting meat. The curtains were engulfed in flames and what little stone furniture that had been in the room was melting in the heat like crayons in the sun.

Maddie gaped in horror. She knew that she had done this. All these people were dying horrible deaths that she had thrust upon them. A woman ran shrieking past her and disappeared through the trapdoor to the rooms below. Maddie let her go and looked frantically around for Mamun and George. George was struggling to his feet and coughing harshly. Mamun lay bleeding near Abiah's screaming corpse. Maddie rushed to his side and tried to lift him up.

There were shouts coming from the trap door and Maddie peered through the smoke to see the manager staring with wild, frightened eyes at the raging inferno. He barked commands to someone on the stairs below him. He came up to the room and hurried towards Maddie and Mamun.

"What happened?" he yelled, putting his shoulder under Mamun's arm and lifted him off the floor. Maddie shook her head. She left Mamun with the man and went to George. He was on his feet before she could reach him. He looked at her with horror.

"What have you done, Tracker?" he hissed. Maddie opened her mouth to reply and suddenly the floor opened up under her. She clutched at George only to find that he wasn't there. She let out a blood-curdling scream and fell forever.

CHAPTER 48

Maddie was still screaming when she it the cold hard floor. The impact drove the air from her lungs and sent stabbing pain along her sides. She gaped stupidly at the dark ceiling and struggled to breathe. Suddenly, there was a blinding flash of light as Fred, George and all of their stuff began to rain down on her. Maddie squealed and covered her head with her arms as she was pelted with clothes, odds and ends, and Fred. She had a moment to wonder what had just happened before Keung's face appeared over her's. He was paler than usual and he looked haggard. She blinked in astonishment at the blood dotting his white collar and wondered, what the hell was going on?

"Get up and get changed, Tracker. You have to be on your way immediately," he snapped. Maddie blinked and tried to gather her wits. She rolled onto her hands and knees and got to her feet. Keung was already leaving the room and she hurried after him. The room was spinning and she hit the doorframe hard. Keung stopped to wait for her and grabbed her arm as soon as she got close to him.

"What's going on?" she gasped as she was hauled through a hall towards the elevator.

"There's trouble," he stopped at the elevator and jabbed at the call button.

"What kind of trouble?" she began to pry her arm out of his grip. He was strong and he was bruising her. The elevator doors slid open and he all but threw her into it. He followed and hit the button for sublevel three. Her stomach pitched as the elevator dropped.

"What is your problem?" she snapped, rubbing her arm.

"There's some trouble with your family. You must go to them as soon as you change your clothes," Keung replied. The elevator stopped too abruptly and Maddie fell down. Keung bent down and hauled her to her feet and dragged her from the little room. He moved so fast that Maddie struggled to keep on her feet until they reached the wardrobe area.

"What's the problem with my family?" she asked gripping the counter for support. Bob appeared, looking ill. He held Maddie's regular clothes in his arms. He dropped them on the counter next to her and waited silently with her shoes and wedding rings in hand.

"The Distari has located your children and is converging on your home as we speak," Keung replied.

"Distari?" Maddie asked as she ripped her clothes off and began to dress in clean clothes. "You mean those things that attacked us when we first got to Iza? What the hell are they doing at my house?" Her voice was rising to an angry shriek. "What the hell are you doing here instead of going to my house and saving my children?"

Keung said nothing. He watched as Maddie jammed her shoes on her feet and rammed her rings onto her finger. She kept giving him scathing looks that told him that she was ready to draw blood.

"The car is waiting in the garage," he said and walked off. Maddie snatched her purse from Bob and ran after him.

"Couldn't you just have had the Threshold take me home?" Maddie panted.

"The Threshold can only cover extreme distances and return them to where they started. It is beyond its abilities to simply send you home through it. Your house is too close. We have to use local means of transportation," Keung replied.

"Well, don't we have a helicopter or something?"

"Yes, and no we can't use it. Too many of your neighbors would notice it landing in your yard."

"Well, don't you think that they'd notice a swarm of demons beating down my front door?" she snarled.

"Yes, but we don't have to hide Distari," Keung snarled back. They had reached the garage without her noticing. A sleek, black car pulled up. It had tinted windows and fancy rims. The Agent behind the wheel wore dark sunglasses and a black suit and tie. Maddie glared at it.

"Oh, yeah, this thing is real discreet," she said dryly. Keung answered her by opening the car door and getting in. Maddie dove in behind him. As soon as she closed the car door the Agent stomped on the gas. The tires squealed on the smooth pavement and the car shot out of the garage. They tore through the city. Cars honked their horns and their brakes squealed as the limo wove recklessly in and out of traffic.

As soon as they broke free of the city, Maddie dug her cell phone out of her purse and called Sam. The phone rang six times before the machine picked up. She swore and strangled the phone before she hung up.

"He's not picking up," she almost screamed. "How could you let this happen? You promised me that you would look out for my family when I took this job! How could you let this happen?"

Keung bent forward and pushed on a panel on the seat in front of him. A gun popped out of the compartment and Keung picked it up. He checked the clip and chambered a round before he handed it over to Maddie. Maddie snatched it from him. She didn't care if the damn thing went off. In fact, she wanted to shoot Keung right now. She set the gun in her lap as he reached into his jacket and produced a rod similar to the one she carried on the mission. Maddie snatched that too and tucked it into her pants.

She had images of her children being torn limb from limb as they drove at high speeds along the freeway. By the time they pulled off at her exit, she was almost certain that she would get home to find her family slaughtered in their beds. Rage and grief poured through her and her skin began to feel hot again. Keung gave her a sidelong look.

"Calm down, Tracker. We cannot save your family if you incinerate us in this car," he said calmly.

"Don't you tell me to calm down!" Maddie screeched. "Don't you dare tell me to calm down. My family is going to die because you are an incompetent asshole! If I set fire to this car and kill everyone in it, it's no less than you deserve!"

The car came to a screeching halt in front of the house. Maddie flung the door open and jumped out before it had come to a complete stop.

"Wait!" Keung shouted after her. "We're missing Agents and we don't know what's going on in there!"

Maddie didn't hear him. She heard the screaming coming from the house. Gunshots split the air and bright flashes of gunfire appeared at the upper floor windows. She held the gun up as she dashed up the front porch steps and ran through the shattered front door.

Horrible, twisted monsters turned towards her as she stepped into the house. They had blood dripping from their mouths and running down their chins. Maddie took only a second to take it all in. She assumed that it was her children's blood on their faces and she lifted the gun and fired a shot into each of their heads.

She was in a cold rage when she turned away from the corpses and ran up the stairs towards the screaming. She moved as fast as she could. The screams meant that someone was still alive. There was still someone left to be saved. Halfway up the stairs, she saw blood soaking the carpet and dripping onto the top step. A mass of broken bones and meat lay on top of the puddle. She stared at it with her heart choking her; afraid to guess which one of her children was lying there.

She hit the landing, her tennis shoes sinking into the carpet with a squish. The blond hair spilled across the blood stopped her cold. A ragged sob tore at her throat as she stared at what she thought was Katie's mangled body. Then a little girl's high shriek echoed from somewhere above her and she jumped and looked around for her daughter. She glanced back down at the body and wondered who it was. It was too big to be Katie and too small to be Sam. The glimmer of a woman's gold watch glinted against the dark blood.

Suddenly, she couldn't breath. Her knees felt weak and she found she couldn't stand up. A sob tore out of her throat as she stared at Darlene's body. There was nothing left of her. The Distari had taken it all and left only the shock of her yellow hair and her gold watch. What was she going to tell her mother? What was she going to say to her children? How was she possibly going to deal with this? Her sister was dead! Dead for the family Maddie should have been home to defend!

"Tracker." The voice was low and raw, but the tone was eager and predatory. Maddie looked up in time to see three more of the beasts stalking down the dark hallway towards her. The screams of her children echoed from over head and she could hear Sam swearing violently at something. She lifted the gun and fired.

The nanopack was working at 100% efficiency and doing its best to manipulate her brain and body to its highest capabilities. She felt nothing. Her anguish and grief had been replaced by cold, logical rage. She could suddenly see in the dark, she saw every detail and every ripple of muscle underneath putrid skin. They leaped for her, their claws reaching out as they shrieked in triumph. Her body and reflexes moved fast and sure. Every shot she fired hit its mark precisely.

There were too many of them to hit all at once, no matter how fast and accurate she had suddenly become. Two leaped over the dropping bodies and reached for her. It was easy to side step them and flip the switch on the rod that had suddenly appeared in her other hand. A long curved blade shot out of the end, and she brought it around with all the strength and force she could muster. Thick, reeking blood arched out as she took the head of the first grunt and then spun and gutted another coming at her from the guestroom. Another leaped at her from the stairs and she simply shot it in the head.

Sam's shouts and the children's screams were becoming more frantic. Maddie faced the battered and broken door. She saw the gaping hole in the dark wood and the pieces of furniture blocking the other side of the door. She lifted the curved blade and hacked into the door. She managed to clear it enough that the door crashed open when she threw herself into it.

Two more Distari were in the room facing the closet. They spun and snarled at her as she lifted the gun. She could hear her children screaming very clearly now. They were terrified and crying for her to save them. Rage, terrible rage, filled her until she thought she would die of it. She fired the gun and dropped both of the beasts and kept firing long after they were dead and until the gun clicked empty. She tossed the gun away and started towards the ruin of the attic ladder.

Sam's head popped out of the ceiling. Even upside down with his hair sticking up and his glasses skewed on his nose, he was a sight for sore eyes. She saw blood on his face and prayed that it wasn't his or one of the children's.

"Maddie?" he said in a raw voice. "Is that really you?"

She rushed to him with her arms out and a glad cry on her lips. Sam didn't wait to greet her. His head disappeared back into the attic. She stood there bewildered as she listened to Sam retreat across the ceiling and come back.

"Help me with Allen!" Sam shouted. Maddie reached up and grabbed the toddler as Sam lowered him out. She examined every inch of him, looking for any sign of injury. Allen was unharmed and she nearly wept with relief at how clean he was. He shrieked and struggled until he realized that he was in his mother's arms. Then he wrapped his chubby arms around her neck and hugged her and refused to let go. Next was Chris. Chris appeared uninjured as well, but he was limp and his eyes were vacant in his sweet face. Maddie didn't have time to give him a closer look. Sam was lowering Katie down and let her drop the last two inches to the floor. Katie immediately began to babble incoherently and threw her arms around her mother's waist. Sam followed by jumping out of the attic and landing heavily on the floor. Maddie moved to hug him but Sam glared at her and shook his head.

"You are going to pay for his," he hissed. Astonished, Maddie opened her mouth to reply.

"Tracker, get out of the house! There are more Distari on their way!" Keung's voice boomed through her head.

"Get out, get out, get out," Maddie commanded, pushing Katie towards the door with her foot. Sam took Chris from her and they ran for it. Katie stopped with a cry at Darlene's body and began to shriek.

"Go on!" Sam screamed at her. "Keep going!"

Katie was too hysterical to argue and she bolted down the stairs, too eager to get away from the horror behind her. Sam and Maddie pounded down the stairs behind her with the boys in tow.

"Who the hell was that?" Sam demanded. "Please tell me that was one of your coworkers and not one of the neighbors."

"It was Darlene," Maddie replied coldly. Sam didn't answer; he concentrated on getting down the stairs without falling down them and dropping Chris rather than digesting the news.

Katie stopped at the bottom of the stairs and let out a bloodcurdling scream. Sam and Maddie nearly tripped over her as they forced themselves to come to a stop. Five Distari clustered around the front door and roared at them. They turned to go back and saw four more coming down the stairs towards them. The Distari were making the bizarre hyena laugh as they came.

"Get down!" Maddie shrieked, letting Allen slip from her arms and onto the stairs. She remembered that George and Mamun had been down on the floor when she had released her fire upon Abiah and they had not been killed. Katie and Sam hit the stairs, taking Chris and Allen with them and holding them down.

Maddie let the heat build in her body and released it in one hot explosion that shattered the remaining windows and blistered the paint on the walls. The wave of heat struck the Distari coming at her from both directions and drove them back. They burst into flames and topped to the ground and flailed about in their desperation to put the flames out. Maddie fed more heat into the fire until they died and cooked in their own juices.

At Maddie's shout, Sam gathered the children and they fled out of the door and into the front yard. More Distari corpses littered the yard. There were Agents everywhere, beating the bushes and firing weapons into the trees. Keung stood by the car with a gun in his hand and staring intently at the darkness. In the distance, sirens wailed louder and louder as they came closer. The police would be here soon.

*　　　*　　　*

Sam sat in the back of the ambulance with the children while the paramedics checked them over. Katie was still sobbing inconsolably while Chris seemed to have sunk into a catatonic state. Allen was doing better. He was sucking quietly on a piece of chocolate that the paramedic had given him and clutching his father's leg. Sam scanned the yard with his eyes. He saw cops everywhere as they studied the scene and shook their head in bewilderment.

The coroners were bringing what was left of Darlene out in a body bag. They were quiet as they put her into the van. One of the detectives was talking to Maddie. She gave him a sharp nod and began to walk towards Sam. He stiffened as she stopped in front of him

"Is everyone okay?" She reached out to touch Chris and ruffle his thick dark hair.

"Don't touch him," Sam snapped. Maddie pulled her hand back and turned angry eyes on him.

"Why not?" she snapped.

"Who are you?" he hissed without answering her question. "What have you become?"

Maddie opened her mouth then closed it again. How could she possibly answer that question when she wasn't sure of it herself? She looked into Sam's accusing face and shrugged helplessly.

"What do you mean by that?" she said weakly.

"I saw the way you responded to what happened to your sister. You barely looked at her. You didn't even see her when you stepped over her body. Darlene died defending us and you act as if it didn't matter," he hissed.

Maddie jerked as if she had been slapped. "I had to get you out of the house. I didn't have time for hysterics."

"You have time for it now," he replied. Maddie sighed and took a step back.

"You've just had a horrible experience and you're still freaked out. I'm going to back off and then we can talk as soon as you calm down."

"No, Maddie, no," Sam said. He suddenly looked twenty years older and very tired. "No, I can't ever talk to you again. I hate you. I hate the way you look. I hate the way you act and I hate the way you look at me. I never want to see you again."

"Sam, you're—"

"No. Just go away. Go away and leave us alone."

Maddie turned and did as she was told, too numb and tired to argue with him. She walked slowly, hoping to hear one of the children call her back. But they didn't so she found herself standing near Keung. He was speaking with Darlene's partner, Cooper, and was feeding the man a flawless cock and bull story about what happened. Maddie watched him play the concerned coworker perfectly and marveled at the change in his demeanor. He seemed almost human now, someone she could actually relate to.

Cooper stepped away from Keung and went about his work. Keung wandered over to her and stopped next to her.

"I have the Agents scouring the area for the Distari lair. I promise you that it will be exterminated," he said softly. Maddie didn't look at him and she didn't say anything. She just stared numbly at the mangled grass at her feet. "I've arranged for a suite for your exclusive use in the Center. You may stay there as long as you wish. Send me the bill for your sister's funeral. We are more than willing to take that burden from your family's shoulders. I'm very sorry for your loss."

The world came crashing down on her then. There were no tears, no wailing and no screaming to the heavens about the unfairness of it all. It was just an awful, hideous numbness that wrapped her in an ugly cocoon and sheltered her from her grief.

CHAPTER 49

The cops were everywhere. They scoured the property for evidence and went in and out of the house in waves. For the most part they worked in silence but when they spoke, they did it in hushed tones. Detective Cooper had taken Maddie's statement. He kept his questions short but full of tact. He treated her gently and showed her as much compassion as he could even though his own grief was crushing him. She managed to confirm that the human remains found in her house were, in fact, her sister before he had to find an excuse to leave.

Maddie watched bleakly as the ambulance took her family away without even saying good-bye. Sam wouldn't let her near the children so she wasn't able to hear what the paramedics said about their condition. She did manage to get Sam to promise to call her and tell her how they were doing. The unfortunate thing about it was that she had to jack his brain a little to get him to do it.

Maddie continued to wander the property and looked around. On occasion, she saw an Agent lurking in the shadows for fleeting seconds before they faded away from view. She stared at the swirling red and blue lights of the cop cars and let them draw her into a meditative state. Her eyes lost focus and everything became a mass of bright lights and dark shadow. She felt everything that she held bottled up for the last forty-eight hours melt away. It made the muscles in her upper body relax. The anxiety, rage, fear and despair emptied out of her brain and left her lighter and remarkably at ease.

Her mind became more open to everything and the thoughts and emotions of dozens of men and women poured through her. Her own numbness shielded her and kept her from becoming crippled by the grief of the people around her. It lay like a reeking fog of death and fear across the crime scene. Maddie observed it from an emotional distance, noticing that many of the cops here thought that she might be responsible for the deaths.

Maddie thought briefly about whether or not spending the rest of her life on death row was worth getting out of being the Tracker. Then she pondered whether or not Keung would even allow her to go to jail for any length of time. She gave it up as a useless thought and went back to what she had been doing.

Her wandering mind found something. It was small and hidden but it was something very different from all the other minds around her. This one was dull and viscous and had an unquenchable thirst for blood. She automatically turned toward it in surprise. It wasn't paying close attention to her. It was staring in the direction the children had just gone and was filled with yearning for the taste of their blood. It drooled and imagined how their tender flesh would taste and how glorious their screams would sound in its ears.

Rage filled her, burning her flesh to a crisp and making the small hairs on her arms and the back of her neck lift away from her hot skin. She took a tentative step towards the evil mind and stopped. She was suddenly very aware of all the soft human minds around her. The more sensitive people were beginning to notice her odd behavior. Maddie paused to consider them for a moment and then discarded them as a potential threat to her or her children. She didn't care if they thought she was weird; their opinion had very little to do with the well-being of her children, whose terrible deaths were being vividly fantasized about in that cruel inhuman mind.

Suddenly, the Distari realized that she was listening to it. It hissed at her in anger. It threatened her with its thoughts and felt confident that it would win a fight with her. She bared her teeth and growled back at it and drew looks of alarm from some nearby cops. She ignored them and concentrated on the awful mind that was daring her to come and get it. Maddie seethed at its smug audacity and was just as eager to do battle with it as it was with her.

Cooper grabbed her arm and she jerked it angrily away. He was talking urgently and adding noise to the swirl of visions and emotions coming off the Distari mind.

"Shut up!" Maddie snarled at him. Cooper blinked in surprise and anger. She turned her attention back to her enemy.

"Mrs. Johnston, perhaps you should let the paramedics take you to the hospital and let someone have a look at you," Cooper said, swallowing his anger for her sake. Maddie shot him a dark look and ignored him. He reached for her again and she shoved him away. The Distari taunted her as it moved away and it dared her to come after it.

"Mrs. Johnston!" Cooper couldn't contain his anger anymore. "If you do not calm down and control yourself, I will have you arrested."

Maddie glared him as if he were dangerously insane and looked away. It was moving at an alarming speed. She knew that she would never be able to keep up with it on foot. Maddie snarled and beat the air with her fists. It was unacceptable that this thing would get away and hurt her babies.

She kept her hold on its mind tight as she turned and began to run for the nearest car. She avoided the cop cars. If she stole one of those, they would follow her and she didn't want cops following her to where she was going. There was a good chance they would all get killed. Keung had taken the car with him when he had left. Which left only the big, gleaming red truck parked at the end of her driveway.

People shouted as Agents seemed to burst out of nowhere and flanked the Tracker. Maddie acknowledged them briefly then focused on getting to the truck. With any luck, Sam had left the keys in the ignition. Cooper stopped beside her window and shouted angrily at her. She stared blankly at him as his mouth opened and closed. Suddenly, he disappeared as an Agent passed a key through the window to her. Three Agents piled into the vehicle as she jammed the key into the ignition and turned the engine over.

She blew the horn to let anyone who might be in back of her know that she was coming and that they'd better get out of the way. Then she threw the truck into reverse and hit the gas. The truck shot out of the driveway and nearly collided with two cars and a person. She threw it into drive and sped out of the subdivision. She drove too fast as she followed the taunting mind, determined to catch it and kill it.

"Tracker?" Keung's voice came as if he were standing right next to her. *"What are you doing?"*

"What you failed to do," she snarled. *"I'm going to destroy that lair and protect my family."*

And she slammed her shields tightly into place and ignored Keung's mental touches to get her attention.

They were getting closer, she could feel it. She drove without really seeing what she was doing. She knew she was being reckless since the usually unflappable Agents jumped in their seats and traffic honked angrily at her. She found herself on Main Street and headed towards the Square. She suddenly knew where she was going. The Distari was headed for its lair beneath the Church Street Bridge. Now that she thought about it, it seemed like the perfect location for such a place. It was dark, rather secluded despite the small row of antique shops and had lots of underground access.

Maddie parked in the Square, which was literally a square about the size of half a city block. She hopped out of the truck and ran towards the bridge without waiting to see if the three Agents were following her. They caught up with her easily and ran along side her as she crossed the square's parking lot and into the darkness beneath the bridge. She examined the street, first glancing at the quaint shops in one direction then in the other direction where the street ended into a bridge support and was generally used for parking. At the foot of the bridge was a massive manhole cover that lay flush with the pavement.

She went for it, feeling the Distari mind that she sought taunting her from beyond it. She reached it and knelt down to examine the huge metal disk. Several grooves were cut deep into the edges of the cover that would make it easy to lever the metal disk out of the opening. An Agent produced her rod and she extended the blade and jammed it into one of the grooves. One of the men had to help her remove the cover while the other two grasped it and rolled it aside.

They gazed down the hole, their vision straining to penetrate the darkness. An oily, rank smell wafted from the depths and it brought with it the stink of offal and unwashed bodies. Maddie paused for only a moment then jumped feet first into the unknown. She landed in ankle deep water as dirty and foul as the air around her. She took a step forward and heard a loud splash behind her. She spun on her toes and prepared to attack but calmed when she saw that it was an Agent.

"Madam Tracker," the Agent said softly in the darkness. "You're hunting Distari for the first time. Perhaps you should allow one of us to go first."

Maddie gave him a hard look. "If I let you go first, then you would get in the way of what I have planned and that means that you will die. If you want to stay alive then I suggest you let me go first."

The Agent looked a little taken aback and then nodded.

"As you wish," he murmured.

Maddie turned and started down the nearest tunnel as she heard two more splashes at the entrance of the lair. She ignored them and stretched her mind out ahead of her. She wanted to know where every single beast skulking in this hideous place was and she didn't want surprises. She had let the monster that led her here go and now she was seeking the nearest victim.

The tunnel shrank around her and she was crawling through twists and turns littered with filth and things she didn't even want to think about when she stuck her hand into them. She paused when she came within a few feet of faint light and counted the minds she felt just beyond the lip of the tunnel.

There were dozens of them. All of them noisy and greedy, and completely mad. They thought of nothing but blood and death, not just for humans and small animals but for the weakest and stupidest of their own kind. They were like people but only in the worst ways people could be. She felt how dangerous and cowardly they were and she hated them. They had to die.

This time, when she released the terrible heat she allowed to build below her skin, she attempted to direct it where she wanted it. There was no finesse to it. It was like using a sledgehammer to squash an ant. All she could do was point it in a general direction and kill as many as she could reach. And she wouldn't incinerate the men who were following her into battle. Which was good enough for her. She wanted every disgusting creature in the room beyond to die horrible agonizing deaths.

The horde of oblivious Distari screamed as the terrible heat touched them. Some of them simply vaporized under the heat of her terrible rage while others melted like wax and those furthest back simply caught fire. She felt their minds either blink out or grow distracted by their pain. She slipped out of the tunnel and continued on her way. Behind her, the Agents emerged cautiously and stared at the carnage around her. They pulled out their guns and began to pick off the stragglers.

As she made her way through the lair, she torched everything she came across. They died screaming and twitching and she simply stepped over their smoking corpses and kept to her pace. She felt no remorse and she didn't spare a thought for their agony. She killed and sought out more lives to snuff and she would only stop when they were all dead.

Too soon, she began to feel cold. She stopped a second and considered the fact and realized that she was using up her own body heat to fuel her flames. After that, she used her blade to slay the small groups she came across and saved her fire for when she encountered groups too large for her to take in battle. Even then, she stole the heat from their bodies or from the rock around her.

It was a hell of blood and flying body parts. The air stank of burnt flesh and evacuated bowels. Fear and rage pelted her brain like rain on glass. It hit her mental barrier and rolled away, unnoticed. She moved blindly, not really seeing what she was killing and only caring if she could find more.

Finally, she found herself standing in front of a pair of massive doors stretching from floor to ceiling. The wood was carved in hellish relief, displaying a horde of monstrous beasts and snarling demons. She stared at the door and thought about what might lay behind it. It was much more complex and elaborate than anything else she saw in the lair. Simple common sense said that the masters of this place lurked beyond. She stretched out her mind and searched for those beyond. She wanted to know what she was dealing with and how smart they were. Behind her, she could feel the Agents picking off the few creatures she had missed. She smiled in satisfaction and turned back to the door.

They knew that she was there. One of them awaited her eagerly, while her boldness enraged the other. Both were strong and both were intelligent. There would be a fight. She shivered despite the warmth offered her by the multiple torches lining the walls. She took a minute to steal the heat. The torches flickered and went out and the heat restored some of her energy. She was still too cold and depleted but it didn't matter. There were two more left to die and she would kill them.

She went to the doors and gave them a mighty heave. They were surprisingly light and they swung easily on their hinges. They hit the wall behind them with a satisfactory crash as she strode into the massive room that was better suited to a medieval castle than in a dirt hole beneath a small Georgia town.

The massive chamber was sparsely furnished with only a large chair before a fireplace large enough to hold a bonfire. A large desk dominated another part of the room and a huge faded, dirty tapestry hung along one wall. Maddie barely noticed any of it; instead, she focused her attention on the two figures standing in the middle of the room.

As she approached them, she drew more heat from the fire blazing in the fireplace until it nearly went out and her body felt like it was going to burst. The hooded one threw his cowl back and glared in disbelief at her. He seemed human enough. He had large dark eyes, a straight nose and a thin mouth. He was handsome enough, if you liked tall dark and scary, and his very black hair fell to his shoulders in waves.

The grinning one was more like a bad caricature of a human. His features were exaggerated so that his eyes bulged, his nose was weird and too big for his face and his mouth and jaws were too big for the rest of his skull. His body seemed all wrong, too, since the limbs were over-long and the huge joints all wanted to bend the wrong way.

"I cannot believe what I am seeing!" the Master gasped. "The Tracker, come to us all on her own!"

His voice was mocking her and it served to enrage her further. She stared him down, yearning for his end. She stopped a few feet from him and waited. He wanted to attack her. He wanted to draw first blood. But he had felt her power shaking the lair and was wary of it. He didn't want to do anything that would bring the fire upon him. She glared at him as he circled her, looking for an opening for attack. She didn't give him one. She waited for the other one to attack while his Master had her distracted but He simply stood to the side and waited with a broad grin on his face.

The Master suddenly lunged at her, moving in a blur of motion. Maddie cried out and staggered, shocked by the speed in which her opponent moved. Her brain tingled with a new download. This one was of an ancient memory. She saw herself facing down another Master in another place. He, too, moved to fast to track, and that Tracker had bled before he cut him down.

Maddie glanced down and saw the blood pouring from her side. She frowned at how little it hurt. A sane voice in her head told her that it was a bad sign. Deep wounds caused shock and shock protected the mind from becoming crippled by agony. Something vital had been struck and that meant she had a limited amount of time to kill her enemy. She pushed it aside and faced her foe again.

"Why don't you use that frightful new power of yours against me?" the Master sneered. She twirled the blade around her in a defensive move and wondered why the Master was so eager for her to set him on fire. The other behind her was laughing softly. She decided then that she would not use flame to destroy this pair. They were prepared for it and most likely knew ways to counteract it and use it against her to deadly effect. Her head ached and nausea was beginning to set in. It was time to end this before she bled to death.

But the Master was in no hurry. He knew that she was in trouble and that it was only a matter of time before she died of blood loss. So she did the only thing she could do. She attacked. The memories guided her; she attacked to the side of the Master, her blade reaching for some vital part of him. He easily sidestepped her, his dark eyes gleaming with cruel laughter. She attacked again and he struck a glancing blow to her already-ravaged side. Her blood pumped out of her body and she was beginning to feel dizzy. He was toying with her, confident that the fight was already over and now he could simply revel in her death throes.

Suddenly her body began to move like it possessed. The blade began to whirl around her head and body. It caught the light and surrounded her with an eerie and deadly aura. The Master began to look uncertain as he watched her advance slowly on him. As she drew closer, he backed away to stay clear of her whirling blade. Then the idea occurred to her. She slowly moved her hands along the spinning shaft so that her fingers grazed the switch as her eyes locked with his. He saw something in her that made him hesitate and he glared with all the hate of his long centuries. She felt her mouth curl in a cold smile and bared her teeth in her own expression of rage.

"Enough!" the Master snarled as he came for her. He trusted himself to be fast enough to reach past the spinning blade and snatch a handful of her organs before she knew what had happened. She watched him tense, her thumbs still dancing along the edge of the switch as she waited for him to move.

Suddenly, he did. He was on her before her brain could register it and his hand was against her belly. But she had been expecting it and she stopped the spinning blade and pressed the switch in one smooth motion. The bottom of the metal shaft hit hard against the Master's chest and the blade ejected from the end and punched through his body. He gasped and his eyes widened in astonishment. Maddie felt her muscles bruise and her insides rupture from the impact of his hand. She paid no attention to it and focused all the heat in her body into a fine point and plunged it into his head.

He clapped his hands together with glee as the Master's head exploded in a shower of brains and bone fragments. The Tracker collapsed into a boneless heap on the floor and lay there moaning in agony. He couldn't believe his eyes! The crazy bitch had done it! He jumped up and down like an excited child and laughed with glee. She managed to lift her head and regard him with dull eyes. Blood bubbled up through her mouth and dripped onto the floor beneath her chin.

"Oh, that was glorious!" he laughed. "That was the grandest thing I've ever seen! I didn't really think you could pull it off at first but you did it! And because you could, I will advance to that of Master! You have my sincerest thanks and I shall grant you something in return."

Maddie watched as He walked away from her and went to the desk. He hummed happily as he rifled through the drawers. He found what he wanted with a cheerful cry and came back to kneel next to her head. He bent and peered into her face, smiling that awful smile and waving a bright and slender blade in front of her face. She followed it with her eyes, bitter that this smug turd was going to be the one to kill her.

"I'm going to grant you a quick and painful death," he said cheerfully. "I know, it feels more like your death is more for my glory. But your injuries combined with the effectiveness of your nanopack will guarantee that your death is slow and painful. So when I kill you, it will spare you a great deal of pain as well as rewarding me with a wealth of personal glory. So you see, everybody wins."

Maddie didn't answer. She relaxed into a sprawl on the floor and waited for him to kill her. He smiled when he saw her submit and he raised the bight blade over her head. He was laughing so hard that his hand shook and he had to take a moment to get a hold of himself. Finally, he grasped the hilt with both hands and stretched himself out to plunge the blade deep into her body. Maddie close her eyes and waited.

An explosion rocked the room and a sharp blast of heat arched over her body and singed her eyebrows. She opened her eyes and saw that He was gone. She turned her head and looked where he had been and saw him writhing on the floor, clutching his throat and gnashing his teeth. Footsteps ran across the room to her and strong arms lifted her up. An Agent's face came into her line of vision. It was difficult to focus on him. She blinked as she tried to see him and groaned in pain and misery.

"You shot him!" she gasped. The Agent smiled gently and nodded.

"Yes, Tracker, I did," he said.

"Make sure he stays dead," she said, her tongue thick. The Agent chuckled at that. More footsteps passed her unseen and she heard more explosions as another of the Agents fired several more rounds into the elite's twitching body. She had enough time to think that it was the loveliest sound she ever heard before the world faded and turned black.

EPILOGUE

Maddie stood beneath a tree and watched as the headstone was set at her sister's grave. It had been an elegant thing, a carved pedestal made of marble with an archangel perched on top. It was graceful and over dramatic and so very Darlene. Her parents and older sister and three brothers stood before the grave. They wept and held each other, completely ignorant of the fact that Maddie was there.

She hadn't been able to face them ever since she had called her mother and told her about Darlene's death. Mom had become irrational and hysterical and was hospitalized for a couple of days. Dad had asked what had happened and she had told him, leaving out anything that gave away the Center's secrets. Which meant she had not been able to give her family the answers they wanted. Now she was unable to face them and so she hid from them. She found other things to do when they wanted to meet her and she soon stopped answering their calls.

Sam had been more of a comfort to them than she had. He had no limits to what he could say and he told them everything. It was then that she learned that Sam thought she was a criminal and that her alleged crimes had played a role in her sister's death. She didn't think that his opinion had been that far off the mark and when she didn't dispute the rumors, the phone calls stopped coming.

The divorce papers were filed quicker than state law usually allowed. Sam was able to prove that she was guilty of child endangerment, thanks to testament from Detective Cooper and some of the neighbors. She was allowed supervised visits with the kids and she supposed that it was better than nothing. She hadn't disputed any of Sam's claims in court either. Hell, she hadn't even shown up.

The crowd at the grave began to disperse slowly, one by one until only Mom and Dad were left. Maddie watched them from afar, knowing that she could never speak to them again. They were too angry with her and she could feel that rage mixed with grief and despair from where she stood. She was well and truly alone in the world. All her ties to her past had been severed in one terrible night and she knew she could never get them back. All she had left was a bunch of people she hated and a job she despised. Still, it was better than nothing. And there was potential at the Center, even if she didn't want to consider it right now.

Maddie let out a deep sigh as Keung approached. He stood silently at her side with his hands clasped properly behind his back. They watched as Dad took Mom in his arms and held her as she wept bitterly and her knees threatened to buckle.

"When's the next mission?" Maddie murmured dully as she watched her parents.

"Soon enough. You must finish healing first, Tracker."

Maddie nodded and contemplated the thick grass.

"It gets easier," Keung said softly. "Soon you will sink into the rhythm of the Center and it will be easier."

She noticed that he did not promise her happiness or that she would regain all she lost. All he offered her was adjustment to something new and that she might find her stride in it, even if she hated it. There was happiness of a sort in that, and she decided that she could learn to live with it.

www.ingramcontent.com/pod-product-compliance
Lightning Source LLC
Chambersburg PA
CBHW031103260626
47172CB00001B/201